THE PERFECT HUSBAND—
OR THE PERFECT LOVER?

Stephen Langley was all that Laura had ever dreamed of
in a man. He was handsome, brilliant, well-born, wealthy—
and on the high road of political power that well might
lead to the White House itself. It seemed like a dream
come true when Stephen asked her to marry him, and she
became his wife.

Eric was everything that Stephen was not. Intensely passionate, extravagently talented, he came from a world
of European culture and sophistication. Art was his life
and love was his gift, and he led Laura to heights she
never imagined existed . . . and to the brink of a betrayal
that she never before considered.

For Eric was the one man in the world who could make
Laura happy and fulfilled. But first she must be willing
to break her vows to the man whose name she had taken—
and now so easily could destroy. . . .

THE CIRCLING YEARS

The spellbinding new novel
by the acclaimed author of *Seventrees*

JANICE YOUNG BROOKS

THE CIRCLING YEARS

JANICE YOUNG BROOKS

AN ONYX BOOK

NEW AMERICAN LIBRARY

PUBLISHED BY
THE NEW AMERICAN LIBRARY
OF CANADA LIMITED

PUBLISHER'S NOTE

This is a work of fiction. Names, characters, places, and incidents either
are the product of the author's imagination or, if real, used fictitiously.

 ONYX IS A TRADEMARK OF NEW AMERICAN LIBRARY

SIGNET, SIGNET CLASSIC, MENTOR, ONYX, PLUME, MERIDIAN
AND NAL BOOKS are published in Canada by The New American
Library of Canada, Limited, 81 Mack Avenue, Scarborough,
Ontario, Canada M1L 1M8

First Printing, September, 1986

   2   3   4   5   6   7   8   9

PRINTED IN CANADA
COVER PRINTED IN U S A

Prologue

The Cottage

*T*HE Thornes always called it the cottage—a pretty designation for what was actually a rude, sturdy settler's cabin. It was one of the first white man's structures in the steeply undulating Ozark mountain land that would someday be known as Thornehill.

The site of the cottage, uncharted, unmarked on any map, had been visited many times by people of several nations and races. In 1541 a group of Spaniards who'd been with DeSoto's expedition stayed there on the sheltered south side of the limestone bluff. In 1686 French trappers discovered the nearby spring and the cold, clear lake it formed and subsequently camped by the bluff to conduct some trading with the local Indians. In 1804 Daniel Boone stopped for a day or two and went away believing the cough he'd had for some weeks might have been cured by drinking the sparkling turquoise water from the spring lake. It was often said, but not proven—for who in the South cared to prove such things?—that escaping slaves had used the spot for the concealment and protection it offered.

In 1850 a settler from Pennsylvania named Yokum built the cabin, setting it so it backed up to the bluff for protection from the north winds in winter. Yokum was a cabinetmaker by trade and he built the cabin as though it were a fine piece of furniture to be handed down for generations, each log dovetailed into the whole, the door and windows perfectly square and true. By the time the cabin was finished, the wife was bulky with pregnancy, but the next year both she and the infant were carried away by a sudden fever. Yokum lost heart and drifted off, leaving everything behind.

The cabin sat vacant for several years. Red squirrels nested in the chimney; mice and moths nibbled through the wife's clothes; spiders spun swags of dusty webs in the corners. The wife's headstone ("Beloved Emily and Child"), not very well anchored in the fertile soil, fell over and chipmunks burrowed under it.

Occasionally a hunter would pass through and stay overnight, appreciating the cold, fresh water from the spring and comfort the cabin offered. After the Battle of Pea Ridge, a trio of Confederate soldiers stopped there to nurse their wounds, and once, four men who'd robbed a train near Hot Springs halted briefly in their flight from the law to count their money on the rough oak table in the center of the main room.

In 1880 Jeremiah Thorne came to Arkansas from Boston. He was forty years old, a widower with a ten-year-old son and immense wealth that hadn't been able to buy off the ravages of crippling arthritis. Jeremiah heard of the miraculous cures claimed by those who'd taken the waters in a makeshift town called Eureka Springs—a few miles from the settler's cabin. Desperate to assuage his pain, he came from Boston to find a cure.

Within weeks he was able to walk upright, leaning slightly on his cane or his son Jack's shoulder. In another month he could walk briskly with only a trace of a limp. He became the willing slave of the waters of Eureka Springs, Arkansas. But clapboard wooden villages were not his style, nor were the inhabitants of them his sort, so he picked a nearby mountaintop that had a commanding view and made his way toward it with the idea of building a grand home there for himself and his descendants. Halfway up this hill, he discovered Yokum's cabin, dirty and overgrown, but still as sound and sturdy as ever. The cabin meant nothing to him, but the nearby spring, cold and clear, seemed a sign of heavenly approval. Surely this spring, so pure and blue, must flow from the same miraculous source as those in the town.

When the building of his great castle-house commenced, workmen used the cabin. They climbed the hill in the morning and labored at constructing Thornehill mansion and returned at night to the cabin to drink, play cards, and sleep. They cleaned it up, installed extra bunks, and added a lean-to kitchen. Two extra rooms were created by hollowing back into the soft limestone bluff the house nestled against. But when the mansion was complete, the workmen left and the spiders and squirrels took the cabin back.

By the turn of the century, it was discovered again and came to be known as the "cottage" by young men—flannel-trousered, boater-hatted guests from the mansion. When croquet had palled, charades grew dull, and the niceties of the houseparty atmosphere became oppressive, they could slip away to the cottage, a place now for lovers' trysts.

In February 1918, it came to the perceptive ears of Grace Thorne, daughter-in-law of the late Jeremiah, that her son Jackson had been employing the cottage for just such a purpose. The same day, workers were sent down from the mansion to rebuild the kitchen addition, repair the roof, and put in modern plumbing. Then Grace Thorne informed the head gardener that he, his wife, and their daughter would take up residence in the cabin.

The next November a child was born there:

Laura.

I

November 10, 1918

MILDRED Smalley watched from the front window of the cottage as the funeral party returned to the mansion. The main drive was some distance away and obscured by intervening trees and hills except in one place. The estate wagon, a lumbering, buslike vehicle, drew to a stop in the clearing, let her husband alight, and moved ponderously along to deliver the other upper house servants. Then, after a long pause, several unfamiliar motorcars went past. Those would be the cousins and Captain Jack's friends. Then two flashy, speeding vehicles, one trailing a woman's shrill laughter. *That*, she thought with a critical sniff, would be young Jackson's friends.

Mr. Smalley reached the cottage and let himself in. "Well, it's done. He's laid to rest right fine. Terrible pity. Terrible."

It was a cold day with a scent of frost in the brisk wind, and this might have accounted for Smalley's reddened nose and smarting eyes. Or it might have been genuine grief. He'd greatly admired Captain Jack and had even offered to give up his gardening and go to war with his employer. But Captain Jack had laughed and said, "Smalley, you're more necessary around here than I am. Thornehill would wither and die without *you*. No, I'll go fight. You stay and take care of the place."

Then Captain Jack had gone off to France and was gassed to death in some field with a name no one could pronounce.

Smalley blew his nose loudly, then hung up his coat on the hook on the back of the door. "What about *her*?" his wife asked, still looking out the window. The emphasis on the pronoun was half-sneer, half-awe.

"What about her?"

9

"Was she there?"

"Of course. He was her husband."

"Did she cry?"

Smalley's heavy features registered distaste at the questions. "Grace Thorne? Cry?"

The last car was passing. No, not passing. It had stopped. The chauffeur was opening the door. "She's coming *here*!" Mildred cried, thrilled at the remarkable prospect of getting to enjoy the widow's grief up close.

She joined her husband in a flurry of tidying up. When the knock at the door finally came, Mildred was flushed with anger at herself for attempting to impress the visitor, feeling Grace Thorne had made her do something against her will.

"How do, Miz Thorne," Smalley said, opening the door and beckoning her to enter.

She stood in the doorway for a moment, as if daring Mildred Smalley to study her. At forty-six, Grace Thorne was an impressive woman. It would be unjust to say she looked older than her actual age, for her skin was still smooth and flawless and her thick, polished cherrywood-colored hair was glossy in spite of the faint veins of gray beginning to fan back from her temples. But there was a ramrod stateliness to her posture and a haughty grace in the set of her head and hands that suggested age and authority, even beauty, although her individual features were quite unremarkable.

She stepped into the room. "It was good of you to come to the service, Smalley. My husband would have been pleased. He thought very highly of you. We will hear the reading of the will in half an hour, if you will be so kind as to come to the house?"

"We was awful sorry to hear about Captain Jack," Mildred said.

Grace Thorne glanced at her as if mildly surprised to find her there. Then she inclined her head slightly, acknowledging the sentiment without deigning to reply. Mildred searched the new widow's face for some sign of crying—reddened eyes, puffy lids, anything. But there was only her tailored black dress ("Clear to her toes, so old-fashioned!" Mildred later reported to her friends) to indicate that she'd attended a funeral, and nothing to say she had been the principal mourner.

"As you might have guessed, I have a specific matter to discuss with you," Grace said to Smalley.

"Yes, ma'am?"

"In the last month, since I learned of my husband's death,

it has also come to my attention that your daughter had given birth to a child. A girl, I believe.''

Smalley flushed, scarlet mottling his wide cheeks. ''That she has, ma'am. She's a bad girl and I've told her so—''

Grace raised a black-gloved hand. ''I haven't come to criticize her morals, Smalley. Nor yours . . .'' She glanced again at Mildred, and the unspoken message was clear: daughters are what their mothers make of them. ''Who is the father of the child?'' Grace asked.

Smalley shuffled his big feet but didn't answer.

''She'll tell me. Where is she?''

''She and the baby have our room just now,'' Smalley said, crossing the main room and opening a door. Grace followed him. Mildred trailed them both, horrified that Grace was going to see the bedroom.

Iris Smalley had fallen asleep nursing the baby. She lay sprawled on her back, one overripe breast exposed. The baby, dried milk streaked across one fat cheek, was asleep beside her, dangerously near the edge of the bed. Mildred pushed forward, hastily yanking the neck of Iris's nightgown into place. ''Iris, Miz Thorne's come to see you. Wake up!''

Iris sat up and casually dragged the baby back toward the middle of the bed. She blinked, rubbed her eyes, scratched at her tumbled and not-very-clean blond hair. ''Miz Thorne?''

Grace stepped closer, hovering over Iris like a black angel. ''Who is the father, girl?''

Iris pointed to Smalley.

''Not *your* father. The baby's father,'' Grace said impatiently.

''Oh . . .'' Iris said, scratching her head again. She was a pretty girl, in a plump, vacant-eyed way. Just the sort a young man might find attractive for an afternoon's entertainment.

''Do you *know* who the father is?'' Grace asked.

''Yes,'' Iris mumbled.

''Then tell me. There will be no punishment, so long as you answer me truthfully.''

Intimidated, Iris hung her head. ''Mr. Jackson, ma'am.''

Mildred gasped, but Grace didn't flinch. She turned to Smalley. ''Do you think this is true?'' she asked him.

He couldn't meet her penetrating gaze. ''I reckon so, ma'am. I caught them here together one day before we moved in. They said they was just lookin' at the cottage, but Iris ain't got no call to be on terms with such as your son, ma'am.''

"But you didn't tell me anyth—" Mildred began, but Grace cut her off with a gesture.

"Why didn't you tell me?" Grace asked Smalley.

"Weren't your fault, ma'am. The girl knows how things are with men and women. No point in upsetting you, what with Captain Jack going to war and all."

Grace nodded and with a rare, affectionate gesture touched his arm briefly. "We must talk."

They went back into the main room. Smalley and Grace sat down at the table while Mildred poured them chipped pottery cups of coffee. "A good friend of mine has a large estate in North Carolina," Grace said. "She has often admired your fine work in our gardens and remarked enviously what your skills could accomplish in their rich soil and mild climate. I would like for you to go to work for her, Smalley." He opened his mouth to protest, but Grace gave him no opportunity. "I shall dislike losing you, but I'm afraid that's how it's to be. Do not feel this is a punishment. I intend to make a very generous settlement on you as a mark of what a great loss I consider your departure. This will be, of course, in addition to any bequest of my husband's. Your wife and daughter will leave immediately, but I would like for you to stay on and select your own replacement. I could trust no other judgment, not even my own, in such a matter."

Mildred nearly dropped the coffee pot. The "generous settlement" part of the speech fascinated her, but on general principles, she felt obliged to register some objection. "The baby ain't old enough to go such a long way, ma'am."

Grace paused only for a heartbeat. "The baby isn't going. It's a Thorne and I can raise it better than your daughter can. This way Iris will have a fresh start in life and no one need ever know she's had an illegitimate child. It will improve her marriage prospects immeasurably." Grace rose, her coffee untouched. "Now, if you will dress the baby warmly, I will take it with me. Smalley, if you would be so kind as to come see me in the morning, we will work out the details of your move. I shall post a letter to my friend tonight, telling her of her good fortune."

As Grace walked down the path a few minutes later clutching the squirming bundle, Mildred said to Smalley, "It better be a lot of money, like she said. Iris'll be needing some new dresses."

Smalley didn't seem to hear her. "The baby will be better off," he said.

Mildred suddenly remembered something and called out to Grace, "Her name's Annie!"

Grace didn't turn around or answer. Instead, she held the baby tighter and said to herself, "Her name is Laura Elizabeth Thorne."

"Where *is* Mother?" Jackson Thorne II asked, pouring himself a second brandy.

He stood at the long windows of the so-called library, actually a trophy room. "The wildlife mortuary," Grace had once commented acidly as her husband cleared another bank of bookshelves to mount a prize moose head. A spacious, high-ceilinged, walnut-paneled room, it was the heart of the house. Nearly every morning since her marriage, Grace had come here and had sat at the cherrywood secretary between the windows to do household accounts, plan menus, and conduct her wide-ranging social correspondence. At noon, her husband, Jack, used to enter and kiss the back of her neck. Like a fairy-tale princess released from a spell, she would stop her work, rise, and depart. For an hour Jack would take his place at the massive oak desk at the far end of the room.

Just what he did there was a mystery. He took little interest in the financial affairs of the estate, leaving most of that to Grace, who both enjoyed and excelled in such matters. Nor was he a great reader, though a Harvard education had provided him with a passable knowledge of literature to make reference to Romeo or Socrates if a social occasion demanded it.

When word came of his death, Grace had opened the drawers of this desk for the first time and discovered that two of them were entirely empty; one contained smoking material—pipes, pouches of specially ordered tobacco, cleaners, and a large crystal ashtray; the remaining drawers were full of sporting magazines and photographs, mainly of groups of well-dressed men standing proudly over various species of dead animals. There was also a photograph of a scantily clad young woman signed "To my own Jackie-bear, Love, Mimi."

It had been eight months since Jack Thorne left, clad in the handsome uniform that so well suited his tall, lithe figure. And for all that time, the chair with the cracked leather armrests behind the desk had been unoccupied. Today, however, a neat, square, fortyish bachelor named Willis Hawkins sat there observing the others as they awaited Grace's arrival.

When Jackson repeated his query, it was Willis who said, "There's no hurry, Mr. Thorne."

"What do you know about it?" Jackson asked.

More than you suppose, Willis Hawkins thought. He was the Thorne family lawyer and the leather satchel on which his small square hands rested contained Jack Thorne's will. They were assembled for the reading of it. The few servants, including Smalley, who were to be given minor bequests, were seated, nervous and prim, along one wall. Jackson's wife, Evelyn, had taken the armchair next to the fireplace. She was looking into the flames and squirming uncomfortably at intervals. A slight, high-strung woman of twenty, she was on the overblown brink of motherhood and this made Willis uneasy. She was so vastly pregnant he feared she might suddenly go into labor and deliver before his horrified eyes.

He hadn't realized he was staring at her until the man across the desk from him leaned forward and said with soft mockery, "She's fine, Will. There won't be a baby crying as you read."

Willis was chagrined, but comforted somewhat by the presence of Howard Lee. He was an old friend of the Thornes', having attended school with Jack. He'd been best man when Jack married Grace Emerson and had, in his professional capacity, attended Jackson's birth as well as the other numerous lyings-in that resulted in nothing but tiny coffins and tears. Willis had always suspected that Dr. Lee was half in love with Grace Thorne, but what man wasn't?

The door to the library opened and everyone turned to look as a thin black woman stepped in. This was Grace's servant, Mabelann. Her "lady in waiting," as Willis thought of her. "Mr. Hawkins, sir, Miz Grace say she be with you in just a minute or so." Her busy brown eyes met his, swept the others, including Jackson, as if defying them to object. Willis noted that Jackson couldn't quite meet her gaze. He shrugged angrily, made an indeterminate noise in the back of his throat, but said nothing.

They're up to something, Mabelann and Grace, Willis thought, then dismissed the idea as the door closed behind the black woman. What could or would they be up to on a day like this? He knew the contents of the will; he knew that Grace had already accomplished what she wanted.

But he was assailed by the thought again when Grace finally entered the room. Not that there was anything overtly excited in her demeanor. Her carriage was erect and dignified, her mien somber and controlled. But there was an aura of repressed energy in her step, a hint of sparkle in her eyes, the merest trace of a smile at the corners of her mouth.

She came to Willis and shook his hand as though they had not met for a long time, even though he had paid his respects at the church and the cemetery only hours before. She was still wearing the sweeping black garments she'd had on then. This surprised him. He'd supposed she'd spent the intervening time changing her dress. As she sat down, he noted that there was even a discoloration on her skirt, a faint streak of white. Unlike Grace—perfectly groomed Grace . . .

"I believe we're all here, Mr. Hawkins," she said. "Jackson, dear, it might be suitable if you were to abandon your drink for the time being."

Willis, still worried to distraction by Evelyn's condition, noticed that she cringed back into her chair as Jackson replied, "Certainly, Mother. Not that Father's ghost doesn't deserve a hearty toast."

Grace didn't even appear to hear him. "Will you proceed, Mr. Hawkins?"

Willis opened the case, drew out the document, and smoothed it quite flat before beginning in a dry legal drone, "Dated this ninth day of January 1918 . . . I, Jackson Matthew Thorne, being of sound mind and body . . ."

The minor bequests were first—stipends for devoted servants like Smalley, sums to a few charities, sentimental gifts of jewelry and paintings to cousins, a favorite gun to a hunting crony. He paused before going on. Grace said, "I think it likely the rest of the will concerns only the family. Perhaps the staff would like to be excused to get back to their duties . . . ?" They rose and trooped out like a Greek chorus.

Now Willis got to the meat of the matter. He began with a lengthy list of the Thorne assets: the mansion itself, the outbuildings, the hundred acres of prime Arkansas land on which it was located as well as four outlying farms and the rents from same.

"Get on with it, Hawkins!" Jackson said.

Willis glanced at him, thinking what a shame it was his manners weren't as fine as his looks. He was a handsome young man, with his dark hair and his startlingly pale eyes. But there was a beginning of a jowl there, a flush that so often presaged the ruddiness of the chronic alcoholic. "I'm bound to read the entire document, Mr. Thorne," Willis said.

He went on reading. Stocks were the last and most essential items. It was the income from this vast investment, accumulated over generations, that kept the Thorne empire afloat. More than afloat—riding the financial crest. The farms barely supported the mansion and staff. The stocks, however, allowed for the fine clothes, exquisite furniture, the travel, the imported liquors. Willis recited the list respectfully, lovingly.

He turned the page and plunged on. ''Having entrusted the management of my affairs to my beloved wife, Grace Emerson Thorne, for the duration of our married life, I see no reason why my demise should be seen to diminish her acute monetary perceptions. I therefore leave all my worldly goods except those otherwise specified above to said Grace Emerson Thorne, with the understanding that she will gain approval of my trusted friends and advisers Howard Lee and Willis Hawkins—''

There was a crash, a splintering of glass as Jackson's brandy snifter shattered against the firegrate. Evelyn squealed. Willis leaned away from her. Dr. Lee stepped quickly to her side. Only Grace was utterly immobile, her features as tranquil as if carved in wax.

''You did this to me, Mother!'' Jackson shouted.

''Jackson, please. The servants—''

''Damn the servants! I don't care who hears. You cheated me. You persuaded him to take away my inheritance. It should have all come to me. I'm of age. I'm his son. How could you!''

''Oh, Jackson—'' from the armchair.

''Evelyn, will you stop whimpering, for God's sake! Hawkins, I'll take this to court, I'll—''

''I cannot advise that, sir,'' Hawkins said firmly. ''Your father was entitled to dispose of the estate as he chose. Had he acted in a bizarre or irresponsible way, there might be grounds for objection, but leaving his assets to his wife, your mother, is a perfectly normal arrangement—''

''When the child is a minor—''

''Yes, that is usually the case, but need not be so. You must let me finish with the stipulations of the inheritance.''

Evelyn was weeping quietly. Dr. Lee was absently patting her shoulder. Grace hadn't moved except to brush her hand across the white spot on her skirt. ''In simple terms, Mr. Thorne,'' Willis went on, ''your mother has full control of the estate for life, with the understanding that at least eighty percent of the total value of her holdings at her death pass to one or more of her descendants. That is, you and/or your children. So, you see, there is no question of you and your progeny being deprived of the ultimate benefits of your father's wealth—''

"Quite the contrary," Grace said, standing. This move and the words accompanying it silenced everyone. "Mr. Hawkins, am I correct in assuming that I have full control of the estate, to do with as I choose?" It was a rhetorical question. No one in the room was ingenuous enough to suppose Grace hadn't been fully familiar with the terms of the will.

Willis suspected, in fact, that she was its primary author, with Jack's agreement, of course. "You do, provided you make no major expenditures without prior consultation with myself and Dr. Lee."

"Then we shall consult. I propose to give Jackson and Evelyn 25,000 dollars a year. If they choose to stay here at Thornehill, they will have no expense for living quarters, food, or servants. That should be an adequate amount for their pleasures. Do you agree, Jackson?"

He'd gotten up and taken a fresh snifter from the cupboard. Pouring a generous splash of brandy in it, he said, "And what's the trick, Mother? You've never given anything away without attaching a chain to it. What's the chain?"

"Nothing," she said, and sat back down. After a long moment she said softly, "Well, there is one thing . . .''

Jackson put his drink down and leaned forward. "Here it comes. Look out, folks. Well, Mother dear, what's this one thing?"

"Evelyn is going to have twins."

Evelyn put both hands to her swollen belly. Dr. Lee said, "Grace, I don't think that's likely."

But his words were drowned out by Jackson's harsh laugh. "Well, Mother, it's beyond me. Consult with God for that one. I'm sure you have his ear. Twins! By all that's holy, you've gone too far in asking that one."

"I don't believe you heard me," Grace said. "I'm not asking. I said that Evelyn *is* going to have twins."

She went to the door and nodded to Mabelann, who'd been standing guard so that none of the other servants could eavesdrop. Grace nodded to her, and Mabelann disappeared. Grace came back and sat down. No one spoke until the thin black woman came in carrying a blanket-wrapped bundle which she handed to Grace.

Willis was astonished to see a genuine smile light Grace's face as she turned back the blanket corner and revealed the sleeping infant. That explained the white spot on her skirt. Willis, a bachelor, knew little of babies, but he understood that powder figured in their lives somehow. Grace had been tending this child while they waited for her. The picture they made would last in his memory for years. The black-clad widow, looking down with sweet, Madonna-like serenity at the round pink face peeking from the swaddling.

"This," she said, not taking her eyes from the child, "is one of the twins."

"Good God! It's a baby!" Jackson said. "Whose is it?"

Grace looked up. "Yours."

"What? Are you mad?"

"I stopped at the cottage and saw Iris Smalley . . ." Her voice trailed off and Willis thought he detected sympathy in her tone.

Evelyn was struggling out of the deep armchair. "What is this all about?"

Jackson's stricken face told all. "Mother, how could you?"

"Jackson, dear, I'm sorry." Her voice was so soft now it was almost a whisper. "I had to. I *had* to!" It was as close as she could come to pleading.

"She had to what? Jackson, what is this baby doing here?" Evelyn was shrill, frightened.

Grace and her son sat across from each other, their eyes locked in silent communication. Jackson was the first to break the gaze. "Blood of our blood," he muttered. Whether this was sarcasm or sincerity was impossible to guess. One thing was certain. He wanted the generous settlement Grace had proposed. Had he inherited, there was no doubt he would have had the foundations for a "dower house" laid down within a week in order to get his mother out of Thornehill. But the tables were turned. Grace was more than willing to let him stay, but at a price. The full acceptance of his bastard child.

He rose and went to Evelyn's side. "Darling, come along upstairs and I'll explain to you," he said.

"Does she mean it? That child is yours?" Evelyn wept.

"I can explain—"

Suddenly Evelyn bent forward and shrieked. Her labor had begun.

The scream startled the baby. She flung out her tiny arms and her face puckered. Grace stroked the firm little cheek and said, "There, there, darling. It's all right. I won't let anything hurt you. I'll take care of you, Laura."

And with those words and that touch of finger to smooth baby skin, the years seemed to fall away for Grace and memory flooded her mind. Another baby Laura, another way of life, and so very long ago. . . .

II

1883

GRACE had been eleven years old on that day—the day that would ultimately set the course of her life.

"I'll take care of Laura," she said.

"Gracie, sit up straight. What will the Sullivans think of us if you slump like a hoyden?" Clara Emerson said to her oldest daughter as she tilted her parasol to evade the Virginia summer sun.

"Yes, Mother. I was just playing pat-a-cake with baby Laura. See how good she's getting?"

"She *is* a smart baby," Clara said, bending forward and chucking the child's chin. Her husband, Robert, sitting at the front of the stylish carriage, smiled fondly at his wife and daughters. He hadn't married until he was well into his forties and was inordinately proud of his pretty young wife and lovely daughters. Well, one lovely daughter, anyway. Baby Laura would certainly be a beauty and Gracie might be handsome enough when she grew up. Not that she was unattractive—not by any means—merely rather plain compared to the radiant golden, dimpled beauty of her mother and sister.

"How far is it, Mother?" Gracie asked.

"Sit down and stop twisting about like that. It's just ahead. We turn at that gate."

"Will I get to eat dinner with the grown-ups?"

"Of course not. You will help Florabel watch baby and you'll eat with them like always."

That was a disappointment. Gracie was beginning to chafe at the restrictions of childhood. She dreamed of having pretty dresses with hoops and getting to use the fine table manners that had been drummed into her all these years. At the same time, it *was* fun to eat with the baby. Florabel often let her feed her adored little sister and they had wonderful games of it. Gracie would fill the spoon with peas or porridge and "gallop" it toward the child's mouth, saying, "Here comes the horsie! Open the stable doors for him!" and Laura would open her sweet little rosebud mouth with a giggle and receive the food.

She was better than a doll. Much better. She laughed and said baby things and could hug back. When she got tired, she'd fall asleep on Gracie's lap and Gracie could pretend she was Laura's mother, not her big sister. And while Gracie rejoiced in Laura's every new accomplishment, she sorrowed, too, because she didn't want Laura to grow up and stop being a baby. She was a year and a half old, and soon she'd be too big to carry around. Even now, she often squirmed out of Gracie's arms and insisted on toddling around on her own fat little feet far too often to suit Gracie.

"Oh, Miss Clara . . ." Florabel moaned from the plank on the back of the carriage where she rode, only the fuzzy black top of her head showing.

"What is it?" Clara snapped.

"Oh, I sick, Miss Clara!" There was an awful retching sound as Florabel vomited in the road.

"Oh, Florabel! Get off the wagon and walk. I can't bear that terrible noise again."

"It's just the terrible heat, Miss Clara, and ridin' backways," Florabel said, slipping off the plank.

"That may be, but I don't want you around the children today."

"But, Miss Clara, who gonna take care of them younguns?" Florabel wailed, stumbling along behind them and wiping her mouth with the back of her hand. "Ain't nobody but me knows how to look after them."

"Mrs. Sullivan will have a servant who can care for the girls. You stay in the servants' quarters today," Clara said.

"But, Miss Clara—"

Robert Emerson turned around and thundered, "Florabel! That's enough. You do as you're told without any backchat!"

With a sharp crack of the whip, they rolled up the long shaded drive, leaving Florabel to walk behind. Gracie liked Florabel and was sorry she was sick, but with her out of the way, Gracie would have an even greater responsibility for the baby. She could tell the Sullivans' servant, whoever she might be, all about Laura's preferences.

Mentally she practiced giving advice. "Don't feed her any black-eyed peas, they give her a rash." "She takes her nap with her calico doll and I just lie down with her for a few minutes. She won't go to sleep unless I do." "If you don't tie the ribbons in her hair real tight, they slip out. She has very fine hair."

As it turned out, all these bits of Gracie-wisdom fell flat. Mrs. Sullivan assigned a slovenly girl named Reecie to watch the Emerson children. Clara was uneasy about her. "Gracie, you'll keep a close eye on Laura, won't you?" she said as the children were led away.

"Yes, Mama," Gracie answered proudly. "I'll tell Reecie how to take care of her."

Reecie, who was only fifteen herself, wasn't the least concerned with what Gracie's wonderful baby sister ate or how she slept, so long as she caused as little trouble as possible. While the girls had their luncheon in the kitchen, Reecie flirted with a young black man just outside the door. She posed and wriggled and rubbed herself against the door-jamb and laughed in such a way that her big breasts bounced alarmingly. Gracie was so fascinated with this display of sexuality that she missed Laura's mouth twice with the spoon and got mashed potatoes in her golden curls.

After lunch Reecie led them up the back stairs to the room where they would take their naps. Gracie took off Laura's pretty little lavender dress and her own yellow one and they got in bed on top of the lumpy white spread. Laura was tired and hot and rather fussy.

Reecie hung their dresses on chairs, then positioned herself by the window with a big palm-leaf fan which she waved lethargically between taking peeks out through the curtain. Gracie started singing to baby Laura, who cooed along for a bit, then fell asleep. Gracie allowed her own eyes to close, just for a minute, and when she opened them, Reecie was gone and the sunlight had a different slant.

Laura was yawning herself awake, her yellow curls stuck to her sweaty forehead. Gracie got up and made Laura use the chamber pot, then dampened a cloth in the tepid water from a pitcher on the nightstand. She kept expecting Reecie to return any moment, but she didn't. Gracie thought about calling her, but the house was still nap-quiet and she was feeling very grown-up, taking care of Laura on her own.

She dressed the baby, making sure each ruffle on her little lavender dress was hanging right; then, as Laura played with a hairbrush, Gracie slipped into her own dress. She brushed Laura's hair, then carried her to the window.

Down a slope in back, they could see a pond with pretty white ducks floating around serenely. "Gucks!" Laura squealed.

"Shall we go see the ducks, dear?" Gracie said, unconsciously imitating her mother's tone.

"Gucks! Gucks!"

Gracie still expected Reecie to turn up at every corner, but there was no sign of her as she took Laura down the steep steps and through the deserted kitchen. She heard the cook talking to someone in the pantry, but she tiptoed across the room and opened the door very quietly. As soon as they were out of the house and away from the shaded veranda, she set Laura down and held her hand. Laura twisted free to walk on her own. Gracie kept a pace or two behind, watching with delight as Laura staggered along, arms held out for balance and curls bouncing in the sunshine. Gracie felt her heart swell with love and pleasure at the sight.

"Gucks!" Laura said as they reached the edge of the little pond and the ducks started paddling around in agitation.

"Don't scare the ducks," Gracie said in her little-mother tone. "Sit down here and we'll throw them some nice leaves."

They tossed bits of leaf and grass into the pond and the ducks eventually became used to their presence and moved closer. One got out, waddled a few feet, and gave a tail-shake that made Laura shriek with delight. One by one the other ducks got out of the water and repeated the performance. Laura was doing so much squirming around that it made Gracie a little uneasy so close to the water. When one of the ducks started to wander off and Laura wanted to follow it, Gracie was glad to let her.

"Be very quiet and we'll see where he goes," Gracie said, making a game of stealthily following the duck. Laura smiled at her and put a chubby finger to her lips, saying "Shhhh," just like Gracie did.

The duck waddled ahead and disappeared into a hedge. Laura made a disappointed face and took hold of Gracie's skirt. Just then, Gracie heard a funny sound and she parted some branches of the hedge to look through.

Just on the other side were Reecie and the young man she'd been flirting with earlier. But Gracie was stunned by the fact that Reecie had her shirt off and her huge breasts were exposed. They looked like halves of eggplants, glossy and black and straining with ripeness. The extraordinary thing was, the young man was touching them. More than that—he was kneading them like huge, satiny lumps of black dough.

Reecie was standing with her head thrown back and her body arched against him. She made a moaning sound deep in her throat and said, "Put it in, Isaac," as she thrust forward and ground her pelvis against his.

Grace let the branches come back together, astonished at such a remarkable sight. She sensed instinctively that she shouldn't have been watching. If Reecie knew, she'd probably be mad—and she might be very unpleasant if she got mad. Gracie decided she'd take Laura back to the house and pretend they were never near the hedge. She reached down to take Laura's hand . . .

Laura?

The tension on her skirt hadn't been Laura's little hand; it was a twig of the hedge. Where was Laura? A sudden bubble of panic exploded in Gracie's stomach. She ran back down the slope toward the pond, but was only halfway there when she could see the lavender blob in the water. *"Laura!"* she screamed.

Ducks scattered in front of her as she ran. Her own scream was echoed as the servants came out to see what was happening. Gracie flung herself into the muddy pond and fought her way through the water. She couldn't run. Her feet stuck in the mud bottom and her clothes dragged in the water, but she kept flailing forward. Someone was right behind her, but Gracie got to Laura first. She was facedown in the water, her golden curls turned to yellow strings floating on the surface.

Suddenly a pair of brawny black arms shot forward and lifted Laura from the water. She hung there limp and streaming with pond water. "Get up there on the bank befo' you drowns you'self," the young man Isaac said to Gracie, grabbing her elbow with his free hand.

"Don't touch her! Don't you touch our baby!" she shrieked.

Gracie was never able, or willing, to remember exactly what happened in the next few minutes. It was all a confused blur of faces, black and white. Sometimes she'd recall only Florabel crumpled on the bank, sobbing into her skirt. Other times she'd remember Reecie clutching her shirt to her chest, her face gray and horrified. Or Isaac with Laura over his knee, pounding on her back, making her limp legs and arms flop. And then Clara—Clara with pillow creases from her nap still crossing one cheek like a pink scar. Clara snatching the lifeless body from Isaac and crushing it to her bosom.

Then Robert was running across the lawn with Mr. Sullivan. "Clara! Clara! What's happened?"

And Clara was looking at him over the top of Laura's head, which hung at an impossible angle from her neck.

"Oh my God, Robert! Gracie let Laura drown!"

III

1890

GRACE was never allowed to forget her transgression. Hardly a day passed in the next seven years that she wasn't reminded. She made a very private peace with her God and her conscience and managed, by virtue of native strength of mind, to avoid being eaten alive by guilt. But she never stopped missing her baby sister. Sometimes, even years later, she'd wake suddenly, having dreamed she was playing with Laura or rocking her to sleep or combing her pretty hair. But she forced herself, in her waking hours when such force was possible, not to think of the baby and what she might have become.

Grace never left home again after that day until she was eighteen and went to stay with her mother's sister in Boston.

"Gracie, you have the perfect complexion to wear fur," Nell Woodline said, fluffing the fur around her niece's face. "Too bad you don't have much occasion to wear it in Virginia."

Nell looked at Grace, assessing the shy girl who had dropped half-unexpectedly into her life. That straight nose would be imperious in another twenty years, perhaps even beaky when she grew very old, she thought. And the fine line of her jaw would someday be intimidating to anyone who came into her presence with a guilty conscience. But now she was all tender vulnerability, youth softening her features into poignant sweetness. How had Clara—selfish, coarse Clara—managed to have a daughter so strikingly attractive and gentle-mannered?

Grace turned from her Aunt Nell and looked at herself in the mirror. The collar of the white fur cape framed her face like a valentine. I look pretty, she thought. How remarkable. Grace Emerson wasn't accustomed to thinking of herself as pretty—largely because no one had ever told her she was.

"I wish your mother were here to see how lovely you are for your coming-out. You don't suppose if I wrote to her again. she might travel up . . . ?"

"I'm certain she wouldn't, Aunt Nell. Her health isn't good, you know."

Nell's hands fluttered like butterflies. "It's a wonder she's still alive. All that tippling is enough to kill anyone. Don't say a thing, Gracie. I've never been fooled by that 'health' business. She's my sister, though I never thought I'd see the day that a Dalton woman let herself go to seed that way. After all, many women lose children—my own son died of typhoid when he was seven—but they don't go to pieces the way she did."

"She *is* very delicate, Aunt Nell."

Nell snorted. "That's nonsense. You forget, child, I grew up with her. Clara could outtalk, outeat, and outrun me any day. She's just used that baby's death as an excuse to avoid her duty and to make a slave of you."

"Please, Aunt Nell . . ." Even after all these years, Grace couldn't bear to hear anyone speak of Laura's death so brusquely. Nor could she stand hearing anyone voice her own woes.

"It's true. Don't shush me. You might as well face it. Your mother's turned you into a slave as surely as they used to do the darkies down there. That's why I insisted on sponsoring you for your coming-out here in Boston. Are you enjoying the parties and the young people here?"

"Oh, yes! I've never had such a good time!" Grace said. It was more the truth than her aunt could have guessed. It wasn't only *more* fun than she'd had before, it was virtually the first time in her life she'd had any fun at all. Nell's conception of Grace's demeaned status only scratched the surface.

Clara had returned from baby Laura's funeral in a state of collapse from which she'd never attempted to recover. From that day, she'd hardly left her bed, much less her room. Sips of spirits to brace her against fainting had turned to whole bottles. She'd become plump from her indolence, then fat, and eventually obese. And it had fallen to Grace—Grace, who "let Laura drown"—to care for the incoherent, bitter, bloated wreck her once-pretty mother had become.

Her father, unable to comprehend or cope with the change in his young wife, had let Grace be enslaved, but in the end, it was he who rescued her. The turning point came on Grace's eighteenth birthday. Robert Emerson had insisted that Clara be brought down to a celebration dinner. She did so with reluctance, fortifying herself generously before allowing herself to be half-carried down the stairs.

As the dinner progressed, Clara became truculent and then abusive. "Bring me a bottle of sherry, Gracie. This food is rancid. What a state you've let the staff come to. It's all your fault. Get the sherry!"

"Mama, I don't think you should—"

"Get it, you little bitch!" Clara shouted, flinging a glass of water in Grace's face.

As Grace sat there, utterly silent, tears mingling with the water dripping from her chin and soaking her new dress, Robert Emerson suddenly saw with blinding clarity what he'd pretended not to see for years. And the sight sickened him. As Grace started to get up, he said, "Sit down, Gracie. This will *never* happen to you again. Not in my house."

He summoned the two burliest house servants to haul Clara back up to her room. When she'd gone, screaming, slobbering, and spitting invectives, he came around the table and took Grace's hand. It was the first time she could remember him touching her since she was a child. "Do I recall something about your Aunt Nell inviting you to Boston?"

"Yes, she has. Several times. But Mama can't get along without me."

"She's going to from now on. I'm writing to your Aunt Nell tonight to say you're coming to stay with her. Have your things ready to go by next Tuesday." He had tears in his eyes.

On the appointed day, he'd gone with her to the train station. Sending her maid ahead to see that all her luggage was aboard, he put his arm around his daughter's shoulders and walked slowly along the platform with her. "I haven't been a good father to you, Gracie. I see that now. But I'm going to give you two rules to follow and you must listen and obey me. First of all, you must never come back here."

"But, Papa—"

"No. I mean it. Never. Go to Boston and have a good time. Try to forget everything here. Find a good man and marry him. Somebody who will never bring you here. And be sure he's young. That's my second rule. Marry a man with all his strength and years and hopes ahead of him. Not an old man like I was when I married your mother. I didn't know what a young woman wanted or needed, nor did I know how to be a father to you. That's the train whistle, Gracie. You must go. Now!''

"Why, you're shivering, Gracie. Are you cold, even with the fur?'' Nell said, bringing her thoughts back to the present.

"No. I'm not cold,'' she said, making herself smile. "Who are these people I'm going to the theater with tonight? I know you told me, but I've met so many new friends, I'm having trouble with names.''

"You haven't met them before. They live next door when they're not at their house in the country. A nice young man named Edmund Bills and his sister Adele. Charming young people. And they're bringing along a cousin of theirs who's visiting from Alaska or Alabama or someplace. His name is Jack Thorne. Ah, the doorbell. Are you ready?''

Edmund Bills was a gangly, fair-haired youth a year older than Grace. His manner was painfully shy, but gentlemanly. His sixteen-year-old sister, Adele, was as sweet and bubbly as champagne. "So you're Grace. I'm ever so glad to meet you. How yummy you look in that cape. I vow, I'd love to wear furs, but my mother says I'd look like a little bear because I'm so plump, you see. But you're thin and graceful. Graceful Grace! How clever of me. I must remember to tell cousin Jack that one. He'll be along in just a moment. He's ever so anxious to meet you—''

"You're giving away my secrets, Adele,'' a soft Southern voice said from the doorway. "I'm glad to meet you, Miss Emerson.''

One of Grace's frequent duties at home had been to read to her mother from Clara's collection of maudlin romantic novels. Grace had doggedly read aloud about sweet young girls who met The Man and fell instantly in love. It was all she could do not to fling the silly books down in disgust. And yet, the moment she saw Jack Thorne, she knew it could happen—*had* happened to her.

He was tall and square-shouldered with thick blond hair and lobelia-blue eyes. He had the long, high-bridged aristocratic nose and the strong, even teeth of a thoroughbred. His voice was deep and slow and tinged by the South—a lazy, not-quite-arrogant drawl that sounded soothing to Grace's

Virginia ears after weeks of clipped Boston vowels. The
marvelous look and sound of him literally left Grace breathless.

"How d-do you do . . ." she started, but the words stuck
in her throat.

"I say, has Adele already stunned you with her chatter?"
he asked, tucking Grace's arm through his in a proprietary
manner. "It's quite natural. Most folks can only take a few
minutes of it before they clap their hands to their ears and run
off screaming that they want to be hermits."

"Jack Thorne! I declare you are the most impossible man!"
Adele pouted prettily.

"I promise you, Miss Emerson, I'll tie something around
her mouth if she keeps it up. Come along, now, y'all. We'll
be late for the play."

Grace never knew what the play was; she spent the next
two hours watching Jack Thorne out of the corner of her eye.
If she'd been only slightly less a lady, she'd have frankly
stared, drinking in the fine sight of him like a desert soaking
up a spring rain. At one point he shifted in his chair and his
arm brushed hers. For the rest of the evening she could feel
her skin tingle where he'd touched her arm.

By the time he and his cousins delivered her to her aunt's
house, Grace was in despair. She'd been too tongue-tied to
utter more than a few words, and each of those, she believed,
was idiotic in the extreme. He'd never want to see her again.
She managed to smile as they said their good-nights, but as
soon as the door closed, she started crying.

Her room at Aunt Nell's faced the Bills house and she
spent the next two days concealed behind the curtains watching for Jack Thorne to come out. And he did. Over and over
again. Sometimes alone, sometimes with Adele and Edmund,
but they always went the other way. Finally, a week after
their evening at the theater, he did come to see Grace. "I've
borrowed some bicycles," he said. "Would you like to come
for a ride with me?"

"I don't know how to ride one, Mr. Thorne."

"I can't see what difference that makes. Neither do I, but
how shall we know if we like it unless we try? And I cannot
allow you to call me Mr. Thorne. Simply can't allow it. My
name's Jack."

"And mine's Grace."

"I know. It's most suitable."

"I'm not sure you'll think so after you see me on a
bicycle," she said with a wry smile.

The bicycling was quickly abandoned, to Grace's relief. She couldn't even get the terrible high-wheeled vehicle to stay upright, and Jack managed to go only a few wavering yards before toppling off. They returned "the monsters," as Jack referred to them after his fall, and walked around the little park across the street from the homes where they were staying. Jack took her hand just as if they were sweethearts. "Where are you from?" she asked him when she could trust herself to speak.

"Arkansas. I'm here attending school. I finish this spring, then I'll go back."

"I've never met anyone from Arkansas. You don't sound pleased about returning."

"I'm not."

"You like Boston better?"

"Lord, no! Arkansas is a beautiful place. My house is grand and has a view from nearly every window that would take your breath away. The climate is generally mild, the hunting's good. It's a fine place. But it's lonely."

"You don't have a large family?"

"I don't have any family, except the Billses. My mother died shortly after I was born and my father passed on three years ago. That's when I came to school, because I couldn't stand the quiet. The house—it's called Thornehill—is enormous. Like a castle or hotel or the like. I've never known what my father had in mind, building it. He didn't remarry, nor did he seem to have any intention of doing so. Perhaps he meant the very size of it to say something about himself to those who saw it. I don't know."

Grace had been picturing a rather gloomy house as he spoke. "Is it not a cheerful home?"

"It could be. But it needs to be full of people. It cries for voices and bustle. Do you understand that, Grace?"

"I do indeed. I've led a very isolated existence too. Just my mother and father and myself. I never want to return to it."

He gave her a quick, appraising glance, then changed the subject.

After that, Jack Thorne came to see her frequently. "When do you attend to your studies?" she asked once.

"Practically never. I have no need to make myself brilliant to get ahead in life. I started ahead," he replied offhandedly. "In another two months I'll have to go back home, you know."

"I know."

The days rushed by and every night Grace went to bed cursing the fact that another precious day was gone. Jack Thorne called on her nearly every day, taking her to dances, plays, card parties. They tried tennis and golf and went to Constitution Hall on the train with Edmund and Adele to see the Liberty Bell.

Sometimes Jack's friend Howard Lee came along. "I'm trying to get Howard to come back with me this summer, but he's determined to stay on and finish medical school," Jack explained to Grace.

Howard grinned through his sandy mustache. "Gotta make a living, old boy, not like some idle rich folks I know."

Jack Thorne was the personification of everything Grace had missed in life. He was laughter and freedom without a care or worry. He was easygoing, outgoing, young, and vital. And if he was a little irresponsible, so much the better. Grace herself was weighted down like a drowning victim by a sense of responsibility. (Was it her sister or she herself who had drowned that day? she wondered for the first time.) Jack's easy unconcern only made him all the more charming. Whereas she had faced life like a high wind to be doggedly endured, he let the breeze take him where it might.

She asked him often about his home, not quite understanding at first his reluctance, but insistence, on going back. "But if you don't like it there, why return?"

"But I *do* like it. I love it. It's just lonely. Other than that, it's probably the most perfect place on earth."

"It's in the mountains? The Ozarks, you called them?"

"Well, not mountains like the Rockies, not craggy and wild and hostile. The Rockies are grandfathers. The Ozarks are grandmothers—gentle, rounded, lush with growth. And the fogs! Oh, Grace, you've never seen such beautiful fog— soft white tatters that drift and billow. And on certain days in the spring the smell of new growth is so pungent it makes you faint with the joy of it." He closed his eyes, breathing deeply as if conjuring up the memory of the fecund scent. Grace was as mesmerized by his words as by his strong, handsome profile.

"And the house?" she asked. "Tell me about the house."

"It sits on the peak of a hill and you can see for miles and miles in every direction. There are a great many windows and the rooms are large and airy. The only thing it lacks is people. My father didn't seem to mind that. He used to just roam around the house, like a king who'd lost his kingdom but hadn't yet noticed. The house has everything but noise, if that makes sense. It needs the voices of children and servants and dogs barking and music playing—then it would be perfect."

Grace sighed, imagining the vast home with the beautiful views and the awful quiet. She was too young and untried to realize she was falling in love as much with a place as a person, but Thornehill and Jack Thorne were one. Equally important, that which he so craved was what she wanted too—a home that was full of life and laughter. Someplace that would forever erase the memory of the silent halls, the darkened room where a mean, obese drunk held court.

Two weeks before Jack's scheduled departure, Adele and Edmund's parents had a going-away party in his honor. Halfway through the party Jack came up behind Grace and whispered, "Meet me out in the garden in ten minutes," then disappeared.

When she joined him in the small, neat backyard that adjoined her aunt's yard, Jack was sitting on a stone bench, his long legs stretched in front of him and the smoke from his cigarette drifting on the night air. He leapt up and ground out the cigarette on the paving stones. "I need to talk to you, Grace. Sorry to be so mysterious. I just didn't want my dear nosy cousin Adele along."

"I don't think she'll miss either of us. She's dancing with Frank Smith," Grace said, sitting down on the bench beside him.

"Good. I think my aunt's going to have a son-in-law sooner than she expected. Grace, I want to ask you something."

For the first time since she'd met him, he seemed nervous. His speech had lost some of the comfortable drawl it usually had. "Is there something wrong, Jack?"

"No . . . Yes. I'm going back to Arkansas."

She laughed. "I know that. It's the reason for this party. I shall miss you." Miss you? I shall die without you, she thought.

"I've thought about staying here, you know."

Grace wanted to ask why, wanted to make him say he longed to remain with her, but instead she said, "You don't like the city. You know you're anxious to get home."

He nodded. "I am. Yes. But, Grace, suppose you were in my circumstances. Suppose you had to go back to your home and there was no one there. What would you do?"

Grace shivered at the thought. Her home would never be

empty, it would be peopled with ghosts. But she made herself think as Jack must. "I'd invite all my friends along to visit me."

He suddenly took her hands in his and she felt as if a magnetic force was flowing between them. "But friends would only visit. They wouldn't stay. They wouldn't become part of the home."

"Then I'd invite other people. I'd invite all the bright, interesting people I knew. Artists, writers—"

"Yes, and so shall I, but I want more than that. Every time I imagine what it's going to be like back there, I know there's something missing. You, Grace. I want you there."

"Well, if Edmund and Adele and their parents come, perhaps Aunt Nell would let me accompany them."

"No, Grace. I want you there all the time. I want you to be my wife. Will you marry me?"

Grace knew she should be coy and reluctant, but answered instantly, "Oh, yes, Jack. Yes, yes, yes."

For a moment he seemed stunned, as if he'd expected refusal or feminine delaying tactics. When he fully realized what she was saying, he dropped her hands and folded her in a crushing embrace. "And we'll fill the house with children, Grace? Promise me that."

"Scores of them! We'll have to name them alphabetically to keep track of them all!"

He threw his head back and laughed. "Thank God. Oh, Grace—my wonderful Grace—we're perfect for each other. How happy we're all going to be!"

Grace believed it was all true, this glowing future they'd invented while sitting in a moonlit garden holding hands. She had to believe it because Jack wanted it and she wanted Jack and Thornehill more than she'd ever wanted anything else in life. She would give him children—give *them* children. They would people their own happy world.

IV

NELL Woodline, suspecting but not fully comprehending the details of what life was like at home for Grace, insisted on having the wedding in Boston. "You and Jack both have so many friends here." At least Jack did—that much was true. "It would be a terrible shame for all of them to miss the occasion. There's never been a wedding in this house before and it's a perfect place with that huge parlor . . ."

No one objected; not Grace, who wasn't fooled for a minute by talk of friends and parlors and was grateful beyond words. Not Robert Emerson, and certainly not Clara, who probably was never sober enough to understand—if she had been told at all. Grace had written and asked her parents to attend, living in dread that her mother might, by some hideous circumstance, decide to accept. Robert replied:

"I am delighted that you have found so worthy an object of your affections as Mr. Thorne seems to be. Your aunt's letter about him only underscores the esteem in which you seem so rightly to hold him. I'm writing to Nell today to thank her for her extremely gracious offer to serve as hostess and sponsor of your wedding in your mother's place. I hope you will further express my gratitude for this generous and thoughtful offer. Your mother will not be able to attend this happiest day of your life, but I will be present."

As stiff as it was, Grace read affection and relief into his words and was pleased at the last sentence—not only the content, but the firm attitude. There was no polite "unfortunately" prefixing it, no excuse, no apology. Just the promise that Clara wouldn't be allowed to spoil the day as she'd spoiled so many years.

It remained to explain the situation to Jack. Grace debated for a long time with herself just what to say. She didn't want Jack to think she was hiding anything from him, nor was she ashamed—although she once would have been. She'd been away from home long enough to realize some very important things she'd have never understood if she'd stayed in Virginia. Her mother's meanness and alcoholism were no reflection on her. She had not, in spite of Clara's years of teaching to the contrary, been responsible for what her mother did with her life. She wasn't to blame for Clara's condition, nor did she think Jack would think less of her for it.

On the other hand, she was reluctant to lay out the whole truth for fear he would pity her. She didn't want pity, she'd nearly drowned in Clara's self-pity, and it was the most thoroughly repugnant human emotion as far as she was concerned. Nor did she want him to think for a moment that she was marrying him out of desperation to escape intolerable living conditions at home. She was marrying Jack out of love, and love alone. That home was a hell on earth was another thing altogether.

In the end, she was honest but spare in her explanation. "My mother is an alcoholic, and that's why Aunt Nell is offering to have the wedding here," she said. "And from my father's letters during my stay here, I think my mother's health is failing. She won't be coming up."

Jack was all familial concern. "Do you want to delay the wedding until she's feeling better? Perhaps visit her first?"

"No! No, she won't ever feel better."

There was so much that could have been appended to that. She could have said: I am under my father's orders never to return, and thank God for that. Or: Seeing me is the very last thing that would make her better. She hates me. Or she might have said: I can't bear a moment of delay. The door that's now open to a happy life might slam shut while my back is turned. But she didn't tell him any of that; she just said, "It's all right. My father is coming and he will tell her all about it."

They went to the train station together to meet Robert Emerson when he arrived the day before the wedding. He looked terrible. Grace had forgotten how old he was, and the aging must have accelerated since her departure. His hair was whiter and thinner, his skin seemed merely to hang in pale wrinkles to the bones of his face. She embraced the rather fragile old man, clinging for a moment as if to impart to him by force of will some of her youth and happiness, and when she stepped back she saw that his eyes had filled with tears. They both pretended they didn't notice. "Now introduce me to this young man of yours, my dear," he said, his voice as dry and crackly as corn husks.

He approved of her choice of husband, there was no questioning that. He studied Jack as if mentally ticking off the requirements—young, handsome, polite, vigorous, well-bred—yes, all of those. "He's just what I wanted for you," he said to Grace when Jack went to get his luggage.

"He's just what I want for me too," Grace said. Then: "How is Mother, really?"

He glanced away, as if physically shying from the mention of Clara. When he met her glance again, his eyes were guarded, as if a transparent screen had come down over them to filter out the truth. "She's well."

She knew he was lying. Clara was not well at all. Of course, she never had been, not since the baby died so many years ago. But this was something more. She was, Grace sensed, very ill. But he didn't want to tell her and she didn't want to force him to. Nor did she really want to know—she didn't want pity reaching its long spindly arm across the miles to clutch at the back of her wedding gown and hold her back. "I'm glad to hear it," she said.

He nodded. They understood each other.

In later years Grace seldom lost full control of her actions, but the wedding was like a marionette show. She and Jack were the marionettes and Aunt Nell had her plump, soft hands on all the strings, jerking them about like mad. A wave of people washed over Grace at Nell's bidding—dressmakers for final adjustments in the gown and veil, caterers clattering through the house, a photographer, a hairdresser, and innumerable other people who seemed to be very busy, although Grace couldn't tell just what they were doing.

Howard Lee, fluctuating between vicarious happiness for his friends and some apparent secret sorrow, served as Jack's best man. Adele, now wearing an engagement ring of her own and dressed in fluffy pink, was the maid of honor. Aunt Nell, in plum organza, played the part of mother of the bride with almost embarrassing enthusiasm. Only Jack himself seemed unruffled, floating through the preparations with the serenity of a cork on calm seas. "After all, Grace, the groom is the least important part of a wedding," he said, smiling. "So long as he's present, sober, and reasonably clean, no one notices him.''

The wedding itself, enacted in Nell's front parlor, was a blur to Grace. The minister kept droning on and on. She had to repeat his words and respond with gravity, when all she wanted to do was say, "Yes, yes, be done with it. Make me Mrs. Jack Thorne and let us get out of here!"

After the ceremony there was a formal dinner to endure, and then, as Grace donned the muted green traveling dress and matching hat she would wear to the train, a talk with Nell. *The* talk. "Since your mother is not here to advise you, I fear the task must fall on my shoulders," she said. Blushing girlishly, she murmured, "I hardly know how to begin . . ." and with a final nervous fidget, she put aside her qualms like a bad melon and launched into a startlingly frank description of bodily parts and functions that left Grace all but gasping with astonishment. Somehow Nell managed to convey, without actually saying so, that these activities could be enjoyable, and even if they weren't, there was duty to be thought of.

Only Robert Emerson accompanied the new Mr. and Mrs. Jack Thorne to the train station for their departure to Arkansas. There was, at Grace's request, no wedding trip. "I just want to see your home."

"My home?"

"Our home," she corrected herself.

Jack tactfully busied himself with the stowing of the trunks and suitcases while Grace remained on the platform a few minutes longer with her father. She kept thinking about the last time he came to put her on a train and the advice he'd given her. Marry a young man and don't ever come back, he'd told her. She'd followed this excellent advice. "About Mother . . ." she said.

"I'll write to you when you get settled," Robert said.

"No, I want to know now," Grace said softly.

He looked around as if seeking an escape route, and seeing none, said, "She's dead, Grace."

"When?" She wished there was at least a trace of sorrow in her voice—he deserved to have his wife mourned. He'd loved her, even if no one else, including her daughter, had.

"Four days before I came."

"Did Aunt Nell know?"

"Not until I got here. She agreed with me that you shouldn't be told. Clara hadn't the right to blight your wedding, not even by her death."

Grace took a handkerchief from her sleeve, not to blot her eyes, but to occupy her hands. "Was she ever . . . nice? I can't remember."

"I'm not sure I do either. Not as nice as you, though. That I'm sure of."

"You'll come live with us, won't you?"

He patted the hands twisting the handkerchief. "No, no, I can't do that. I have a home of my own. It will be very quiet and peaceful there now."

"Please come with us. Jack won't mind." Now the tears started.

He took the handkerchief, touched the corners of her eyes with it delicately. She remembered him doing this once before when she was very small. "I think you're right; he wouldn't mind. But you know I can't do that. Don't fuss at me about it."

"A visit then? At least a visit?"

"Perhaps."

But she knew he wouldn't come. He was old and tired and going back to Virginia to die. And she couldn't stop him. She sensed the subaural thunder that signified the rolling over of a generation. She was no longer the child, nor he the father. She was a woman grown and married, might soon be a mother herself, and he was an old man who, standing at her side earlier in the day, had fulfilled his last responsibility by handing her life over to Jack. She'd never loved him so much.

Jack returned and shook his hand. Robert Emerson, as if underlining his earlier ceremonial action, placed Jack's hand in Grace's. "Be happy," he commanded with a hint of the strength Grace vaguely remembered from childhood. "Be very happy."

In spite of all her resolve, Grace began crying as soon as she lost sight of her father standing on the platform waving at the departing train. Jack held her and comforted her, thinking no doubt that this was natural for a young woman leaving her home and family behind. Still she couldn't tell him that it was a home the recollection of which was a nightmare. She did, however, tell him that her mother had died and the information had been kept from them in order not to interfere with the wedding.

Later, Jack left her alone, claiming to be going for a brandy, actually giving her time to compose herself for bed in privacy. When he came back, he put out the lights, leaving as the only illumination the occasional flash and flicker of lights from farmhouses and villages the train was passing through. He was gentle, solicitous, and courteous about this strange animal thing Nell had told her about. But for Grace, exhausted and emotionally drained, there was only the mild discomfort Nell had warned her of, a deep sense of embarrassment, and a curious feeling afterward like being hungry but unable to find anything in the larder to satisfy the appetite. But Jack was apparently satisfied and that was all she really wanted. She must have misread Nell's hints that this might be pleasant. It was neither pleasant nor terribly unpleasant, only necessary.

"When will we see the house?"

"That's the third time you've asked," Jack said with a smile. "We'll get a glimpse of it in just a minute. No, you're looking the wrong way. Over there just beyond the trees—"

"I see it! Jack, I see it! Oh, Jack, it's enormous!"

"I told you it was."

They were still too far away to discern details, and in a moment the house disappeared from view. "Hurry, Jack. Hurry!" she said as they went along the winding road. They passed, without Grace's taking any particular notice, the overgrown track that led down to the cottage.

And then the house was revealed again. It was perfectly situated at the very peak of the hill and looked like a French château that had inexplicably found itself in Arkansas and had settled in to make the best of the location. The facing stone was a rich bluish-gray with white limestone around the windows and doors. The architect had managed to graft on a weather-practical two-story columned veranda along the center front without making either the house or the veranda look uncomfortable. This center section was like the crossbar of a very short H, with three-story wings on each side. The center had three levels with copper-flashed roofs that had mellowed to a distinct lichen green.

"What do you think?" Jack asked, grinning.

She could hardly dredge up words at all, much less any that expressed her immediate and profound love of this place. She'd never seen it before, never even seen anything like it. And yet it was vaguely familiar, as if from a recurring childhood dream. This was Thornehill at last. Her home. "How could you have ever left here?" she asked.

"I had to," he replied. "To find you."

"Oh, Jack . . ." She meant to laugh, but it came out a sob instead. "Let's never leave here. Not even for a minute."

They'd hardly settled in before the guests started coming. Jack had made many friends while in Boston and invited all of them at one time or another. People said laughingly that an invitation to Thornehill was really a summons, there was no turning it down. There were always people around. Servants— far more than necessary—bustled about tending to the needs of the never ending stream of guests. There were luncheons and dinners and picnics on the grounds, with bright umbrellas and wicker baskets of food. Jack put in tennis courts and a small covered dock on the spring lake just below the house. A friend with landscaping skills helped lay out a pattern of graveled walkways to make strolling the grounds more pleasant. There were hunting parties and fishing parties and card parties, dances and masquerades and charades after dinners that could have fed twice as many and would have if Jack had been able to find more individuals to sit at table. At first, it was all as they'd imagined.

In a little less than a year Grace was pregnant; seven months later she miscarried. "Maybe you counted wrong," Jack said as she clutched her abdomen at the first sudden pain.

But she knew she hadn't. And she knew the child wouldn't live.

"I'm sorry, Jack," she wept as he came to her room after it was done and the small bundle that might have been a child had been taken away. She'd wanted the child and could feel the ache in her arms from wanting to hold and cuddle an infant. But she hadn't wanted it nearly as much for her own sake as for his.

"I'm sorry too, but there'll be other children. We're young. There's plenty of time."

"Yes, Jack. We'll have dozens and dozens of children. I promise."

He'd hired a nurse, months ahead of her anticipated need, painted a room for her and the baby, brought a crib down from the attics where it had been stored. "It was mine," he'd told Grace as he polished it and tested the smoothness of the rockers. Now the nurse went back to Hot Springs, the room was closed, and the crib was covered with a dust sheet—but not taken back to the attic.

She kept apologizing to Jack until he became irritated. "It wasn't your fault, Grace," he said almost snappishly. "It was just a hateful little trick of nature."

And even before she'd left her sickbed, he'd invited more people to visit them as if their harsh adult voices might somehow cover the silence of missing babies' cries. Grace didn't mind their presence, but didn't need it as he seemed to. For her the world was ringed by Jack and hope, which was enough. But as time went by, the doubts came in black inches; the guilt started dropping a gauzy curtain over her days and nights. And every time a new month was marked with her blood, she despaired anew. Would she never fulfill her part of their loving bargain?

Adele came to Thornehill as one stop on her wedding trip. Edmund stayed a whole summer and never seemed to look up from his books, though he claimed, quite sincerely, to be enjoying himself. Aunt Nell brought a widowed cousin and the two older women had a grand time learning to fish, and even baited their own hooks before the visit was over.

The one person who didn't come to visit was Robert Emerson. At one point he seemed almost convinced. "Please, Father, just for a day or two at least. I won't try to hold you here if you don't like it, but I want you to come," she'd witten in response to his last letter.

He didn't reply; Nell did with a telegram. "Robt. Emerson passed on peacefully yesterday. Letter to follow."

There wasn't time for the long train trip before the funeral. Nell went to Virginia to represent Grace, and Edmund Bills went along with her at Grace's request.

"Are you sure you want Edmund to sell the house and land for you?" Jack had asked, surprised at Grace's request.

"Will he mind?"

"Not in the least. But don't you want to go back yourself before turning it over to strangers? See it once more?"

"No. My house wasn't like yours, Jack."

"Mine?"

"Ours."

Though she grieved the loss of her father, she felt a strange sense of freedom. The last tie to the past was broken now. She and Jack had nothing but future. And if they could just have a child, then everything would be perfect.

V

1895

"SIT you forward just a bit, Miz Grace, and let me plump up them pillows. There now, how's that?"

"Very comfortable, Mabelann. Thank you," Grace said, lying back and pulling the covers up.

"You ready to see the doctor now? He been downstairs talkin' with Mr. Jack while we been gettin' you fixed up."

"He waited all this time? Yes, please, send him in."

Howard Lee came in a few minutes later. He'd finished medical school six months after Grace and Jack had married. He'd set up practice in Eureka Springs with his father, who hardly waited until the gloss was off Howard's instrument bag before retiring to Arizona. Howard had taken over his office, his patients, and his dignified mien. Now he sat in the needlepoint chair by Grace's bed with his legs crossed and his long fingers laced on his knee. "How are you feeling?" he asked her.

"Is that a medical question or a social one?" Grace asked.

It was an oddly bitter remark—for her. But understandable, he supposed, under the circumstances. "Social, mainly. I can tell to look at you that you're well. Your color is good and you don't seem to be in pain."

Grace looked away for a moment. "Oh, Howard . . ."

"I know. You're upset. You got your hopes up in spite of all my warnings that it couldn't live."

"Not 'it,' Howard. 'She.' My daughter."

"No, Grace. A premature infant who couldn't have survived more than a few hours."

"I named her Laura. That was my sister's name." For a second she was on the brink of telling him about her baby

43

sister. She'd almost said: I let her drown. She felt her eyes filling with tears for this Laura and the long-dead one both. No, she thought, always brutally honest with herself, the tears are for me.

"Grace you're torturing yourself unnecessarily. There will be more children. You're young. Only twenty-three."

"But this is the third time. I can't seem to carry a child to term. What's wrong with me!"

He'd heard women say this before, but he'd never heard them mean it quite the same way. "Nothing's wrong with you, Grace. It's merely an accident of nature, not a personal failing. You must not think that you are to blame. Blame God or the medical profession or the phases of the moon if you want, but not yourself."

Grace was silent for a long moment, then reached out to him. He took her hand in his and patted it avuncularly. "Don't try again too soon. Give yourself a long rest without worrying."

"Howard, I can't wait. I can't!" she said.

"Why not? There's all the time in the world."

Grace couldn't tell him. Close as they were, she couldn't say that she believed Jack married her primarily for the children she'd promised him, and without children, she had a fear bordering on phobia that she'd lose Jack's love.

If she ever had it.

"You sleep a little longer and I'll come back to see you again this evening," Howard said, rising. "Jack's gone into town to . . . make arrangements. For the burial."

"Thank you for everything," Grace said, closing her eyes and pretending to obey his orders.

But sleep wouldn't come. How many more times would Jack select tiny coffins before he realized that he'd made a bad bargain marrying Grace Emerson? Was this it? Was this the time he'd return from the undertaker's and look at her in a new way?

He wouldn't divorce her. That she was sure of. He was too kind, too honorable, and too fond of her. Yes, he *was* fond of her. He laughed at her jokes, fussed over her when she was ill, noticed and complimented her skills, and sympathized with her failures. He respected her. He admired her mind, her looks, her morals, her management of the household.

Why wasn't that enough? It was all Grace had imagined the perfect marriage to be. And yet, she'd have happily given it all up for one thing—even though she wasn't sure what that one thing was. The missing element was only a hazy concept in her fevered mind. She couldn't define it. Only feel it—or rather, feel its absence.

The mysterious void was most apparent to her on those nights when he came to her bed. It had been the same ever since their wedding night, little had changed. Jack was politeness itself, giving her subtle warning that he would join her, dousing the lights before undressing to spare her the shock of seeing an unclad male body, never referring to their activities in a direct or vulgar way. And always she wondered why he bothered at all. It had to be because this was the only way to beget children. For all the sticky evidence that he'd found relief, he didn't seem to actually enjoy it any more than she did. Not *really* enjoy. He never laughed, or even smiled when it was over. If anything, he was mildly apologetic.

Grace had decided there would never be anything in it for her, but wanted to make it more pleasurable for him, hoping in some way to buy a larger stock in his heart to make up for the lack of children. But she was a well-brought-up young woman of generally eccentric but sexually conventional antecedents and had no idea of how to make him happier in bed. She might as well have tried to converse with him in Sanskrit.

So they had gone from year to year, performing a duty that was cool and necessary for him, perplexing and frustrating for her. She might have just accepted the situation as being natural, like the majority of women of her generation did, except for a remark Mabelann made.

Mabelann had come to Thornehill the year after Grace did. Sixteen years old, sassy and self-confident, she claimed to be a widow. "Lynch mob, ma'am," she explained with a cool detachment that Grace couldn't fathom. "Said he broke into a barn and stole a chicken. He never did no such thing! We had our own chickens. Nice little flock of Rhode Island Reds. He didn't have no need to steal none." The injustice of the accusation seemed to bother her more than her husband's actual demise.

"How terrible for you!"

"Yes'm, Miz Grace, 'specially at night. He was one powerful good buck in bed."

Suddenly realizing this was an inappropriate way to talk to her employer, Mabelann stopped. Grace, shocked, pretended not to have heard. Nor would the most exquisite torture device ever have made her raise the subject again, but she thought about it. Often. What *could* Mabelann have meant?

Apparently she was referring to the same act that Grace and Jack performed, but from a completely different viewpoint. It seemed, if Mabelann was to be believed, that a woman could actually enjoy intercourse.

It was like hearing a rumor that someone had dropped a diamond down the drains. All common sense argued that the search would be long and fruitless and the diamond, if found, might turn out to be paste, but still the image of finding it kept coming back at odd moments. A sparkling, unattainable goal.

Grace turned over gingerly, putting a hand to her aching womb, and finally fell asleep wondering if Jack would remember to have "Laura" put on the tombstone.

When she awoke, he was sitting on the edge of the bed. "Feeling any better? Howard says you can get up in a few days."

They didn't talk about the baby's death. Not directly. Nor did Jack mention the funeral arrangements. As before—too often before—she wouldn't be well enough to see the child buried. In a month or so Jack would take her to the gravesite and they would pray together. For now he talked about Grace's health as if she'd had some vague sort of operation. When the subject had been exhausted, he turned the conversation to other matters. "Robert and Emily had to leave. They wanted to tell you good-bye, but you were sleeping. The Ravenwoods are going home tonight and I've sent word to the Joneses that you're ill and we'd like to postpone their visit."

Grace had nearly forgotten about their houseguests—part of a steady stream of horsey, outdoorsy people Jack knew and populated the house with. "They weren't due to come until next month, were they? I'll be fine by then—"

Jack shook his head. "I have other plans."

"Oh?"

"I've been talking to Howard. He suggested a rest would do you good and I think a change of scenery would be a tonic."

"I could move into a room on the other side of the house," Grace suggested, puzzled.

He laughed. "That's not the sort of travel I had in mind. I want to take you on a real trip. We've never been anywhere."

A cold blob formed in the pit of Grace's stomach. "A trip? Where? To visit Adele and Edmund in Boston?"

"No, we're going to Europe!"

"Oh . . ." Grace said weakly.

"You don't want to?" he asked, looking for all the world like a child who's offered up his best toy and had it rejected.

"I . . . Of course, Jack. That would be . . . nice," she said, forcing the words and a matching smile. But inside, she was in turmoil. A trip. Going away. A long, hot drive. Strange people, strange places. Danger. A sudden picture of wet yellow curls and muddy lavender cotton flashed through her mind and was gone before she could identify it. Going away meant disaster.

But Jack wanted it. Jack wanted to give it to her. This plan was an undesired gift she must accept graciously after disappointing him so grievously. So repeatedly. "When will we go?" she asked.

"As soon as you're on your feet again. Two months? Three? We'll take it in easy stages so you won't tire. Oh, Grace, it'll be wonderful. Like a honeymoon. We've never really had a wedding trip, except to come here. We're turning into a couple of fusty old moles, burrowed in here. I know all sorts of people we can visit. Friends from school, family acquaintances, even a few distant relatives. We won't have to stay in hotels. We need a trip. Both of us."

It's the one thing we *don't* need, she thought.

"I can't wait," she said.

"You will come with us, won't you?" her English hostess asked peevishly.

"I'd be delighted, Lady Abigail," Grace answered with as much false enthusiasm as she could muster. "I've just got a little paperwork to finish." One of the companies in which the Thornes held considerable assets was considering a merger and there were proxies to deal with. Jack, disinterested as usual, had asked her to sort it all out and prepare the paperwork for his signature. She had started marriage handling only the domestic accounts—servants' wages, minor house repairs and such—but quickly discovered that a greater realm of family finance called to her. Jack had taught her what he knew about the stock market, seemingly glad to cast off this knowledge and responsibility. Grace had eagerly taken it up, to please him and because she enjoyed the challenge.

"Oh, very well, but I can't imagine how you can do all that boring business. I'm ever so glad John attends to all that." Her words were bland, but her expression was critical, implying that such "boring business" was somehow unfeminine.

"I suppose he enjoys it, as I do," Grace said to the rebuke.
"My husband doesn't, so I try to spare him the nuisance."
She glanced out the window at the rain, the perpetual London
rain, and wished for a pleasant day. She could at least get out
of here for a walk or a quiet ride in the park.

"Who are these people Mr. Thorne has gone to visit?"
Lady Abigail asked. She was a young, silly woman with
frizzy hair and pale lashes. Normally she seemed vapid and
vain, but as she asked this question her face assumed a distinctly sly look.

Grace studied her for a moment, then answered, "I didn't
catch the name he mentioned. Some sort of distant cousins. He'll be back in London tomorrow."

"He'll be sorry he missed being here. He and John have
been to the musical show several times and found it most
entertaining. Of course, it isn't the sort of place ladies normally go. Ever so scandalous, but I adore shocking people,
don't you? I'm so glad John finally agreed to take us. Now,
you just *must* come along and show everybody how modern
Americans are."

Please come back and get me out of here, Jack! Grace
thought when her hostess had finally gone. Such an utterly
useless, silly girl, and her husband was no better. But they'd
probably stay on another week as planned because Jack—for
reasons surpassing her understanding—seemed to like them
both. More surprising, he enjoyed their life. The morning
visits, the endless male talk of shooting, the drinking, the
gluttonous meals with more servants than served, the evenings when the ladies stayed home and gossiped and the men
went out on the town—all of it seemed so pointless to Grace.
But Jack was supremely happy.

Grace was prepared to hate the music hall and it lived up
to, or rather down to, all her anticipations. It was crowded,
noisy, and stifling hot. The music was loud and discordant
and the "entertainment" was alternately boring and distasteful. Lady Abigail was busy being shocked at herself and kept
emitting little squeals of delight. Her husband roared like a
bull elephant at cockney jokes that Grace couldn't hear, much
less understand. They were having a delightful time, preten-
tiously "slumming," and Grace was embarrassed for them
and for herself.

Finally the master of ceremonies announced that someone
named Mimi was next on the bill and anyone who didn't quiet
down and behave would be thrown out. There was a vast

cheer accompanied by foot stomping and whistles. The master of ceremonies shouted above the din, "Here, for your entertainment and education, straight from the stages of Gay Paree, the beautiful, the incomparable . . . *Mimi!*"

She was beautiful, in a voluptuous yet fluffy, kittenish way. She came onstage in a little rickshawlike wagon pulled by two burly men. She hopped down with a careless flip of her skirts that revealed shapely plump calves and well-turned ankles and began a song. It was all about an innocent country girl coming to the city and was full of naughty double entendres that missed being vulgar because of her charm. She giggled and winked and pranced delightfully. Her voice was both husky and childish and she had the barest hint of a lisp. Her generous bosom bounced as she danced, and almost fell clear out of her dress when she bowed. She stood up, looked down, and said, grinning, "Oopsy-daisy! I didn't mean to shock the little boys!"

The men stood and clapped again, shouting, "More! More! Encore!"

She did two more songs, each a little more blatantly risqué than the one before, then pranced off, petticoats flipping. The audience begged for more, but she came back only for one quick, breast-revealing bow, then disappeared.

The show was over—thank heaven!—and the crowd started to depart. But as Grace and her companions reached the aisle, a scuffle broke out. She was pushed against the wall and lost her grip on Sir John's arm. Voices were raised and people started pushing.

Rather than struggle against the crowd, Grace backed up and ducked through a doorway next to the stage, intending to wait a moment until matters were straightened out. She found herself in a small dark alcove at the bottom of some steps that apparently led to the dressing rooms.

"Oh, I don't think I was a bit good tonight," a husky voice said somewhere behind her. Mimi's voice.

"You were wonderful, as always," her companion replied.

Grace froze in place as her heart turned over in her chest. It was Jack who'd answered.

Jack!

No! It couldn't be! He was down at Rye visiting cousins.

"Oh, you're just saying that," Mimi said with a giggle. "What a naughty big man you are. Give us a little kiss, lovey."

Grace turned, her body stiff as sun-dried leather and almost creaking with the effort. She stood in the dark, staring up at the scene at the top of the stairs for a long moment, though it had taken her only a second to confirm her fears. Jack had his hands on Mimi's tiny waist and was bent, his lips touching hers.

"Come on, ducky," Mimi said, pulling away a few inches. "I'm dry as a beached whale. Let's go have a drink and a bit of eats, then we can go to my place and you can tell me how you liked it—dinner, I mean," she added with a laugh.

"I'll be glad to tell you exactly how I like it—dinner and everything!" Jack replied.

And to Grace's vast relief, they moved off. She'd been horrified that they'd come down the stairs and find her cringing there. She felt guilty at having penetrated Jack's secret, as if she were somehow at fault for his indiscretion, not he. And indeed, she did believe the fault was mainly hers. If only she'd been able to engage his whole heart, he wouldn't need to be here.

She didn't notice the door open until Sir John took her arm. "That was quick thinking, slipping in here," he complimented her. "It's all clear now. Just a spot of fisticuffs. Nothing to worry about. Why, you're pale as a sheet! Sit down here on the step for a moment—"

"No! I want to go home. Right now."

Lady Abigail had joined them. "Oh, my. Are you going to faint, dear? I thought Americans were used to this sort of thing. You're not hurt, are you?"

Hurt? Grace felt as if a molten knife had slashed through her innards. But she would *not* make a scene for fear Jack might still be near and find out she'd seen him with Mimi. "No, I'm just fine, thank you," Grace said, straightening and touching her hair. "But I would like to get home soon."

VI

"*P*RETTY l'il place . . .." Jack drawled ironically.

Grace, startled by the remark after such a long silence, dutifully looked out the carriage window at the house revealed in the valley below them. It was enormous, almost institutional in size, though not architecture. Nestled in a valley a few miles from the fashionable English resort town of Bath, Huntleigh Manor was quite the most impressive private residence Grace had ever seen. Its mass made even Thornehill seem trivial and transient. The core of the manor house was early Tudor, but newer wings sprawled gracefully in all directions. To the west, a Stuart staircase graced an addition that looked like Charles II might have overseen its construction; to the north an enormous Georgian brick block of rooms enclosed a courtyard; on the south side an addition almost as large as the rest of the house was newly, brashly Victorian and narrowly missed being vulgarly ornamented.

While Grace was suitably impressed, she'd have gladly traded the whole place to be back at Thornehill. This trip had become a daily, hourly agony for her. Especially since the night two weeks earlier when she'd seen Jack with the musical-hall girl. She'd cried herself sick that night, wallowing in sorrow until she loathed herself. The next day Jack had returned, hangdog and snappish.

"How were your relatives?" she'd asked, trying very hard to keep the sarcasm out of her voice, but unable to quell the question.

He might have heard the bitterness in her voice, or noticed her puffy eyelids beneath the thick coat of rice powder, or it

51

might have only been his own guilt, but he looked at her for a long moment before answering curtly, "Very boring."

A hundred times she'd come to the crumbling brink of confrontation, and each time she'd drawn back in horror. She wanted to fling herself at him, slash him with accusations, let out the leaden sobs that kept blooming in her chest. She wanted to say: I love you more than myself! How dare you cut my heart apart this way? And yet she feared such an action might be the very thing that would drive him away permanently, slam shut any doors that might still remain ajar between them. Jack liked life easy and pleasant. He liked people to be happy. If she behaved like a screaming shrew, he might utterly reject her. And that, she could not bear. The knowledge of his infidelity, horrible as it was, was only the second most terrible thing that could happen to her.

Of course, he had rejected her by having an affair. But as long as she pretended not to know, there was hope. So Grace decided that first night. The worst—the absolute worst—was when he came to her in bed as if nothing had changed. Their sexual relations were torture to her. She kept thinking: He's done this with her. How? What did he say, what did she say, where did he touch her, did she like it? Did he? Will he go back to her and compare us? Since then, she had thought about almost nothing else. And she'd come to some other conclusions.

Jack had prefaced his proposal for this trip to Europe with the warning that they'd become "fusty old moles." It wasn't true of him, but had he really meant her? Possibly. He'd always claimed to admire her intelligence and she had reveled in the praise, trying always to live up to his expectations of her mental abilities. He'd commented favorably on her tranquillity, her serenity, and she'd nurtured the qualities like hothouse flowers for the sake of pleasing him. But had she gone too far? Had she become too stiff, too intellectual, too boring? An admirable woman, but unlovable?

She watched him closely during the next week of parties and dinners. It was always the silly, fluffy women who got his attention. He helped the helpless ones, laughed at the giggly ones, killed spiders for the shriekers, and carried hatboxes for those who were too dainty for the job. Often, in privacy, he would sum them up as useless fools, but did he mean it? Or did he say it to dissuade her from feeling any inconvenient jealousy? Up until two weeks ago, Grace had never questioned the former. Now she leaned to the latter.

So when he told her three days earlier that they'd been invited to a huge houseparty at Huntleigh Manor, Grace had made some difficult resolutions. He had married her in haste and was repenting at leisure. He liked silly women, so she would be one. No matter what it cost her.

Reminding herself of this vow as the carriage rolled down the steep road, Grace smiled brightly and said, "I hope I've got the right sort of clothing for this party. My goodness, a party that lasts a whole month. How extraordinary. I should have done some more shopping. I don't want everybody to think I'm just another frumpy American."

She cringed inwardly, knowing she wore coyness as awkwardly as she would have worn Wellington boots. But in time she'd get better at this.

Jack looked at her questioningly. "Whatever are you talking about, Grace? You have the most superb taste of any woman I've ever seen."

"Oh, Jack, you're just saying that," she said with a moue.

He stared at her as if she'd just come out with chickenpox. "I *am* saying it. And I mean it."

I'm not doing this well, Grace thought, trying not to blush and failing.

He took her hand. "Grace, are you ill?"

"What a thing to say! Do I look ill?"

"You don't seem yourself, somehow. Perhaps we shouldn't have come. We can turn back right now if you like. Go back to London or on to Paris . . ."

Back to London and your Mimi! she thought bitterly. Not on your life, Jack Thorne! "I wouldn't dream of it. I'm looking forward to have a perfectly wonderful time here."

Their host was a man in his forties named Robert Shirehouse. His father had made a fortune in rope and bought the then-crumbling manor house from the family who'd owned it for centuries before falling on hard times. The father had purchased everything he could for Robert, including a very expensive education and an even more expensive duke's daughter for a wife, an inbred, horse-toothed woman named for her second cousin, the queen. Robert Shirehouse might have been the reincarnation of Henry the Eighth in appearance—big, rufous, hearty, and slightly pig-eyed. Fortunately, he lacked the late monarch's scheming, egocentric personality and had, instead, a mild, chatty, and somewhat earthy disposition.

Oddly, he had such an extremely upper-class accent that it seemed he was trying to talk around a mouthful of peach pits.

"Servants'll show you to your rooms, don't you know. Freshen up, what? Long journey and all that. M'wife Victoria'll join us for sherry later. Say the library at six? What? Little printed maps in rooms. Get the layout of the place, eh? Har-har-har!"

A maid in starched black and white and a footman in green-and-gold livery were waiting discreetly at the door for a summons to show the Thornes to their rooms. They seemed to walk for miles through halls that twisted and turned, finally reaching a door with a beautifully printed card afixed: Mrs. Grace Thorne.

The footman and Jack went on while Grace went in her assigned room to freshen up. Her baggage had already been brought up and unpacked. The maid stayed on to help Grace out of her traveling clothes. She drew a hot, scented bath in the adjoining *salle de bain*, which she insisted on pronouncing "sally dee bane." Grace bathed and then dressed in one of the new frocks she'd bought in London. It was a deep fuchsia silk with clinging narrow sleeves, and a plunging neckline bordered by wide, draped ruffles. An exquisite dress, but very unlike Grace's usual tailored, modest style.

Grace dismissed the maid, studied the printed houseplan, and went in search of Jack. Each door in this wing had a card like hers identifying the resident, but she had to turn two corners before finding her husband's room. "Did you think they'd put me up somewhere in Wales?" he asked when she recounted the difficulty she'd had in finding him. "You look wonderful, dear. New dress? And you've done something different with your hair, too. Mmmm, nice scent," he added as he took her arm.

It's working, she thought. The outrageous price of the dress might prove to be worth it.

But her hopes lasted only until they entered the library. The room was full of guests, several of whom were quite beautiful women. And she saw in several sets of eyes that hungry, acquisitive look that so often came over women meeting Jack. He was all smiles and charm and was instantly absorbed into a group of ladies who claimed to want to hear all about the United States. "Do you have red Indians around your house?" one ringleted blond asked, taking his arm.

Grace accepted a glass of sherry, endured a round of introductions, and settled herself on a Queen Anne chair near the fireplace. He's forgotten me, she thought miserably, watching a woman in black lace flirt with Jack.

Across from her, half-concealed in the shadow of a deep wing chair, a man sat observing her, a lazy, calculating smile on his long, distinctive face. "You deserve better," he finally said, sitting forward for a moment so she could see him.

"I beg your pardon?" she said, surprised at his presence and confused by his remark.

"Any man who would leave you sitting by yourself to give his attentions to that one is a fool of the first order. I'm Frederich VonHoldt, Mrs. Thorne," he said, leaning back again as if giving her time to absorb this important information.

He was quite remarkable-looking, with hair even lighter than Jack's, startling blond against his tanned skin, and eyes so pale they had an eerie look, as if he might be able to see things with them that were invisible to others. His face was long, with sharp angles at jaw and cheekbone. In repose, it was the austere, almost ugly face of a medieval saint. But when he spoke, there was a languorous sensuality to his voice and the cast of his features that negated the saintliness. "He's your husband, I assume." His speech was English-public-school, but with something faintly glottal and Teutonic lurking in the consonants.

Grace felt strangely alarmed, but excited, by him. "How is it you know my name, but aren't sure that's my husband?"

"Unlike the English gentlemen, I have no interest in men, but I'm never in the room with a beautiful woman for long without knowing who she is," he replied with a slow smile. "You, for instance, are Grace Thorne of America, lately from London, destined for the Continent. I have not yet penetrated further. Perhaps you will enlighten me. Or need I make pointed inquiries of others?"

Feeling like a rabbit caught in a snake's gaze, Grace answered, "Why should you take that much interest?"

"Because you are beautiful and unhappy. I appreciate the beauty and can alleviate the unhappiness."

"How? I mean, what nonsense. I'm not the least unhappy."

He ignored the addendum and answered her question. "I shall fall in love with you. We will have a brief, but doomed, affair of the heart. We shall both leave here better for it. Temporarily saddened, perhaps, but with memories to last a lifetime."

Grace came to her feet, nearly spilling her sherry. "I find you rude and offensive—"

He rose from the chair like a fast-growing vine, lithe and serpentine. "I've been too forward, lovely one. My misjudgment. I had assumed that American women were as forthright as their men. I take back—but only for now—what I said. But we will speak of it again when you are ready. And you *will* be ready."

There had been guests at Thornehill at most times since Jack and Grace married, but it was a far different situation from this. At Thornehill, three or four couples at a time came and led a leisurely, unpressured existence for a week or more. It was understood that Grace spent her mornings privately and was not generally available to act hostess until luncheon. There was always something for company to do, but they were more or less expected to find it themselves. Each day, Grace would plan some single activity—a picnic, a long walk, a shopping trip to Eureka Springs, or a special dinner with music afterward.

Here, however, a houseparty was a very busy affair in the manner currently so favored in France. There were, Grace estimated, twenty-eight guests. Each evening, as the maids turned down the beds and put out nightclothes, they also left a schedule for the next day. For the men, there was always a hunt of some sort in the mornings—stags, pigeons, ducks, foxes, or whatever could be aimed at without retaliating. Many of the ladies attended as well, largely for the sake of showing off their sporting costumes.

The days were built around meals. Breakfasts ranging from kippers to kidneys with everything conceivable in between were the beginning. A midmorning snack was usual, in spite of the fact that everyone would soon be offered a gargantuan luncheon when the hunting element returned from their labors. Later in the afternoon, sometimes following hard on the heels of lemonade and cookies on the terrace, there was a high tea with six or seven kinds of sandwiches and as many sorts of cake. There was then an interval in which one might rest, change, and get ready for the formal dinner that began the evening's activities.

Every occasion required a different kind of dress, jewels, and hair arrangement, and making these changes could have absorbed the rest of the time, except that there was a great deal of other organized socializing. There was riding and racing on horses, boating and fishing on the estate lake, even bathing in its frigid waters for the more daring. For those who disliked nature, but wished to be energetic, there were exercise sessions and bicycle riding on the terrace.

Lady Victoria also had a steady stream of "experts" who taught classes in a wide variety of subjects. One could learn cooking—not, of course, in order to perform the skill, but to better instruct one's cook—heraldry, history, poetry, watercolor painting, singing, harp playing, and literature. The days were hectic, energetic, and passed quickly.

The nights, on the other hand, were for flirting—eating, dancing, music, and moonlight strolls, not to mention those myriad forays through darkened hallways after everyone was ostensibly asleep. No one was ever so blatant and vulgar as to refer to such activities directly, but everyone, even Grace, knew what was happening, if not exactly by and to whom.

Through all this, the ladies gossiped, and Grace, unable to participate by circumstance, unwilling by nature, still found herself listening and was irritated with the avidity of her interest when Frederich VonHoldt's name came up. And he was mentioned often.

He was, she learned, in his early thirties, German, and unmarried, though there was rumored to be a great beauty waiting for his eventual return to Berlin. He had been educated in England and was tolerated in English society by virtue of family connections and enormous amounts of money. His people, descended from the same Hanovers who'd provided England with its monarchy when the Stuarts died out, had been rich and influential for centuries. Within the last few decades they had augmented their already substantial fortunes by getting into the manufacture of heavy machinery and ammunition.

This ominous note only added to his mystique. The other women, Grace soon observed, regarded him in somewhat the same way she did, with fascination edged with an emotion akin to fear. There was something inherently alarming about him, something about those icy eyes and angular jaw that precluded the sort of open flirting that could be engaged in with other men. It simply wasn't *safe* to take him too lightly.

It was soon apparent, as well, that he had no interest in any of them but Grace, and the expression of that interest was as perfectly aligned as a gun sight. Where she went, he was. Often their arrival coincided or he contrived to be there first, so she could make no legitimate claim that he was following her. His remarks were attentive, vaguely suggestive without being improper, and totally flattering. He always knew how to stop one word short, one gesture short, once second short of pushing her too hard or pursuing her too ardently.

But pursue her he did. And Grace's injured heart bloomed under the attention, even as she told herself it was dangerous to allow herself to listen and be attracted to him. But when Jack went in to dinner with a ginger-haired lamprey attached to his arm, how nice it was that Frederich was there to smile at Grace, take her hand, and say, "Now to the meal, lovely one, and afterward I will take you aside and tell you some highly amusing stories about Mozart. Then you will tell me more about yourself."

At first, Grace told herself she was interested in Frederich only in relation to Jack; that is, if she pretended to be fond of Frederich, Jack would notice and find her more desirable himself. Jack, however, seemed to be nearly the only person present at the houseparty who was utterly unaware of the flirtation. Grace had never been very good at lying to herself and soon admitted, if only in a secret, quiet place in her own mind, that she was drawn to Frederich for his intellect, his strangely attractive appearance, his wry manner, and, most of all, for his suave, unrelenting seduction of her.

One night two weeks into the visit, Victoria Shirehouse staged an impromptu play. All afternoon the ladies rummaged through a roomful of costumes kept just for such occasions. Grace, risking and incurring a certain degree of enmity, refused to take part. "I could never remember my lines," she demurred.

"Nonsense! No one can. That's part of the fun," her hostess said.

Grace tried to think of another excuse, and failing to find one, said simply, "I'd prefer to be part of the audience, thank you."

The play turned out to be as frightful as she had feared. The other young women had decked themselves out in perfectly outrageous outfits and pranced about like fillies at the auction block. Grace, not wishing to further offend the hostess, had stayed back to help with costumes and slipped into the back of the tiny private theater when the "production" was under way. Jack, at the end of the front row, was in her line of sight.

A young woman with auburn hair and a voluptuous figure— Grace thought her name was Priscilla—was clearly performing especially for him. She kept sidling to the side of the stage nearest him and presenting her lovely face and awesome bosom in flattering profile while sneaking him looks. Finally, near the end of the so-called play—a torturously mangled version of *As You Like It*—she flung the rose she carried to Jack. The men guffawed as Jack stood, pressed the rose to his own shirt front in mock lovesickness, and tossed it back to her. A look passed between them that was almost tangible in its promise.

Grace rose quickly, her knees trembling. To the footman at the door she said, "Tell Mr. Thorne I've gone to bed, should he inquire."

She returned to her room, but found she could not bear the closed-in solitude. She grabbed a cloak and went down the winding stairway to a door that led out into the gardens. There a chessboard in two shades of granite was laid out with surrounding ranks of topiary chess pieces. She slipped between a yew-king and yew-queen and walked on toward the smaller of several lakes visible from her window. There was a stone ha-ha with benches. Cloak and skirts billowing, she sank onto a bench and buried her hot face in her hands.

But tears wouldn't come. They would have been a relief. Instead, she felt a cold anger. And she was too absorbed in attempting to analyze it to hear the soft footfalls of Frederich VonHoldt until he stepped into the ha-ha. "You found the entertainment distasteful? Of course you did," he said, sitting beside her without any polite inquiry as to whether she desired company.

It was good that he didn't ask permission. She would have felt she must ask him to leave, when, in truth, she wanted him there. And when he leaned back and slipped his arm around her shoulders, she knew she should move away, should chide him, but instead marveled at how she could feel the warmth of his arm through the fabric of his garments and hers. She had once had that experience with Jack, but she'd been young and innocent then, free of the unsatisfied hungers that haunted her now.

He murmured something in German. She turned as if to inquire as to the meaning—no, she turned so her lips might be closer to his. But he didn't press the advantage she offered. Not right away. "You were wise, not putting yourself on the sale block the way the others did tonight."

"The sale block?"

"Do not pretend naiveté, dear Grace. You are unsullied, but not stupid. You know my meaning."

"Is the play over?"

"It was over before it began," he said with a soft laugh that raised the hair on her arms for a reason she couldn't discern. "I would have been gravely disappointed if you had participated, but I knew you would not. To be so young and beautiful and yet have such a sense of dignity and self-worth, Ah, it is rare and wonderful."

"You're quite wrong. I have no self-worth," she blurted out.

"Then you have been ill-used."

"No, I haven't."

"Then . . . unused."

Grace, suddenly ashamed of the intimacy of the conversation, turned her head. But he took her chin in his long fingers and brought her back. At that moment, a rumble of distant thunder rolled over them and a closer flash of lightning illuminated his face—his strange, angular, handsome-ugly face—and Grace leaned against him, as though propelled by a hand at her back.

Then he kissed her, his lips finding hers unerringly in the sudden darkness following the brief illumination.

It was as if she'd never been kissed before, but had been preparing for the moment all her life. His touch was light, tempting, promising. He put his long, angular, sensitive hands to the sides of her face and examined her features with his lips—eyes, cheeks, brow, temples, jawline. Grace closed her eyes, reveling in his attentions, shaken by his physical presence as she never had been by Jack's. And yet, even in this strangely exhilarated euphoria, she knew better than to call it love. It was no such thing. But it was, on this evening, a very good substitute for a woman who'd never suspected there was a substitute.

She had no idea how long they stayed there, kissing, caressing, uttering soft, meaningless syllables. But when Grace became aware of her surroundings again, the storm had moved to the eastern sky and the lights of Huntleigh Manor had flickered out. "We will go inside now," Frederich said. It was a promise, freighted with meaning, which Grace understood.

"Yes."

He took her directly to her room. Of course he knew, even in a nearly dark hallway, which was hers. At the doorway, she paused a moment, her hand on the knob. "You are afraid?" he whispered.

"No, not afraid," she replied, surprised that it was quite

true. Her half-fear of him had fallen away. If she feared anything, it was herself.

The room was dark; the maid had gone. Frederich crossed to the dressing table as if he knew his way and lit a tiny paper-shaded lamp, then turned to her in the dim glow. "You have raindrops in your hair, like stars." he said, coming to unclasp her cloak and let it fall, unheeded, to the floor.

Grace laughed. "Was it raining?"

"Only a little," he said, reaching around behind her and expertly unclasping the buttons at the back of her dress while nuzzling her neck. "You tremble."

"Yes," she admitted.

"You need not," he said, slipping the shoulders of her gown down and smoothing his hands down her arms.

Grace closed her eyes and leaned against him, savoring the warmth of him, the contrasting textures of fabric and skin as he shed his own clothes. By the time he carried her to the high bed, she was nearly whimpering with anticipation. And he didn't disappoint her. He was an expert lover; gentle and powerful both, willing to suit her pleasure with touches, kisses, pauses.

And while it was happening, Grace was aware of two of herself. One Grace who lived at Thornehill, loved Jack Thorne, and knew what she was doing was utterly and completely wrong. But another Grace, a bruised, confused young woman, was half an earth from home and surety. She was not loved by the man she adored, but was desired by this highly desirable man. And that Grace had a hunger for love that superseded all common sense and Victorian morality.

That woman put herself in his hands, figuratively and literally. She was, for a few unforgettable hours, his slave and master, his student, his lover, his woman. And in being all those, she discovered a hidden capacity for pleasure in herself that had, like a lion cub in a secret den, grown to fearful proportions without her knowing its existence. She wasn't to realize until later that she was hardly thinking of Frederich at all. She was too astonished at her own reactions to even wonder about his. Only his skill and obvious experience were of concern to her during that long night.

The clock on the fireplace mantel of her room was striking four when he left. They didn't speak as he dressed, nor after he gave her a last lingering kiss before departing.

*　　*　　*

Jack came to her room late in the morning. Grace was still in bed, but awake, with a belated breakfast tray on her lap.

Somehow, he knew.

And she knew he knew, though she never found out how the revelation came about. It might have been the uncharacteristic disorder of her bed, or the way her dress was still heaped on the floor where it had fallen. Or it might have been something he saw or heard during the night. Or it might have been simply the look of wonder and satisfaction on her face.

"Grace, we're leaving."

"Leaving?"

"We're going to London and then straight home."

With that, he turned to leave, but paused at the door. "You cam make your good-byes this morning, can't you?"

It was an innocuous remark—or would have been in other circumstances. Grace hadn't time to reply before he was gone. She set aside her untasted breakfast and hurriedly dressed. The hallway was blessedly empty when she tapped quietly on the door of Frederich's room. He opened it immediately, still clad in a blue brocade dressing gown. "Grace!"

"My husband is taking me away," she said. "Today."

"Ahh, he is not as stupid as he appears," Frederich said, pulling her in and shutting the door behind her.

"He's not stupid at all," Grace said, instinctively defending him. "What am I to do?"

Frederich left her standing there while he went across the room and took up a pipe. "How extraordinary that you should ask me . . ." he said between puffs as he held a match to the bowl of the pipe. He didn't look up. "But since you do ask, the answer is quite obvious. You will go with him. What else would you do?"

Grace was dumbfounded. She waited for him to go on, and when he didn't, she said, "That's all you have to say?"

"What else should I say, Grace dear?"

"You don't want me?"

"Want you? Of course. Otherwise would I have pursued you so ardently? Had you remained with the houseparty I would have been utterly 'true to you'—as the English so sentimentally say—for the duration. But this is not to be."

"For the duration . . . ?"

Then he looked up, annoyance in his angular features. "Certainly you were not believing otherwise. Did you imagine I would try to take you away from your husband? This is not my way. Grace, you knew what you were doing . . . this was an *affaire*. That's all. You knew that from the beginning. I was sure you understood, otherwise I would not have become involved. Last night was delightful, and it's a pity there are not to be more, but . . ." he finished with a shrug.

Grace couldn't have been more shocked if he'd thrown a pail of boiling water on her. She all but sputtered in her shock and indignation. "You are contemptible! You used me!"

"I? Don't be any sillier than you have to be. I did *so* admire your serenity and dignity. We were both using. You needed flattery and romance. I gave them to you in full measure. In return, you opened your . . . door"—he said the word with such sly vulgarity that she shuddered—"to me. It was a bargain. Understood by you. Go home, American lady, and teach your husband to flatter and romance you. But do not linger here and create a scene that will do neither of us a service."

Grace was blind with humiliation. She fumbled madly with the doorknob and finally managed to yank the door open. She turned back to say something hateful and devastating to him, but he was relighting his pipe and she was so choked with emotion that she couldn't speak.

When she got back to her room, the maid was tidying. "You may be excused," Grace said in a voice shaking with fury. "Please tell my husband and the hostess that I have a headache and wish to spend the day undisturbed. We will leave at first light tomorrow. Until then, my door will be locked."

When they departed the next day Grace was white with exhaustion and red-eyed from crying. But she had herself under rigid control. She had replayed the scene in Frederich's room a hundred times in her mind, loathing him and herself more each time. But she'd finally managed—after hours of fruitless hysteria—to dig into her heart for the truth. She had gone to his room without consciously examining what she expected to transpire, but later she'd been honest with herself and realized she'd wanted him to beg her to leave Jack and come with him. She wanted, desperately, to be wanted. And she knew, as surely as she knew her name, that she would have gently, ever so kindly refused. She even knew the phrases she would have used to reject him without destroying his honor.

It was not her heart that was injured, for her heart had not been involved. She hadn't ever loved him. She had feared him, been fascinated by him, been enormously attracted to him, but love had never entered into it. It was her pride that had suffered a near-fatal wound. He had used her, used her abominably and with her full cooperation! She had played the whore for a few pretty compliments.

Despicable!

She hated herself, but she hated him with a loathing that was physically painful, for she had been innocent. Stupid beyond belief, but innocent. But he!—he had known her innocence, her sexual ignorance, and he had exploited her to the fullest measure. He had stolen from her an irreplaceable measure of her self-esteem and then had the earth-shaking nerve to discard her as if she were no more important than a soiled glove.

And for this ignomy she had risked her life with Jack.

They rode to the railway station in Bath in complete silence. Grace couldn't trust herself to speak and Jack stared resolutely out the window of the carriage. Once aboard the train, Grace considered how to open the subject. She considered confession, reveling in self-loathing, imagining that if, in abject contrition, she could gain his forgiveness, she might eventually grant her own, but there was no real privacy on a public conveyance. Perhaps on the ship, she thought. Then we will have time by ourselves, without danger of interruption.

But by the time they were on the sea, she'd changed her mind. Jack had never alluded to the events at Bath, even by implication. Partly through common cowardice, partly through genuine concern, Grace decided this was his way of telling her he didn't want to know the truth. She decided to say nothing, but to concentrate on making a superhuman effort to regain whatever happiness they'd had together before this disastrous trip.

By the time they crossed the Atlantic, spent two weeks with Edmund and Adele in Boston, and returned to Arkansas, Grace knew she was once again pregnant. She knew, too, with a sick combination of dread and anticipation, that she would carry this child to term.

There was, however, one important thing she didn't know: one question that kept her awake nights and assailed her like a physical blow when she least expected it. That one thing was the most important. Whose child was it?

VII

IT was the worst pregnancy of all. Grace was listless and nauseated from February through August. She lost weight, her hair and skin grew as dull as her spirits, and the more miserable she was, the more solicitous Jack became. "You know how sorry I am that you're feeling unwell, darling," he said, "but perhaps it's a good sign. You've never been like this before. Maybe it means . . . something."

She knew what he was trying to say. That maybe this time she'd carry the child to term. Maybe it would live. Not maybe: surely. For she knew that her misery wasn't biological. It was a mental state. Recognizing the cause should have resolved the problem. but it didn't. Uncharacteristically, she almost enjoyed being sick. She deserved it, after all. It was, in fact, rather mild punishment for her stupidity and inexcusable moral lapse.

And when, in the middle of July, she began spotting, she was filled with a mixture of elation and terror. Was she losing the child? One moment she was in despair—she sensed that this might very well be her last pregnancy, her last chance. The next moment she was thinking what a relief it would be. She'd never have to know, or ever wonder, whose child it was. But Howard Lee prescribed absolute bed rest and the spotting stopped.

Grace nearly burst with the terrible secret that was growing inside her with the child. The fear was like a child itself, a twin to the one who inhabited her womb. And when the child moved, it was as if the wicked twin reached up a cold hand and clawed at her heart. She had no one on earth but Jack to confide her fears in and he was the single person she could never tell. His joyful anticipation of this birth was too great. There was a great deal she didn't know about him, but she did know for a certainty that he would be devastated by the news that it might not be his child she was carrying.

The only person who seemed to understand her misery was Mabelann. It was not, of course, the sort of thing that could ever be discussed between mistress and servant; neither of them would have considered breaching the rules to that extent. But somehow Mabelann knew. Knew everything, Grace suspected.

"You carryin' that there boy low," Mabelann said often toward the end. "Gonna be a boy, I can tell, and a right big boy, just like Mr. Jack. Bet he gonna look just like him, too."

It was her way of reassuring her employer. "Thank you, Mabelann," Grace said. And for a moment their eyes met and they understood each other perfectly. Then Mabelann dropped her gaze and went back to her work.

It was a surprisingly easy birth, considering the agony of the gestation. At first Grace was afraid to even see the child—a boy, as Mabelann had predicted. But when Howard Lee presented the squalling bundle to her, Grace courageously examined the little features for an answer.

There was none. He didn't look like Frederich VonHoldt, but neither did he look like Jack, nor anyone else. He was just a baby. A plump, soft, extremely cuddly baby.

"How he got to be so fat when you hardly ate a thing all these months is a mystery to me," Howard said, taking his usual chair and watching as Grace looked over her baby. "Grace, this is the healthiest baby in all of Arkansas."

"He'll live? This one will live?"

"Live? He'll stick around till he's a hundred! And he's going to lead you a merry chase. I can see that now. You've got to get your strength back and do it pretty fast if you're going to keep up with him. This boy is going to be a handful."

Grace looked up at him. "I've never seen anybody grin the way you're doing, Howard. You mean it, don't you?"

"Of course I mean it! And if you think I'm grinning, wait till you see Jack. He makes me look downright morose."

"Has he seen the baby?"

"I took him out in the hall to meet his daddy while Mabelann was changing your bed and prettying you up. I've never seen a man come so close to fainting from sheer pleasure. He's downstairs writing up telegrams to the world now. Said to tell you he'd be up in just a minute."

Jack bounded into the room moments later and he didn't stop bounding for years. For the first few weeks he hardly slept. Every time Jackson cried, stirred, or even sighed in his sleep, Jack was at his side, cooing and fussing. He brought him cases of toys—drums, lead soldiers, wooden horses, everything he imagined a boy would ever want. He invited everybody he'd ever known to visit the house so he could show off his son. "Jack, I've never heard you mention these Harringtons who are coming next week," Grace said at one point.

"Well, I haven't exactly met them," he explained sheepishly. "But they're friends of the Worthings and don't have children of their own and I thought they'd really appreciate getting to know Jackson . . ."

I've done it, Grace thought contentedly. Even if I can't give him a houseful of children, I've given him one who is the center of his life. And if, as Jackson grew up, she was a little jealous of the bond between father and son, she ignored it. It was the proof she needed, the moral validation of her son's paternity.

It didn't take Grace very long to forget her worries on that score. Her health improved, her spirits soared, and she threw herself into motherhood with very nearly the same giddy passion that Jack exhibited. They were a very, very happy family.

For four years.

It was a freakish storm. There was seldom much snow before New Year's and this snow wouldn't last very long under the bright Arkansas sun, but they were getting the best of it before it melted away. Jack had unearthed an old sled from his own childhood in the cavernous basements and Grace had bundled four-year-old Jackson into mittens, boots, heavy pants, and a hand-knitted hat that tied down around his ears.

"You look like an Esquimaux baby!" Jack said of his son. With his round, bright face, he did.

"I'm not a baby, Daddy," Jackson said, stomping in the snow.

Grace watched this exchange and her heart ached with love for both of them. The chunky little boy looking up, and Jack—handsome Jack, his fair hair shimmering in the sun—

bending at the waist to listen to the child. "We promised your mother to show her some fancy sledding, young man," Jack was saying.

They set up the sled at the top of a slope and Jack sat down, trying to arrange his long legs to accommodate the child on his lap. But there wasn't enough snow. With Jack's weight on the sled, the blades kept running aground and bringing them to sudden halts. After one abortive run, they came back up the hill, hand in hand. Jackson's round face was pink. "Mommy, sled won't work."

"Let's build a snowman, then," Grace said, laughing at Jack's attempts to get the sled rope disentangled from his feet.

"Good Lord, I think the thing's got a life of its own!" Jack said, stepping backward and nearly falling.

Grace showed Jackson how to start a snowball rolling so it turned into a bigger and bigger ball. "Let's build him outside the library window, so we can see him from inside," she said. She and Jack lifted the middle ball into place, then Jack lifted the child up to put the head on top. "But he needs a face! Come on, Jackson, let's go to the kitchen and find him a face."

They got a carrot nose, and peach-pit eyes, and Jack let them stick in one of his old pipes to indicate a mouth. "But he'll be cold, Mommy," Jackson said.

"You silly boy," Grace said, joining in his giggles. "He's supposed to be cold. He's made of snow."

Jackson took off his hat. "He'll like this, Mommy. Can he have your scarf?"

"Of course." Grace put the hat on the snowman and wrapped her plaid wool scarf around the snowman's neck. She put her arms around the structure and said, "Oh, what a handsome snowman." She kissed its frigid face and made a production of shivering violently. "Oh, he's too cold to kiss. I'd rather kiss a warm little boy!" She turned and scooped Jackson into a hug. "Mmmmm, what a boy."

His face *was* warm. Hot, in fact, and filmed with a sheen of sweat. His hair was damp, too. "Come on, honey, you better get inside."

"I want to make another snowman!"

"Next time it snows. You've gotten overheated."

He still was warm when Grace went in to tuck him into bed that night. "My head hurts, Mommy."

"You've just had a big day and you're tired. You get to

sleep and you'll feel fine tomorrow," Grace said confidently, smoothing back his dark auburn hair. But her confidence was less when she talked to Jack later. "He's a bit feverish. Do you think we ought to ask Howard Lee to come by and take a look at him?"

"Howard's coming in the morning anyway to do a bit of hunting with me. You're a worrier, Grace. The boy's just overexcited. He'll be fine."

But he wasn't fine. By morning he had a definite fever and his breathing was raspy. Howard Lee looked him over and said, "I think it's just a bad cold, but I can't be sure yet. Keep him bundled up and in bed. We'll see."

"I shouldn't have let him take his hat off yesterday," Grace lamented.

"You said he was already hot then. That had nothing to do with it," Howard said in his usual bluntly comforting way.

Grace sat by the child's bed all morning while the men were out. At noon Jackson was sleeping fitfully, tossing and whimpering. Howard checked him over again, then talked to Grace and Jack outside the room. "We may be dealing with pneumonia here. I still can't be sure. It could be one of a hundred things. He'd be better off in a hospital if there was one near, but I think a long trip would be detrimental. I'm leaving some medicine and I'll look in again tonight."

But Jackson continued to get worse. For days the fever rose higher and higher. His breathing was labored and Grace held him on her lap, rocking him, wanting desperately to help him and unable to do anything. He refused to eat and had to be forced to drink anything. His weight dropped alarmingly, as if his small body was literally consuming itself. He'd been a chubby child; now, in a matter of a few days, he'd become all ankles and elbows and knees.

Jack and Grace took turns with him. Each sat for four hours at a stretch, bathing his hot face, holding his hands when he reached out, trying to soothe him when he thrashed about attempting to escape the misery that had locked in around him.

Grace was frantic with worry. Nothing Howard Lee could say about the chances of the child's survival could ease her worry. The irony of it was terrible. To have waited so long for a child, to have conceived him under such questionable circumstances—circumstances they'd never alluded to, either of them—and then, after four happy years, to face the possibility of losing him was too much. Dear Lord above, she'd promised Jack children and she'd given him only one. Don't let the one be taken from them. This little boy was the only thing that held them together, the only reason Jack cared for her . . .

"I'm not as worried about the disease itself—whatever it is—as I am about the secondary effects," Howard Lee said one afternoon. "The dehydration, the possibility of . . . well, starvation. I've never seen a child use up his own body weight at such a rate. If the fever would only spike and fall, we might be in the clear. As it is, there could be permanent damage if this keeps up. I know that's not very comforting, Grace. I wish I could work a miracle for you."

That night it happened.

Howard Lee had stayed the night. Grace knew this meant he expected Jackson might die before morning, but no one talked about this. "It's such a long drive back to town, just to come back first thing. I think I'll just camp out in the boy's room," was how Howard put it. "You can both get some rest for a change. I'll keep an eye on him."

But Grace stayed with him too. Around four, Jackson began to whimper and throw his arms around. The sweat poured down his face, his lips cracked with the fever, and a tiny tickle of blood ran down his chin. He started trembling violently. "Get some cold water and cloths!" Howard ordered, and Grace, stumbling with exhaustion, raced to obey. When she got back to the room, Jackson was in convulsions. Howard was trying to hold him.

As Grace came in, Howard threw back the covers and hauled the child out of bed and onto the floor. "Cool him down. Fast!"

Grace dipped a cloth in the water and started to wring it out. "No, not daintily, for Christ's sake! Like this." Howard grabbed the dripping cloths and sloshed it over Jackson's face. Then he lifted him, dragged his nightshirt over his head, and started slopping the cold water all over his naked body.

Jackson shuddered, took a long gasping breath, and lay still. "We've either killed him or saved him," Howard said, leaning down and putting his ear to the child's chest. Jackson took another deep, gasping breath. "Quick, Grace, blankets. Dry blankets! I think we've done it."

Howard wrapped him up and laid him gently back on the bed. He took his pulse, lifted his eyelids, and peered. "Put your hand on his head. Feel. He's cool."

"Is he . . . is he dead?" Grace asked.

Howard grinned. "No, far from it. Here, Grace! Don't you go fainting on me. Sit down."

Howard, after several more reassurances, went back to his own room to change his rumpled clothes, leaving Grace to sit by the child's bed. She closed her eyes for a moment. The next thing she knew, Mabelann was shaking her. "Miz Thorne, ma'am. The doc say I can sit with the youngun now. You gotta get you some rest. You 'bout dead on you feet. That boy, he gonna make it."

Grace went to the side of the bed and looked down at Jackson, sleeping normally now, his chest rising and falling with smooth regularity. But as she glanced at his face, she was shocked. All the baby fat had fallen away during his illness and now, with the flush of fever gone, his pale skin and thin face told her the thing she had dreaded knowing—the truth she had almost forgotten hung over her. The thin nose. The angular jaw. The hollows above his eyes.

This was Frederich VonHoldt's child.

Jack came to her room that afternoon. "Jackson's temperature is almost normal. Howard's gone back to town. He says to make sure he stays warm and eats as much as we can get in him."

His voice was dead and flat.

"You've seen him?" Grace asked, looking at him in the dressing-table mirror.

Jack nodded.

"You know?"

"I know. He was a very distinctive-looking man."

It seemed to Grace that the world had slammed to a stop. She could almost feel the lurch—or was it her heart? "I'll go away. You can keep Jackson." Why did those last words come so easily to her lips?

Jack turned away. "Why him, Grace? Why anybody?"

"Why Mimi?" she countered.

"Who?"

"The dance-hall girl. I saw you with her." Suddenly the old pain of it swept over her as if it had been only moments ago, not five years. She turned away from her reflection to face him. "You had an affair with her."

"I tried to have an affair with her. It seemed the thing to do. But I couldn't go through with it. Never even got my clothes off, nor hers."

"Oh, Jack, I thought—"

"But you, Grace—how could you get involved with that man? Why anyone? Wasn't I good enough for you?"

"Good enough! Oh, Jack, you're much too good for me. I thought you were tired of me, disappointed in me."

"Tired of you? Disappointed? In what way? How could you think such a thing?" Jack had turned back and was facing her angrily.

"Because I didn't give you the children I promised—"

He threw his arms up in a furious gesture. "Children! Are you mad? I didn't marry you for children. I married you because I love you so much I couldn't stand to be away from you for more than a few minutes without feeling like something in me had died."

Grace stood up, her knees nearly buckling. "Jack, do you mean that?"

"Of course I mean it, you idiotic woman. Are you honestly wrongheaded enough to think I'd marry anybody just to have children? Or was that your idea? Is that the reason you accepted me?"

"Oh, God, Jack! What a muddle we've made of things. No, my darling, I accepted your proposal because I loved you. Still love you so much it hurts. I adore you. I can't look at you without wanting to touch you . . ."

He looked as stunned as she was at her frank words. "But why . . . ?"

She knew he meant the houseparty and Frederich. "Because you liked all the pretty silly women. I thought I should be one of them to make you love me."

"Like them? Of course, just as I like a pretty picture or a well-crafted gun or a game of whist—for the sheer amusement of it. But that has nothing to do with love. Nothing. If I'd known you were upset, I'd never have even looked at anyone else. I'd have worn horse blinders. But I didn't think you minded. I didn't think you cared enough to mind, and you're so damned dauntingly sensible and efficient, I never dreamed—"

"Sensible? Efficient? But I thought you admired—"

"I *do* admire that in you. I've come to depend on it as well, but, well . . . I've always felt you had a certain contempt for me because I'm not that way."

"Contempt? How on earth could you believe that?"

"Well, I know you don't think much of my hunting and card-playing friends. They bore you. But, Grace, I'm one of them and I'd come to feel I was something of a disappointment to you."

She bowed her head, overwhelmed by this conversation, these ridiculous revelations. "Jack, we must be the greatest fools who ever lived. Think of the years we've wasted. Years of doubts and insecurities—both of us . . . Oh, how blind and stupid we've been! Jack," she said, lifting her head and opening her arms to him, "listen to me now. I adore you. I worship you."

He came to her and folded her in his strong arms. "Grace . . . darling, darling Grace . . ."

His lips came down on hers and it was as if they had never touched. She was jolted by the passion that suddenly coursed through her. "Jack, would it be shocking if I suggested we go to bed? Now?"

He smiled broadly. "I've always wanted to make love to you in the afternoon."

Later, they talked about Jackson.

"It doesn't matter who fathered him," Jack said a little too emphatically. "He's our child. Yours and mine. That's all that matters."

"No one else will ever know, and we don't care!" Grace added.

But she knew they were both lying to themselves.

Jackson, the little boy they'd both loved so dearly, had become a symbol of the near-destruction of their love. He would always represent the sorrow and misunderstandings and infidelities of the past. Facing the truth had brought Grace and Jack together at long last, but that same searing truth had excluded Jackson from that bright new circle that was their love. Neither of them would ever look at him again without consciously or unconsciously thinking of Frederich VonHoldt.

VIII

1918

GRACE yawned, stretched, and sat up. When this wedding was over she was going to burrow under the covers and sleep for a week. Beside her, Jack rolled over and put his arm around her waist. Smiling, she toppled over into his embrace. "What time is it?" he mumbled into her hair.

"Seven."

"Seven? It's still dark and you're getting up?"

She shivered with pleasure as he nuzzled her neck. "It's not dark. The drapes are drawn, and yes, I'm getting up. So should you, you lazy man. The house is positively teeming with guests who expect to find their host bright-eyed and wolfing down breakfast with them."

"Then they are doomed to disappointment. Why do we have to have this damned wedding here? Those giggling bridesmaids and their bossy mothers are driving me to madness. Aren't girls supposed to get married at their own homes?"

She snuggled in closer. "You know Evelyn's parents had that awful fire a few months ago and the place isn't fit for guests. Besides, they've visited here so often they feel like Thornehill is almost their home. And the bridesmaids are all half in love with you. You should be flattered. Oh! Jack, don't do that. I've really got to get up."

"Another half-hour won't matter so much, will it?" he said into the hollow of her shoulder.

"Mmmmm, I guess not—"

"Do you realize we could be grandparents a year from now?"

"What a time to mention such a thing!"

74

"You'll be the youngest, most beautiful grandmother in the world."

"And you'll be the most dashing grandfather ever."

By nine o'clock Grace was at her desk in the study, going over some of the lists of things that still remained to be settled for the wedding. Howard Lee's wife, Meg, had been a big help. She was a great list-maker and since she and Howard were themselves childless, she'd come out of her shy shell to help Grace with the wedding plans, saying, "It's the closest I'll ever come to marrying off one of my own."

Grace remembered being rather surprised at the remark. Though she liked Meg in a vague way, and they'd spent a great deal of time together over the years because their husbands were close friends, she'd never felt that she and Meg were anything more than friendly acquaintances. And then to discover that Meg felt motherly toward Jackson—well, it seemed strange.

What was she sitting here wondering about Meg Lee for? Grace asked herself, picking up her pen to mark what remained to be done. There was the seating for the dinner, tricky because of private quarrels that kept below the boiling point so long as certain individuals weren't placed in close proximity to each other, the arrangement of the flowers that were being brought in from New Orleans, if only they arrived in decent condition, the . . . "Yes, Mabelann?" she said as the slim black woman came in and put the newspapers on Jack's desk where he would read them later.

"Most of them boys didn't git theyselves down to eat."

"They had a bachelor party last night. That's supposed to be quite the fashionable thing to do, though I suspect it's just one more excuse to get drunk and rude."

"Doan I just know! Singin' and yellin' till all hours. That Mr. Jackson, he didn't never come back till an hour ago."

Grace set her pen down. "Oh? Where was he?" Mabelann had an uncanny ability for knowing where everyone was most of the time, especially when they didn't want to be located. It made her a valuable confidante to Grace but heartily loathed in other quarters.

"I hear he was down at that cabin place near the spring. Them boys go down there a lot, Miz Thorne."

"Why have you never told me this before?"

"Well, it's just high ol' spirits. Boys and all."

"What do they do there?"

Mabelann gave her a knowing look. "They's girls round here doan mind a little foolin' round with them rich boys what come here."

"Thank you, Mabelann."

Grace sat thinking for a few minutes, then got her heavy coat and went down to look at the cottage. She'd nearly forgotten its existence. There had been an incident five or six years earlier when a rather flighty woman guest had claimed to have seen a ghost staring malevolently from the window, but it proved to be a squatter who was given a job on the grounds and evicted. After that, the cottage was locked up, but Grace supposed it would be a simple matter to break in.

The cottage was dusty and neglected, but there were abundant signs of its having been used. There were empty whiskey bottles strewn about, a pair of suspenders hung over the back of a bedroom door, and old bed linens in a state to defy all washing. Well, she'd put a stop to his. If the local girls thought they could run a whorehouse on Thorne property, they were badly mistaken.

She went back to the house and took an interval from her wedding arrangements to put a number of people to work fixing it up. She also called Smalley, the gardener, in and instructed him that his family could have use of the building. She didn't give it much more thought until after Jackson and Evelyn's wedding, when Jack said, "I understand you've had the cottage fixed up."

"I told you about that, didn't I? I'm sure I did, you just weren't paying attention. Do you mind?"

"Not in the least. I just wondered why you bothered. Smalley tells me you put his family in there. I'd have arranged for it myself if I'd known how awfully pleased he'd be."

"I'm glad he is. Jackson and his friends were using it for questionable purposes. I just thought it wise to remove the temptation."

"Grace, there's something we need to talk about."

She knew instinctively it had nothing to do with the cottage. "What's that?" she asked warily.

"About the war . . ."

She had lived in terror of this. She'd watched Jack read the papers, discuss the war news, and she knew that this conversation would take place someday. And yet she'd hoped desperately that somehow it would end without involving them.

"No! You can't go, Jack. You promised you wouldn't leave here."

"No, darling. I promised I wouldn't make you leave. I know your superstitions about staying at home."

"It's not superstition. Please, Jack. Let's don't talk about this anymore."

"I'm sorry. We have to. Grace, I had visitors yesterday. Representatives of a group of men throughout the county who are going to join up and asked me to go with them as their commanding officer. It's important that I agree. We've always tried to set a good example in the community, and they're counting on me."

"Jack, no. You're too old, for one thing."

"I'm only forty-eight. Grace, I have to go."

She threw herself at him and clung ferociously. "Jack, it's dangerous. It's a war. You'll be killed. I can't live without you."

"Now, Grace. You're exaggerating. I'm going to be very careful. I'll be back. I promise you that. This war is winding down anyway. I wouldn't be surprised if it's not over before I can even get there. You'll see. I'll get a long, boring trip to Europe and just have to turn around and come back. But I'll have done the right thing, made the right gesture—"

"No, you're going to die!"

He shook her. "Grace, you're being hysterical and maudlin. It's not like you. I was depending on you to accept this with dignity."

Suddenly she realized what he really meant. He was terrified of dying too, for all his brave, unconcerned words, and was relying on her to inject him with added courage. She drew a deep breath, stood up straight, and said, "You're quite right. It was just such a surprise. Yes, the news from the front is encouraging. You'll probably be starting back before I've even got the spring cleaning attended to. I'm sorry I behaved so badly. It was very silly of me."

"That's my girl. Now, let's take a little walk before dinner and forget all about it for the evening. Tomorrow I'll tell the men my decision."

He left on April 1. "An April Fool for certain," Grace said, trying to sound as though this were nothing but a mild adventure. She studied him as he buttoned his crisp uniform jacket. He looked very handsome and dashing, she had to admit.

He studied himself in the mirror for a moment. "I wonder if every man has the secret yearning to see himself in a uniform just once in his life? All boys are soldiers at heart, little warriors. But I thought most of us grew out of it. Now I'm not so sure. Don't worry, Grace. I'll be back before I ever get it dirty."

The telegram came on September 3.

Unlike the majority of the common soldiers who were gassed in the same battle, Captain Jack Thorne's body would be shipped home. The others would be buried there, in a foreign land where they'd fallen. But Jack had made special requests for that arrangement, and the Army, in gratitude for his service and his substantial voluntary financial support of his unit, was honoring his request.

Grace never disgraced him with a public demonstration of her grief, but in the privacy of her room she was nearly insane with sorrow. Jack, gone. It was inconceivable. He'd been the core and center and reason for her life for as long as she could remember. She had no existence before him. No life without him. There was no question in her mind as to *how* to get along alone. She had no intention of facing life without him. Her life, like his, was over. It was simply an academic question of how and when to end it.

She would have to live, of course, until his body was brought home. She would see to the funeral arrangements, the headstone selection, and all the rest of it. Then she would join him. In her room at night, she indulged her agony, shrieking her loneliness and grief into her pillow. Then in the morning she'd leave the essence of herself there to mourn while she moved about, an empty shell, functioning as mistress of the estate.

Family and friends saw little change in her, for she'd always been gracious and dignified and rather cool. There was only one person left in the world who knew her intimately enough to sense her suicidal resolve and who cared enough to attempt to abort it.

Mabelann brought her the telegram informing her that Jack's body had reached the States and was now on a train on its way to Arkansas. Grace read it, cold-eyed. "Will you tell Jackson and Evelyn that we should be able to have the service on the tenth?" she said.

"Yes'm."

"Very well," Grace said. Then, noticing that Mabelann

had made no move to leave, she said, "Is there something else?"

"Yes'm. That Iris Smalley done had a baby yesterday."

"Iris Smalley? Oh, yes. The oldest daughter. I didn't know she was married," Grace said dully.

"She ain't married, Miz Thorne."

"Oh? What a shame for Smalley. Is that all, Mabelann?" Grace said, picking up her pen to resume her correspondence.

"No, not quite. It's the baby's father . . ."

"Who *is* the baby's father?"

"Nobody know for sure. But, Miz Thorne, I seed Mr. Jackson out in the woods with that Iris a couple times. And at that ol' bachelor party before Mr. Jackson's wedding—"

"Are you telling me Jackson is the father of the baby?"

"I just saying, could be. I figure you oughta know, Miz Thorne."

Grace was still too preoccupied with her sorrow to give this much thought. A pity, of course. Smalley was a good man, an upright Christian, and a hard worker. Shame his floozy daughter had to embarrass him this way with an illegitimate child. But it wasn't really her problem.

But still, she found herself coming back to the thought as the days passed. Jackson's child . . . would it look like the Thornes? She'd have to ask Mabelann if it was a boy or a girl. She hadn't said. And every time she caught herself speculating about the baby, she tried harder to push the thought away. It was a threat, this little creature of her blood with nothing but future. And precious little future, at that.

Of her blood . . .

A Thorne . . .

No, she couldn't concern herself. Her life was over. As soon as Jack was properly buried, she would end it. An eternity of blissful nothingness. No more of that horrible lurch of the heart when she woke up in the morning and realized again every day that he was dead. No more terror that she would suddenly go into a frenzy of grief, as she nearly had so many times, at the sight of one of his pipes, found by accident behind a curtain, at the imagined sound of his footsteps in the hall, at the heat of his touch in dreams.

Oh, God, Jack, how could you have left me?

The funeral was a living nightmare, worse—far worse—than she had imagined. Grace had always felt that funerals and marriages really ought to be very private, intimate occasions, and felt it vaguely distasteful and voyeuristic of others to intrude. And yet, she knew they had come as a measure of their love of Jack and respect for her. Even Evelyn, her skinny frame ballooned with child, went through it all. And friends—dozens of them from all over the country—had come. The roads to Eureka Springs were crowded that day as local people poured in to pay their last respects.

"My boy Will was hurt bad the same day, Miz Thorne," one ragged hill woman said to Grace. "He wrote me every week before that and always said what a good man Captain Jack was to them. I'm right sorry about him dying."

"Is your Will back home yet?" Grace asked, forcing the discussion into another channel.

"No, they said they'd send him home when the war was over. That's right upon us, ain't it?"

"Tomorrow. It'll end tomorrow."

That was somehow the worst of it. Burying Jack the day before the official end of the senseless conflict that had killed him.

"Mabelann," she whispered to the black woman who had been relentlessly at her side for the last few days. "Get that woman's name and address. We'll want to help them out when her son gets home."

Finally it was over. Jack had been buried, not in the family plot, but in the community cemetery. "He died for them, in a sense. It's only reasonable," Grace had said. Jack was gone. Dead. His spirit would be with her for the short duration of her life, it didn't matter where his body was.

She stood by the gravesite, not for any sort of final communion with him as others might think, but merely to let everyone go on ahead of her so she could have some peace and quiet to start making her plans.

She got into the chauffeured car at last and discovered that Mabelann was there, waiting for her like a sentry. No, like a protector—to protect her against herself. Grace knew, even though no words had passed between them, that Mabelann sensed her intentions and was determined to keep her from going to join Jack. She would have to take that into consideration. Whatever she did would have to be quick and irreversible or Mabelann would save her.

"You gonna go right straight home, Miz Thorne?" the black woman asked.

"Of course. Where else would I go?"

"Dunno. Thought you might take to stoppin' by and seein' that there baby at Smalley's."

"I have *no* interest whatsoever in Smalley's bastard grandchild."

Mabelann looked out the window, saying nothing for several miles. Then she said softly, "It's a girl child."

"I don't care."

"Right pretty little thing, I hear."

"I don't *care!*"

The car seemed to be going awfully fast as they turned into the long drive. "Slow down a bit," Grace ordered, ignoring the faint smile she thought she saw at the corners of Mabelann's lips.

Ahead of the turnoff to the cottage, Grace tried to look away, but her eyes were drawn to it. In a moment, they'd be past. She'd never come this way again. Never have to think about it again.

"Stop here!"

Grace almost thought it was Mabelann who had spoken, but of course it was her own voice. She turned to the servant, whose expression was deliberately bland. "You wait in the car. I'm just going to make sure that Smalley knows he's required at the reading of the will."

"Yes, Miz Thorne," Mabelann said, looking down at her hands folded in her lap. "I'll wait."

Grace could hear sounds of scurrying as she reached the door. That slovenly Mildred Smalley must be trying to clean the house.

"How do, Miz Thorne," Smalley said, opening the door and beckoning her to enter.

"It was good of you to come to the service, Smalley," she said. "My husband would have been pleased. He thought very highly of you. We will hear the reading of the will in half an hour, if you will be so kind as to come to the house?"

"We was awful sorry to hear about Captain Jack," Mildred said.

Grace felt a prickle of annoyance that this woman, this mean-spirited, pig-eyed woman, should even have the right to speak Jack's name. It was the first time in months that Grace had felt anything so common and healthy as ordinary annoyance.

She ignored Mildred and addressed Smalley. She'd heard, she said, that his daughter had given birth to a child and she wanted to know who the father was. She was vaguely surprised that Smalley would not say, but that itself almost confirmed what Mabelann had implied. "She'll tell me. Where is she?" she demanded.

She was ushered into the main bedroom. There lay Iris, barebreasted and torpid. And beside her, the baby. Grace felt as if her heart had made an extra beat and something almost forgotten surged through her.

Familiarity. She'd seen this baby before. She'd *loved* this baby before. She'd watched a tiny blond cherub like this grow and learn and eventually toddle to her death.

"Who is the father, girl?"

Iris pointed to Smalley.

"Not *your* father. The baby's father." The girl was really remarkably stupid. But she was pretty enough in an over-blown way, and Grace could imagine how Jackson might be attracted to her. "Do you *know* who the father is?" she asked her.

"Yes," Iris said. It was a kitten-mew.

"Then tell me. There will be no punishment, so long as you answer me truthfully."

"Mr. Jackson, ma'am."

It wasn't until some moments later that Grace recognized what her own thought processes had been all along. It was as if another being had been working behind some curtain in her mind and was only now revealed as the director of Grace's actions. She explained to Smalley and his wife that she would get them a good job far away, thinking on a conscious level that such a plan would get this baby out of her sight, thoroughly out of her life.

- But when Mildred said, "The baby ain't old enough to go such a long way, ma'am," Grace realized in her own mind what she'd really intended all along.

That child is mine, she thought.

"The baby isn't going," she said.

A few minutes later Mildred brought the baby to her and unceremoniously dumped it into her arms. Suddenly an emotion long dormant unfurled in Grace's heart, like a fern come quickly to life in a spring rain. It was painful in its aching sweetness.

Grace turned away before Mildred Smalley could see the tears welling in her eyes, though the overwhelming love she felt for this child must surely show in every line of her face, every cautious move of her body. She walked along the path to the car, clutching the baby, her chest heaving with emotion.

Mildred's voice, shrill and whining, penetrated her turbulent thoughts. "Her name's Annie!"

Grace looked down into the wide blue eyes that gazed up so trustingly at her. She'd seen those eyes before, too many years ago to count. She'd felt the firm little defenseless body in her arms, she'd watched with amazed adoration every change and development.

"Her name is Laura Elizabeth Thorne," she said softly.

And as Mabelann ran to meet her, her face nearly lost in her smile, Grace knew that she had committed herself to go on living. This child was the future—her future. And she would not only go on living, she would enjoy life for this child's sake and because this child was with her.

"Grace?"

A hand touched her arm, but her reverie was so deep that it took her a moment to respond. The baby in her arms was sound asleep, one tiny fist curled at the side of her face. "Yes, Howard?" Grace said.

"Evelyn is doing fine."

Grace smiled. "So I can hear." Evelyn's shrieks, muffled by intervening doors and walls, were audible even in the library.

"She's making a lot of it, of course," Howard said, returning her smile. "But she's coming along nicely. Grace, are you sure you want to do this? Pass these children off as twins?"

"What else could I do?" Grace asked. Mabelann, as usual, was hovering silently in the background. Grace rose and gently handed her the sleeping infant, and Mabelann faded away. "Leave the baby, this Thorne child, with the Smalleys? Have you met that girl? She's barely human."

"Of course I've met her. I delivered the child. But, Grace, you must think farther ahead. Will you tell her the truth of her parentage? Will she really be any better off with Evelyn as her nominal mother?"

Grace picked up a crystal paperweight from the desk and pretended to study it rather than meeting Howard Lee's perceptive eyes. He knew her too well. To a stranger she could have defended her actions without any trouble at all, but to Howard? Jack's oldest friend, the man who had delivered her babies? Who had stayed with her that night so long ago when Jackson almost died. "Howard, I don't know if it's the right thing to do. I don't even care. I only know that I had to do it.

And if Evelyn's not a good mother—frankly, I can't imagine her being very good at anything—it won't matter. I'll watch over the child. I'll love her. She's the daughter I never had—''

"She's *not* your daughter, Grace," Howard said. He took the paperweight from her and set it down on the desktop.

When she looked up, there were tears in her eyes. "Howard, don't turn against me."

"Turn against you? Oh, Grace, how could you say that? I'll stand by you whatever you decide. But there's still a chance to change your mind about this. You're setting up a situation that you must live with the rest of your life—the rest of Jackson and Evelyn's life. And the child's."

"There's nothing else I can do! I couldn't let that stupid, sluttish Smalley girl keep the baby. Don't you understand? They didn't even care. Any of them. They were willing, even eager, to sell her to me. That's what it was, you know. All Mildred and the girl cared about was the money."

"I know. And I agree to that part. But why keep her yourself? Meg and I would adopt her. Meg's always been sorry we didn't have children and she'd be a good and willing mother."

"Meg is too old to start motherhood," Grace said, pulling a handkerchief from her sleeve and dabbing at her eyes.

Howard laughed. "Listen to yourself! Meg's a year younger than you are!"

He expected at least a smile in response, but instead Grace gazed at him with an intensity that was almost frightening. "I *want* this child!"

For an instant she looked just as she had all those times he'd come to her bedside when she was younger and told her that her babies had died. Those eyes were still the eyes of the disappointed bride, the best friend's wife he'd been half in love with, the patient he'd wanted to comfort and didn't know how. Of course she wanted this baby. This was the Laura who had touched her life so many times and then stolen away. "Very well, Grace. If you're sure . . ."

IX

1924

ON November 11 America celebrated the end of the War to End All Wars. But at Thornehill quite a different sort of celebration took place on that date every year. It was the birthday of Laura Elizabeth Thorne and her twin brother, Jackson Thorne III, known as Sonny.

For this birthday, the twins' sixth, Grace had hired a small traveling circus. The weather turned bad that morning, so the tent was brought in and set up in the mansion ballroom. "They wanted to drive their tent stakes into the floor," Grace said to her late husband's cousin Adele, who was visiting for the occasion.

"No! What did you do?" the other woman exclaimed.

"I stopped them," Grace said simply.

"That's why the ropes are tied around sandbags," Evelyn said. She and Grace had adhered rigidly to the bargain they had struck the day of her confinement—or rather, the bargain Grace had imposed. Evelyn allowed the world to think she was Laura's mother, though less-than-shrewd observers could detect an obvious lack of warmth in her regard for Laura. In return, Grace supplied an extremely generous allowance, which Evelyn and Jack went through with relish. A large portion of the money was used for Evelyn's clothing, which was stylish and expensive but always appeared not quite to fit her small, nervous frame. "Oh, look," she said, "Sonny has spilled some ice cream down the front of his little suit. I'll have Mabelann take him up to change his clothes."

"Never mind, Evelyn," Grace said, arresting the younger woman as she was halfway out of her chair.

Evelyn subsided, but said, "You had Laura's clothes changed when she got punch on her skirt."

"Girls are different."

The three women sat silently for a few minutes, watching the children play, Grace keeping an eye on Laura, Evelyn on Sonny, and Adele trying to sort the others out. "Why do those two boys limp?" she asked Grace in a hushed whisper.

"They have new shoes, Adele. They are the sons of one of the grooms. If I didn't invite them to the party every year, their parents might not buy them shoes at all. They're hill people, or were until I hired their father to work in the stables."

"And those little nigger children—such sweet faces. Who are they?"

Grace stiffened. "Adele, that's a word we never use here."

"I do beg your pardon, dear, but I thought in the South—"

"Thornehill is not the South. It is Thornehill. Jack and I never felt the need to adopt the prejudices of this region just because the house is here." This wasn't strictly the truth; Grace had spent years eradicating the word "nigger" from her husband's vocabulary. She glanced at Adele and thought she saw tears threatening. "The Negro children are Mabelann's nephews and nieces. Her sister is a laundress in Eureka Springs. They come out frequently."

Adele sniffed and smiled. "Do you have such a grand party every year for the twins?"

Grace smiled as Laura made a ringer with a wooden horse-shoe. "We didn't have any party the first year. The Spanish influenza was still raging. You remember. Then the second year we had quite a large gathering. Evelyn wanted it."

There was a sour note, but Evelyn didn't notice. "Yes. I put a notice in the local paper that all the town mothers of two-year-olds were invited to the mansion for the birthday party."

"And they all came?" Adele asked.

"They did indeed!" Grace said. "Dr. Lee was here that day. He said he'd never seen so many big children for their age and that he distinctly remembered delivering some of them as many as four years earlier."

"Still, it was charming," Evelyn recalled.

"Charming? If you call Sonny getting ringworm from one of the children and both the twins coming down with chickenpox a few weeks later charming," Grace said. "After that, we limited the invitation to family members and the children of the staff with whom the twins are in contact already.''

"What about their schoolmates?''

"Schoolmates?'' Evelyn came as close to snorting as a lady could and still remain ladylike. "They don't attend the local school. We have tutors for them. Sonny's far too bright for public school and Laura's so susceptible to every nasty disease that goes around.''

"It was Sonny who had the ringworm,'' Grace reminded her.

Sonny and Laura had gone behind the circus tent to look at the wooden monkey she'd won at the horseshoe toss. She had turned it over to Sonny to take apart and see how it worked. "Are Mama and Gram fighting again?'' she asked.

Sonny dropped a leg of the monkey as he peered around the corner of the tent where the three women sat. "No, I don't think so. They don't really fight. Not like me and you. No hitting or anything.''

"We're not supposed to hit,'' Laura said.

"But we do. Sometimes.''

They both grinned.

"Last birthday I hit you and you threw up,'' Laura reminded him cheerfully.

"Gram said it was because I ate so much candy,'' Sonny said, pulling loose the string that held the rest of the monkey's limbs together. "You could put his feet on his arms.''

Sonny's tinkering was the despair of the household. Any object with articulated parts was in danger of dismantlement. He had once taken apart a music box of Grace's with such thoroughness that it was hours before anyone figured out what all those tiny parts had once been part of. On another horrifying occasion, he had invaded the gun cabinet in the library and reduced a pistol to random mechanical bits.

Laura didn't share his curiosity, but was his willing accomplice. It was she, in fact, who found the key to the gun cabinet for him. Sonny lacked interest in putting anything back together, but Laura continued to happily sacrifice her toys to his investigations.

And when he got in trouble, she insisted on sharing that as well. As a result of the pistol episode, Sonny was confined to his room on bread and milk for two days. During that time Laura willingly incarcerated herself, only coming out to eat and then restricting herself to bread and milk as well.

Neither Grace nor Evelyn had foreseen that such a bond would grow between the children, and neither was entirely happy with it. But it was a natural result of the way the twins lived. Overprotected, largely isolated from their peers, and in a household that shimmered with a constant undercurrent of repressed strife, they could only have loved or hated each other, and they had chosen love.

Like some real twins, they were very unlike each other. Sonny was an owlish boy with a deceptively frail-looking body that would be some years catching up with the size of his head, hands, and feet. He had the same straight dark hair and clear blue eyes his father had had as a boy. Laura was a full two inches taller than he, with fair hair that curled slightly and would probably turn dark to match her brown eyes. They were both shy almost to the point of secretiveness.

It might have seemed suspicious that twins should be so different in appearance, except that Sonny was obviously his father's son and Laura's features bore a remarkable resemblance to Grace's. People often commented, in fact, on the similarities between the little girl and the portrait of her grandmother as a bride—the portrait that hung in the dining room, seeming to watch the twins' table manners even when Grace herself was not present.

Sonny was still tinkering with bits of the monkey when Jackson came around the back of the tent. "There you two are. Your mama and gram were worried about you."

"I gave Sonny my monkey to take apart," Laura said, pointing proudly to the wooden arms and legs they'd put in a pile on the floor. Jackson didn't pay any attention, so she nudged the parts with her foot and said, "Look, Daddy."

"That's a baby toy," Jackson said, taking the torso and string out of Sonny's hands and dropping them. "I have something really exciting to show you. The circus man has some ponies outside."

Sonny took a step toward Laura and went pale. "I don't like ponies."

"These aren't big horses, just ponies. You'll like them," Jackson said. But the pleasant wheedling tone went out of his voice as Sonny edged behind Laura. "Get your coat and come outside. Act like a man, son."

"He's not a man, Daddy. He's a little boy."

"When I need your opinion, missy, I'll ask for it. Now, Sonny, you come along and ride a pony."

"I don't want to!"

"I didn't ask you if you wanted. I'm telling you you're going to do as I say, young man."

"I'll come too." Laura offered. Sonny was beginning to cry and she knew when he cried Daddy got really mad and sometimes spanked. "Ponies are just little things," she told Sonny confidently as they went up the stairs to get their coats. "Like dogs," she added. She'd never been on a pony. but she'd heard they were small horses and she'd always imagined them about the size of a collie dog.

They both found out how wrong she was when they got outside. If the ponies had been eight feet tall and had flames shooting from their nostrils, they couldn't have been more frightening. Sonny started crying in earnest and Jackson grabbed him by the arm and marched him up to the animals. "Which one do you want to ride?"

"I don't wanna—"

Jackson smacked him on the shoulder. "*Which one?*"

"The white one," Sonny sobbed.

"Me too. I want to ride the white one. Can we ride together?" Laura asked. Her knees felt all trembly and she jumped as the pony snorted.

The pony's owner was a swarthy, beetle-browed man who was used to this scene—fathers trying to force sissy little boys to ride against their will. The sooner over, the better. Without waiting for the culmination of the dispute, he scooped Sonny up and deposited him on the back of the scruffy white animal. Then the little girl in front. He tugged on the reins and started walking across the wide lawn. Jackson ambled along behind them.

It had rained that morning, a cold slow drizzle. Now the sun was out, but the lawn was spongy-wet and the pony's feet made funny sucking sounds with every step. Laura wished Sonny would stop whimpering so she could hear it better. Actually, this pony business wasn't so bad, she was deciding. Letting go of the pommel with one hand, she reached out and gently touched the wiry white mane and watched with fascination as the fur on the pony's neck rippled in reaction. His fur was rough, not like her stuffed animals. And had an interesting smell. Not like soap or perfume, but not really bad.

They came around the side of the house and were in sight of the ballroom windows. "Wave at Mama and Gram, Sonny," Jackson said.

Laura glanced at the windows and raised her free arm. "Wave, Sonny!" she whispered.

"I can't let go. I'll fall off," he replied, both arms wrapped so tightly around her she could hardly breathe.

"Yes, you can. Just one arm."

Sonny tried, but it was a disaster. As he hesitantly waved, the pony bobbed its head and snorted again. Sonny flung his arm back around Laura with such force that she jumped, inadvertently kicking the pony in the side. The animal bolted forward, ripping the reins from the owner's hands. Jackson shouted, a faint trio of screams wafted from the ballroom window, the pony's owner cursed, but all was drowned out by Sonny's unearthly keening and the squashy pounding of hooves.

Laura was terrified into absolute immobility, unable to do or think anything. Neither she nor Sonny had their feet in the stirrups, and she became aware that they were gradually slipping to the left—or rather, Sonny was slipping and dragging her along with him. She tried to bend forward for a better grip, but Sonny, still shrieking, was holding so tightly to her waist that she couldn't move.

The pony, not having had this much exercise in years, quickly tired and slowed. By the time he stopped, Laura was hanging onto the pommel sideways and Sonny had only his knee still hooked over the animal's bony back.

Laura let go and they tumbled off into a muddy patch under a tree. They lay there in a heap for a long moment. Sonny had run out of sobs and was taking deep, shaking breaths. Laura lay back and felt the cold mud ooze into her hair. Suddenly she started giggling. Giggles turned to laughter, then into joyous yelps as Sonny joined her. Every time one of started to say something, the world got funnier before the words were out.

By the time Jackson and the pony's owner caught up with them, the pony was munching contentedly on a bush and the twins were mud-soaked and gasping for breath. "I'll kill that bloody, vicious creature!" Jackson was shouting as he ran toward them. He knelt in the mud and cradled Sonny's head. "Are you hurt, son? Can you talk?"

Evelyn, the most spry of the women, was the next one to get to them. She'd broken the heel off her shoe, her skirts were splashed with mud, and her face was as pale as a sheet. "Dear God!" she exclaimed, throwing herself on the gorund next to her husband and son. "What's he broken? Can he speak? Sonny, darling, speak to Mama!"

Laura turned away, resting her cheek in the mud. The laughter had turned to racking sobs. In a moment, she felt a hand on her shoulder and heard Grace's voice saying softly, "Laura, where are you hurt?"

Laura sat up and clutched at her.

"Everywhere, Gram. Everywhere."

Grace picked up the leggy little girl, and heedless of her weight and dirty condition, carried her to the house. A gardeners assistant offered to help, but she said, "Thank you, but she needs me."

When they reached the house, Grace allowed Mabelann to take Laura upstairs to her room and followed them. While Mabelann ran a hot bath, Grace undressed Laura, looking for bruises or cuts. There were none.

As Laura stepped into the hot, soap-slick water, she said, "Why don't Mama and Daddy love me?"

Grace's answer was prompt and brisk. "They do, dear. How could anybody not love you?"

"They don't. All they care about is Sonny."

"No, dear. It just seems that way sometimes because they worry more about him," Grace said, scrubbing Laura's face with a washcloth. "Sonny isn't as big or smart as you and so they have to take a little better care of him. You see that, don't you? Besides, lots of other people love you a great deal."

"Who, Gram?" Laura asked, wriggling as Grace ran the cloth over the bottoms of her feet.

Grace smiled. "Well, Mabelann loves you."

"Who else?"

"Let me think . . ."

Laura was laughing again. "Come on, Gram. Who else?" Grace leaned forward quickly and nuzzled her soapy neck. "Me! I love you, Laura-bunny."

"Oh Gram, look ! You have a bubble mustache!"

Grace had a warm smile on her face as she left Laura, but as she made her way quickly to Evelyn's room, the smile turned to a grimace, the warmth to anger. "How is Sonny?" she asked in a manner that a more perceptive person than Evelyn might have recognized as perfunctory.

"Terribly shaken, of course. But unharmed. Thank God! He could have been killed. Animals are so unpredictable. My parents would never let us have pets, for exactly that reason. I resented it then, but I see their wisdom now—''

"Have you anything else to say about the nature of animals?" Grace asked bitterly.

At this Evelyn stopped short.

"You haven't asked about Laura," Grace said.

"How is she?"

"Do you care?"

"Well, of course I do!"

"It's not very apparent. That was a disgraceful thing you and Jackson did out there—falling all over Sonny and ignoring Laura."

Evelyn had little spirit, but this brought it out. "No one else needs to bother with Laura. She has you."

"She needs a mother who cares about her—and shows it!"

Evelyn's jaw tightened. "She *had* a mother of her own. That slut you put under Jackson's nose—''

"Evelyn! Do you think for a moment that I wanted Jackson to be involved with that horrible girl?"

Her daughter-in-law was slightly chastened, but still had stored-up grievances to air. "Well, you certainly didn't approve of me."

"Since you seem to feel this is the time to open our hearts, I'll do the same. I never cared one way or the other about you, Evelyn. And to be frank, I still don't. Nor do I expect affection from you. But we had an arrangement. A business arrangement. You and Jackson live a life of leisure; you have no responsibilities, no work you must do, and the only price you pay is to act the part of a loving mother to Laura."

This bluntness was too much for Evelyn. Unskilled at verbal sparring, she took the only escape route available. She burst into tears. Exasperated, Grace fought down the urge to grab those bony shoulders and shake some sense into her. Instead, she sat down and waited with deadly calm until she stopped her sobbing. "Evelyn, I shouldn't have spoken so harshly. But the fact remains that Laura needs you. If you can't feel genuine affection for her, you must at least try to act as though you do. Can't you at least do that?"

"I suppose," Evelyn whined, "I can try harder."

Grace gave up and left her. She went back to her room wondering what held her daughter-in-law together and upright. It wasn't character; she had none. Nor did she have an inch of spine. She'd be more likable if she even had the wit or strength to stand up for herself.

Oh, well. Someday Laura would grow up and Laura would be everything Grace hoped. That would make up for Evelyn and Jackson and so many others who had disappointed her.

The next day Laura and Sonny explored the scene of their adventures. The pony droppings hadn't been cleaned off the lawn yet and the children squatted down in the grass to examine them. "I wonder why they're so round," Laura speculated, daintily poking at one with a stick.

This phenomenon wasn't sufficiently mechanical to interest Sonny. "Let's go down to where the pony threw us."

"The pony didn't throw us. We fell off," Laura said.

"Daddy told everybody the pony threw us off."

"Well, he couldn't. The pony didn't have hands, silly. You can't throw things unless you have hands. Besides, Daddy wasn't there. He was running someplace behind."

"Here's some of the pony's footmarks," Sonny said, following the path they'd taken the day before. "Mama said it was lucky we weren't killed."

Laura considered this. "I don't think ponies can kill you. Not unless they ran on top of you, but we were on top. I kinda liked the pony, until he started running. I wonder if we could have our own pony someday. We could go places faster than walking."

"I don't want a pony. I want an automobile, like Daddy's got." He made steering motions with his hands.

"Where would you go?"

Sonny thought about it. "Nowhere. I'd just drive around and around."

"I'd go to Boston. That's where Aunt Adele lives. Then I'd go to France like Daddy and Mama did last summer. But I'd go with Gram."

"And me! But I don't want to go with Gram."

"We can't go anyplace by ourselves. We don't have any money," Laura said.

"We don't need money. Not if we don't go shopping."

There was a flaw in this, but Laura was still puzzling it out when Mabelann's voice came across the lawn. "Sooonny! Lauurra! Where you naughty children gone? I swear, you two be the death of me yet! Always runnin' off. Your mama skin you and me both if she saw you walkin' away by yourselfs."

She caught up with them, took one little arm in each hand, and headed them back to the house. "Where would you go if you had an automobile, Mabelann?" Laura asked.

"Me? Child, I don't want no newfangled thing like them automobiles. But me, if I was to go anyplace, it'd be Hot Springs."

"But the spring is just down that hill right there," Laura said. "We aren't allowed to go there, but Gram would let you. You're a grown-up."

"No, honey, I don't mean that ol' spring. I mean a town called Hot Springs. Here, you, Sonny-boy, you wipe off them dirty feet before you goes inside."

"I don't wanna go *anywhere!*" Sonny said. He marched off, his too-big head held high and defiant.

"I'll go to Hot Springs with you, Mabelann," Laura said.

"Will you now, child? That's right nice. 'Bout as likely, you *or* me."

X

1929

*T*HERE was a sheltered spot behind the cottage where some wildflowers had escaped the season's first frost. Miss Hawkins picked a handful and said, "Ahhh, these are perfect examples. Now, children, sit down here with your sketchpads and make your drawings before they wilt. Then tomorrow I will expect you to be able to label all the parts: stamen, pistil, anther—you have the list in your notebooks."

Sonny and Laura, ten years old and still summer-brown, sat down side by side on the fallen headstone where a shaft of autumn afternoon sunshine had warmed a place. Miss Hawkins was the niece of Willis Hawkins, the family lawyer. She'd left home to attend Vassar and returned with fashionably bobbed hair, a raccoon coat, and almost in spite of herself, an excellent grounding in science and math. She'd come back with every intention of marrying well, but bobbed hair and raccoon coat notwithstanding, she hadn't gotten any proposals, so she was forced to fall back on her academic achievements and was now filling her time tutoring the Thorne twins in biology and arithmetic. While they made their sketches, she puttered around the front of the cottage, humming, "Five Foot Two, Eyes of Blue."

"All done!" Sonny crowed, waving his sketchpad in the air.

Laura glanced at his drawing and snickered. He'd cleverly drawn the flower with a silly face and petals that looked like the tutor's frowsy hair. Miss Hawkins wouldn't think that was very funny. Laura grabbed his sketchpad and flipped the front cover over so she wouldn't see his page, then did the same with hers. "I'm done too, Miss Hawkins," she said.

"Let me take a look," the teacher said.

"I'm getting cold," Sonny said, knowing this would abort any attempt on her part to delay their return to the house. Grace and Evelyn were both fanatic about the children's health, and woe be to anyone who endangered it.

"Very well, we'll go back," she said, setting out briskly.

The path from the cottage to the main drive was becoming overgrown after ten years of disuse, and weeds slapped at Laura's legs. She picked her way slowly, and Sonny held back to keep pace with her. Miss Hawkins stopped at the drive and rerolled her stockings while waiting for them.

When they got to her, Laura stopped and looked up at the main house. This was the spot where one got the first good look at it on the way up the long winding drive, and Laura never outgrew the surprise she felt seeing it whole and from a distance. "How old is Thornehill, Miss Hawkins?" Laura asked. She knew the tutor took a keen interest in local history and it was an excellent way to get her mind off the biology assignment. There was still some danger she might ask to see their drawings when they got back to the house.

"Your great-grandfather Jeremiah built it in 1880," she said. "At least, it was finished that year. If you'll just hand me your sketch—"

"But he didn't live very long after that, did he?" Laura asked. She remembered that part from previous lectures.

"No, he lived only seven years in this house before his demise. Then your grandfather Jack, his only child, inherited it. He was only seventeen at the time. A few years later, he married your grandmother. They were a very young couple to have such a responsibility," Miss Hawkins said.

"Someday it will be my house," Sonny said, kicking a pebble along the drive.

"It already is. We both live here," Laura said.

"No, I mean I'll own it. When Gram dies it'll belong to Daddy and when Daddy dies it'll be mine."

"You mustn't talk that way!" Miss Hawkins said.

"What way?"

"About people dying. It gives the false impression of eagerness." Miss Hawkins knew all the rules about not appearing eager.

They got back without any further reference to the wildflower sketches. Normally they would have gone directly to the schoolroom they used on the third floor, but it was apparent that something was amiss. Both the big maroon

Hispano-Suiza and the Minerva Landaulet were at the front door, piled high with luggage. But the current guests, part of a never-ending succession, were not due to leave for several days yet. Inside, there was an insidious atmosphere of worry. Evelyn passed through without even noticing Miss Hawkins and the children, and Mabelann was trying to stack and sort a disordered pile of newspapers someone had dropped in the front foyer. Laura glanced at Miss Hawkins, who had become infected by the odd mood. "What's the matter, Mabelann?" the tutor asked.

The black woman looked up. "Not for me to say, Miz Hawkins. Don't rightly understand it myself."

"Is someone ill?"

"No, it's got sumpin' to do with money."

"Oh, well then, nothing serious, I'm sure," Miss Hawkins replied. Everyone knew the Thornes were about the richest people in Arkansas. Nothing to do with money could be that serious. "Come along, children. We'll have our arithmetic lesson, then luncheon."

The remainder of the morning passed as usual, but luncheon was a strange experience. Usually it was the best part of the day, with Gram and Mama and Daddy all serving themselves from the generously laden sideboard. Miss Hawkins and the afternoon tutor, Mr. Watkins, ate in the kitchens with the staff, and the twins were allowed to mingle with the family and whoever was visiting—and there was always somebody visiting, mostly friends of Mama and Daddy. The ladies were all exotically beautiful, often attending luncheon in the Oriental gowns they wore to play Mah-Jongg. They talked about cars and fashion and drinking and dancing—sometimes getting right up from the table to demonstrate some new variation of the Charleston.

But today the hectic flappers with their rouged knees and bangle bracelets were absent. So were the handsome silent men with the Oxford bags and slicked-back hair that they all believed made them look like Valentino. The children ate alone from trays that Mabelann brought from the kitchen. "Why have they all gone?" Laura asked Sonny when Mabelann left.

"Doan know. Maybe there's another war, like when Grandpa Jack died and we were born."

"No, Mabelann said it had something to do with money."

Sonny lost interest. "I don't think Mama liked that lady with the silver hair and all the jewelry, do you?" he said, veering off to a topic he'd been brooding on all morning, but had been unable to discuss in Miss Hawkins' presence. Sometimes Mama took strange dislikes to the lady guests, usually the same ladies Daddy liked best.

Normally this sort of speculation was fascinating to Laura, but today she didn't care about the lady with the silver hair. "I'm going to find out what's wrong."

She gave Sonny her uneaten slice of cherry pie and went to the library. Opening the door very quietly, she slipped in and sat down on a Chippendale chair. She didn't hide, but she didn't make any effort to draw attention to herself either. Nobody seemed to notice her, not even Gram, whose eagle gaze seldom missed anything.

Grace was at the big desk, which she had taken over a year after her husband's death. Evelyn was at the long window, looking out and twisting her hands. Jackson was pacing in front of Grace. The desk was uncharacteristically disorganized, with telegrams, ledger books, bits of paper, and newspapers littering it. One of the papers had fallen on the floor and Laura could see half the headline: "RKET CRASHES!"

"I still say it's just a newspaper trick to sell more copies! Journalists are such dogs, not caring who's upset so long as they have a headline!" Jackson was saying.

"I suppose the telegram people are in on it too," Grace said acidly. She grabbed a handful of yellow sheets and flapped them at him. "Can't you read, Jackson? Look at these! Johnston didn't even answer the one I sent him. His secretary did, to say he'd jumped to his death from the office window. You might as well face it. The market has collapsed. Most of the Thornes' stocks are virtually worthless. American Telephone and Telegraph down twenty-eight points yesterday, and today . . . who knows? I just thank heaven we hadn't bought anything on margin. We've lost a lot, but at least we don't owe anything."

"But why don't you just sell everything and we could live on the cash until this is straightened out?"

"I refuse to sell stocks at a tiny percent of their value for cash to live on—for cash to reinvest, possibly, but never to spend without a return."

"What is there to reinvest in, then?"

"Nothing, now."

"So we might as well paper the lavatory with the stock certificates," Jackson said.

"Not quite. Some might stabilize and eventually recover,

but there won't be dividends again for years, if ever. Dear Lord, I should have seen this coming. We all should!''

''But what about our allowance?'' Evelyn asked, getting directly to the only aspect of the national economic crisis that interested her.

Grace shrugged. ''It's gone, Evelyn. We'll be lucky if our total income next year is half what I've been giving you and Jackson.''

''But there are still the farms,'' Jackson put in, as if just remembering them. ''We have income there, or we could sell the property.''

''The income is barely enough to support the normal operation of this house and the ongoing repairs. As for selling, I would oppose the idea under any circumstances. All other investments can turn into phantoms, as this catastrophe proves, but land is land. It can't disappear overnight. We'll keep the farms.''

Stung by her condescending manner, Jackson said, ''Well, then, what are we to do? Since you have such a firm grasp of the situation, Mother, tell us what we're going to do about it!''

Grace rose and walked over to the window Evelyn had abandoned. She clasped her hands behind her back and stared outside. Laura thought her face looked just like a cameo silhouette, all pale and sad. ''I don't know, Jackson,'' Grace finally said. ''I have no idea. But we'll stay here. That's certain. We'll learn to live frugally. And we'll survive this—somehow.''

Laura slid off her chair and silently left the room.

Late that evening Howard Lee came to see Grace. She was just asking the telephone exchange to call his number when Mabelann announced that he was coming up the long drive. Dear Lord, I'd hoped for a few more minutes to prepare myself, Grace thought with dread.

He came into the library and for the first time Grace was aware of the years that had passed. She still thought of him as the sandy-haired young man she'd first met in Boston so long ago, and he'd never seemed to change. He'd worn his age lightly. Until tonight. There was very little white in his hair, just a distinguished sprinkle at the temples. Nor had he lost his boyish figure—he didn't even have a trace of the potbelly a man his age might be entitled to. But the laugh lines around his eyes looked like age lines tonight, and his normally tanned skin was pale. "You look tired, Howard," she said with more concern than tact as he sat down facing her across the desk.

"I'm a hundred and four," he said as he stretched his long legs forward in an obvious attempt to relax. Grace could tell the attempt was doomed to failure.

"How is Meg?"

"How is anybody with terminal cancer? Sorry, that was unnecessarily rude."

"You can be as rude to me as you want, Howard."

"She's having a bad day. I'm sorry now I urged her to have the surgery. I knew—we both knew—it wasn't a cure, just a delaying tactic, but it seemed worth it for a few more months of life. I didn't know how miserable those few more months were going to be. I should have let her go peacefully."

"You're a doctor. You couldn't let anybody go, peacefully or otherwise. You know that."

"I know."

They sat together in companionable silence for a long time, Howard with his eyes closed in a moment of respite, Grace watching him and wishing there was something, anything, she could do or say to ease his suffering. When she'd first learned of Meg's illness she'd thought it was fortunate for Howard that he'd never appeared to love his wife with a real passion like she and Jack had experienced. They had always been very fond of each other, of course, and Meg had obviously worshiped him, but Howard hadn't seemed to feel anything more than respect and affection for her.

But now, after watching him try to extend her life if not save it, she'd changed her mind. He not only had the sorrow of losing the companion of most of his adult years, but he had the added weight of guilt—or so Grace surmised. Without his ever having said so, she sensed that he had a terrible need to make up for that lack of passion. He hadn't let his practice slide since her illness; he was still as hardworking and compassionate as ever, but he'd turned all his previously leisure hours over to attending her. No more hunting, no more socializing, a complete withdrawal from the civic activities that had always interested him. No more sleep, from the looks of him this evening.

"Can't you bring her here to stay?" Grace asked. She'd made the offer before and been turned down. She expected to be turned down again, but it was all she had to give. "Mabelann and I would be honored to help you with her care."

"Thank you, Grace, but she wants to die in her own home. And if that's what she wants, that's what I'll give her. Lord knows it's all I *can* give her now."

The silence fell again, but it wasn't as peaceful this time. Howard finally leaned forward and picked up the newspaper still lying on the desk with its half-headline glaring. "Let's get the bad news over with," he said bluntly.

Grace folded her hands and looked down. "It's true. I'm sorry. Some of your stocks haven't fared quite as badly as ours, but still . . ."

Howard shrugged as if it didn't matter, and at the moment, it didn't. "It was only money."

"Howard, I can't tell you how awful I feel—"

"No need. You didn't make it happen. God only knows what did, but I'm certain it wasn't you."

"But I'm the one who urged you to invest in stocks instead of buying that property you were thinking of."

"You only urged me. You didn't twist my arm. Besides, you know that land flooded last spring and took out all the best topsoil. I was fated to lose either way."

Grace wanted to weep. "I can't bear to hear you say things like that! You aren't fated to lose. None of us are."

He stood up suddenly. "I'm not good company anymore, Grace. Don't try to cheer me up. It's impossible. Good night."

She sat at her desk for a long time after his abrupt departure, remembering having felt the same way once. When Jack died. But Laura had saved her. Who would save Howard?

Many years later, when Laura's own daughter asked about the Great Depression and Laura attempted to describe those first weeks and months, she realized it should have been a frightening experience for a child—having life turned inside out without the slightest understanding of why. But Laura hadn't found it frightening; rather, it was an exhilarating period, with every day bringing some interesting alteration in the way they lived. The first change that touched Laura's life was on her birthday a week and a half later. Normally she received a great many new dresses and sweaters. Part of the birthday routine involved putting these in the closet after removing those dresses that had gotten too short. These outgrown clothes, many hardly worn, were then given away.

But on her eleventh birthday, there was only a Hunting Stewart plaid dress, a warm red sweater with matching skirt,

and several pairs of cable-knit stockings. Later, when Grace
went through Laura's closet, clothes were chosen for length-
ening and letting out, not for discard. As Laura hadn't yet
reached the age to care much about personal adornment, she
didn't mind. But Sonny, who did care, was outraged when
he realized his new navy knickers were actually a pair of his
father's golfing trousers that had been cut down for him.

The big black Hispano-Suiza and Jackson's sporty Packard
runabout were put on blocks in the stable. The oil, gas, and
water were drained from their engines and heavy canvas was
thrown over them. "What's the use?" Jackson stormed. "You
might as well sell them and be done with it."

"I would do so, if I could find a buyer," Grace said. "As
it is, they can wait out our troubles under wraps. We'll keep
the Minerva in working order."

"But it's so dowdy-looking," Evelyn objected.

"So it is, but it cost over twenty thousand dollars, and the
only way we can get our money's worth out of it now is to
use it. It's larger than the others, which means Mabelann can
do all the weekly shopping with it, and it will come in handy
for picking up the farm produce."

"You're going to let the maid use a Minerva automobile to
haul vegetables?" Jackson exclaimed.

"I'd use it to plow the fields, if I could," Grace answered.

Eating habits changed, too. At first beef and pork appeared
on the table almost as regularly as before, but in far smaller
portions. "Sonny, don't take that chop unless you plan to eat
every bit of it," Grace would say, or, "No, Laura, you may
not be excused until you finish your dessert. We cannot
afford waste." They had game more often. "If you're going
to spend so much of your time shooting at things, they might
as well be things we can eat," Grace told Jackson.

The cook was put to work thinking of inventive and palat-
able ways to prepare less expensive meats and, in general,
made a good job of it, though even Grace could not stomach
squirrel or possum and declared that one appearance of these
on the table was one too many. But she insisted on frequent
rabbit. "How *can* you bear to eat that?" Evelyn asked one
evening when Grace took a second helping of rabbit stew.

Grace smiled. "I see it this way, Evelyn: if I weren't
eating this rabbit, he'd be out fathering more little rabbits and
in the spring all those little rabbits would eat the sprouting
peas. I love fresh peas and if I want any next May, I've got to
eat as many rabbits now as I can."

Even Jackson laughed at this.

There weren't any visitors during the first few weeks after the stock market collapsed, but on the day after Thanksgiving, Grace sent for Laura. "I'm going into town to meet the train. Do you want to ride along?" she asked.

"Oh, yes, Gram."

"Then run up and put on your red sweater and skirt. We want to look as cheerful as possible."

"Why, Gram?"

"Because we're picking up your Aunt Adele and her brother, Uncle Edmund. Do you remember Aunt Adele? She came once when you were little."

"I don't think so. Why are we going to look cheerful? Is she sad?"

"Yes, dear. She probably is. But she won't be for long. We're going to make her happy again."

"Sad" was hardly the word. "Morose" was closer. Adele Bills Smith stepped off the train clutching a sodden handkerchief to her reddened eyes. Laura vaguely recalled her as she threw her plump arms around Grace. She was in her mid-fifties, as plump and sleek as a well-corseted pigeon. She had on a good but very conservative fur coat and the sort of expensive ugly shoes only the rich could afford or wanted to wear.

"Ruined, my dear! Utterly ruined! Everything is gone. I couldn't even get the steamship line to pay me back for the tickets I'd bought. Edmund and I should have been in France by now if it weren't for . . . Oh, Grace . . ." she finished with an incoherent wail.

"Adele, dear, you mustn't cry about it. It's completely against your nature! Everything will be fine now." She put one arm around Adele and extended her other hand to the stately gentleman who'd been standing, statue-stiff, beside her. "Edmund, I'm so glad to see you. You look wonderful. You never change. I've regretted all these years that the children couldn't know you better. Here's Laura. You'll meet Sonny when we get back to the house."

Laura stepped forward and said, "How do you do, Uncle Edmund?"

He took her small hand. His grip was firm, but his skin was soft—the clean, uncallused hands of a scholar. "I'm very well, my dear child. You look very like your grandmother. Grace, the resemblance is quite clear and takes me back many

years. Now, Adele, you must stop this weeping and help me
identify the luggage.''

On the ride home along the hilly, winding roads, Laura sat
in the back seat with Uncle Edmund. He was a tall man with
a shock of white hair, an immaculately groomed walrus mustache, and a professorial habit of pausing and weighing each
word as if it were gold before uttering it. Laura liked his
deep, rumbly voice and fresh, soap smell, but was shy of his
direct gaze. She wished he'd talk more, but his sister Adele
dominated the conversation on the way back to Thornehill.

Laura listened as Adele described what the catastrophe on
Wall Street had done to them. Uncle Edmund, having put in
many years teaching college, had finally retired. They'd sold
their cozy little house in Cambridge and planned the long-
awaited trip to Europe, intending to spend a year, then return
and live out the balance of their lives well endowed with
dividends and memories. ''I thought sure it was some sort of
mistake at first. It didn't seem possible. The family has
always had money without having to even think about it. It's
just there. But everything's gone now. Edmund and I together
barely had enough for the train fare. Oh, Grace, I shouldn't
be carrying on like this to you. I'm sure you're in as much
trouble as we are. I never thought to see the day when Jack
Thorne's wife would have to drive her own car. What *has* the
world come to!''

Grace flashed her a smile. ''Don't jump to conclusions,
Adele. I'm driving because I enjoy it. We haven't had to
dismiss the chauffeur. He's just down with a touch of flu.''

Laura stared at the back of her grandmother's head, astonished. She'd never heard Grace tell a lie. Busby, the chauffeur, wasn't sick at all, he was on the roof repairing a leak.
Gram used to hire people to come in and do things like that,
but now everybody did funny jobs they hadn't done before.
Uncle Edmund patted Laura's hand and she jumped. The way
he was looking at her, it was as if he could read her thoughts.

''You're not to worry about a thing,'' Grace was going on.
''We're delighted to have you come join us.''

''We hate imposing on you—''

''You couldn't impose if you tried, Adele. We have more
room than we know what to do with at Thornehill. Besides,
you're family. It's as much your home as mine.''

Uncle Edmund let out a dry chuckle. ''That's taking gra-
ciousness too far, Grace. Jack's father and our mother were

brother and sister. That gives us no right whatsoever to your home.''

"Rights or not, I'm glad you're here and I want you to stay as long as you want. Forever, if possible.''

That night Grace came in to tell Laura good night. Now that there weren't guests to entertain, she often did this. "You looked very grown-up today, Laura. And I was glad you used your best manners without being asked.''

"You mean the soup spoon?'' Laura asked. She'd been allowed to eat dinner with the adults, and after careful thought had selected the right spoon.

Grace had been watching, and winked at her minor victory over the treacherous labyrinth of etiquette. A lump gathered in her chest at the thought of how proud she was of Laura. She was everything Grace had hoped for—pretty, bright, well-mannered, thoughtful of her elders. Everything a woman could wish for in a child. If only her own child had been as lovable. If only she could have loved him as she loved Laura. "The soup spoon and everything.''

She sat down on the bed next to Laura and leaned back against the headboard. "It's been a long day, hasn't it, Laura-bunny?''

"I like Aunt Adele and Uncle Edmund, Gram.''

"So do I. Very much.'' She closed her eyes and took a deep breath.

"Gram? Do you really like to drive the automobile?''

"No, but I didn't want Adele and Edmund to feel guilty about coming here. Guilt is a terrible thing,'' she said fiercely.

"I don't understand. Why would they feel guilty about coming here?''

Grace put her arm around Laura and pulled her close. "Laura, they've lost everything.''

"So have we. I heard Daddy say so.''

"Oh, no, Laura. We've only lost money. We still have all the important things. We're healthy; we have each other; we have Thornehill and the farms. It will be a pesky nuisance, not having so much money, but that's all. But Adele and Edmund have only what they brought in their suitcases. We must make them feel like they're doing us a favor, staying here. As they are.''

She was quiet for a long moment; then she added, "It's nice we like them, but that isn't the reason I invited them.''

"It's not?''

"No, I invited them because it was the right thing to do.

Even if they had been awful people, it would be our responsibility to take care of them. You understand that, don't you?''

"Why would we do things for them if we didn't like them?"

"Because they're in need, and because they're Thornes."

"But Uncle Edmund's name is Bills and Aunt Adele is Mrs. Smith. I heard you tell everyone that."

"You don't have to be named Thorne to be a Thorne, bunny. I meant . . . well, that they have a stake in Thornehill. Just like Mabelann does, and Miss Hawkins. That's why Busby is doing other work now on the house. You see, when this awful money thing happened, we agreed to pay him because otherwise he might not get another job. Many businesses in Eureka Springs are closing down. Then his family couldn't buy clothes and food. So we keep him on and he, in turn, must do more valuable work for us. We're all helping each other. All the Thornes."

"Do you pay Miss Hawkins?"

Grace tried to stifle a yawn. "Yes, I do."

"How much?"

Grace rose, smiling. "Not nearly enough, I suspect. Considering how many questions you must ask her."

"I'm sorry, Gram."

Grace scooped her into a hug. "Don't be sorry, Laura-bunny. Ask me all the questions you want. But tomorrow. Good night, love."

Were it not for Grace's dogged good cheer, Christmas would have been a dreary, stingy occasion. She found the thought of parties with nothing to celebrate and gifts with nothing to spend extremely depressing, but knew the rest of them took their cue from her. If she gave in to the inclination to lament the change in their lives, so would they. Even if she were willing to let the adults sink into a morass of self-pity, she must not ruin the children's holidays.

"I have an excellent idea I think we should try this year," she announced. "We should have a rule that no one is allowed to purchase a gift. That way we'll all have to work our brains and hearts, which is what Christmas should be about."

Grace and Evelyn, working together for once, invaded the attic of the mansion and turned up a number of long-forgotten treasures: an ivory-handled riding crop for Jackson, Jeremiah Thorne's pocket watch for Sonny, and a pair of opera glasses for Laura. There was a tiny jade figure whose head unscrewed to reveal a slim corridor for sewing needles for Adele, and a lovely silver bookmark for Edmund.

Adele knitted hats and gloves for everybody, and Edmund went through his trunks and carefully selected appropriate books for everyone from his vast collection. Sonny, who had some slight talent as an artist, which he imagined to be a great talent, made drawings for his family.

Laura, however, was in despair until she hit upon giving promises. She wrote up each in her best hand and then colored fancy paper frames. To Grace she promised always to use the right silverware. To Jackson she promised not to help Sonny take anything apart. As a sop to Sonny, she promised to do his math homework for him on any five occasions of his choosing. She promised Uncle Edmund to shine his shoes for a month, since he set such great store by personal neatness. It wasn't until she got to Evelyn that she realized how little she really knew about the woman she called Mama. She racked her brains for days and finally wrote out, "Dear Mama, I promise to crank the Victrola for you anytime you want."

Christmas dinner itself was a festive occasion. In the past, Grace and Jackson traditionally had a brief reception for the staff in the library on Christmas morning, during which generous gifts of money were distributed before the family had their own gift giving. This year was different only in the amount of the gifts. "I'm sorry it can't be more," Grace said to the cook, the grooms, the chauffeur-turned-handyman, the two maids, the gardener and his assistants as she slipped each an envelope.

Another tradition remained unbroken as well. Dr. Howard Lee and Willis Hawkins took dinner with them, one sitting on each side of Grace. "Like the queen and her courtiers," Evelyn mumbled to Jackson as she took her place next to him. Laura knew that Dr. Lee was only going to stay for the main course, having heard him say to Gram that his wife was doing very well that day and that she'd insisted that he attend Christmas dinner at Thornehill while a neighbor sat with her.

The usual caviar and shrimp cocktail were missing and the oyster dressing lacked oysters, but everyone made a sincere effort not to notice. In addition to a rather stringy turkey, there was a magnificent ham, which Mabelann carried in on an enormous silver platter.

"Grace!" Howard Lee exclaimed with something of his

old bonhomie, "if I didn't know you were an honest woman, I'd wonder how you came by such a thing."

"If I *were* altogether honest, I wouldn't have it. It's a gift—from our bootlegger. A charming fellow who calls himself 'Big Al.' He's supplied us for years now and I suppose he's under the erroneous assumption that we somehow survived the crash, although I was quite forthright with him when I canceled our standing order."

"You did what?" Jackson said, blanching.

"Don't worry, dear," Grace said with a twinkle in her eye. "I've got a wonderful recipe for dandelion wine I'm going to try out."

Jackson grinned. "I'd take the cure before I'd drink any such thing! As if being poor weren't bad enough."

But for that one day, being poor wasn't so bad.

XI

*I*T was going to be another hot day—August in Arkansas always was. This year it was so dry, even in the hills, that lips parched and wood paneling cracked and split. Laura sat on a high stool on the front veranda. Aunt Adele stood behind her with a comb and glass of water weaving Laura's hair into brutally precise French braids, as she did every morning. This was the sort of job that Mabelann used to do, but hard times had brought a great shuffling of duties. Mabelann now helped in the kitchen, as did Grace and Evelyn. Today they were canning corn, having started at dawn to get as much as possible done early in the day.

Miss Hawkins had finally gotten the long-hoped-for proposal three months earlier and left Thornehill. Uncle Edmund had eagerly stepped into her role. "I've been a teacher all my adult life, Grace," he'd said. "No point in being on the dole here when I could make myself useful." He was a superb instructor, but Sonny and Laura weren't always happy with the change because it wasn't possible to manipulate him as they'd done Miss Hawkins.

"I don't see why we have to study in the summer," Sonny said. He was sitting in a wicker chair with his feet on the railing watching as Laura endured the daily torture of having her scalp raked. "Other children only go part of the year."

"Other children have to work in the fields, or have jobs in factories," Adele said. "You're both fortunate to have such a fine teacher who's willing to give his time to you. Laura, if you'd stop wiggling we'd be finished sooner."

"I'd rather work in a factory than study," Sonny said, taking a sip of orange juice he'd brought out from the breakfast table. "Stupid old arithmetic! I can't see what good it'll ever do me to know that stuff."

"Don't let your grandmother hear you say a thing like that," Adele warned. Then she hugged Laura. "There. Done. I see the postman down the drive. Why don't you two go meet him and bring the mail up before you start your lessons."

Laura slid off the stool and Sonny leapt up. "Thanks, Aunt Adele," Laura said. "You'll tell Uncle Edmund why we're late?"

"Wait! Put that stool back in the kitchen before you go. And did you leave that pair of dungarees out to be mended like I asked?"

"Yes, ma'am!" Laura shouted over her shoulder. They dragged the errand out as long as they could. But their attempt to engage the postman in conversation wasn't very successful, as he had long rounds and, like everyone else, wanted to get the job done before the hottest part of the day. "Do you like your job?" Laura asked him after he handed her a string-tied bundle of letters.

He took off his cap and wiped his forehead with his sleeve. "I like having a job. There's lots that don't. Y'all run along with them letters now."

They took the letters to the kitchen. Evelyn was cutting the juicy corn off the cobs, which were then put out in the sun to dry. Jackson had heard they could be burned as fuel in the winter. Mabelann was funneling cut corn into one batch of mason jars and Grace was screwing the caps on others, holding the hot jars with a tea towel. "Thank you, dear," Grace said, taking the packet of mail from Laura and glancing through it. "Mmmm, India McPhee . . ." she said, holding one envelope out at arm's length to study the return address. "Who in the world . . . ? Oh, yes. My cousin's daughter. I haven't heard from any of them for ages. Put these in the library, Bunny, on your way. I'll read them all later."

The schoolroom was on the third floor of the central part of the house, where the maids would have slept, had there been an extensive staff. Both the maids they'd had at the time of the crash had married and left. Grace had accepted their resignations with apparent sorrow, though everyone knew she was glad of two less salaries to pay. It was stifling hot and by midmorning even fastidious Edmund was sweating. "We'll take our books outdoors this morning," he finally said.

They found a shady place near the kitchen door and settled in around the base of a tree, each with a palm-leaf fan. Before he could resume the lessons, Laura said, "Uncle Edmund, this morning the postman said he was lucky to have a job. That lots of people don't. Why is that?"

"It's the Depression, child. Vast numbers of people are out of work."

"But why? Did they lose their money in the stock market like we did?"

"No, not so very many people had money in stocks. A few people, like your Aunt Adele and myself and your own family, had a great deal invested. No, I think the crash was more a symptom than a cause."

Laura picked a long blade of grass and started idly shredding it. "Then why don't people have jobs?"

Edmund didn't answer for a moment. How could he explain to a child what most adults, himself included, grasped only hazily? He fanned himself a bit and said, "It started, I think, with overproduction. Making too many things, too efficiently, in a sense. Then a number of big companies had to cut their production. That meant putting a lot of people out of work."

"Why didn't they just get other jobs?"

"They tried. But many of them couldn't, because other companies were having the same trouble. Suppose, Laura, that you have a town with a big factory and it fires fifty people. Well, maybe ten of those people had new stoves and they were paying for them on time. Now they can't pay anymore and the man they bought the stoves from can't get the money—"

"He could get the stove back. That's what happened to Mabelann's sister. I heard her tell Gram the store had taken back their icebox."

"Yes, that happens, but what good does it do the man with the stoves? He gets them back, but they're old and used and nobody will pay the full price for them again. Besides, there probably aren't another ten people in town with extra money. So the stove man goes broke. And so do the icebox man and the man who sold those people radios and automobiles. Then those men, in turn, can't pay their bills and so other people don't get the money that's owed them. They can't pay their debts and the bank doesn't get the money back that they've loaned and it goes on and on . . . ."

Laura sucked on the end of one of her braids. "Then how does anything ever get better, Uncle Edmund?"

He continued to fan himself. "I don't know, child. I just don't know. I'm not sure anyone does."

Grace screwed down the last lid and spread a cloth over the bottles. "We'll have to give this up for today," she said.

"I done turned off the stove, Miz Grace," Mabelann said.

"Don't forget your mail," Adele said as Grace took off her apron.

"It can wait. If I don't bathe before lunch, I'll 'offend' everyone for miles away," Grace said, all but staggering from the kitchen. Once upstairs, standing under a refreshing stream of water from the shower, she recovered her spirits to some extent. "Howard had the right idea," she said aloud, letting the water strike her shower cap and run down her face.

Howard Lee was in Canada. "My last trip," he'd said when he stopped to see her before setting out. "I might not even have the money to get back, but I certainly won't be able to afford it by next summer. I haven't been paid in actual cash money for months. Remember how Jack and I used to pack for these trips? Lord, but we looked like a safari ready to set out into the wilderness for a year-long trek!"

It was nice to hear him talk like his old cheerful self. He'd been a sort of stranger since before Meg's death in January and well into the spring following. But then in late June something had happened to him—he said it was delivering the Yokum triplets, for which he was paid six bushels of corn—that made him raise his head and look around at life again. He'd once again become a frequent visitor at Thornehill. Wednesday nights he'd come up and have dinner and listen to the radio with the family until ten. Sundays he came at noon and spent the afternoon hours fishing with Edmund at the spring. Then he'd have a cold supper with them and stay through the evening again.

He fit in easily with the family—in fact Grace often forgot that he wasn't actually one of them. He taught Sonny to play cribbage and even let him win often enough to maintain his enthusiasm. He brought along a quilt his mother had made and gave it to Adele, who was fascinated with the pattern. But his interest was mainly in Grace herself.

He's courting me! she'd thought at one point when he asked her in a surprisingly formal way if she'd enjoy going into town to see a movie. "That's great!" Sonny had shouted. "Let's all go!"

"I'm asking your grandmother, young man," Howard had replied.

Grace, watching him, thought she detected a hint of a blush and then chided herself for her foolishness. She was just turning into a lonely old lady, imagining flattery where none was intended. But now, standing under the shower thinking about it, she wondered again. She didn't feel old and her mirror told her (most of the time) that she didn't look at all bad for her age. A few lines around her eyes, a slight sag at breast and hips that wasn't detectable to anyone but her. Hair and skin that had preserved amazingly well considering how little attention she'd paid to such things most of her life.

Nor was Howard Lee in his dotage. In fact, he was a remarkably handsome man with his lean, athletic figure, tanned skin, and outstanding teeth. Even Jack hadn't possessed such wonderful teeth, Grace thought a little guiltily.

She turned the shower off, hung her shower cap up, and toweled off. After she'd put on her underwear she stood for a minute studying herself in the full-length mirror on the back of the bathroom door. No, not too bad, she thought. Suddenly she felt embarrassed for herself. What if someone could read her mind? What sort of grandmother considered such things?

Grandmother! she thought, as if the idea were brand new to her. How had she come so far in such a short time? Where had all those years gone? She wondered if everyone felt this way at her age, like a twenty-year-old who just happened to have lived nearly three times that long! Did anyone ever feel old inside? Did anyone ever give up hoping that someone might find them attractive—even romantically so?

Romance . . . She *was* too old for that, wasn't she? And yet, she'd been flattered, even a little . . . well, excited (she turned away from the sight of her own blush) when Howard began paying so much attention to her. She hadn't even allowed herself to consider such things since Jack died. How long had it been now? Twelve years? That many? In some ways it seemed like centuries ago, like that grieving widow had been another person Grace hardly remembered at all. And other times, most often in the dead of a lonely night, it seemed no more than days.

Jack . . .

Dear God, how she missed him. Still.

She wouldn't be thinking of her age if Jack were alive. He wouldn't have let her. She'd still be sharing a bed with him, sharing her body with him, basking in his looks and words and waking every morning with the anticipation of another day . . .

She grabbed a brush and took an almost savage whack at her hair. Enough foolishness! Enough! "The heat is turning your brain to tapioca, Grace Emerson Thorne!" she said out loud.

She got her hair into order without letting her imagination run away again and hurriedly dressed for lunch, picking up her mail where she'd left it on the nightstand when she came upstairs. Maybe there'd be some good news or even a really shocking bill in it to take her mind off . . . off such "fanciful" thoughts.

Grace didn't get around to reading her mail until luncheon was almost over. "We're going to have a visitor later this week," she said.

"Oh?" Jackson brightened. He, more than any of the rest of them, had missed the continual rounds of guests who had characterized their life-style before the Depression.

"My cousin's daughter India. Her mother and grandmother, my Aunt Nell, died of the Spanish influenza. India was twelve or thirteen at the time. I wrote to her father then, inviting her here to live, but he said his people would take care of her. I haven't heard a word from any of them since then."

"Why's she coming here?"

"Her letter says she's on a tour of the country and wants to stop in for a few days. I certainly hope she's not a hearty eater," Grace added, watching as Laura and Sonny both reached for the last spoonful of black-eyed peas.

Once again Laura was invited to ride to the station. Normally they took a stroll through town on such trips, but today was too hot. The train was late and they sat quietly in the meager shade of the platform roof watching the heat shimmer over the rails. Grace dabbed at her upper lip with a lacy handkerchief. "You look pretty, Gram," Laura told her.

Grace was surprised. "How sweet of you to say so, bunny."

It was true. No matter how hard Grace had to work, she always made the effort to look thoroughly the lady when she left the house. Today she had her hair in a loose knot at the back of her head and wore a stylish and appropriately wide-brimmed straw hat with a single silk poppy at the brim. Her well-draped summer dress was cream-colored like the straw, with red piping around the collar, button plackets, and breast pockets. Her shoes matched the hat and her wrist-length poppy-red gloves brought the whole ensemble together.

Grace's self-assessment in front of the mirror a few days earlier had been accurate, if not as modest as she would have wished of herself. Except for the white in her hair, no one would have guessed she was in her mid-fifties, for her figure and bearing were those of a woman in her early thirties. There had been occasions, in fact, when Grace was wearing a hat that concealed her hair that she'd been taken for Laura's mother rather than grandmother. The error had pleased her on several counts.

"Ah, here it comes. At last!" Grace said as the sound of the approaching train carried along the tracks. They waited patiently for the Missouri & North Arkansas (the MNA or "May Never Arrive," as the town called it) coach to pull to a stop. As the conductor hopped down and lowered the steps, several people were waiting to disembark. "What does cousin India look like?" Laura asked.

"I have no idea. I've never seen her. Perhaps that's she," Grace said as a rather plain, homebody young woman stepped down. Grace went forward. "You must be India," she said, putting out her hand.

The young woman ducked her head, shaking it in denial.

Just then a voice cried out from behind them: "*Aunt Grace!* Oh, it *must* be you! How *divinely* beautiful you are!"

Grace stepped back so suddenly she trod on Laura's foot. They were facing a vision. India McPhee was nearly six angular feet tall with protuberant eyes and big horsey teeth with a wide gap between the front two. But if she was less than attractive, she seemed utterly unaware of the fact. She wore a shimmering emerald-green turban that gathered into a bow the size of a cabbage at the side of her head. Her vivid floral-print dress was almost concealed beneath the black-fringed, jet-beaded shawl she wore flung around her body and over her shoulder. The corner nearly touched the ground.

She dashed forward, all but swallowing Grace in a gigantic, effusive hug. "How *very* dear of you to meet me, Aunt Grace."

It was the first time Laura had ever seen her grandmother disconcerted. She emerged from the embrace with her hat askew and a stunned look on her face. Adjusting her headgear, she pulled herself together and said, "India? India McPhee? How nice to meet you, my dear. This is my granddaughter, Laura Thorne."

"Laura Thorne! *What* a melodious name. Laura Thorne! It's like poetry. *Such* a pretty child," she exclaimed, and without any shyness, knelt on the platform to look at Laura closely. Even kneeling, she towered. She grasped Laura by the shoulders and stared into her eyes for a moment, then closed her own and put her fingers to her temples as if stricken by a headache. "Ahhh, what a *lovely* aura she has. I'm sure she's divinely intelligent. One can tell, you know, if one just opens one's mind to the vibrations."

Suddenly her long, bony arms shot out of the shawl and she hugged Laura. She wore a heavy patchouli scent. Laura was so overwhelmed she hardly noticed the beads on the shawl pressing into her cheek. "Oh, I'm so *terribly* thrilled to be here," India said, rising and lunging for Grace again. Grace sidestepped her this time. "We're going to have a perfectly *heavenly* time getting to know each other, aren't we, darlings?"

By the time they'd loaded her four suitcases, humpbacked trunk, six hatboxes, picnic hamper, and endless loose parcels, Laura was deep in her first crush. This was beyond any doubt the most exotic, vivacious individual she'd ever met or dreamed of. "Isn't she divine?" Laura asked Grace as India dashed back to tip the porter.

Grace cocked an eyebrow. "Divine?" And after a long moment, she smiled and said quietly, "She looks like she has a good appetite."

India McPhee met with a mixed reception at Thornehill. Jackson found her amusing and provoked her into ever more outrageous behavior. Evelyn was frankly agog, especially when India took her hand and proclaimed that Evelyn's aura positively glittered with beauty and good fortune. "Men must simply *flock* around you, darling. So *exciting*. So divinely mysterious. Your vibrations remind me of a dear friend of mine. She was aboard the *Titanic*, flung into the sea and rescued. *Such* a thrill. Just a child, you understand, but marked for *life* by this divine aura of mystery. You weren't on the *Titanic*, were you?"

"No, I'm afraid I wasn't," Evelyn replied, flattered and flustered.

Aunt Adele didn't like her. At one point during dinner, India leapt from the table to run to the kitchens and tell the cook how divine dinner was. Adele leaned toward Grace and muttered, "Quite insane."

Edmund, not hearing this remark, addressed Adele. "Interesting young person. Reminds me a lot of you as a girl, Adele." To which his sister replied with a glare.

Grace said nothing, but observed closely what large portions of everything India took and how much remained on her plate when she folded her napkin and sat back. "You must eat all your food, cousin India," Sonny said.

She gave him a toothy smile. "Nonsense, you little dear. Food is merely a bodily need. We must be more concerned for what nourishes our spirits."

"But you didn't eat your chicken leg." Sonny pursued the original subject, undeterred by ventures into more spiritual realms.

"May I have it? I'm still hungry," Laura said. She was so full the thought of another bite made her almost gag, but she knew there would be repercussions if the chicken leg went back to the kitchen.

After dinner, Grace went into the library to listen to the wireless and Adele joined her with a pile of mending. Jackson, Evelyn, India, and Edmund went onto the veranda for a rubber of bridge, and Sonny and Laura went to the stables to see a new batch of kittens. But the mother cat hissed and spit and they gave up trying to get close enough to handle the blind little balls of fur. Walking back, Laura said, "Isn't cousin India wonderful?"

"No, she's silly. She kissed me and said I was sweet."

"But Mama says you're sweet and you don't mind."

"That's different. Besides, she uses too much scent. I can't even breathe around her."

"I think she smells heavenly."

"Wanna help me take my bicycle apart?" Sonny offered, bored with the subject of their visitor.

"No, I think I'll go watch them play cards. Maybe cousin India will teach me how to play."

"That's stupid. And you're stupid."

After a week Grace was asking, "How long are you going to be able to stay with us, India?"

"Oh, only a day or two more. I don't want to wear out my welcome. So *hard,* tearing oneself away from such divine company."

After another week Grace was leaving train schedules in prominent places and Adele was making remarks like, "How your friends must be missing you, India. I'll bet they're just clamoring for your return.''

But India stayed on . . . and on . . . and on. She and Evelyn stayed up half the nights with her Ouija board or impromptu séances (which Grace positively forbade Laura to attend) or playing cards. India seldom appeared before noon. Then, as often as not, she strolled around the grounds of the estate all afternoon in her flowing, flapping, brilliantly hued clothes. Sometimes she let Laura come along when she could escape from her lessons. "Listen to the *dear* little birds, darling. So sweet and melodious. I think I was a bird in a previous life. I almost seem to understand what they're saying sometimes. Hear that? Yoo-hoo, yoo-hoo!'' she trilled, imitating a chickadee.

Laura, wanting to join in the spirit of this, picked out the sound of a white-crowned sparrow and imitated its distinctive call. "Poor Sam Peabody, Peabody, Peabody!'' she sang.

"Yes, dear, that's it perfectly. I do believe you were a bird as well. A parrot, perhaps. No, not quite so colorful. Though I'm sure *I* was an eagle. Soaring *ever* so high and doing all *sorts* of delicious swoops and dives. I can just *feel* it still. The heavenly freedom from all that's earthly and common.''

One rainy, dismal day in October Laura had a stomachache and Uncle Edmund sent her to report it to her grandmother. "Dr. Lee is back and she might want to ask him to come up and see you. It's Wednesday, he'll be along anyway.''

Laura went to the library, where Gram had been working on accounts all week, but the room was empty at the moment. There were papers all over the desk. Laura considered going to look for Gram, but decided to wait instead. She sat in the chair by the desk for a little bit, but her stomach still hurt and she decided she'd feel better lying down. At the other end of the room was a sofa that faced the fireplace. She curled up there and pulled an afghan over herself. She wasn't cold, exactly, just in need of the comfort. Not surprisingly, she fell asleep.

She didn't hear Grace come in, but woke when there was a tap on the door and Grace said, "Come in.''

"Aunt Grace? Mabelann said you wanted to see me.'' India's voice.

"Sit down, India. I have a letter here that concerns you. It's from a lawyer in New York State who says he represents a brokerage firm. He seems to have done some pretty thorough investigating and discovered that we are relatives of yours. He is inquiring as to whether I know anything of your whereabouts. According to his letter you owe one hundred and twenty-five thousand dollars to the brokerage firm.''

Laura was frozen. She'd been quiet too long to reveal herself now for fear they'd think she'd deliberately hidden there, but she wanted to leap up and come to her beloved India's defense. She didn't understand just what the letter really meant, but she knew it was bad and it couldn't be right. Cousin India couldn't owe anybody that much money.

But her thoughts were interrupted by a horrible sound like an animal choking. Laura scooted along the sofa horizontally until she could just peek around the edge.

India had collapsed in the chair across from Grace. She had her head buried in her hands and her wide shoulders were shaking with sobs. "He told me the stock would go up. *Up!* I sold everything Papa left me and bought all I could. The broker told me it would go up. Then . . . then the market did that terrible thing. I'd bought it on margin. He'd said that was the best way, because I could get so much more than I had the money to buy. But it dropped and dropped and I sold it. Then the bastard called me in and said I owed him all that money!

"Aunt Grace, how *could* I owe him money when I didn't have any? It wasn't my fault. I'd sold it and didn't have anything left and he kept saying I owed him the money. He said he'd have me put in jail—*jail!* Aunt Grace, I didn't know what do to, so I just packed everything and came here. I didn't tell anyone where I was going and I didn't think anybody would guess . . .''

Grace folded the letter and slid it under the blotter. "How much money *do* you have, India?''

India dragged a handkerchief out of her sleeve and blew her nose mightily. "Forty dollars. Oh, God! They're going to send me to jail or the poor farm. I'd rather *die!*''

"No, India, nobody's going to put you in jail. How long were you intending to stay here?''

India looked up, her protuberant eyes red and streaming. "Until you threw me out. Are you going to?''

"Well . . .'' Grace leaned back and tented her fingers, resting her chin thoughtfully on them. "I can't pay your debts, you know. That would go beyond my responsibility, even if it were possible. Which it isn't. But you *are* family. I'll write to this lawyer and say I lost touch with you when your mother died and have no idea where you might be.''

"Oh, Aunt Grace, thank you, thank you . . ."

India leapt up and was about to run around the desk to show her affection, but Grace raised her hand, stopping her in her tracks. "Sit down, India. We aren't through talking yet. I don't want your gratitude, but I must have your cooperation."

"What do you mean?" India asked, subsiding and blowing her nose again.

"India, you seem to have blinded yourself to the fact that we're in grave financial difficulty here—"

"I had *no* idea!"

Grace half-smiled. "I fail to see how you could have missed it. Be that as it may, we must live very frugally and you have been most wasteful and frivolous. You've sent back perfectly good food, you've wasted the motorcar's gasoline on pointless trips to town, you've created extra work for Mabelann. If you're to stay here, that sort of thing can't continue."

"I really didn't know," India said miserably.

Nothing was "heavenly" or "divine," and if Grace possessed an "aura" at that moment, it was far too gloomy for India to mention. "I'll do better, Aunt Grace. I promise."

"Have you any useful skills, other than playing cards and conducting séances?" Grace asked bluntly.

India held her hands out. "None that I know of. I paint and I've done some very pretty stenciling on furniture—"

"Hardly what I'd hoped for, but we shall eventually find you a niche, I suppose."

India stood up. "Are you going to tell the others? I'd hate for Evelyn to know."

"No, I'm not. You are."

"Yes, I can see you're right. I should." India thanked her again and fled the room, unaware of the sound her clay feet made in Laura's ears.

Grace got up slowly when India was gone and walked to the windows. She pulled the draperies open and looked out at the rain. Watching her from her concealed position, Laura could only see her profile and couldn't tell if the expression on her face was pain or amusement.

For a moment Grace felt that she was eighteen again, sitting in a garden listening to the music and laughter of the going-away party. The promises she'd made that night! The innocent courage and anticipation she'd felt about the future. It was a good thing she'd had no way of knowing what life was going to dish up for her. She might have run away then if she'd realized that someday so many people would depend on her strength and judgment.

Finally Grace spoke very softly. "Well, Jack, it isn't the way we intended, but I'm finally filling up the house with people." She blinked rapidly, then turned away, letting the heavy draperies fall back into place.

XII

*I*T was the first truly warm day of spring; the air was heavy with the fecund scent of new growth. India was sunbathing, her angular white body sprawled on a comforter on a flat section of the roof of Thornehill. Laura was next to her on a fraying quilt Adele had repaired. She was watching a bead of sweat trickle from India's temple into her spiky, lacquered hair. It made Laura tickle to watch and she wondered why India didn't feel it. Turning on her back, she closed her eyes.

It was a fine day for lazy thinking, the sort of aimless speculation that is the stuff of childhood. I wonder what it would be like to be blind? Laura thought. Only the week before, she'd gone to Eureka Springs with Mabelann and had seen a blind woman there. She had a cane that she tippy-tapped the ground with as she walked. The extraordinary thing was, the woman was smiling. Not big-grin-smiling, just happy-smiling, like there was something special going on that pleased her.

Laura made an effort to tune in her senses, like Sonny did when he fiddled with the wireless in the library. What could she hear if she were blind? Birds, of course, some of which she'd learned to identify by sound from a record Uncle Edmund had given her. There was the startled squawk of the flicker, the twittering of goldfinches, and the bubbling scarlet song of the redbird. But the air was full of the sound of warblers as well, those transient voices that passed through in the spring and autumn on their way to strange climes. Where did they all go, and why?

She could hear the wind sighing and by listening very carefully, she could pick out the sound of voices, too. Sonny's voice and Uncle Edmund's somewhere below, too faint to tell the words. From very far away there was the muffled "pop" of a gunshot. Daddy shooting, probably. She'd seen him go out early with his gun. Suddenly there was a sound close by and Laura jumped.

India. Snoring. Laura giggled.

The best thing about pretending to be blind was the smells. By concentrating, Laura could pick out a great many. There was mainly a damp green earth smell. It had rained for several days previously and today's sun was steaming the moisture out of the earth. There was a faint scent of lilac laced through. A slight breeze brought the smell of chickens, a distinct acid sort of smell. She could catch a faint whiff of cigarette smoke from time to time and could pick out the scent of India's shampoo. She thought she detected the odor of a gasoline engine as well, but that might have been her imagination.

If I really were blind, she thought, I'd have a pretty silver cane. She pictured herself on the streets of town, lightly tapping along, graceful and helpless. People would step out of her way, look at her gentle smile, and nod with admiration of her spirit. A very handsome man might come along and help her step off a curbing. "You're very brave and beautiful, miss," he would say. "Oh, no, sir. Not brave at all. One does what one must do," she would reply, unconsciously using one of Grace's often-repeated phrases.

She changed the scene, toying with it in her mind. What if she were crippled instead of blind? She could have a lovely chair with fancy scrolls and big wheels on it. But that didn't work very well. Negotiating the hills of Eureka Springs or the stairs at Thornehill would be an insurmountable problem. No, suppose it was just a very mysterious limp. A graceful limp, of course. But Laura couldn't quite imagine a graceful limp, hard as she tried.

She could be deaf. That was pretty good. Deaf people didn't look different that she knew of. Of course, she'd never met a deaf person, but she'd read a story once about a girl who was deaf and she'd been able to tell everything people said by watching their lips. Yes, that provided interesting possibilities. She would go away to school and nobody would know. She would laugh and talk with the other girls and only later they'd find out she couldn't hear. They'd be astonished and amazed at how clever she'd been to keep it a secret. But again, there was another side to this. Laura pictured one of the girls (she had red hair and freckles) telling secrets with another, but they had their backs to her and she couldn't see what they were saying. No. Deaf was out.

She could, of course, have a broken arm with a lot of plaster and a splint, and everybody would make a fuss over her. No—a broken arm might really hurt. Mabelann had stubbed her toe and broken it once and she'd complained of the pain for weeks. Laura sat up and rubbed her eyes. It was so boring to be healthy and ordinary. Nobody thought you were brave and wonderful if you were just normal. Of course, all the adults did say nice things about how smart she was. But smart wasn't fun, it was just easy to do arithmetic and things.

If only she could be beautiful. That wasn't as good as brave, but it would be nice. Some years later *Life* magazine was to declare her "a dead ringer for Hedy Lamarr" on the same week that a *Time* writer said she had "the wistful profile of Vivien Leigh," but that was long after the day when she looked down in disgust at her long, skinny legs with the knobby, scarred knees. Janet Gaynor's legs never looked like that. Neither did Norma Shearer's. Laura was sure of it. Nor did they have teeth that looked like they belonged in somebody else's face. ("Your face will grow up to fit them," Grace had told her, smiling when she complained.)

And her figure! Well, that was hopeless—utterly hopeless. She'd never get breasts, she feared. Here she was, thirteen years old—*thirteen*, for heaven's sake!—and her chest was still as flat and ribby as Sonny's. If she chopped her hair short like India's, nobody would even know she was a girl.

Now *that* was an interesting idea. Suppose she dressed like a boy. She could do all sorts of interesting things. Or could she? What did Sonny do that she couldn't? He wasn't allowed to swim in the little cold pond the spring formed, but that was because Gram was afraid of children near water. He wasn't allowed to play football either, but that was because of his asthma. But he didn't have to wear dresses to meals and keep his knees together, and if he got a little loud, nobody told him to keep his voice down like a lady. Nor did he have to endure the daily tortures that were involved with long hair—the shampoos, the awful pinch and pull of the rags Aunt Adele used to curl it for special occasions. Nor did he have to take piano lessons because it was "a ladylike skill," in Gram's words.

Of course all of this had another side, too. Sonny wouldn't ever know how thrilling it was to move your fingers on the keys and make music. Nor would he ever experience the slippery cold feel of silk slip or the wonder of having everyone say, "Laura, how pretty you look with curls."

Maybe if she'd learn to curl her hair herself . . . She turned over just as the door of the roof opened and Aunt Adele said, "I've been looking everywhere for you, Laura. Didn't you hear me calling? Have you gone deaf?"

"No, Aunt Adele," Laura answered sadly. "I'm not deaf. Or blind. Or beautiful. I'm just ordinary."

Adele put her hands on her hips. "India McPhee! What have you been filling this child's head with? Ordinary, indeed! Hrmph! Nobody here is ordinary. Come along now, Laura, and help me change the beds. That's certainly a more valuable activity than lolling about turning yourself into a brown lizard!"

Adele repeated this conversation to Grace later. Adele attached no particular importance to it and merely told the story to fill in a lull in the conversation. But Grace, though she said nothing to chide Adele, found food for thought in what she'd said. How strange that she and Laura should have grown up in such very different circumstances and yet were so alike. Laura had a large, lovely extended family, whereas Grace had grown up in the presence of her alcoholic and abusive mother with occasional awkward brushes with her father. Grace remembered thinking of herself as ordinary, but how could Laura feel that way? Laura, who was so special!

She watched her granddaughter closely at lunch, looking for signs of distress, ready to take her aside and investigate her unhappiness with an eye toward eliminating it. But she was pleasantly disappointed. Whatever had been disturbing her, it must have been momentary, for Laura was cheerful to the point of good, healthy silliness.

Grace ended up chiding herself. Laura was only being a perfectly normal child, undergoing the occasional pains and doubts of growing up. If only Grace's own childhood had been as normal, she would not be such an alarmist. But just to be sure, she took time from her work that afternoon to show Laura how to play gin rummy, and when she'd mastered the basic points, said, "Is there anything bothering you, Laura-bunny?"

"Yes, I think there's a seven missing from this pack," Laura said, and didn't understand why Gram thought that was so funny.

*   *   *

Grace was still smiling to herself about Laura that night when Mabelann came to her room around nine to say that Dr. Lee was asking to see her. Grace had been planning on going to bed early, as much from a satisfied sense of boredom as any other reason. "Is there something wrong, Mabelann? Did I forget he was coming?"

"You din' say nothin' to me, Miz Grace. Don't look like nothin' wrong. He all spiffed up, though."

Suddenly Grace had a feeling she knew why he'd come and was half-sorry she couldn't in good conscience plead some excuse. Reluctantly she took out the two pin curls she'd put in before the interruption. "Tell him I'll be down in a minute, would you? And stop grinning like that!"

Mabelann bobbed her head and disappeared.

Howard was waiting in the front hall instead of the library, where the rest of the family was still congregated for an evening with the radio. "I hope I'm not disturbing you too late," Howard said. "I meant to come by later, but Mrs. Yokum's crowd all came down with chickenpox—"

"It's not late. I'm sorry I kept you waiting."

"Grace, may I speak to you privately?" His voice was portentous.

Grace had a momentary urge to say: Yes, I mind. Please don't say what you're going to say. But she quelled it. "We can go out and sit on the front steps. It's a warm evening."

He opened the door, waited until she'd settled herself on the low stone edging before clearing his throat and saying, "Grace, we've been friends for a long time and . . . and I've come to think of you as more than just a friend these last two years . . ."

Grace's heart sank. She'd hoped she was wrong, but he was saying just what she feared. The courtship had been a slow, dignified ceremony as befitted their ages and stations. She'd become accustomed to it, had come to believe it was a static situation, a perpetual hiatus between friendship and love. Until a few moments ago she'd assumed that Howard was perfectly satisfied to let it remain that way.

"You must know I've always loved you . . ." he was saying.

"No!" Grace said, startled.

"Since the first day Jack introduced us in Boston. I thought then that you were the most gentle, beautiful girl in the world and I've watched as you grew into the strongest, most handsome woman. I even hoped—it sounds ridiculous and selfish now—that something would happen between you and Jack, and I could carry you off."

"Oh, Howard . . ." she said, torn between equally strong urges to laugh and cry at this syrupy remark. The entire conversation was so out of character for him—or was it? Had she just thought of him as she *wanted* him to be all this time, the stalwart friend, compassionate doctor, respected civic personage, not a man who could love.

"I'm quite serious, I'm afraid. I got over it, though, after that year Jackson almost died and later you and Jack changed. I didn't know what it was, but suddenly you were like parts of one person, not separate individuals. That's when I married Meg, you know. Six months later."

"So you did," Grace said softly. She'd never made the connection before.

"She never knew she was my second choice," Howard said. "At least I hope she didn't. When Jack died, well . . . it was almost as bad for me as for you, in a way. I knew how devastated you were and I couldn't do anything. I was a 'happily married man' and had no right . . ." His voice trailed off for a moment in recollection. "I had no right to say or do anything I wanted to. That's why I helped you with your scheme to pass Laura off as Sonny's twin. I'd watched you that month, nearly fading away with grief. If it hadn't been for Meg, I'd have moved in here then. Slept by your door, followed your every step—"

"I wanted to die," Grace said, the memory stabbing at her briefly, then retreating. "I planned to die—"

"I sensed that. But when you came back from the funeral with the baby, I knew you'd survive. And thrive." He'd been sitting next to her. Now he stood up quickly. "I didn't mean to get into all this. It's past and done. I just wanted you to know."

"I'm glad you told me. I wish I'd known then. No. I don't wish that."

"I felt, when Meg got the cancer, that God was punishing me for loving you, for being a little bit glad when Jack died. No, that's not really true. I loved Jack, in a different way, as much as I loved you."

"I understand, Howard. You don't have to say all this."

"No, I suppose not. But it's been a burden for a long time and I wanted to unload it. You know what I really came here to ask you?"

"I think I do."

"Will you marry me, Grace?"

She didn't answer right away. Why had she put off making a decision so long? She had known this night would come, this question would be asked. She should have been ready. Now the moment had come. Did she want to marry Howard Lee?

She *should* want to marry him. It was oh-so-sensible. They would be each other's companions in their declining years—except that she had no intention of "declining" for a very long time. He was kindness, intelligence, stability, everything she should want. But when, waiting for her reply, he took her hand, she knew the answer and knew it made no sense. She didn't want to sleep with Howard Lee. She'd had that kind of love in full measure and it was over. Jack was gone. She never wanted another man that way, no matter how good a man he was.

And there was another reason, too. A reason she couldn't quite put the words to. It had to do with making room in her heart as well as her bed. Howard, as beloved friend, had a place. But Howard as husband? She thought not.

"Oh, Howard . . . I can't. I really can't. I've been a widow too long. I've learned how to live alone—or as alone as anyone can be in this house. I'm too set in my ways to change. I don't ever want to share a bathroom with anyone again!" She said this last with a smile, hoping he'd find it amusing, but still realize what she was really trying to convey—that intimacy was a thing of the past.

He looked disappointed, but not as crushed as she'd feared. "You're sure?" was all he asked.

"Howard, I don't . . . I . . . Oh, why are you asking me! What man in his right mind wants a fifty-nine-year-old bride, for heaven's sake!"

He smiled. "A sixty-one-year-old man who's loved her for a long time!"

The tension was broken. She started giggling, then laughing outright, and he joined in. "Howard! You're glad I turned you down."

"No, I'm not!"

"You are. I'm sure of it."

He put his arm around her shoulders, a friend's gesture. "Maybe a little."

"It does seem like something we ought to do, doesn't it?"

she said. "Laura asked me once if I was going to marry you."

"She did? What did you say?"

"I said you hadn't asked me. Howard, you'll stay my friend, won't you? You're very important to me."

"Not half as important as you are to me. All of you, actually. The Thornes are my only family; Thornehill is more my home than the house I live in. Jack and I used to race each other up and down these steps when we were boys. I have a scar on my scalp from falling into this very ledge . . ."

"Come live here then," Grace said.

"No, not now."

"Someday?"

"Maybe. When my broken heart has healed." He said it with self-mockery.

"That ought to be about thirty seconds from now."

He didn't reply for a long time and finally said, "I meant it, you know. About loving you."

Grace nodded silently.

If Laura hadn't been late for dinner the next night, Mabelann would have answered the door, but Laura was just coming down the front stairs and heard the knocking—hesitant but insistent. She flung the door open and was confronted by a man and boy. The man wore faded and much-patched overalls, boots with one toe out, and a greasy-brimmed hat that he was holding with both hands. His face was narrow and almost brutish with ravaged pride. But he was clean-shaven and his hair was neatly combed. The boy was obviously his son, a small carbon of the man minus the hat. He met Laura's eyes for a fraction of a second, then looked down at his feet as his father said, "We're looking for work, miss."

Laura stared at them, then past them at their vehicle—an automobile with the front end cut off and a mule hitched up. A "Hoovercart," people called such things, just as they were starting to call old newspapers "Hoover blankets," and empty pockets turned inside out "Hoover flags."

"I'll ask my Gram," she said, and started to close the door. Then she caught herself. With the realization that sometimes enlightens the very young, she knew that these people didn't deserve a door shut in their faces. "Come with me. You can ask her yourself," she said, flinging the door wide.

They hesitantly followed her into the dining room. Dinner was already under way and out of the corner of her eye Laura

saw the boy lick his lips at the sight of the bowls of food.
"Gram, we have company," Laura said. Her voice was
unsteady. Now that she'd come this far she wasn't so sure it
was the right way to have handled things.

Evelyn gasped, "Laura!"

Sonny said, "Who's that dirty boy?"

Grace glanced at the man and the boy, then at Laura, who
was nervously twisting a handful of her skirt. Then she said,
"Sonny, you may be excused now."

"But I'm not through eating—"

"Yes, you *are!*"

Laura would normally have gone to Sonny's defense, but
she'd seen a look of agony in the boy's eyes at Sonny's words
and was glad her brother was being sent away. Grace rose
and came to the strangers with her hand out. "How do you
do? I'm Grace Thorne. I don't believe I caught your name,
sir?"

The man carefully wiped his hand on the leg of his overalls
and shook Grace's. "I'm Isaac McHenry, ma'am. And this is
my boy Howie. Stand up straight, Howie."

"Will you join us for dinner?" Grace asked, pointedly not
noticing the various sounds of surprise from the family.

"We'll be mighty pleased, ma'am, but not at table with
your family and not unless we could do our share of work for
you. We don't want charity. I notice you got a chimney with
some loose bricks up on the south side of your house. I'm a
bricklayer by trade. I'd be pleased to fix it up for you."

"You're very observant, Mr. McHenry. And enterprising.
That sounds like a fair trade to me. But it can wait until
tomorrow when you have proper light. Please join us for a
meal. We'd be honored."

McHenry was reluctant, but Grace was determined to be
hospitable. She seated Howie at Sonny's abandoned place and
had Mabelann set a place for the father. After introducing the
rest of the family, Grace engaged Edmund in a discussion of
Plato until the visitors had taken the sharp edge off their
hunger. Laura watched the way they ate, as if they were
desperately hungry but resolved not to show it. She also
noticed that Gram didn't help herself to peas, so there would
be plenty for Mr. McHenry.

Finally Grace turned the conversation back to McHenry.
"Where are you from?"

"Oklahoma, ma'am. On our way to Washington, D.C."

"That's a very long way," Edmund said. He'd been the

first to recover from the shock of having these tattered strangers join them for dinner. "Are you going to visit family?"

"No, sir. I'm going to see the President. Mr. Hoover himself. I'm a veteran, you see. Fought in the Great War for my country. Now I want my country to give me what's owed. See, they passed this law that they'd give you money for what we did back then—"

"The Adjusted Compensation Act," Edmund said. "I just read a piece in the paper about it this week."

"That's right, sir. But they say they aren't gonna pay it until 1945. We need it now, you see. And it's owed us. I figure Mr. Hoover needs to be told in person why that is."

"Do you think he'll listen?" Grace asked.

"Hoover? Listen?" Jackson put in. "The same man who says there's no problem with the economy?"

McHenry smiled for the first time. "The same man. Reckon I've got a lot to tell him."

Laura listened as she ate, fascinated by the man whose clothes were so shabby but who believed the President needed his advice. She, and possibly Howie, were the only ones at the table, however, who shared McHenry's view that President Hoover might want a firsthand report from an Oklahoma bricklayer.

As soon as dinner was finished, the man and boy excused themselves. "I'm glad of your offer for a room tonight, ma'am. But me and Howie are used to sleeping in the car. We'll stay there and I'll get to work on the chimney first thing in the morning."

Grace showed them to the door and had just come back when Evelyn said, "Jackson, do you suppose your mother intends to invite every hobo in the country to sit at table with us? If so, I'll just have to excuse myself from such an ostentatiously democratic activity! Laura, haven't you any sense at all? Inviting those people in—"

Grace closed the door firmly. "Evelyn, your attitude brings shame to all of us. I most certainly do not mean to invite every 'hobo' to meals. But that was a proud, hardworking man. And his boy had better table manners than yours. That nincompoop in the White House is going to turn him away without a hearing and it's not right that we should also. As for Laura's sense—she's got something far more important. A heart. Not to mention a courteous spirit."

"Mother, stop this high-minded rhetoric and be sensible," Jackson said. "We haven't even got enough for ourselves, and you're feeding strangers. Did you see how much that boy ate?''

"He was hungry!" Grace snapped. "We're not. Oh, we're hungry for luxuries, but not one of us has ever been truly hungry. That man and his boy deserve all the help they can get. They made me realize how morally lazy we are.''

"Lazy?" Adele said. It was the first time she'd spoken, and there were incipient tears in her voice. She'd spent the whole day mending and ironing sheets. Her cheeks were still flushed with the effort.

Grace reached across the table and took her hand contritely. "I didn't mean you, Adele dear. It's just that Mr. McHenry is doing something. It's tilting at windmills, of course. Foolish and doomed. But at least he's trying to help better his lot in life. We're just treading water. Canning, hunting, mending, scrimping—all so necessary, but essentially pointless. We're so busy trying to stay in place that we never think of improving our lives, or anyone else's.''

"What is there to do?" Jackson asked, as if she were blaming him for the situation they were in.

Grace rubbed her eyes and sighed. "I don't know," she said. "That's part of the reason I'm upset. When Mr. McHenry was talking, I suddenly remembered something Jack said to me when I first knew him. About how he didn't have to get ahead in life because he was already ahead. We've all been like that. All our lives. I fear that ambition and initiative have been bred out of us.''

India, silent throughout this, was lacing her napkin through the tines of her fork. Adele was staring at the portrait of Grace as a bride and blinking back tears. Evelyn gazed at Jackson as if expecting some answer from him. No one spoke. This speech was utterly unlike Grace and it shocked them. She was their spine, their keel, the one person who kept them upright and steady against the fear that lurked in dark corners. Grace never showed fear and despair. She had reacted to their reduced circumstances with anger, sarcasm, and sometimes humor—anything to keep the sense of defeat and hopelessness at bay. It was as if Mr. Hoover's Depression was a personal insult to be ignored, laughed at, revenged, or coped with, but never given in to.

Now Grace had shown a moment of weakness and it frightened them all. She realized she was letting them down, and felt resentment bubble up. She knew and felt the great weight of her role in the family, but why must she always be the strong one, the sensible one who smoothed life out and told them all would be well if they would just do this and this and this? Mr. McHenry had made her feel jaded and weary and she needed someone to pamper and encourage her, not vice versa.

But it wasn't going to be that way—ever. She might as well accept it. She forced a dazzling smile and rose briskly. "I'm so stuffed I can hardly move. I need a good long walk. Who will come with me? Laura-bunny?"

Laura had trouble getting to sleep that night. She kept thinking about the McHenrys trying to be comfortable in their car and about Gram's strange behavior at dinner. Maybe if she'd go talk to Gram and maybe sleep in her room, she'd feel better. She dragged her pillow and light summer cover off the bed and started down the hall.

But the light was on in Gram's room and Laura could hear her father's voice raised in anger. ". . . counted it all up," he was saying. "I can add, even if you can't or won't. If you'd sell that stock, even a part of it, we could live decently. It's not right, abusing Evelyn that way, accusing all of us of laziness when we're working so hard at helping you scrimp, while you've got all those stocks, just piled up in a drawer. We're living like goddamn white trash, all patched clothes and slop for supper."

"Don't you dare speak to me that way," Grace said with deadly calm. Laura turned to go back to her room, but found she simply couldn't. She didn't want to hear them fight, but was unable to stop listening.

Grace had acute hearing and it was an old house that creaked. She should have been aware, if not by sound then by instinct, of Laura's presence. But she was tired; her defenses were down. She simply wanted this confrontation to be over so that she could rest and think things out. "See here, Jackson—"

"Don't try to bully me like you do everyone else, Mother. I'll speak my mind any way I choose. I've gone through your desk and tallied up the stocks. We don't need to live this way. The stocks alone are worth at least forty thousand dollars, even as deflated as the value is."

"Do you know what those same stocks were worth before the crash? At least ten times—"

"I don't *care*, Mother. I'm not talking about before. 'Before' is as dead as a fossil fern. I'm talking about now."

"And I'm concerned with the future. Yours, mine, Evelyn's, the children's, the relatives', the servants'. If we were to sell the stocks to buy fancy food and new clothes, in two years we'd have nothing left. Nothing! Would you like to cut up the Minerva and all of us could pile in and go looking for work that isn't there that we don't know how to do?"

"If it were up to me—"

"It's *not* up to you, Jackson. And I thank God for that. It's a good thing your father left everything in my control, otherwise you'd be frittering away our only assets." She shouldn't have said those words and she knew it, but she was too angry, too deeply involved in the dispute to withdraw an inch by apologizing.

"Oh, yes, he left it to you. Every damned penny. How did you do that, Mother? I've never understood the hold you had over him. Sex, I suppose. They say the ice-maiden types are the hottest in bed—"

Grace slapped him, the first time she had ever touched him in anger. She was as shocked as he.

Unseen in the hallway, Laura gasped and clapped her hands over her ears, but that didn't keep her from hearing what came next. "God! I don't know why I said that," Jackson said in a broken voice. "You drive me to it. Mother, when did you start hating me?"

"Don't talk nonsense, Jackson. I don't hate you. You've just had too much to drink." Why couldn't this stop? This eternal wrangling with him. She didn't want it and she sensed he didn't either, really. But they were helpless, both of them. Caught in a whirlpool of anger and guilt.

"I haven't had anything to drink tonight," he said.

Then, after a long pause, he went on: "I remember when you loved me. You and Dad both. I'll bet you didn't realize that. One day especially stays in my mind. I still dream about it sometimes. I was very little. It snowed and we all went out and played. You built me a snowman, just my size, and you put a jacket of mine on it. You pretended to kiss it and then you shivered and said you'd rather kiss a warm little boy instead. Do you remember that day?

"No, I can see you don't. But I've never forgotten. But what I can't remember is when or why you stopped loving me. What did I do? What *could* a child do? How did I lose you? Or did you just start loving someone else? You know, I don't think you're able to love more than one person at a time. Just like when Dad died and you focused all your attention on Laura and she wasn't even—"

Oh, she remembered that day. How could she ever forget? God wouldn't let her forget, or forgive herself. But even now, so many years later, it was something she couldn't talk about, not to anyone. Especially not to her son. "Jackson! You must get a grip on yourself. It's very late and you're saying things—"

"Things I'll regret? God, Mother, you have no idea of how many things I already regret. All right. We won't talk about anything from our hearts. Good night, Mother dear," he added with his usual sneering tone. "We'll just go on playing 'happy family.' You turn the crank and we'll dance to your tune. Like a bunch of monkeys."

Laura grabbed the pillow she'd dropped and ran back to her room. She wasn't the only one at Thornehill who cried herself to sleep that night.

It took Isaac McHenry a day and a half to complete the repairs to the chimney. His pride in his work was so great that Grace even donned trousers and climbed out on a sloping section of roof to inspect and praise the job. She sent him and Howie off with invitations to stop again on their way back from Washington. They never returned and Laura often wondered what became of them and how far along they got before discovering the hamper full of food that Grace had slipped into the back of the Hoovercart.

Laura feared another outbreak between her father and grandmother, but whatever they felt about the heartbreaking conversation she'd overheard, they kept to themselves. Jackson drank more than usual for a few days, spoke more curtly to everyone, and spent most of his time away from the house, but Grace gave no sign that anything of import had transpired.

On the first Sunday in June, they all got dressed in their best and piled into the Minerva to spend the day in Eureka Springs. This had become a tradition and Laura looked forward to it for weeks. The first stop was St. Elizabeth's Church, where the women and Sonny attended services. Though not a religious family, they never skipped church on this day, largely because it was the only church in the world built on such a steep slope that one of the entrances was through the bell tower.

Just above the church was the elegant Crescent Hotel with its formal gardens and paths. Jackson and Edmund always took a leisurely stroll there while waiting for the others to come out of St. Elizabeth's.

"Where shall we lunch?" Grace asked when they rejoined the men. As usual, there was disagreement. Sonny wanted to go to the Basin Park Hotel, which advertised that it had "eight stories, each a ground floor," because of the wooden walkways that joined the back of the hotel to the almost vertical park behind it. Jackson and Edmund preferred the New Orleans Hotel with its fancy wrought-iron front. But Grace, Adele, India, and Laura outvoted them and they ate this year at the Crescent. During most of the year it was an exclusive small college for women, but in the summer it was a hotel. This Sunday marked the season's opening and the building still smelled ever so faintly of gym shoes, books, and biology experiments.

"Tell me about what the town was like when Great-Grandpa came here," Laura asked Grace when they were seated at a long table with a view out over the town.

Sonny groaned. "You ask that stupid question every year."

"I like the answer," Laura replied.

They placed their orders and Grace said, "Your grandfather Jack was about your age when he and his father came here. At first there were only covered wagons and a few people who came to the springs for their health. Then more and more people came from all over, and they started building little wooden houses that climbed up the sides of the hills. In a year or so there were thousands of people and much nicer houses. By that time, your great-grandfather was building Thornehill."

"Then Carrie Nation came here to live," Laura put in, getting ahead of the story.

"No, she didn't come until after I moved here. She had a stroke and died a few years before you children were born."

"Carrie Nation herself?" India exclaimed. "What a perfectly divine aura she must have had. All white and milky, I should think. Did you ever hear her speak, Aunt Grace?"

"Yes, but I couldn't tell you a thing she said. I know she meant well in her own way, but she was such an extraordinarily unattractive woman I couldn't do anything but stare at her. Oh, dear, that was an unkind thing to say. Especially on a Sunday."

"Tell India about the first lawsuit," Jackson said.

Grace laughed. "I'm sure it's just a joke, but they say the first lawsuit was against a housewife who threw a pail of dishwater out her kitchen window and right down her neighbor's chimney.''

India laughed so loudly that several tables of diners turned to look at her. She didn't notice. "What a remarkable town. I don't see how anyone ever learns their way around."

"There's one house that has four different addresses on four different streets and it's not even a big house," Grace said. "Someone counted up and said there are over two hundred and fifty streets and not a single right-angle intersection."

After luncheon, they set out on foot to explore the wonders of the town. To Laura's distress, signs of the Depression were everywhere. Whole blocks of shops had closed, the sidewalks were in poor repair, and potholes were developing in the steep streets. Private houses, too, were becoming shabby because the money for repainting was no longer available. No one mentioned any of this, but they all noticed, and of mutual, unspoken accord, cut short their usual day-long visit.

There was little talk on the way home. Laura was sitting next to Evelyn, who was rummaging in her oversize handbag for a lost cigarette. "I must have the catch on my cigarette case fixed," she muttered, pulling out various odds and ends. Presently she came to a letter. "Dear Lord! I forgot to even open this!" she exclaimed. "Jackson, dear, we got a letter yesterday from Chic and Marta Parker."

"Good old Chic, best poker player in Chicago," Jackson said fondly.

Evelyn tore into her letter and in a moment shrilled, "Oh, Jackson, they're coming to visit next month. How marvelous. I've missed them so."

Grace was sitting in the back seat and said quietly, "Perhaps we ought to turn around now so you can make reservations for them at the Crescent or the Basin Park."

Jackson, at the wheel, touched the brakes lightly and swiveled his head to look at his mother. "What do you mean by that? Why should our guests stay in a hotel?"

"Because we can't afford to have them, of course. I remember the last time they were here. For a whole month, plus a day or two. We nearly had to hire on extra staff to take care of them. Special foods, Marta changing clothes six times a day and needing things ironed at hourly intervals, and that awful little dog ruining the carpets. No, we can't afford them again. Or anyone else, for that matter."

The tires squealed as Jackson took the next corner. "That

really takes a hell of a nerve! Having those damned dirty Okies at our table and refusing to have personal friends.''

''By those dirty Okies, I presume you mean the McHenrys. Well, they paid their own way. Valuable work for food. Now, if your rich friends want to pay for the trouble they cause, plus a neat little profit, they're welcome,'' Grace answered coldly.

''Pay? Dammit, Mother, you'd turn our house into a hotel if you could.''

Grace stared out the car window.

XIII

NOTHING more was said about Chic and Marta's visit, but Laura presumed her mother found some way to keep them from visiting, because they never came. Grace hardly spoke the rest of that Sunday, nor the next day. But rather than an ominous quiet, this was almost a cheerful silence. She was preoccupied at meals, gazing into the middle distance and giving answers that sometimes had little to do with the remarks addressed to her. "Gram's acting real funny," Sonny reported to Laura. "She let me have a candy bar before lunch. I asked and everything, and she said it was okay." And Adele told Edmund, "She was humming while we weeded the garden this morning. I've never known her to do that. Swear, sometimes, but never hum."

Privately Adele confided in India that she thought Grace's strange behavior had to do with Dr. Lee. "I heard her calling him this morning on the phone. I couldn't distinguish a word she was saying"—her disappointment in this was evident—"but they were on the phone a *very* long time. Do you suppose they are 'up to something'?"

"Wouldn't it be divine if they were! I thought you were a better eavesdropper."

"Me! I never eavesdrop!" Adele sniffed and dropped the subject.

On Tuesday morning Sonny so thoroughly botched his arithmetic assignment that Edmund excused Laura for the morning so he could force-feed the information into Sonny without interruption. Laura went to the library and found Grace there, kneeling on the floor surrounded by huge sheets of crackling paper. "What are those, Gram?" Laura asked, carefully sitting down next to her.

"They're the architect's plans for the house. See, on this one. Here we are." She pointed out the library. "And this sheet is the second floor. There's your room, and mine, and India's."

Laura leaned forward, resting her elbows on the carpet and her chin on her hands. "What's that funny little square? Oh, I know. The closet. And that must be a chimney. These are fun, Gram. What are you doing with them?"

"Just studying them," Grace said. "Speaking of studying, what are you doing here?"

Laura explained about Sonny's academic difficulties. "So I thought I could do something with you, Gram. Can I?"

"*May* I."

"May I, please?"

Grace stood and started rolling up the blueprints. "Well, I believe I could put you to work. Would you like to be my secretary this morning? Get your tablet and a pencil and meet me in the front hall. You will take notes for me. But no questions, Laura-bunny. And don't mention to anyone else what you're doing."

They spent the day investigating the house. First they made a cursory inspection of the central part, the bar of the H. The ground floor had the big entry hall with powder room and cloakroom opening off it. "Make a note, bunny. That corner section of tile is stained," Grace said. Next to it was the formal dining room ("Those draperies need to be replaced, but maybe they could be turned and patched instead") and then the kitchen and the room overlooking the gardens where they usually had breakfast. On the other side of the entry was a large storage area where a few broken bits of furniture, a painting or two, and some battered suitcases were kept.

On the opposite side were the library, a well-furnished but stuffy parlor, and a room they called "the writing room" and never used except to pass through, as there was a narrow back stairway that opened into it. Grace looked around in here, then went back to the dining room to measure the table. "Gram, what are you—?"

"Remember, bunny, secretaries don't ask questions."

Upstairs in the central wing were the bedrooms—Grace's suite of bed-, bath-, and dressing-room in the center front. To one side was Laura's room, then India's, with a shared bath between. On the other side was the small room Adele had adopted, and a big walk-in linen cupboard that was actually a small bedroom converted to the purpose. Across from these rooms were Edmund's book-filled lair, Jackson and Evelyn's suite, Sonny's room, a large bath, and an empty bedroom. "Quite the nicest carpet in the lot," Grace mumbled. "Make a note of that, Laura."

More empty bedrooms were on the third floor—they'd been intended for maids and other servants. Many had been in use before the crash, when a great deal of entertaining had been done at Thornehill, but now all but the cook's room and Mabelann's were dusty and forlorn. "Including the two rooms we use for school, there are ten up here," Grace said.

Something about the phrasing of this worried Laura. The rooms *we* use—yes, it was the "we" that made the goose bumps come up on her arms. Who else would or could use those rooms? Good heavens! Could Gram possibly mean to *sell* the house? The thought was awful and Laura tried to shrug it off, but it refused to go away.

Leaving the central section, they went to the west wing. It was roughly a square, extending beyond the central wing at both front and back. On the ground floor were all the rooms for specific activities, designations much beloved by wealthy Victorians. There was a gun room, holding all the weapons, decoys, and mackinaws that guests might need for a bit of shooting. ("Just needs some airing out. You could mildew to death in here," Grace said.) There was a billiards room, a smoking room, and a large room fitted out for exercise. "I don't imagine anyone's been in here since Jack died," Grace said to herself, running a finger through the dust on top of an equipment cabinet. "There's a spot in the flooring that's warped. I hope it won't all have to be taken up."

On the second floor of this section were the bedrooms where guests had always been put up. Grace counted beds, had Laura record the total, and moved on to a brief look at the third floor, which was open attic space. Grace stood at the top of the stairs, looking in at nearly fifty years' accumulation of belongings, and shook her head. "I don't know where we'd ever put all this!" she said in a voice of despair.

Laura's heart sank. They *were* going to move away! Otherwise there would be no reason all these treasures couldn't remain where they were for another generation or two. Her agile imagination ran amok. Where would they go? To Eureka Springs? It was the only place she'd ever been, and

therefore the only place she could think of. Would they live
in a little house there? All of them together? Surely they
would stay together; Gram wouldn't make the relatives go
away. But in a little house in town? There wouldn't be a
view, or secret places to play hide-and-seek, or room to keep
ducks and chickens, or a barn for kittens to be born in. And
she and Sonny might have to go to regular school with
teachers who didn't know them!

Laura loved going to town, but she didn't want to live
there. She didn't want to live anywhere but here where she'd
always been. "Gram, where are we—?"

But Grace didn't hear the question. "I wonder which are
the keys to the east wing . . . ." she said, flipping through the
small tin box she'd brought along in her dress pocket.

This was so remarkable that it momentarily diverted Laura's gloomy thoughts. "The east wing? I've never been in
there. It's always locked."

"Well, you'll see it today. Ahh, I think this it it. I hope the
locks haven't rusted shut. You've been in the ballroom."

"Yes, but never upstairs," Laura said, trotting along behind her grandmother.

As they made their way along the second-floor hallway to
the wide double doors that Laura had never seen opened,
Grace explained about the history, such as it was, of that part
of the house. "Your great-grandfather had it built with
the rest of the house, but he just had the outside walls and the
floors done. When I married your grandfather, we had the
ballroom finished and put in walls upstairs. I was never sure
just why, except that he seemed to feel it was the thing to
do."

That wasn't strictly true, but it was adequate explanation
for Laura. There was no need to tell her that the rooms had
been intended for all the children she and Jack were going to
have, and to house the nannies, governesses, and tutors that
were to have been necessary. Grace could remember as if it
were yesterday how she and Jack had gone through the
unfinished rooms, imagining what they would be like filled
with children and laughter and schoolbooks and pets. Instead,
the rooms had been abandoned, left to fill with dust and
spiders and unfulfilled dreams.

"I don't think I've been on the upper floors more than two
or three times since then. Only when there was some sort of
roof repair or something and the workmen had to go through

this way. My, but that lock's stiff. We might have to get the doors taken off the hinges . . . There, we did it!''

The doors swung open and they faced down a hallway with three doors on each side and a large uncurtained window at the far end. Laura ran ahead and looked out. ''Oh, Gram, you can see the spring from here. Isn't it pretty?''

To Laura it was an exciting peek into the past; to her grandmother it was a disconcerting look into a future that might have been and never was.

Grace came to the window, putting her arm around Laura's shoulders. ''Hmmm, the spring. I'd forgotten all about it. A nice gravel path running down there, maybe a bathhouse and some tables and chairs . . .''

''And there's the roof of the cottage! Gram, this is fun. I didn't know you could see so many things from up here.''

Grace turned away. ''Get your pencil ready, bunny.''

The rooms were all the same, with finished floors and plastered but unpainted walls. The plumbing was merely stubbed in and there were old-fashioned gas outlets, not electric lights like the rest of the house. In one room a squirrel had fallen down the chimney, and in a frenzy to escape, had chewed away chunks of woodwork around the window. Its pathetic skeleton lay curled in a corner. ''Can I . . . may I give it to Sonny, Gram?'' Laura asked, excited at the prospect of what fun Sonny would have with all those neat little white bones.

Grace came over and looked. ''I guess it's been dead long enough that it can't be too nasty. Scoop it up on that piece of lath.''

Laura took the squirrel carcass back to her room, then rejoined Grace. They spent the rest of the day taking a thorough inventory of the house. Laura recorded in her tablet the conditions of curtains, rugs, and toilets. She helped Grace count beds, pillows, and linens. They tallied light fixtures, light bulbs, and they made notes about loose stair rails and squeaky treads.

True to her promise, Laura didn't ask questions, even though she felt they were battering against the back of her teeth. Nor did Grace offer any explanations.

When they were done, Grace took the tablet sheets, nodded approvingly, and said, ''You've a very neat hand, Laura, and you've been most helpful. Now, run along and finish up your schoolwork before dinner. Have you got a kiss for Gram?''

Sonny was thrilled sick with the squirrel skeleton. ''Look

at the ribs! And see, I can make the jaw move. Its teeth are still sharp. Where did you find it?''

"In a room in the east wing," Laura answered listlessly.

"Liar. Nobody can go in the east wing."

"I'm not a liar. That's where I got it. Gram took me there."

"Why?"

"I can't tell. It's a secret."

"C'mon! You can't keep secrets from me. That's not fair. I tell you everything."

"You do not! Remember the time you had the whole box of candy canes you ate without telling me you had them? Anyway, it's not my secret. It's Gram's, and I don't even know what it is."

Sonny gazed at her speculatively. "You *sound* like you know."

Laura sat down next to him and stroked a bit of fur that still adhered to the squirrel's tail. "I guess I can say what I think. As long as Gram didn't say anything. Sonny, I think Gram's going to sell the house and we're going to move away from Thornehill."

"*No!*"

The words were hardly out of Laura's mouth before Sonny was on his feet. "*No!* I won't go! I'll stay here. I'll hide and they'll have to go away and leave me. I won't go. I don't want to live anyplace else. This is going to be *my* house when I grow up. Daddy said so!"

Laura was horrified at the vehemence of his response. She was sad and upset herself, but he was nearly hysterical. "Stop yelling like such a big baby. Everybody will hear you!" she hissed.

"I don't care. I hope they do hear. I won't go away from here. Not even if they tie me up and make me go. I'll run away and come back."

What had she unleashed? Sonny was making toward the door, undoubtedly with the intention of discussing this with anyone and everyone he could find. Laura was frantic. Without really meaning to, she'd given away the secret Grace had entrusted to her. "I expect I got it all wrong," she said, trying desperately to sound calm.

But Sonny wasn't to be mollified so easily. He put his hand on the doorknob and Laura said, "Sonny, if you say anything, I'll tell on you."

"Tell what?"

"I'll say you . . ." She rifled her memory for some recent and sufficiently horrible transgression to threaten him with. Finding none, she said, "I'll say you put some of the squirrel bones in your mouth! I'll tell Gram that and she'll make you throw it away."

"I wouldn't do an icky thing like that!"

"But I'll *say* you did. Gram will believe me," she added, playing a trump she'd never used before—never even been consciously aware she held in her hand.

Sonny's hand dropped to his side. Laura felt terrible. The words had left a hateful taste in her mouth. "Sonny, just don't say anything about what I said—about moving away. I just made it up. It was stupid and I didn't mean it."

Sonny went to the window seat and flopped down with his back to her. "Go away, Laura. I don't like you very well today."

Neither do I like me today, Laura thought. She wanted to pat him or something, but knew he'd probably hit her if she did. She got up and went out, closing the door as softly as she could.

"What's the matter with you, Sonny?" Jackson asked toward the end of dinner that night.

"A cold, I suspect. Have you taken his temperature, Evelyn?" Grace asked.

"I'm not sick!" Sonny said. He'd been sniffling miserably throughout the meal and had refused seconds, even of dessert.

"Then what's wrong?" Jackson asked irritably.

"Nothing!"

"Nothing? You're eating with your chin in your plate for no reason at all?"

Sonny looked up at Laura, but she refused to meet his gaze. She'd hadn't been able to look him in the eye all through the meal. Now that they were all harassing him, she was in a fever of anxiety. Suppose he blurted out what she'd told him?

"Leave me alone!" Sonny said, flinging his napkin on the table.

"See here, young man, I won't have this sort of rudeness at meals," Jackson said, matching his gesture. "Now, you'll explain yourself, or you'll eat in your room until you do."

Laura suddenly realized it was all going to come out one way or another. She couldn't bear to see Sonny take the blame for something that was really her doing.

"I told him, Gram," she said. "It's my fault."

Grace laid her knife on her plate and looked at her granddaughter. "Told him what, bunny?"

Laura felt the tears welling and spilling down her face. But she plunged on. "Oh, Gram! I didn't mean to tell your secret, but I did it anyway. I'm sorry. I told Sonny we're moving away from Thornehill—"

The rest of her apology was drowned out by a sudden babble of voices from the others. But Grace quickly quelled them all. "Quiet! Please. Laura, I haven't the faintest idea what you're talking about. Nobody's moving away from Thornehill."

"We're not? Promise?" Sonny asked.

"Of course not. That's the silliest thing you two have come up with yet," Grace answered. "Laura, stop that crying. You too, Sonny."

"But, Gram, when we went around the house, I thought—"

"Oh, I see! You jumped to your own conclusions. Well, we're not going anywhere. I'd burn this house to the ground before I'd leave it. Believe that, Laura."

"What *is* this all about?" Adele asked, touching her napkin primly to her lips. "A table full of weeping children, all these mysterious remarks about moving or not moving . . . ?"

"I didn't intend to say anything just yet, but I suppose I must now. If we're all through, let's adjourn to the library and I'll tell you all what Laura and I have been doing that she so sadly misinterpreted."

By unspoken accord, Laura and Grace stayed behind as the rest left the dining room. "Gram, I'm really sorry I told," Laura said once again.

But Grace, normally yielding and indulgent where Laura was concerned, was not about to forgive so easily this time. "I hope you mean that, because it was very, very bad of you. Not just because you gave away a secret, but because you gave away incorrect information. You jumped to a completely false conclusion—a conclusion that was upsetting to everyone— then spread it about as if it were truth."

Laura was crushed, especially since she knew she deserved every word of Gram's criticism. And she knew she'd make it worse by blubbering like a baby, so she sat up very straight and said, "I know it was wrong, Gram."

Grace studied her for a moment. "I wonder if you have any idea *how* wrong you were. Come here, bunny. Sit by me. Listen carefully. You'll never, *never* have to leave here.

Thornehill belongs to Thornes and always will. We'll do whatever we have to in order to keep it. Do you understand that?''

"Yes, Gram," Laura said, but she wasn't actually sure what Grace meant.

Grace took her hand. "Come along. The others are waiting."

And they were, with various degrees of impatience. Jackson was drinking a Scotch and a soda as he paced the length of the room. India was mixing gin fizzes for herself and Evelyn. Edmund was making a pretense of reading a newspaper, which he flung aside as soon as Grace entered the room. Beside him, Adele was perched on the edge of a chair, her normally busy hands uncharacteristically idle in her lap.

Grace sat behind Jack's desk. "I regret the confusion and mystery," she began. "I had no intention of being secretive. I merely wished to keep my thoughts to myself until I was sure of some facts."

"Sure of what facts, Grace?" Adele asked.

"Sure of what we have to do to survive. I'm going to be very frank with all of you. We've made many economies and sacrifices, but it's not enough. We've been living on the dividends of the family stock, and as you must all know, they've all but disappeared. Jackson has urged me to sell some stocks for the cash to live on, but I don't want to do that."

"Quite right, Grace," Edmund put in. "Terrible thing, dipping into capital. You never recoup the loss." Jackson shot him a deadly look, but Edmund didn't notice. "Not unless you reinvest."

"That's just what I intend to do—with your agreement, of course. All of you."

India sat forward quickly. "Aunt Grace, you don't mean to speculate in the market, do you? Please say you wouldn't do that. Look what it did to me."

"No, I'm not going to speculate in the stock market. I'm going to speculate on Thornehill and all of us. That is, *if* you're all willing."

They *had* to be willing—without being told what truly dire financial straits they were in. This was beyond even Grace's capabilities of pushing through on her own. Without their agreement, even enthusiasm, they stood to lose everything. But she didn't dare tell them that.

"Willing to do exactly what, Mother?" Jackson asked coldly.

"I want to turn Thornehill into a hotel."

There was a terrible silence.

Jackson stopped his pacing mid-stride. India slumped back in her chair as if she'd been struck. Edmund picked up the paper he'd discarded and started folding it, and Sonny dropped the toy car he was getting ready to take apart. Grace held her breath, forced herself not to meet anyone's eyes for fear she would see failure and defeat. Laura alone managed to speak.

"A hotel, Gram?"

"Yes, a luxurious hotel." She addressed the whole group. "Now, I know this is a new idea, but before you form an opinion, let me tell you my thoughts so you may consider them. First, the house itself is ideally suited, both in layout and geographical location. We have the most magnificent view for miles, we have the spring on the property. There are at least a dozen unoccupied bedrooms, and space to expand the number. The kitchens are adequate for preparing food for large numbers, and the ballroom would make a perfect dining room. This has always been a favored area for Eastern vacationers."

Still no one spoke.

Grace's voice rose like a tightened violin string. She wanted to scream at them: This is the only way to save ourselves! But that would panic them. This one time she must use honey instead of vinegar. "Of course, there's a great deal to be done before we could be ready for guests. The rooms in the east wing have to be finished and furnished—"

Jackson came to life. "I presume we're to whittle the furniture for them with our own little hands? I'll hew the trees, how's that? Edmund can saw them into lengths, and Adele can weave some nice homespun bedspreads in her spare time."

"Don't be ridiculous!" Grace snapped. She took a deep breath, forcing herself to regain her calm. She must act as though this were simply an idea she was proposing for them all to decide on. But God help them all if it were rejected!

"I? Ridiculous? This, for a woman who maintains that we can't afford to buy fuel or decent clothes and yet wants to work a major renovation on the house? You'd actually have to sell some of your damned precious never-to-be-touched stocks."

"That's precisely what I mean to do," Grace said.

Jackson sat down, his whiskey splashing over the lip of the glass. "You mean that, don't you?"

"I do. It would be a reinvestment. A suitable use of the money. Let's deal with that—the financial question. First, the conversion to a hotel would create income. That's our primary aim. But in addition, the changes would be permanent, increasing the value of the house for years to come—its value to us, personally. When things improve and we can bring the house back to private status, we'll have a much nicer home for ourselves and our friends."

Grace paused for a moment, glancing quickly around the room as if taking a silent straw vote. "There's another aspect to this that I've thought about a great deal. You see, we'd not only be helping ourselves, we'd be adding something to the welfare of others. We'd hire workmen to make the changes— men in the community who have no work now; then, when we're in operation, we'll provide employment for local people as cooks, waitresses, bellboys, laundresses, and so forth. We can even have Howard Lee come live here as the hotel doctor. His practice is nearly bankrupt. We could help him and he could help us. In fact, I already have asked him."

"To come here? In what capacity?" Adele asked eagerly.

"Friend," Grace said firmly. "I've talked to him about this at some length."

"What did he think?" Edmund asked.

"He thought it might work. As I do."

As gently and insidiously as woodsmoke, a change was coming over the room. Adele was staring at the floor, ticking off something on her fingers. Jackson was looking out the window, eyes squinted with thought. Edmund had leaned forward and India's generous mouth was touched at the corners with the beginning of a smile. Even Sonny had stopped fidgeting and was staring at Laura as if to gauge her response before deciding his own.

Grace knew where and when to plunge the sword. She shrugged her shoulders and said in a low, unconcerned way, "It's up to you, of course. If you'd rather, we could just go on as we have been and hope we'll have food left on the table when the Depression is over."

"People would bring their children along?" Laura asked.

"I should think they might," Grace said, smiling at her.

"And we could play with them," Sonny added. "We could have bicycle races and play Indians and maybe they'd bring their toys . . ."

The tide had turned and was lapping at the legs of the desk where Grace sat. She knew better than to press her point.

Edmund cleared his throat and essayed, "There would probably be some of my contemporaries as well. Not meaning to insult the lovely ladies of the household, but I do long for the company of old men like myself. Talk about books and the old days, you know."

But Jackson was not won over. "It won't work. There's nobody left to pay the sort of rates we'd have to charge. Everybody's as badly off as we are."

Grace started to reply, but fortunately it was India who forestalled her. "No, Jackson. That's not quite true. I'm always seeing accounts in the papers of rich people who are taking the most divine round-the-world cruises and giving expensive debutante comings-out. I don't know how, but there are people who still have simply gobs and loads of luscious green cash."

Edmund nodded. "Some friends of ours in Boston are still in fine circumstances. Saw it coming, I suppose, and put everything into gold. Living high on the hog, as they say out here."

Adele ignored Jackson's objections and proceeded as though the decision was already made and agreed to. "Grace, dear, I'll take charge of the housekeeping—the maids, linens and such. I've always had a rather absurd longing to run a large household. I suppose I flatter myself to imagine I'd be good at it, but I'd certainly like to give it a try. I might even know of a cook."

"And you can't have a hotel without an elegant little gift shop," India put in. "I can just see it. A divine little cubbyhole with ever such exquisite artifacts. Paintings, dear pieces of handmade jewelry. Perhaps some pottery, too. All quite fashionable, of course. Nothing with too, too much of the homemade about it, you know."

Even Jackson was caught up by this time. "I suppose I could take a few fellas around and show them the best hunting and fishing spots. And it would be pleasant to have some real card playing—other than bridge. Some serious poker . . ."

Evelyn wordlessly rose from the sofa. For a moment there was something so majestic about the fluid motion and her disdainful expression that she held the floor. "And what about me, Grace? Where do you suppose I fit into this? The laundry, perhaps. Nobody's mentioned that. I could have a 'divine little cubbyhole' in the cellar with an array of washtubs. Or perhaps you see me in some other role. Cleaning toilets? Scrubbing the odd floor? For God's sake! What do you expect of me?''

Like spectators at a tennis match, everyone looked at Grace, fully expecting a volcanic reply. None of them present had ever heard Evelyn openly defy her mother-in-law, if indeed she had ever done so.

To the general astonishment, Grace said nothing at first. She was thinking of the times she had chided Evelyn for her lack of attention to Laura. The weapon she'd used was the financial support she provided Evelyn and Jackson. But now there was no support; there had been none for some time and Evelyn had never thrown it in her face. Fair was fair! she told herself. Swallowing a considerable amount of pride, she got up and came around the desk to Evelyn and took her hands as though they were old and dear friends. ''I expect nothing of you, Evelyn. Nothing. You are simply to be gracious and enjoy yourself as if you were a guest. We made a bargain a long time ago. You have upheld your end, at some personal cost. I, however, have reneged on my part. I owe you something. This is all I can give.''

The atmosphere of confusion in the room was as cloudy but palpable as chalk dust. Adele, Edmund, and India exchanged questioning glances and Sonny said to Laura, ''What's she talking about?''

Me, Laura thought. She had no reason to think so, but she knew. It wasn't that they looked at her, more because both women were making such an effort not to. A bargain? What sort of bargain? But as quickly and surely as the realization took her, it released her. ''I don't know,'' she answered Sonny in a whisper.

But the rest of them in the room might as well have been in Siberia for all the attention that Evelyn and Grace paid them. Jackson came to stand by them like a refereee who's arrived too late for the first round. Evelyn seemed to be struck utterly dumb. Her eyes filled with tears and she said softly, ''It hasn't been as hard as I thought it would be, Grace. But I thank you for understanding.''

Edmund said, ''Are we allowed to know what you two are talking about?'' It wasn't belligerent, merely an academic inquiry delivered in dry, professorish tones.

Only then did Grace look at Laura, a glance as bright and fleeting as a meteorite. ''No,'' she said, shifting her gaze to Edmund. ''I'm afraid not. It has to do with . . . with Evelyn's marriage settlement and I'm afraid it's confidential.''

"I see," he said, unoffended.

Grace went back to her position behind the desk. "Well," she said lightly, "are we agreed then about turning the house into a hotel? It would take many months of work. We might be able to open in the fall. Should we be entirely democratic and vote?"

"Oh, let's do vote. Voting is ever so much fun!" India cried. "I'll make little ballots and we can write 'aye' or 'nay'!"

Grace gave her a fond, exasperated look and said, "Very well. Make the ballots, India."

That summer and fall were the most exciting of Laura's life. The mansion buzzed with activity like a beehive with a new young queen. There was always someone to watch—carpenters in the east wing, furniture salesmen with samples of their wares, and town merchants hoping to make a profit. One enterprising plumber set up an array of bathroom fixtures in the front hall for Grace's inspection. Sonny strolled through the hall some hours later and put a lumpy chocolate bar in the empty, unattached toilet, which upset Mabelann horribly.

There were family conclaves to decide such weighty matters as high gloss or medium gloss for refinishing the ballroom floor, whether the trim in the bedrooms should be eggshell white or oyster white, whether pleated or gathered draperies were more appropriate, and how to place and furnish what would be the front desk. India, the artistic member of the clan, usually had the last word in such matters.

Adele planned to take Laura along on a trip to Hot Springs to pick out the linens, but Laura developed a nasty cough the day before the scheduled departure and wasn't allowed to go. While Laura behaved as if she were crushed, she was secretly relieved. She hated the thought of missing anything going on at Thornehill, even if the alternative was the long-desired trip.

Plasterers, painters, electricians, stonemasons, glaziers, carpenters, carpet layers, and plumbers came with their helpers—fetchers, carriers, and holders. They brought their tools and often their families as well. The grounds were frequently littered with women and children who, having little access to free entertainment in these hard times, took advantage of the spectacle being offered.

Sonny and Laura fretted like tiger cubs in a zoo in their schoolroom every morning, and spent the afternoons and evenings in an orgy of play with the visiting children. Laura fell in with a group of girls who were obsessed with skipping rope. She joined them with such fanaticism that her ankles were swollen and tender for several days.

Sonny made friends with a banker-turned-hod-carrier's son who'd accumulated a vast toy-soldier collection in better years and they spent endless hours conducting wars under a green-skirted willow by the driveway. They alternated this activity with making pests of themselves around the rope-skipping contingent.

Uncle Edmund appointed himself assistant to Grace in matters of supervision and payroll of the army of workmen. For a man who'd spent his life cosseted in academic circles, he showed a surprising critical judgment in just how much of any work ought to be accomplished within a given number of minutes. "I could have gnawed that woodwork into shape with my teeth in the time it's taken you to do it with a saw," Laura heard him say one day to a carpenter who was being paid by the hour.

Only Adele was unsurprised by his skills. "A man doesn't spend his life with college freshmen without learning something about human nature," she explained placidly.

India wafted and swooped through the clumps of women, assessing the various homemade artifacts they'd been commanded to bring along for her inspection. She was almost hysterical with joy when she discovered a girl of seventeen with two babies, missing front teeth, no education whatsoever, and a "positively divine way" with a potter's wheel.

Adele bustled. Continuously. No one was ever quite sure what she was doing at any given moment, but dinners appeared on the table at the proper time; sheets were changed and smelled of sunshine; clean, pressed clothes hung in the closets—and they all sensed that she was responsible. Months before the scheduled opening of the house as a hotel, she was interviewing prospective maids with the fervor of a Grand Inquisitor. Many of the rejects left in tears.

Jackson was in charge of the grounds. All that was planned to go on outdoors was his ken. He was to see to the purchase of horses for the riding stables and the general sprucing-up of the area around the spring. He took a trip to Bennett Springs, Missouri, and came back on the train with slopping tanks of fingerling trout to stock the spring stream. "Can't I *please* keep one as a pet!" Laura begged, watching the slithering, iridescent cloud of fish in one of the tanks.

"A pet!" Sonny scoffed. "A fish is a rotten pet. You can't

brush it or teach it tricks or take it around with you. Who'd want a dumb pet like that? These are for eating. They'll get big and fat and we'll have them for dinner.''

Laura burst into tears and vowed never to eat fish.

In spite of her initial objections to helping, and Grace's assurances that she need not, Evelyn chose to become involved in a way uniquely her own. She got out her old engagement books and started writing letters. *"Darlings,"* such letters would run, *"It's been simply aeons since we've seen you. This terrible Depression business has made havoc with travel plans and I'm beginning to feel like an absolute hermit. You simply won't believe what my mother-in-law's done. She's decided to improve the economy herself by hiring people. The problem was that she had nothing for them to do, so she's turning the house into a hotel! Can you believe it? Plans are to open up in the fall (Only two months! How the time has flown!) to the public. Actually, it's rather amusing, though I do shudder at the idea of strangers in the house. I do hope you'll manage to visit us soon. It will be a bore, of course, having to pay, but we more or less have to humor Grace. She's so terribly firm-minded, as I'm sure you remember."*

In this way, Evelyn was able to join in the family effort and save face at the same time, pretending the hotel business was simply the good-hearted whim of a dotty older woman. In a way, Evelyn typified the prevalent attitude of Americans toward the disaster that had drowned the country. It was one thing to admit that conditions were wretched. It was quite another to admit that one's own finances were diminished. Throughout the country, men would dress in business suits to leave the house, then change somewhere across town to beg, or sell apples, or do any number of heartbreakingly menial jobs. Sometimes it was their wives they were attempting to deceive, sometimes it was the neighbors. Most often it was themselves.

Grace's first move in the renovation had been to get the money. Not trusting the post office—or anyone else but herself—to convey anything so valuable as the Thorne family stocks and bonds, let alone money, she decided to hand-deliver the certificates. Stacking and rolling them, she put the documents that meant the family's future into a blue-and-white-speckled pressed-paper canister meant to hold knitting needles and yarn. For authenticity, she put a tiny ball of green yarn in and let the end of it trail out through a hole in the top.

The cash she received, tens of thousands in twenties and fifties, came back the same way. If anyone on the train to New York wondered why the oddly quiet woman seemed so attached to her knitting supplies without ever knitting, they didn't ask. It was a time when people did strange things, and it was discourteous to pry.

It seemed an extraordinarily long trip to Grace. She'd never been out of the states of Arkansas and Missouri since she and Jack went to Europe years before. And now she was not only a long way from home but also burdened by the entire Thorne fortune. And it was a terrible burden. Everything Jack's father and grandfather had worked for was represented in the pressed-paper canister. Everything her parents had left her on their deaths was there too. In that prosaic container were the fruits of several lifetimes. And she was going to spend it! The magnitude of what she was doing nearly sickened her with fear.

The work progressed by uneven stages. One week it would seem that nothing had been done. The next week the advances would be obvious and startling. Toward the end, the level of excitement grew. India's gift shop was nearly stocked and ready to do business. The maids were being trained. The new beds were put into place a week later and made up with crisp, sweet-smelling new sheets. The ballroom floor was a glassy expanse, perfect for children to run and slide on stocking feet. The stables were stocked with oats and fresh hay. The gravel walks had been raked into pretty patterns.

Evelyn had worked at sprucing up her wardrobe until her fingers were sieves of pinpricks. Jackson had been too busy to drink his normal quota and was looking and feeling better than he had for years. India's protuberant eyes glittered with anticipation and Adele was happily frazzled.

Only Grace, pacing the floor of her lonely bedroom at night and walking down the drive to meet the mailman every day, was gray-faced and stiff-jointed with worry. Grace Emerson Thorne, who had never even bet pennies at bridge, had gambled the Thornes' future—perhaps generations of futures—on this venture. If it failed, they would all be true paupers. As the rest of the family swirled around her, reporting on their efforts on behalf of the soon-to-be hotel, Grace nodded and smiled and kept her secret to herself. But soon they would all know.

No one had made a single reservation.

XIV

*I*N the end, it was Big Al, the bootlegger, who saved the venture, and in spite of all that eventually happened, Grace was always grateful to him. He'd come to pay a call on her two weeks before the planned hotel opening. "Well, Miz Thorne, you got the place fixed up good. We need to talk about how your liquor supplies are. I wanna be sure and treat you right and get you the best in plenty of time." He leaned back in the leather chair, picking contentedly at his teeth with a silver toothpick. He was a big, fair-skinned man, a literal redneck whose family had been making and selling moonshine for generations.

"Mister . . . ah, Big Al, what are you going to do if Prohibition is repealed?" Grace asked.

He grinned expansively. "You figure when the law 'gainst liquor goes out the bootleggers are gonna be out too? Naw, don't you worry about me," he said, never considering the possibility that Grace Thorne wasn't the least worried about him. "They make liquor legal again and the feds'll go to puttin' great whackin' taxes and the like on it, just like before. There's still gonna be room for good common 'shine. Not enough to keep a man in five-dollar cigars, mebbe, but a little somethin' on the side, like. 'Sides, I seen it comin'. Folks don't like no government tellin' them what they can drink. Can't feature why they put up with it as long as they have. So I got me a few other business things going. Now, Miz Thorne, about your order . . ."

"I should have checked with my son before you got here, because I'm not just sure exactly what we'll need. Suppose I telephone you later?"

The affable smile faded; the toothpick tapped on the arm of the chair. "Miz Thorne, I thought we was friends, in a business sorta way. And now you're stallin' me. Naw, don't you trouble to deny it. I seen some of the best stallin' there is and I know it when I see it. You got you another supplier? If that's it, you better tell me who the skunk is, 'cause this is my county and if someone's nosin' in—"

"No, no. Nothing like that. I . . . well, I suppose I've got to be honest with you, under the circumstances. I hope this conversation will go no further than this room. My own family doesn't even know."

"Somethin' secret, huh? You just ask around. Folks'll tell you there ain't nobody better at keepin' his trap shut than Big Al. You just spit it out, Miz Thorne."

Grace leaned forward and said very quietly, "No one has made any reservations at the hotel. I've placed ads in several magazines and my daughter-in-law has written to all her friends, but no one has responded. I'm afraid our grand-opening day is going to be a rather deserted affair. That's why I don't want to order very much liquor."

Big Al got a thoughtful look, which did his unlovely face scant good. "Magazines, huh? Letters? Naw, that ain't the way. Word of mouth. That's how you get folks. You get you a couple of customers, make 'em real happy, and they'll tell everybody 'bout the place."

"I realize that fully. It's the first stage that has me stymied. I've run out of ideas for soliciting the initial guests. I'm so sorry. I have no right to inflict my problems on you, but it's a tremendous relief to be able to talk about it. Thank you for listening," she said, getting up to see him to the door.

He waved her back to her chair. "Naw, we ain't through, Miz Thorne. Big Al helps his friends, 'specially when the friends is also customers. Lemme think on this a minute or two. I gotta lot of friends and connections, you know."

Grace sat down slowly, some of the lines of worry easing from her face. "Connections? Other customers of yours . . . Of course!"

"Customers . . . and others."

Suddenly he stood up and jammed his fedora on his big square head. His diamond pinkie ring glinted. "I'll take care of it, don't you worry. And I'll figure out your liquor order myself, if that'd suit. You just sit tight, Miz Thorne. Won't even charge you for it till you get your feet on the ground, in a manner of speakin'. Fact is, this is gonna work out right nice for everybody.''

That evening Big Al walked into a small business establishment in Hot Springs, Arkansas, called the White Front Cigar Store. A lanky man in a police uniform was sitting at a table at the end of the counter. In front of him was a cigar box full of money and a small ledger book in which he was making cryptic marks. Big Al strolled over and dragged out a chair across from him. ''How's it goin', Dutch?''

''Fair to middlin', Al. Only problem is, Miz Palmer's girls must all have the clap. That, or somebody's cheatin' on the receipts. I'll find out soon enough. Where you been, Al? Tried to get you this morning for some more of that 'shine from the last batch you sold Solly. Good stuff.''

''Got a case left. I'll send it over tomorrow. Listen, Dutch, I been out in the country . . .''

The policeman looked up. ''The heat's on you?''

''Naw, nothin' like that. Just business.''

''Good. I'm getting real nervous about those feds been watching the cigar store. I wish there was someplace our boys could go when times are touchy like this. Kansas City's a far piece to travel—''

''That's just what I wanted to talk to you about, Dutch. I think I found us a safe house. Just a few hours away, and a real nice place, besides. Up by Eureka Springs.''

''Pretty country,'' Dutch said, as if he were a devotee of scenery. ''What's the setup?''

''Hoity-toity dame name of Thorne. Got a goddamn castle of a place. What with hard times, she's turnin' it into a hotel, but she ain't got nobody to come stay. Kinda desperate. Put a fuckin' lotta dough into fixin' up the place and whatnot.''

''She into anything herself?''

Big Al looked shocked. ''Naw, Dutch! She's straight legal. Probably ain't never broke a law in her life. Real classy broad, too. The boys'd have to clean up and behave themselves. Couldn't send along any of the kind who'd try to lift the silver.''

''Did you talk to her about it?''

''Sorta mentioned it. Said I had friends wanted a place to go. She thought I was talkin' about other customers, so I let her think it.''

''She'll squeal when she figures it out. Our boys ain't exactly high society.''

"Naw, she won't squeal. Not if they act nice-like. She'll know—she ain't stupid—but she needs the dough bad. Long as they don't bring trouble with 'em, she won't go lookin' for it."

The policeman closed the cigar box and drummed his fingers on the top. "Hmmm, sounds okay. What about the town? We don't know nobody there. Might have some goddamn eager-beaver sheriff."

"Town don't figure in it. This place is four, five miles out and all off to itself."

Dutch was nodding approval. Big Al went on, "Who's around here now?"

"Not much of anybody big. Ma Barker and the boys is supposed to be comin' by in a few weeks . . ."

"Ma Barker cleans up real good. If she'd keep her big yap shut, it might be a good place to put 'em until those fuckin' feds get tired of hangin' around. Tell you what, let's send some of the boys up there and see how it goes."

When they grew up, Laura and Sonny referred to the period that started in the fall of 1932 as the Year of the Hoods. They rubbed elbows with many of FBI Director Hoover's list of Public Enemies. Many of them were dead within another year and a half, but before then Laura accepted a candy bar from Pretty Boy Floyd and was patted on the head by John Dillinger. Sonny learned some very interesting words from a man who called himself Bob Smith, a small, vain man with dark hair, a spruce mustache, and a fidgety manner. He was easily recognizable later when the more sensational newspapers ran photographs of the bullet-riddled body of Baby Face Nelson.

Grace had thought she was prepared for anything and everything. The house was lovely, the family happy and occupied with their various assignments, and Howard's presence, now that he'd moved in to become an official part of the household, was such a joy that she found herself wondering if perhaps she'd made a big mistake in not accepting his one proposal. Unfortunately, he didn't seem on the verge of repeating it. Except for that one personal miscalculation on her part, life seemed to be falling into perfect order for the first time in years.

On the opening day, however, Grace was stunned by her own naiveté. Though she had endured many hard things in life, she realized how much the innocent she was socially.

She'd always moved among her own class of people and her servants and employees. She'd never fully comprehended that there were such people as those who were now coming into her own home. The very first group to register, in fact, set the tone of what was to come.

There was an old man with a face like a toothless ferret's and breath that could have removed wallpaper. With him was a porky, flashily dressed man who introduced himself. "Howdedo, ma'am. I'm Four-Finger Jake. Pleased to meet-cha!" He held out the hand that was missing the digit. "This here is my old man and Velmaline. C'mon, honey, shake hands."

Velmaline, an undernourished girl of twenty or so with badly bleached hair, a slight case of rickets, and an inch crust of makeup, gave Grace a limp clammy hand and whined, "I sure hope you got indoor plumbing in this joint. Last place we stayed I had to piss in the backyard."

As Edmund showed this group to the rooms they had reserved, Grace stood clutching the desk with white-knuckled fingers. "Dear God in heaven," she whispered to herself. "What have I done?"

But by that night when she talked to Howard, she'd started to accept the situation. She knew there was no going back. The decision had been made, the money spent. "These people, loathsome as they are, are here to stay," she said to him.

"I've been trying all day to find a crumb of comfort in this," he said wryly. "I think I've located it."

"For heaven's sake, share it with me!"

"There are people worse off than we are," he pronounced.

She looked at him, eyebrow cocked. "Name four!"

After a moment she added more seriously, "I hate to think what Jack would say if he were to look down and see what I'd brought into his house."

"He'd say you're doing your best and he loves you for it."

Grace felt tears spring to her eyes, the tears she'd been fighting off all day long. "Thank you, Howard."

To Laura the opening weeks in the house as a hotel meant the friendship of Eddie March, a plump, pudding-faced man of fifty with a voice as rough and rumbly as an old tomcat. He was quietly cheerful and unfailingly polite. Best of all, he loved children and was the essence of grandfatherliness. "Miz Thorne," he said one day shortly after his arrival with a group of exceedingly questionable men from Chicago, "I hear there's a pretty spring down the hill. Would it suit you if the children showed me the way?''

Grace was nearly undone by the influx of obviously unsuitable guests and the way her grand plans had gone awry. She was grateful for even a crumb of courtesy. ''The children aren't normally allowed to go to the spring, but if you'll stay with them . . .''

Laura learned the fine art of fly-casting under Eddie March's direction and Sonny built a fine boat which the old man's scarred and knotted fingers helped whittle. Eddie told them how he'd always wanted grandchildren just like them, but it hadn't worked out. His wife, Shirley—bless her memory— hadn't given him children and it was their greatest sorrow. Shirley had died ten years earlier as a result of injuries sustained in a knife fight in a bar in Cicero. ''Not that Shirl was fighting, mind. She was too classy for that sort of thing. She was just trying to help out her girlfriend whose husband was knocking her around. Poor old Shirl, always trying to help her friends.''

''Why didn't you marry some other lady then?'' Laura asked.

''Aw, I just never found anybody else like Shirl. She had a heart of gold, she did. And the prettiest red hair. There was some as said it came out of a bottle, but I always figured, what the hell. Looked real good, however she got it. A real looker, Shirley. Still miss her.''

''That's very sad, Mr. March,'' Laura said.

''Honey, you just call me Uncle Eddie.''

''What do you do for work, Uncle Eddie?'' Laura asked.

''I'm a sort of assistant to Lucky Anderson.''

''That man with the real curly hair?''

''That's right.''

''What do you do for him?''

''Oh, just keep track of things. You know—protect him and keep my ear open for things he oughta know. Been with him for four years now.''

''What did you do before that?'' Sonny asked.

''I was a jug-marker. Worked for myself, mostly.''

''What's a jug-marker do?'' Laura asked. She had a mental picture of someone putting labels on bottles and couldn't figure how you'd do that for yourself.

''Watch out, honey. You're gonna get that hook in a tree or the back of yourself if you fling it around that way. That's better. A jug-marker is a fella who knows all about banks.''

"About how to run them, you mean?"

"No, how to rob them."

Sonny dropped his boat with a thud and looked at Eddie with eyes full of wonder. "You robbed banks?"

"No, I didn't rob 'em myself," Eddie answered.

Laura said, "Good. I don't think Gram would approve of robbing banks."

"Well, honey, I wouldn't say nothin' 'gainst your grandma. She's a fine, upright lady and you ought to pay close mind to what she tells you. But she might not know this: there's banks that need robbin'. Just cry out for it, don't you see? There's mean folks, see, who sometimes own banks, and they take people's money and won't give it back, and they loan poor folks money, but make them give up their farms and houses for it. That's called mortgages and they're bad things. So these bad banks deserve to be robbed."

The children nodded, convinced of the wisdom and essential justice of this point of view. "But you didn't rob them yourself?" Laura prodded.

"No, I just went around and got to know all about them. How they was laid out and where the safes was and what days of the week they had the most money on hand and like that. Why, at one time I could have drawn you a picture of the inside of more'n a hundred banks. I sold that information. Sorta like a newspaper sells you information every day. But I didn't tell just everybody. Only gangs figuring on making a good heist. I'd help them out and then they'd give me a share of what they got. It used to be real interesting to find out about different banks. One time I pretended I was a reporter for a big-city newspaper when this little podunk bank opened. President wanted to brag about it and took me all around, let me take notes and draw plans and everything. Easiest two grand I ever made."

"I might be a jug-marker when I grow up," Sonny said.

"No, it ain't what it used to be. Nobody respects a good jug-marker anymore. They just get their equalizers and their fast cars and do it any which way. That's why so many people get shot. Careless work . . . gives bank robbing a bad name. Back in the twenties, those were the days when they did it right. I worked once with Baron Lamm, you know."

"Who's Baron Lamm?" Sonny asked.

"You've never heard of Baron Lamm?" Eddie asked, amazed. "He was the best organized bank man there ever was. Working with him was like being in a theater play. A real wonder. He'd bring his jug-marker right in to work right with his boys—that is, when he didn't do his own casing. He'd make maps and plans and little model things of the bank and they'd practice over and over just who was gonna stand where and who was gonna say what. They all wore watches that said the exact same time, and when it was time to go, they went! Even if they didn't have all the loot yet. The getaway driver would be waiting outside with a map on the dashboard and the tank full. See, the Baron would've driven all the escape routes himself beforehand and the route would be marked with arrows which way to go it something went wrong."

"Why don't you still work with him?" Sonny asked. He'd abandoned his whittling and was utterly absorbed in Eddie's story.

"Well, son, he got himself killed. Too many things went wrong once. He was pulling a bank job and got a driver who wasn't the best he oughta been. They got the loot and piled into the car, then this vigilante fella comes tearing down the street with a shotgun. The driver lost his head and made a U-turn in the road. But he knocked against the curb and the tire blew out."

"Why didn't they just take another car?" Sonny asked.

"That's just what they did, son, but this car they took belonged to an old geezer whose son had put a speed governor on it to keep the geezer from going too fast. They got a little ways, of course, before they figured out what was wrong. Meantime, they've picked up a couple dozen cops on their trail."

"What did Baron Lamm do then?"

"Well, the way I heard it, they got rid of that car and stole a truck, but the truck didn't have no water in the radiator, so they went a little bit and took another car. But *that* car didn't have but a gallon of gas in it. By the time they ran out, they were out in the country surrounded by about two hundred cops and vigilantes and the like. They tried to run for it, but they were cut down."

"Cut down?" Laura asked.

"Shot up. Now, I better get you two back to your grandma or she'll be worried. Reel that in, honey. Maybe we'll catch some fish tomorrow, now that you know how to cast."

The family was divided in opinion as to the success of the hotel operation. The one thing they all recognized and agreed on was the financial benefit. Their guests were, almost without exception, extraordinarily generous. Sometimes even a small favor or errand earned a twenty-dollar gold piece or a crisp bill. ("They can afford to be generous," Grace told India. "It's not their money. Or at least it wasn't until they stole it.")

But the guests were also, in their own crude way, both gracious and grateful. Many of these men and their women were outcasts from their own homes and society and appreciated the domestic atmosphere of Thornehill. And they did behave, to the best of their limited ability. Whatever excesses—sexual, criminal, or otherwise—they indulged in, went on behind the doors of their individual rooms. In the public rooms they "put on the dog," wearing their gaudy best clothing and using what they believed, sometimes quite laughably, to be upper-crust manners.

But there were problems for the Thornes.

Jackson didn't find the hoodlums to be the hunting-and-fishing companions he'd hoped for. "For God's sake! They'd rather shoot people than quail!" he lamented. "There's not one of them who hasn't got more ammunition in his suitcase than we've got in the gun room."

Adele found her own, quite different cause for complaint. "The laundry is overwhelming. Those floozies they bring along wear so much lip rouge and powder that I'm hard put to keep up on the table napkins and pillowcases. And the stains on the sheets"—she leaned close to Grace and lowered her voice—"surpass belief. Animals!"

India was disappointed too. Her elegant little gift shop wasn't working out at all. "They don't want to buy anything that doesn't say 'Souvenir of Thornehill' on it. Their tastes are abominable. That awful woman with the pinkish hair came in the other day and bought a lovely landscape. She brought it back an hour later to show me what she'd done to it. She'd cut up a photograph of herself standing in front of a beat-up car and holding a shotgun and she'd actually pasted it onto the painting."

Evelyn all but turned into a hermit, so great was her desire to avoid the guests. She, like Grace—like most of the family, for that matter—had never moved outside her own circle of the educated and wealthy and she found the guests shocking and upsetting. Unlike Grace and the rest, however, there was no adaptability in her. Grace sensed that Evelyn would be happier if she made some effort to understand and perhaps even sympathize with these strange people, but true to her promise not to ask help and fearing that such interference might be thus interpreted, she made no effort to impose this view on her daughter-in-law.

Not everyone was unhappy. Howard Lee, knowing of Grace's distress, sympathized with her, but on his own behalf was quite content. He was always busy with the sort of everyday things he was used to—ingrown toenails, broken fingers, and colds—plus a number of unsavory but interesting ailments particular to these guests. He was often asked about plastic surgery, and treated more syphilis than he'd seen in all his previous years of medical practice. There was also a generous quota of requests for abortions, which he positively refused to do. In spite of this, he was treated with tremendous respect, which was gratifying.

Edmund, oddly enough, rather enjoyed the hoodlums too. They weren't what he'd wanted or anticipated, but his curious scholarly mind found ample fodder in their unusual speech, mannerisms, and morals. Though the family took their meals in private, Edmund usually ate in the ballroom, which had been converted into the guests' dining room. He'd linger long after he'd finished dinner. Making leisurely work of a cigar, he'd chat or cavesdrop, sometimes shaking his head in delighted wonder at the outrageous things he heard and saw.

Laura and Sonny were in heaven. Sonny took to swaggering in such a way that the men would say, "He's a cute kid, ain't he?" And Laura was liked by both the men, who would tweak her braids and give her candy bars, and the women, who would sometimes let her try on their makeup and jewelry. One woman named Lil liked to hear Laura read. "Pretty voice you got, honey. Bet you could be a singer if you wanted. That's what I wanted to be, but my old man knocked me across the windpipe when I was about your age. Ain't never been able to sing a note since then."

"Your father hit you?"

"Sure, he was mad, see, 'cause I'd gotten myself knocked up and he didn't want another brat around the house. But I lost it anyway, so it didn't make much difference, 'cept I can't sing good now."

Laura loved the bustle in the hallways, the chatter and clink of plates in the dining room, the billows of cigarette smoke when the billiards room door opened. She begged to have her hair permed and dyed blond like so many of the women guests—to no avail. And though she hadn't formulated it in words, not even in her own mind, she loved the relative neglect. All the Thorne adults were too busy to be as oppressively attentive to the twins as usual. Fingernails weren't checked before every meal as they once were. Lessons were sometimes missed when a crisis popped up, and minor lapses in manners were frequently ignored.

This enviable state of affairs lasted, however, only until a sleety day in January. Edmund was in the kitchen, his towel-draped head over a pan of boiling eucalyptus water to break up his cold, and lessons had been suspended. At loose ends, Sonny and Laura had roamed the house getting in people's hair until Adele finally ordered them out of the way. "Go see if your father is in the barn. If he's not, you can clean out the stables. You two need something useful to do. Scat!"

Nobody was in the barn, so they took the canvas cover off the Hispano-Suiza and played "Bonnie and Clyde." They were in the midst of a getaway, Sonny in the driver's seat, Laura firing at the lawmen behind them with a broken rake handle, when they noticed that they had an audience. "Oh, Gram, I didn't hear you come in," Laura said, climbing down from the car.

Grace was standing next to a bale of straw, half-leaning against it. Her face was set. "What *are* you two doing?"

"We were being Bonnie and Clyde, and we just robbed a bank. I was gunning them down with my equalizer and—"

"Dear God!" Grace whispered. "I thought you were immune. How stupid of me."

"What did you say? Are you mad, Gram? We aren't having lessons because Uncle Edmund is sick—"

"I don't care about the lessons. What's an equalizer, Laura?"

"A gat, a gun, you know."

Grace's expression was grim. "Put the cover back on the automobile and go to your rooms. Stay there until I come and tal to you."

"But, Gram, we were having fun. What's wrong?"

Grace put her hand on Laura's shoulder and looked directly into her eyes. "You really don't know, do you? Where did you learn this sort of talk? Equalizers? Bank robberies?"

"Why, from everybody, mostly Uncle Eddie," Sonny said before Laura could answer.

"Uncle Eddie?"

"You know, Gram. Mr. March. He's stayed here a couple of times and took us fishing and things."

Again Grace spoke more to herself than to them. "And *he's* the best of them. Dear Lord . . ."

Sonny was starting to put the canvas cover back.

"Never mind that. I'll get someone else to do it. Go to your rooms, both of you."

"But, Gram—" Laura started.

"Now!"

They ran all the way to the house. Halfway up the stairs, Laura said, "I don't see why Gram's so mad. She never said we couldn't play in the automobile."

"I don't think it's that," Sonny said thoughtfully.

Laura went to her room and sat down in the window seat, watching the rain. Maybe Gram was angry because they were playing so childishly. In her heart, Laura knew she was too old for that sort of thing. Her body was finally that of a young woman, with the long-awaited breasts and the face that matched the size of her teeth. But her mind and heart were still fighting the change from child to adult. Sometimes she'd go straight from wanting real high-heeled shoes to wanting a nice quiet game of jacks. Or from longing for a date to longing for a pony of her own.

Growing up should have been like climbing over a single, well-defined fence. Instead, it was a long field and she was crossing it blindfolded in slow stages with unseen forces sometimes dragging her forward, sometimes jerking her back. There were whole days when she could hardly keep from crying, without any idea why. Other times she caught herself giggling almost hysterically for almost no reason at all. Because she had no close friends of her own age but Sonny, Laura had no way of knowing this was a perfectly normal pattern for a girl to follow.

Grace didn't come to her room for nearly an hour. When she did, she was smiling, but it was a forced, anxious smile. "May I join you, Laura-bunny?" she asked, sitting down at the other end of the window seat.

"Gram, I don't know what I did, but I'm sorry."

"You didn't do anything, darling. I did. I allowed myself to get so wrapped up in one aspect of your future welfare that I neglected another. I've been talking to India. You and she and Sonny are going to go live at the cottage down by the spring. I've already sent some men down to start getting it fixed up and ready for you."

"Why?"

"Because I don't want you associating with the people we're forced to entertain in this house."

"Like Mr. March?"

"Like him, yes. I have no doubt he's a good-enough man in some aspects, but his ways simply aren't our ways. And you and Sonny are at a very impressionable age. He and his sort are not the impression I want made on you."

"There's nothing wrong with Mr. March," Laura said defensively, remembering the picnics he'd taken them on, the wonderful stories he'd told, the gifts he'd given them.

"Oh, yes, darling. There's a great deal wrong with him. I've talked to Sonny. He told me all about the jug-marker business."

"But that's not the same as actually robbing banks."

"It *is*, bunny. It's criminal and immoral. It's the planning of a crime—a crime that all too often results in the death of innocent people. I don't think you fully comprehend what that means. These people are very callous and have somehow justified to themselves that human life has less value than their own self-interests. I can't risk having them pass that way of thinking on to you. Now, I want you to start thinking about what you want to take to the cottage. Your winter clothes, schoolbooks, and other favorite things."

"Can't we come here at all?"

"You and Sonny may come up to the house with India for dinner and for the evening, so long as you keep out of the public rooms. You may not play on the grounds up here where you might run into any of the guests."

"Not even in the stables?"

"No."

"But, Gram—"

Grace became very stern. "Laura, I will tolerate no arguments on this. If you disobey me, I will have to send you farther away. I would hate to do that, but your safety and well-being are more important than your feelings or mine. Do you understand? Do you?"

"Yes, Gram."

XV

SONNY regarded it as a year of the most bitter and unde-
served exile. Many times during the first weeks he sneaked
back to the mansion and was discovered in his old room.
Grace believed the worst—that he wanted to be around the
guests. But Laura knew it was the house itself that drew him.

Laura was content enough. She liked the cottage, always
had enjoyed the solitude and vacation flavor of the smaller
house. She had no idea, of course, that it was the place of her
conception and birth, nor had she any conscious premonition
of the other events of her life that would take place there. But
she enjoyed the cozy feeling of the rooms, the sound of
birdsong that made constant background music, the damp
earth and forest odor that permeated the atmosphere, the way
the air itself seemed to take on the color of the forest—green
in summer and golden rose in autumn.

Life fell into a new pattern. Every morning Edmund came
to the cottage and they had lessons while India went up to
tend to her gift shop. In the afternoon Adele often joined
them, bringing her mending and a vast store of memories of a
childhood in Boston which she shared endlessly and entertain-
ingly. Several times a week they took dinner with the rest of
the family at the mansion; the rest of the time Laura and India
cooked at the cabin—the job falling most often to Laura
because India's recipes were shockingly creative.

India's passing enthusiasms made every day interesting, if
not always enjoyable. For a while they endured vegetarian-
ism. But there came a day when the main course for dinner
was stewed pears with alfalfa sprouts and Laura and Sonny
rebelled. Then India went "solitaire happy." They got a book

that explained a hundred different ways of playing single-handed card games and for a month every flat surface in the cabin had one game or another laid out at all times. It was India herself who tired of this, and one day they gathered up fourteen decks of well-worn cards and returned them to the mansion.

That winter, when the family finances began to ease—thanks to the guests Grace feared and hated—India was given the use of the Packard, which had been brought out of storage. This enabled the three of them—still virtually banned from the house—to range more widely. India became "movie mad," and every time the bill changed at the Eureka Springs movie house, they piled into the car and went. India learned to do a passable imitation of Mae West (which she had the good sense not to perform in front of Grace) and Laura fell in love with Clark Gable. Sonny drove them all nearly insane reenacting the Marx Brothers' exploits.

By spring, the movie mania had dampened down through simple lack of fuel. The Eureka Springs movie house didn't change their fare often enough to keep the flames fed. India, whose flamboyant personality craved new interests, sought in vain for something to "take up." Finally, at the end of June, she found it. She came dashing into the cabin waving a handbill she'd picked up on her weekly shopping trip. "Children, get ready! We've got to be there early to get a good place!"

"A good place where?" Sonny asked.

"At the revival. See, the Reverend Johnny Heaven is coming to town tonight."

"Who's that?" Laura asked, putting aside a sock she was darning for Adele.

"Who's that? Laura, dear, you do have your head in the clouds. Remember the newsreel we saw of him? Healing thousands of people in that baseball stadium? It'll be madly entertaining to see him preach. He's supposed to be terribly attractive."

"I can walk! Lord, see me walk!" Sonny exclaimed, leaping up and pretending to throw away crutches and totter forward, his hands clasped in fervent prayer.

"Sonny, that's disrespectful," India said. "He's a great Christian leader. They say he's healed thousands of people all over the country."

"And he drives a white Rolls-Royce."

"What a very cynical thing for a child to say," India

sniffed. "Of course he does, he'd the head of the Church of Heaven on Earth. It's only fitting."

"He's a charlatan."

"And you're a priggish little boy who knows too many big words for his own good," India said, smiling. "Laura, you'll come with me, won't you?"

Laura considered only a moment. It was a question of going with India or spending the whole evening darning socks. "I'll come."

"When you get back, you'll be able to see," Sonny said.

"I can already see."

"I know."   .

There wasn't a large enough flat place in town to accommodate Reverend Heaven's tent, so the revival was held a few miles out of town in a field next to the railroad track. It was a big blue tent with white clouds painted all over it. On the siding, there were three railroad cars painted the same way; one of them was the reverend's personal quarters, the second carried the tent and his Rolls, the third was for his staff.

India had to park several hundred feet away, in a field already packed with cars. The tent was half full, but India hovered like a hungry falcon until two unwary souls got up to stretch their legs; then she swooped in and got their seats—on the aisle, only four rows back. The former seatholders were livid when they came back, but she silenced them with a haughty look and the admonition, "Be careful how you speak to a Christian woman in the House of the Lord."

It was another hour and a half before the revival began, but the crowd kept surprisingly quiet. Here and there people prayed; small groups started up *a cappella* hymns; friends greeted each other in hushed, reverent tones; many just sat and tried to keep cool fanning themselves with paper fans that were being sold with pictures of Jesus on one side and Reverend Heaven on the other.

The reverend's Heavenly Helpers moved up and down the aisles, restoring order wherever confusion threatened to break out. These Helpers were apparently chosen for height and looks as much as spirituality. All of them were quite tall, attractive young men. They wore white suits with the single word "HEAVEN" stitched across the back of their shoulders in glossy blue thread.

Suddenly there was a burst of sound from a hidden organ.

Within a few blaring notes, Laura recognized the song—"When the Saints Go Marching In"—and the crowd surged to its feet, singing and clapping. Then, at the back of the tent, there was a commotion. Heads turned, necks craned, someone cried, "Praise the Lord!"

Reverend Heaven came down the center aisle. He, too, was dressed in white, but his clothing was of satin with sparkling sequins around the collar. He wore a white cape with an iridescent blue lining that showed as he strode forward, cape billowing. He walked up and down the aisle several times, shaking hands and saying in a booming voice, "Bless you, brother! Bless you, sister. Praise the Lord. Bless you all!" And still the organ blasted on.

Finally he went to the front and mounted the white stage, pausing to let everyone get a good look at him. He had artificially glossy black hair, transparent blue eyes, and feverishly pink cheeks. He was an adorable "naughty boy" grown up. A trifle overweight, he exuded a raw sex appeal in waves. After a moment, he held his arms up high, the blue lining of the cape framing his sturdy figure. A woman in the front row gasped. He closed his eyes, his lips moved silently; then, as he quickly brought his hands together over his head in an exaggerated attitude of prayer, the organ fell silent abruptly.

The Reverend Johnny Heaven, *né* Ralph Edgar Paggenpohl, had been, in his earlier years, a hog-caller, an auctioneer, a circus barker, and eventually a vaudeville ticket seller. He knew how to work a crowd. When the organ stopped, he called out, "O Lord, *O Lord!* Hear us, your miserable sinnin' flock. We've got together here tonight to praise you. To tell you how much we all love you and your Heavenly Ways. Is that right, brothers and sisters? Is that right? Tell the Lord. Let him hear you."

There was a murmur of "Praise the Lord."

"That's right. Lord, hear us. Hear how we love you, how we sorrow over our sinnin' ways, how we're gonna follow in your Righteous Path from now on. We're sorry, Lord, that's right, soooorry 'bout the bad things we've done. We've sinned. Sure, we've sinned. We're human beings. We've done bad things we're ashamed of. Haven't we, brothers and sisters? Say Amen, brothers and sisters. Let Our Lord hear you. We're like children. Always straying from the Path, but we want to come back to you, Lord. Let us back into your Heavenly Good Graces. So we've all come here tonight at the Church of Heaven on Earth to pray for forgiveness and to promise you from now on, we're gonna be as good as we can. Amen, Lord. I say *amen!*''

"Amen, Lord!" the crowd replied.

By this time, Laura had a charley horse in her leg and was glad to be able to sit down and rub the knotted muscle. "Isn't he grand?" India whispered. Laura wasn't sure if she meant it or was trying to be funny, so she didn't answer.

When everyone was seated, the Reverend Heaven began the real business of the meeting. Later on, he said, as if promising a treat, his Heavenly Helpers would move through with offertory plates and people would get to contribute to the traveling church. "But not now. *No,* not now. You'd just say now, 'Who's this Reverend Johnny Harrison Heaven? How do I know he's a godly man?' No, sir, you put that wallet away. No, ma'am, you quit lookin' in your pocketbook. No, I won't let you put your hard-earned money in the collection now. *Noooo!* Brothers and sisters, we'll have our collection later.

"But I'm gonna talk about money for a while. Nothin' wrong with that in the Lord's House. No, brothers, nothin' wrong with it. Our precious Christ talked about money sometimes, sure he did. He went among the moneylenders, didn't he? Didn't he? Luke 6:32—*I came not to call the righteous, but sinners to repentance.* Amen! Well, seems everybody's talking 'bout money these days with this Depression goin' on. Don't you think the Lord knows about it? Don't you think it's the Lord's doin'? No, brothers, that ain't no blasphemy. Don't you look at me like I'm sayin' bad things about Our Lord. I'm tellin' you he wanted it this way. And do you know why? I'll tell you. Reverend Heaven'll tell you right here and now.

"Listen, brothers and sisters, the Lord did this to us because of our wicked ways. Jeremiah 13:27—*I have seen thine adulteries, and thy neighings, and the lewdness of thy whore-dom, and thine abominations on the hills in the fields. Woe unto thee, O Jerusalem!* Like a lovin' parent sometimes has to spank a little child, the Lord's spankin' us. He's sayin', 'My children's lost their way. Got too uppity and wicked and forgot me. Gotta remind them I'm here and I'm watchin' them.'

"Oh, I know. I read the papers, listen to the radio, I know what those politician fellas say—all kinds of talk about banks and deficits and production and all those other highfalutin words. But we know better, don't we, brothers and sisters?

We know it's just the Lord smackin' us over the knuckles so we'll remember him and follow in his Heavenly Steps. Deuteronomy 12:28—*Observe and hear all these words which I command thee*. Do you hear me, brother? Do you hear me? Amen. Say 'Amen.' I can't hear you, brother. Speak up! If I can't hear you, how's the Lord gonna hear you? Amen . . .''

It went on for nearly two hours. Reverend Heaven's words started as animal growls, ended in orgasmic cries. He paced, he strode across the stage, he pointed, he made dramatic, cape-sweeping gestures, he raised his hands to heaven, he knelt on the stage, banging his fists and imploring God to listen. His voice was by turns as thick and sweet as a bowl of warm tapioca, and as sharp and deadly as a fish-skinning knife. Laura, like everyone else in the tent, was swept up in his magic. She perched on the front of her seat, joining in the ''Amens'' and ''Praise the Lords'' that punctuated the sermon. Her dress became soaked with sweat, her hair fell loose, her breathing became faster.

Reverend Heaven talked about the godly and the ungodly, inventing families to illustrate the difference. The godly family prospered. They were clean, happy, healthy, their fortunes increased by meeting misfortune with prayer. Their children were beautiful and obedient and blessed. They increased the stars in their crowns by spreading the Word of God. They were beloved in their community.

The ungodly family withered. They wilted under ill health, they were scorned by their town, their children despised them and were despised, their material and spiritual poverty knew no bounds. They were Job-like figures of tragedy upon tragedy.

The real message was buried in layers and layers of vivid inspirational stories. ''I knew a little girl,'' Reverend Heaven cried, ''a sweet little girl who wanted to make music. Oh, Lordie, how she wanted to make music. Her mommy and daddy sent her to take lessons on the piano, but as hard as she tried, she couldn't never make her fingers work fast enough. So after some years, she gave up. Then one day, she came to see me at a meeting just like this one. And she came to Know the Lord. She was saved, brothers and sisters. *Saved!* And Christ Jesus came to her, right here in this very tent, and she saw his Glorious Light and she knew she could play. She came up here—right up here on this stage—and she came up to me and she said, 'Reverend Heaven, let me put my hands on your organ.' ''

India snickered and was hushed by a woman next to her.

" 'Let me play music, Reverend Heaven,' she said. Well, I'm here to tell you, brothers and sisters, she walked up to that old organ right over yonder and she put her hands on the keys and the Light of the Lord shone in her eyes and she made music. *She made music like you've never heard before!* Glorious music. You've been hearing that music tonight. Yes, Lord, that same little girl is a grown-up woman now, a good Christian woman—amen!—who's given up her life to come with me to play music for you good folks.

"Now, we're gonna let the Heavenly Helpers pass among you while we sing and pray. You give those boys whatever the Lord tells you to. Maybe he'll tell you to give a nickel, or a dime, or maybe he'll say to you, 'That Reverend Johhny Heaven is a godly man who needs your money to take his ministry to other folks who need to get the Light of God. Other folks who are suffering in the darkness of ignorance.' You feel free—*free*, brothers and sisters—to give as much as you can, because God will pay you back tenfold. Tenfold!

"Let me tell you something—I was in Saint Louis last year, having a meetin', just like we're doing tonight, and a man came up to me. He said, 'Reverend Heaven, I seen the Light. I've accepted Jesus Christ as my Savior. I got a hundred dollars here, I been saving to go to Chicago and get me a job in a factory with my brother-in-law, but, Reverend Heaven, I'm gonna give the Church of Heaven on Earth that money. The Lord's told me to.'

"Well, that man went home to his family, four hungry little children and a wife, and he told his wife what he'd done. Lordie, Lordie, how she carried on. But he shut her up, told her it was the Lord's Will and the Lord would take care of them—Praise Jesus!—and do you know what happened? Do you want Reverend Heaven to just tell you what happened to that Christian man? Let me hear you! Well, I'll tell you. That man had an old uncle—a wicked old man who'd made a fortune selling dirty magazines—and the next week that old uncle died and left all that money to that man. Half a million dollars! Half a million! Can you imagine that? Matthew 10:41—*He that receiveth a prophet in the name of a prophet shall receive a prophet's reward.*

"So when I say to you, 'Listen to the Lord and you shall be repaid tenfold,' you think about that man, brothers and sisters. Now, as the Heavenly Helpers pass among you, open your hearts and hands and help us take this ministry on to the next town. We're gonna play some music now and sing and pray. If there's those among you who are afflicted in some way, come on up and we'll pray for you. If you've been to some doctor who's said, 'I'm sorry, brother, but you're not gonna get well, you're not gonna walk, or see, or hear,' you come on up here and put yourself in God's hands. We'll pray for you.''

One by one, people started coming to the front. Laura found herself wishing she had some handicap that would give her the right to go forward. If India hadn't been there with her, she might have pretended an affliction. She was dizzy with the thrill of it all. The tent had grown hot, the air potent with breath and sweat. People crowded forward, squashing her up against India, who was clapping and singing. The organ grew louder, the singing more fervent. A mob of people were now in front of the stage. Reverend Heaven went among them, leaning down, putting his hands on their heads and shouting for God's attention.

Laura climbed up on the chair so she could see. An enormously fat woman who leaned heavily on crutches raised her arms and let the crutches fall away. ''Oh Lord! I can stand up! Lord be praised! Bless you, Reverend Heaven!''

''Bless you, sister!'' Reverend Heaven cried. ''Oh, Sweet Jesus, we know you're there, watchin' us. Blessin' us. Thank you, Lord, for giving back this woman her legs. Thank you, Savior! Amen. Say *'Amen,'* Brothers and sisters!''

''*Amen!*'' the crowd screamed. They surged forward again and Laura was knocked off her chair.

Suddenly the steaming pink haze of religious fervor was replaced by a thick black panic. Laura had her foot twisted in the rungs of the chair and could see nothing but legs. Fat legs, skinny legs, hairy legs. *''India!''* she screamed, but somehow India had been swept away. Laura tried to get up, but someone stepped on her hand and somebody else was standing on her skirt. She screamed—the mob swallowed the sound—and freed her hand, then jerked on the skirt, feeling it rip.

''Praise the Lord, brothers and sisters!'' Reverend Heaven screamed.

''India!'' Laura shouted, clawing her way up a red print skirt. Once vertical, she was little better off. Jammed between two adults, she could hardly get her breath. The bony man in front of her smelled of pungent body odor, the woman behind her of cheap perfume and unwashed underwear. Laura felt the

bile, bitter and hot, rising in her throat. She gagged, tried to twist free, and gagged again.

Suddenly the bony man leapt forward, creating a momentary space between Laura and India. Laura threw herself at India, who'd been looking around frantically for her. "I want to go home!" she sobbed, clutching at her relative. But she knew India couldn't hear her over the din of the crowd.

India—dear tall, strong India—understood though. She bent, grabbed Laura around the knees, and hoisted her up above the crowd and started plowing through the people toward the exit. Laura, facing backward, saw Reverend Heaven lead a blind woman onto the stage. He put his palms to her eyes. She shrieked, grabbed at him, and collapsed in a dead faint.

A willowy Heavenly Helper was standing at the door holding out an offertory plate. "Get out of my way, you stupid faggy bastard!" India growled at him. When he didn't move, she brought her fist up under the plate, causing a waterfall of coins and bills.

"Pra-a-a-aise the Lord!" Reverend Heaven screamed.

"Amen!" came the thundering response.

India plunged through the door and out into the field of cars before she put Laura down and ordered, "Take a deep breath, honey. That's it. Again."

When they found the Packard and started home, India said, "We'll tell anyone who asks that you tore your skirt on the car door and you keep that hand out of sight until the scratches heal. Can you move your fingers? Good, nothing's broken. Your Gram will have to know, of course."

A few miles later, after a long silence, India said, "You saw that preposterous fat lady throw away her crutches, didn't you?"

"She was healed," Laura replied.

India smiled, her horsey teeth gleaming in the moonlight. "I saw her get off the train this afternoon when I went into town to get some face powder. She could walk as well as anyone then. She's part of the show."

"Reverend Heaven didn't cure her?"

"Honey, the only thing he relieves people of is their money."

When they got home, Sonny was waiting up. "How was he?" he said, all but pounding on Laura, who was keeping her hand out of sight.

"Who?" India asked, grabbing his shoulders and pointing him toward his bedroom.

"The Reverend Billy Bob God or whatever his name is," Sonny said.

India winked at Laura.

"We decided not to go. We just took a nice quiet ride in the country instead. Didn't we, Laura? Now, off to bed, both of you."

India waited until they were asleep before going up to the house to tell Grace what had happened. "She's not hurt," she finished, "and I don't think she'll want to talk about it, but I thought you should know."

Grace was quiet for a long minute. "Poor little bunny, she must have been terrified. I remember one time I was in a theater and a fight broke out . . ."

She fell utterly silent. India waited, but Grace said nothing more. "Were you hurt?" India finally asked.

"Oh, yes. But not by the crowd."

"What do you mean?"

Grace seemed to suddenly become aware of India's presence. "Oh, nothing. It was nothing. Just a silly memory . . ."

But after India had gone, her mind kept coming back to a night in London.

XVI

"WAKE up, Laura!" India said, shaking her shoulders. "It's just a nightmare, honey. Wake up. Everything's all right."

"Oh, India!" Laura sobbed, clinging to her in the dark.

India patted and crooned until Laura had calmed down. Then she lit the bedside lamp and got a cool damp cloth to bathe her face. "What is it you dream about, honey? You've been doing this for months now."

"I don't know. It's just a bad dream," Laura answered.

It was a lie. Laura knew full well what the dream was, for it was always the same and it was more vivid than reality. She was at the revival again. Again and again. She was pressed between people who seemed to be swelling up, their hot, sweating, stinking bodies ballooning. They pressed closer and closer until finally they started melting together into one obscene flesh, with her embedded in it. The crowd became a single bloated creature with thousands of legs and arms and eyes. And she was in the center, and at the same time she was outside it and able to observe, horrified, as Reverend Heaven baited the monster.

He shouted words she could hear and recognize and yet never understand. He was exhorting them to some action, some movement, and Laura tried frantically to understand, and thus escape. But it was impossible. And there was an element—how to define it? how to put into waking words what she was too young to understand?—an element of sexuality so rampant and yet so repressed that it boiled furiously, like a volcano, just under the rotting surface.

The monster started to move, roiling, shambling on its

thousand feet, waving its multitude of arms. Reverend Heaven was in front of them/it. His voice rose and fell seductively, rising to frenzied shrieks of exhortation, falling to primeval appeals. He backed up, gesturing, writhing. And the monster mob followed him, coming toward her now. She tried to run, but she was mired in some sort of slime the mob exuded in its vanguard.

And as it almost reached her, its heat searing her, its stench stifling her breath, its sound deafening her, she always woke, sweating and screaming, with heart-stopping terror.

India tucked her in and folded the washcloth, slapping it absently against the palm of her hand. "I'm going to talk to Grace. I think you need to be back at the mansion."

"No, don't do that," Laura said sleepily, snuggling down into the covers. But she was too exhausted to object strongly.

As it turned out, Laura and Sonny's return to the big house was fated before India had an opportunity to speak to Grace about it. Late in August they had, as always, a combined birthday dinner for Jackson and Adele. Laura was allowed to come to the house in the morning to help in the kitchen. She spent the day cutting up and stirring together the fruit for a compote and managed to lick so much cake icing off her fingers that her appetite was utterly destroyed.

Late that afternoon Mabelann said, "Honey, what's this label say?"

Laura studied the fruit jar in question. "I dunno."

"It your Gram's hand. I gotta use the oldest first. Go ask her what it say. She in the lib'ary."

Laura went in search, clutching the slippery jar in both hands. But when she opened the door to the library, she was astonished to see not Grace, but several strange men. Guests, she supposed, though there was a sign above the door saying "PRIVATE." Before they noticed her, she quietly shut the door. As she stood frozen in the hall, wondering where to find her grandmother, Grace came down the steps. "Laura-bunny, are you through in the . . .? What's wrong?"

"Gram, there's men in the library."

"There *are* men," Grace corrected absently. "What men?"

"Guests."

"What are they doing?" Grace asked, starting for the door.

"I . . . I don't know," Laura replied, thinking the truth sounded too absurd to be correct. Certainly she was mistaken, but it *looked* like they were counting out stacks of money.

"Run on back and help with the cake. I'll take care of it."

Laura thought little more about the incident except to wonder how anyone could have the nerve to invade the part of the house that Gram made clear was private. But Gram would straighten them out, but good!

Later she wasn't so sure. Grace was preoccupied at dinner. After the cake and presents, Grace roused herself and said, "It's time for a family conference."

Sonny stiffened. There had been some talk lately about him going away to school. Nothing very definite, but frequent enough mention to make him wary. "What about, Gram?"

"The house. The hotel, rather."

That she would instantly acquiesce to his rather rude demand for information was alarming. Adele quietly folded the gift-wrapping paper for another use while everyone else—as was their habit these days—cleared away their plates to the kitchen.

When they reassembled in the library with Mabelann outside to keep away any listeners, Grace picked up a newspaper. "Have you read this? Today's paper?"

The headline was about a bank robbery in a small town in Oklahoma the day before. There was a mercifully fuzzy photograph of a pool of blood in front of a teller's cage where a customer had been shot to death. "Let me see, Gram," Sonny said.

"You may read it later, young man. You're here on sufferance because you're getting old enough to be informed of family decisions. But you must be quiet."

"Yes, ma'am," Sonny said, sitting down angrily on the floor.

"I read the piece this morning," Edmund said. "Why do you point it out?"

"Because the men I feel quite certain committed this robbery and murder are staying here."

Everyone looked uncomfortable. Each had, in one way or another, accepted or learned to ignore the fact that their "guests" were probably responsible for a great many crimes. But none of them was easy of conscience about it.

"Up until now I've told myself that what our guests do elsewhere is none of our concern. I don't entirely believe it, nor do any of you, I suppose. But this afternoon I found that three men had made themselves at home in here—"

"No!" India exclaimed.

"Their presence was upsetting enough, but when I came in

to roust them out, I discovered that they had stacks of money spread about on my desk, dividing it up among themselves.'' Grace paced in front of the desk, her long fingers laced tightly together. ''And with that act, they have brought their crime to us. I feel I've been made a party to murder.''

''Quite right, Mother,'' Jackson said, rolling the newspaper up and tapping it on his knee. ''I know you refer to a moral position, but I think you—any of us—might even be held responsible in a legal sense as well. Accessory after the fact. Isn't that what it means?''

''I'm not certain, but I'm not going to ask anyone about it for fear of implicating myself,'' Grace said.

Laura's heart was pounding. She wasn't quite following this except to realize that Gram was terribly upset and nobody was making any attempt to ''jolly'' her out of it. It must be serious indeed. ''Gram . . .'' she said, but could get no further. She wanted to ask if Gram was going to go to jail, but couldn't get the words out.

It was Evelyn who first managed to speak. ''What are we to do about it?''

''They must go. All of them!'' Grace said.

There was a babble of agreement. All of them felt the same fear and distaste Grace did. Naturally it was Adele who first came to her senses and made a practical inquiry. ''I agree with you entirely, Grace, but how are we to live without the income? Edmund and I will, of course, move out and try to find something elsewh—''

''You'll not leave,'' Grace said with firmness that approached snappishness. ''I spent the afternoon going over our books. We have made quite a bit of money since we opened the house as a hotel. Enough, at any rate, to repay our original investment. Not a fortune, certainly not by Thorne standards . . .''

Laura suddenly realized that Gram was a bit of a snob, that they all were, and that it was comforting in a strange way. A tribal sort of comfort.

Grace must have seen a change in her granddaughter's expression, for she smiled and said, ''We're used to being financially secure and I feel obligated to restore the family status.''

''We understand all that,'' Jackson said shortly. His mother's missionary zeal to restore the onetime Thorne fortune was a source of irritation to all of them in practice, but the would-be results were desirable to all. ''But you're talking about eliminating our source of income. You, of all people, aren't proposing to live on the principal, are you?"

"Of course not!" Grace said, stung. Then, catching the sarcastic glint in his eye, realized he was making a joke. "No, I have another proposal. We allowed these highly undesirable people to come here because we had invested everything in the renovations and had to take whoever would come. We're in a slightly different position now. The renovation costs have been recouped, and then some. We can afford to close down while we determine how to attract a different class of people."

There was that comforting snobbism again, Laura realized, feeling her tense muscles relax. Gram had decided something, and the problems would be solved. She didn't and might not ever understand just how, but she was sure of the result.

Evelyn wasn't so sure. "How do you intend to do that?"

"I've got some ideas, but I'll get to that later. First I have a problem I can't solve. You must all help. Our first duty is to get those horrible people out of here. How are we to do that?"

"We could say we're closing for repairs," India suggested.

Adele made the ladylike snort that she habitually used to respond to so many of India's remarks. "They'd just expect to come back when we're done."

"Then you must have a better idea," India responded archly.

"We could simply tell them we're closing down the hotel permanently," Adele said. In her eagerness to put India in her place, she hadn't thought before speaking. The moment the words were out of her mouth she saw the error and criticized herself before India could. "But they'd find out and come back."

"You could just ask them to leave," Edmund said, but this was so patently impossible that he shook his head grimly as he spoke. They were dangerous enough when they believed the Thornes to be friends. To make enemies of them would be folly.

Forgetting his earlier put-down, Sonny spoke up. "We could have Director Hoover come from Washington and flush them out!"

"What lurid things you must read!" Grace said. " 'Flush,' indeed. Whatever does that mean?"

"It means come in with his G-men and arrest them all,"

Sonny said, mistakenly thinking Grace was seriously considering this suggestion.

"Sonny," she said with remarkable patience. "the last thing we need in this house is a gunfight! That is precisely what I'm trying to avoid."

Jackson had been sitting and staring at his rolled newspaper during this discussion. Suddenly he spoke up. "Melvin Purvis!"

He was sitting next to Laura and she was so startled by his outburst that she almost jumped.

"I beg your pardon?" Grace asked. It was apparent from her manner that she'd expected intelligent conversation and was getting nonsense.

"Don't you know who he is?" Jackson said. "Next to Hoover, he's the most important man in the FBI, and though the papers don't ever say so outright, it's clear that the two of them hate each other and are in competition. Purvis is a really outstanding person and has made some pretty serious inroads into the Capone gang in Chicago, while Hoover is sending vast mobs of men out to catch two-bit toughs. Purvis is, I believe, a much more serious threat to the criminals than Hoover, and I think they know it."

"Very interesting, I'm sure. But what has it to do with the matter at hand?"

"Simply background, Mother," he said, unperturbed by the coldness of her tone. "You let it be known that he's coming here."

Grace stared at him. "I was somewhat surprised that I had to explain to Sonny how foolish such a remark is. I'm astonished at you."

"Mother, you're not listening to me."

"How preposterous! Besides the physical danger to all of us if such a person were to come here, think of the legal jeopardy we'd put ourselves in just asking him to come. We'd have to explain that we've been harboring most of the 'Most Wanted' list for some time and have changed our minds."

Jackson stood up, finally goaded to anger. "Mother, be quiet a moment and listen. You who are so damned precise about words should understand. I said, ' *Let it be known* that he's coming here' "

Laura wanted to curl up in a safe ball. The only other time she'd heard her father use that tone with Gram was the awful night she'd overheard the conversation between them in Grace's room. She was terrified that something terrible was going to be said.

But her worry faded somewhat as she watched her grandmother. Grace's face was a study in fury at his overbearing manner, but as the meaning of his suggestion became clear, the scowl disappeared. "You mean . . .?"

"Exactly. You and I have a discussion at the front desk about some reservations for a man named Purvis from Chicago while some of the current guests are around. We can pretty it up with mention that he's bringing a party of ten men with him and it must be some sort of business convention or something. Act as stupid as necessary—"

"—and they'll think he's discovered their hiding place. They'd never dare come back for fear he's keeping an eye on us!" India put in. She came out of her chair and lunged at Jackson to shake his hand. "How utterly, divinely clever of you! It solves all our problems! I'm so impressed!"

"And you, Mother?" Jackson asked, his voice suddenly bitter. "Are you impressed with me?"

She looked up at him, angry at being forced into the admission. "Yes. It seems a good-enough plan."

"Good enough!" Jackson said. "Good enough?"

"*Don't!*" Laura suddenly cried out. "Don't talk awful to each other."

Grace and Jackson exchanged sheepish looks. Grace drew a deep breath and said, "Jackson, it's an excellent idea. You and I can rehearse our act tonight and play it out tomorrow."

"And what about the rest of your plan?" Edmund asked. He'd risen and come to sit next to Laura and was patting her hand.

"The rest? Oh, yes. Well, I think we must make a study of other nice hotels that cater to the sort of clientele we wish to attract. India, you keep track of social doings. Will you help me select the places?"

"Of course, cousin Grace, but to what end?"

"I'm going to have to visit them," Grace said.

Jackson hooted with laughter. At his mother's surprised expression he explained, "You sounded exactly as though you were saying you were going to have to go to Tibet, shave your head, and become a monk for ten years."

"That's precisely how I feel. You know I don't like to leave Thornehill." For an instant she sounded almost girlishly vulnerable, as if she were saying: I'm terrified of this. Please don't make jokes at my expense!

Her panic must have touched Jackson, for he said, "Then why don't you let Evelyn and me go? We'd enjoy it."

Grace hesitated. "Because . . . because I know exactly what I want to find out and—"

"You don't trust us?" Jackson was angry again.

"No, that's not it. I think I may have to do something rather dishonest and I don't want to ask anyone else to be a party to it."

"That sounds very mysterious," Evelyn said. Her disappointment at not getting a long-desired vacation was evident.

"It must be, in case I fail," Grace said with a rare burst of self-deprecating honesty. "I'd rather everyone didn't know what sort of fool I'd made of myself. Now, there is one other thing we need to discuss . . ."

Everyone shifted and eased into more comfortable positions now that they felt secure that things were about to change for the better. Sonny, unaware that his fate was about to be altered, flopped down onto his stomach and started making parts in the design of the carpet.

"Jackson and Evelyn and I have made arrangements for Sonny. Jackson, would you like to explain?"

Sonny was suddenly sitting bolt upright, spring-loaded. "What arrangements?"

"For school, son," Jackson said, beaming. "Your grandmother and I have been corresponding with the headmaster of Phillips Academy in Andover—that's where I went to school, you know, and you're to start next month."

"I won't go," Sonny said.

"You will." Grace replied.

"You've gotten as good an education here as possible so far, but you must have a few years in school before you can enter Harvard," Jack said, not realizing that this wasn't the time for logical explanations.

"I won't go away," Sonny repeated, his voice beginning to rise as he realized that any plan endorsed by both Grace and his father—who seldom agreed on anything—was impossible to defeat.

"I'll go with you," Laura offered.

"You can't," Jackson said. "It's a boys' school."

"There must be a girls' school near it, then. I could go there and Sonny and I could see each other a lot."

"Laura-bunny, there's no need for you to go away," Grace said.

"There's no need for me to go either!" Sonny shouted.

Laura noticed that Evelyn was wringing her hands as she finally spoke. "Sonny, don't speak that way," she said, her voice near breaking. "It's the necessary thing. All young men of your class must be properly educated."

"*No!*" Sonny yelled, running from the room.

"He'll come around," Jackson said. "Be the best thing for him. Make a man of him. Laura, stop that sniffling!"

Howard Lee had been out making calls that evening and found a note on the door to his room when he got back. Responding to the request in the note, he went to Grace's room. "Is something wrong?" he asked.

"Oh, Howard, I was getting worried about you being so late. Yes, as a matter of fact, there is something wrong." She explained about the men in the library and the discussion the family had had earlier.

"Melvin Purvis! That's a marvelous plan."

"You think it will work?"

"I'm sure of it. They talk a little more openly around you than around me, you know. I've heard his name a lot. Threatening that he's coming here ought to clear the place out like a bomb!"

"And what about you?"

Howard strolled over and sat on the window seat, stretching his legs out in a gesture that reminded Grace of Jack. It was a measure of the very real friendship that had survived between them that he could be so comfortable alone in her room with her. "What about me? What have I got to do with it?"

"Well, we—the family—are prepared to yank the rug out from under ourselves financially by emptying the hotel. But it doesn't seem fair to do so without warning you."

"Warning me? Oh, I see. You think I'll starve!"

"No, I was afraid you'd leave."

"I'm not going to do either. Not unless you throw me out with the guests."

"Howard, I wish you'd stop being so flip! This is serious!"

"Of course it is, but you're just looking for extra things to worry about. There's no need. I've maintained my local practice, you know, while treating your guests. So long as you leave me a roof over my head and feed me at fairly regular intervals, I'll have no reason to leave unless you want me to."

"You know I'll never want that."

He stood up then, and took her hands in his. "It's worked out well, hasn't it, Grace? For us, I mean."

"Does that mean your broken heart has healed?" she asked with exaggerated lightness.

"Completely! Well, Grace dear, I'm tired and had best get along to bed."

She stared at the door as he closed it behind himself and then said, "Dammit!" But as she got ready for bed, she started laughing at herself.

Sonny never "came around" to the idea of boarding school, but he did go away to Andover on schedule. He put up a valiant fight with Laura at his side every step of the way, but there was no hope of reprieve. Laura found herself wondering once or twice if Gram was really sending him for the reasons she gave or whether it was simply to get him out of the house, but that seemed such a traitorous and cynical thought that she couldn't maintain it.

The day after the family conference, Grace and Jack staged their "Melvin Purvis Act," and it worked magnificently. Within an hour four parties of guests had hurriedly left. By nightfall only two remained and they were gone at first light. Later that morning Grace faced her most perceptive critic. Big Al came to see her.

"Miz Thorne, you shouldn't otta've invited Purvis here," he said, more in sorrow than in anger.

"Invite? I didn't invite him," Grace replied evenly. She'd been putting paperwork into order at the front desk and Laura was there helping her straighten up. Laura crouched down and pretended to be cleaning out a bottom drawer for fear her own face would give away whatever lies her Grandmother was going to have to tell. "I had no idea who he was," Grace went on, "until everyone started leaving and I asked my cousin Edmund what was wrong."

Big Al harrumphed. "Well, I done what I could to help you out, but you understand I can't send any of my friends here anymore."

"I do, and I'm deeply sorry"—How can she say that and sound so much like she means it? Laura wondered—"but there's nothing I can do about it now. If I refused him admittance, he'd surely sense something amiss."

Laura spent the rest of the day roaming the nearly empty halls. The maids were still at work, though many of them, of necessity, would soon be laid off until new guests started coming—if they did start coming. The adults—Grace, Adele, Edmund, and Jackson, at any rate—were in the library all day, making plans for further changes. Evelyn had taken her lap desk and deck chair to a shady spot on the grounds to resume her communication with old friends who might, this time, be persuaded to come as paying visitors. India was busy cleaning out the tackier gifts from her shop, now that she no longer had to stock the flashy trash the gangsters and their women had so liked. "Do you want to help me, honey?" she'd said, seeing Laura's glum, displaced look.

"No, not unless you need me."

"Not a bit. You're looking for Sonny, aren't you?"

Laura nodded.

India leaned close, her ylang-ylang scent nearly choking Laura. "If you won't tell, I can guess where he might be. Agreed? Look down by the spring."

"We're not allowed to go there," Laura said.

" 'Allowed' and 'done' aren't always the same thing, honey. And if you tell your Gram that I said anything about this, I'll deny it."

"Thanks, India."

As India predicted, Sonny was at the spring. "We're not supposed to be here," Laura repeated, suddenly thinking how priggish she sounded.

Though Sonny had gone to brood, he'd had the foresight to bring along a bag of stale bread and was lethargically feeding a flock of ducks. "Yeah? So what? How's Gram going to punish me—send me away?"

"She'll have to send me away too," Laura offered.

"Like hell!"

"No, I'm going to convince her. If India will take me to the library tomorrow, I can look up a girls' school near you where I can go."

Sonny lobbed a bit of bread over the ducks' heads, causing them to back up. "You're being a baby-brain, Laura. She'll never let you go. Anywhere. It's kinda funny—you wanting to go places and not getting to, and me wanting to stay and being sent off."

"They say it's for your own good. I don't see how—"

"It's for everybody else's good. Mama can tell her hoity-toity friends I'm in a good school. Dad can convince himself I'm becoming a 'man'—why can't he understand that I can't play football or traipse all over the damned woods when I'm having trouble with my asthma? And Gram will have you all to herself."

"What do you mean?"

"Oh, Laura, don't be so dumb. That's her main reason for getting rid of me. When people around here take sides, you always take mine. Don't you know how she hates that? Her dear Laura-bunny, in the enemy camp—"

"Now you're being stupid! Gram's not your enemy. She loves you just as much as she loves me," Laura said, knowing as the words tumbled out what a lie they were. She'd never realized it before—not consciously. Gram would do anything to protect, defend, and provide for Sonny, but she didn't love him.

Laura dug into the sack of bread crumbs so Sonny wouldn't see the tears that had come to her eyes. "Mama loves you more than me. So does Dad."

"Yeah, I guess they do," Sonny said with the bluntness that was common coin between them.

Laura tossed a few bread crusts before saying, "So? What are you going to do?"

"I'm going away to school, of course. I'm only fifteen. I can't win."

"It'll only be for a while—"

"Years and years. God! How I hate this! We'll both be grown up by the time I come back. And everything will change."

"You'll be back. Summers. Christmas. And you'll make lots of new friends," Laura said, determined to make him happy, or at least less miserable.

"I don't want lots of friends."

Laura got to her feet. "Then I'll just have to persuade Gram to let me go too. I'll do it. You'll see."

"It'll never happen, Laura. She's afraid she'll lose you if she ever lets you go away. You might learn to love other people. Depend on other people besides her."

"That's not true!" Laura said, turning away.

But it was true. And it was the germinal stage of Laura's realization that Sonny—whatever his failings—would always understand more about human nature than she did. Laura did everything she could in the limited time available to convince her parents and grandmother to send her away to school near Sonny. When reason failed, she tried pleading, nagging, bribes, and crying. India, whose opinion didn't count anyway, was on her side. "I think she should be allowed to go. My years at Foxcroft were simply heaven! Some of my best memories." No one paid the least attention.

Evelyn, in a fit of irritation, finally said, "Oh, for Lord's sake, let her go! I cannot bear this carrying on."

To which Jackson replied stiffly. "We can't afford it. Not two of them at once. Besides, what need has a girl for an expensive Eastern education? You were educated at home, Evelyn. Most women are."

Evelyn shrugged, her interest already absorbed in what she would wear to dinner.

But Grace was adamant. "I need you here, Laura-bunny. To help me out when I get back from this trip. Besides, you've always had excellent tutors. No school could have a better teacher than your uncle Edmund."

Grace had to work hard at not saying what her heart was crying out: You can't leave me, Laura! You're the reason for my life. The purpose of my days. The joy of my existence. I'll have to part with you someday. I know that. But not so soon. Not now. I'm not ready yet. But she knew that to express that sort of love would be frightening and overwhelming and so she kept aloof and firm and gave cold practical reasons in place of the passionate truth.

And after each round, Laura retreated—defeated and relieved. She was becoming dimly aware that hers was an unnaturally sheltered existence, which was the reason she wanted to get away and also the reason she was terrified lest Gram eventually give in to her demands. For all her vivid imagination, Laura couldn't really picture life anywhere else. Here she was surrounded by adults who'd known her all her life and cared about every detail of her life. Even her parents, who didn't feel the affection for her they did for her twin, were concerned with her welfare.

A world of strangers, people who cared nothing for her or—worse yet—disliked her, was horrible to contemplate. Strangers were, in her mind, like the people at the revival. A faceless mob who might absorb nand crush her if she stood between them and their own interests.

So her pleas had a tidal quality—sometimes heartbreakingly sincere, other times perfunctory and half-afraid she'd get what she was asking. And in the end it made no difference. On a bright Monday morning the whole family piled into the big car to take Grace and Sonny to the train station. Howard Lee was going with them as far as St. Louis, where he was interviewing a young medical graduate who was interested in joining him in his practice. Grace would go on to

Massachusetts and see Sonny settled in school, then continue her mysterious trip.

When the others had waved them away, they got back into the car. Jack drove, with Evelyn beside him. Edmund and Adele were in the middle seat and India and Laura were crammed together at the back. India put her arm around Laura and said, "It's hard to tell who looks saddest. Sonny, of course, but I think Grace was nearer tears than she'd want us to know. And you, honey—why, you're a mess." She leaned closer. "I bought a henna hair rinse yesterday we can try on you. Your grandmother will be gone long enough for it to wash out."

Laura made herself smile at this, but it was an effort. This day marked, she sensed, the end of a part of her life. How could things ever be the same without Sonny?

XVII

GRACE had left specific instructions for changes that were to be made during her absence. Odd things, Laura thought, like putting up the hardware for attaching small name cards to the doors. The front desk was to be dismantled—"so it doesn't look like a hotel," Grace had said.

To which Laura replied, "But, Gram, it *is* a hotel."

"Of course, bunny, but we don't want to remind people of it. Our new guests will prefer to pretend they're staying in a private house."

Just who were these new people going to be? Laura wondered. And why would they want to pretend something that wasn't true?

After a few weeks, reservations began to trickle in for the coming spring. "Look at the family name on this one," India said, pushing a letter across the table at Adele. "I knew their cousins at boarding school. Really fine family. I wonder how Grace did it?"

The truth of the matter didn't come out until months later.

In the meantime, Laura got through the loneliest winter of her life. She had three calendars in her room, just so the passing of each day meant getting to cross it off three times. Edmund's morning lessons were augmented by afternoon lessons in math and science with a man from Hot Springs who lived in the cottage for the winter.

The climate itself seemed to be a reflection of the dismal frame of mind Laura was in. One day in early November, she woke with a dry cough and noticed that the windows of her room seemed grimy. Later that afternoon she stood on the porch with the rest of the family and shivered at the sight of the first great dust storm of the thirties rolling toward them. At first it was only a gray rim on the horizon; an hour later it was a towering brownblack cloud engulfing the land.

"Lordie, Lordie," Mabelann said, holding a handkerchief over her nose, "looks like 'most half a Oklahoma done picked itself up and come here."

It continued to pour in for days—long twilight days when they had to leave the lights on inside the house at noon. The dust sifted in on everything. Hair felt gritty an hour after washing. A glass set on a nightstand left a clear ring minutes later. The autumn foliage, usually such a joyful sight this time of year, turned drab with dust.

They put tape around all the cracks in the windows and put sheets over the best furniture. Adele covered the fireplace openings with oiled brown paper, but still the dust—as ubiquitous as the air—seeped in. They breathed it, they ate it, it covered the floors, their books, their plates. It got under beds and fingernails. Bedspreads, bathwater, and biscuits turned gritty brown. It sifted into cupboards, closets, socks, and most of all, their spirits. If they had known then that this horror would recur for years to come, they might have all gone mad with it.

On the eighteenth, they had a birthday party for Laura. "Chocolate icing, honey, so the dirt don't show," Mabelann said. It was an evening of forced gaiety, everyone trying to make Laura forget that it was her first birthday away from Sonny. Grace arranged a long-distance telephone call to him, but the study-hall proctor wouldn't allow Sonny to come to the phone. Laura went to bed stiff and red-eyed and even forgot to bring her presents up to her room.

It seemed years until Sonny got to come home for Christmas vacation. It was an unsatisfactory visit all around. The very brightness of the anticipation withered the actuality. Laura wanted to hear all about his school and new friends. That was the single thing he didn't want to talk about. "I've gotten away from the damned place, Laura, don't keep harping on it!"

"But you must have met all sorts of interesting people. The boys in your classes—"

"They're a bunch of boring rich brats. Tell me everything that's happened here."

But there wasn't much to tell. "Aunt Adele cut her finger on a carving knife and we had to drive her to Eureka Springs to get stitches," she offered.

"Yeah, I know. But what else have I missed?"

"Not very much," Laura said, trying desperately to think of something interesting to tell him. But all the interesting things seemed to have gone out of life with the departure of Sonny and the gangsters.

When he went back to school, grim and sullen about having to leave, Laura still knew next to nothing about the life he had away from her. She spent a whole week barely speaking to her parents and grandmother as a protest against their sending Sonny back to school. They appeared not to notice. But Laura was crushed with disappointment. She'd looked forward to Christmas for months because Sonny was going to come home and things would be as they always were. Instead, he'd been half-angry the whole time, like a sulky stranger. She felt a terrible fear that something important that bound them together had been severed.

Grace came to her room late one night in January. "You're not speaking to me, bunny?" she said, sitting down on the side of the bed.

Her voice was so soft and understanding that Laura forgot all her resolve and threw herself into her grandmother's arms. "Oh, Gram!" she wept. "Everything's changed. Sonny doesn't love me anymore . . ."

Grace patted her head. "Of course he does. You know how silly that is. He's just having trouble growing up and getting used to changes, and so are you. You'll see. Everything will be fine when he comes back this summer. I promise. You both just expected too much of this vacation and there wasn't time enough to get over the disappointment and appreciate how things really are."

"Why can't Sonny stay here?"

"Oh, bunny, we've been over that before. He must get a good education and he needs to get it under disciplined surroundings. You are quite able to learn from Edmund and the tutors we've hired over the years. Sonny needs a little more. He needs to be away from all of us to learn."

For all the intensity of Sonny's belief that Grace simply wanted to be rid of him, he was wrong. In those moments when she was being brutally honest with herself, Grace had to admit that life was a little easier in some ways with him gone, but she was sincere in her belief that he needed to get away from Thornehill for his own good. The Depression had proved that life could be turned upside down for no good reason. Sonny had to have some preparation for making his own way if he had to, and he would never learn about competition at Thornehill. That was the best part of their life—the lack of competitiveness between family members. And yet it was, she felt, necessary to know how to fight for what you wanted.

"He doesn't want to be away from us."

"I know that. But you're old enough to realize that what we want isn't always what's best for us. You didn't want to take all those piano lessons when you were a little girl, but look how much you enjoy playing now."

"But that's different."

"Not very," Grace said, smoothing back Laura's hair. "You must trust your parents and me to know what's best. I know that isn't easy when you're young."

She paused, smiling at Laura as she lay back and wiped her eyes with the backs of her hands. "Shall I tell you what I did on my trip east? It's a very embarrassing example of doing what you have to do even if you don't like it."

"Oh, yes, Gram. Please tell me," Laura replied. The household had been rife with wonder about Grace's mysterious trip and she'd never offered any explanations to anyone.

"Well, I made reservations at several very fancy hotels where the wealthy go to vacation. First I spent a few days at each place looking at how things were done—how many maids there were and how the rooms were furnished and such. Then I started a sort of acting job."

"Acting?"

"Well, lying, actually. I'd make friends with people who seemed to travel a great deal and I'd urge them to tell me about the different places they'd stayed. I pretended I knew about them too. And then, after they'd talked for a long time, I'd say, 'Well, of course nothing I've seen holds a candle to Thornehill.' They'd ask what that was, of course, and I'd say, 'Oh, I'd have thought you'd be familiar with it. Of course, it's terribly exclusive . . .' That would get their backs up. You know, as though they thought: If she's good enough to stay there, what makes her think *I'm* not! I'd go on and on about how it's not like a vulgar hotel at all. That you feel just like a guest in a private house when you stay there—"

"But, Gram!"

"I know. What's going to happen when they get here and find out that that snooty woman who told them all about it actually runs the place!" Grace leaned back, looking both sheepish and a bit proud.

"Are they going to be angry?"

"They might be, but they can't turn around and go right away and by the time they've been here a day they'll know that everything I said about Thornehill is true. Besides, I don't think most of them will remember or recognize me. You see, I dressed for the part. I bought a number of terribly fancy hats. There's nothing like a showy hat to make people fail to notice your face. And I used my maiden name."

Suddenly Laura had a mental picture of her grandmother dolled up in one of India's flamboyant hats, simpering that she was Miss Emerson of Virginia. She started giggling and so did Grace. They got louder and louder until finally Adele opened the door and said, "The rest of the household would really like to get some sleep!"

"Sorry, dear, but Laura and I were telling secrets. We'll be quiet now. I promise." Grace said. She sounded like a girl herself.

Adele went away, readjusting a pin curl and shaking her head over the strange relationship between the child and her grandmother.

The late-winter months went more quickly than the fall. Everyone was living in anticipation of the reopening of the hotel. All signs of the gangsters were eliminated and small elegant touches were added. One particularly fascinated Laura and seemed to epitomize the changes. Jackson designed a family-crest symbol and had it cast on an openwork metal plate, like a trivet. It had a handle on the back and became the property of Mabelann's brother-in-law, Nathan. His job, when the hotel opened, was to keep constant watch on the ashtray stands that were placed throughout the house. They were filled with pristine white sand which he would wash every few days. In the meantime he would keep ashes and cigarette butts sifted out and press the trivet into the sand several times a day to imprint the fake family crest.

One of Laura's jobs was to help Adele sew hundreds of "lemon caps," little muslin hats with elastic edges to place over the cut side of a lemon so it could be squeezed without squirting anyone in the eye or dropping seeds into the food. "Why can't they just pick out the seeds with a fork like we do?" she asked.

In late April guests started arriving. True to her prediction, or perhaps too discreet to mention it, none of them appeared to recognize Grace as the behatted Virginia spinster who had recommended the hotel. "How nice to see you," Adele or

Grace or India would say to people as the chauffeured car brought them from the railroad station. "We hoped you'd have nice weather for your trip. So uncertain this time of year. We've put you in the green suite with the west view, if that suits you?" they'd say, just as if they were old family friends who were, naturally, quite familiar with the house.

It had been decided early to knock many of the individual bedrooms together into suites. "We'll charge them six times as much for three times the room our 'previous guests' used to have," Grace had said, referring as always to the gangsters in euphemism. "These are the sort of people who feel it isn't good enough for them unless they're being robbed blind."

India grinned. "We used to be of them—all of us. Now it's 'us' describing 'them.' How things change!" It seemed to Laura that India was glad of the change.

Another radical change was in the eating arrangements. There would be nothing so common and hotellike as a restaurant or menu or—God forbid!—mention of money in connection with food. An enormous banquet table was set up where family and guests would eat together every night. Since they were charging so much of fewer guests, it was possible to put all the visitors and one or two of the family members (on a rotating schedule) at the dining table.

"What if someone doesn't like what we're having for dinner?" Laura asked.

"There'll be at least two choices for each course," India explained. "If they don't like any of it, they can suck on the lemon caps."

The illusion that this was a private home was kept up in every possible way. The "DOCTOR" sign came down from the door of the room Howard used. Instead, he opened, with his new assistant from St. Louis, a small office in town where he went three mornings a week. He still lived at Thornehill and still treated guests who were in need of medical care, but he lived as a guest and their treatment was discreetly tacked onto their bill at the end of their stay.

The maids left printed cards in each room during dinner listing the activities that would be available for participation the next day. "Picnic luncheon by the spring—one o'clock in the afternoon," they would say, or, "Car going into town for shopping—ten o'clock in the morning." At least once a week the cards announced charades after dinner or dancing ("black tie") or a bridge tournament. And the family was required to attend.

For the most part, this requirement was a treat that made all the work behind the scenery worthwhile. Evelyn, who had retired to her room and hardly been seen in the hiatus, was completely in her element. Many of the guests were in fact friends of hers, women she'd known as a girl in New York, or distant relatives. And she had no trouble pretending that they were truly houseguests. Jackson, too, enjoyed the companionship of men whose background was like his and who could talk endlessly of horses and hunting and the more respectable sports, like polo.

India learned early on, through the gossip, that the stockbroker who'd been so eager to recoup her stock losses and the lawyer who represented him had been apprehended in an extremely shady attempt to manipulate the market and had fled the country the year before. "I feel like I've been let out of jail!" she told Grace exultantly. "I've been living in dread of it all catching up with me."

Adele was happy, too. Her duties in keeping the staff on their toes were mammoth—just the way she liked things to be. The more harassed she was, the pinker her cheeks and brighter her eyes. She had dozens of girls in crisp black-and-white maid's uniforms to supervise, and a chef ("No, Laura, you must never call him a cook. He might quit!") to consult with several times a day.

One evening after dinner while they all sat on the flagstone terrace behind the library, Adele said, "I think I was born into the wrong time or place or class or something. I should have been a general or housekeeper in a castle or—"

"Or you should have been born a man," Grace said softly. "Men are expected to manage people."

"Boss them, you mean?" Edmund asked wryly.

Edmund, too, was finding much to his liking. Though he had found the gangsters interesting simply because they were so utterly foreign to his previous experience, he was finding mental stimulation aplenty in the current crowd of visitors, thanks to Grace.

She had indulged herself in her choice of victims when she played her Virginia-spinster act. Besides the purely wealthy, she had made the acquaintance of a number of artistic and intellectual individuals. Several minor poets and painters were among the guests in those first months and she had even set aside a room with a good light for the artists to use if they wanted.

Only Laura was less than delighted with the alteration in clientele. These people were—although she wouldn't have thought to use the word—brittle. The women were terribly thin and anemic and had an air of overbred horsiness that was very different from the healthy. straightforward vulgarity of the gangsters' women. Whereas skepticism used to be expressed with wide-open mascaraed eyes and a "Shit, Harry, ya' don't mean it!" now the same emotion was expressed by the delicate flare of a nostril and a chilly "Oh?"

The men were either chunky and bland or downright effeminate in their arch wittiness. Most of them seemed, for reasons Laura couldn't define, vaguely sad—as if having money and leisure had somehow deprived them of something else. She mentioned this to Uncle Edmund. "It has, my dear. It's deprived them of the need to excel. There is no point to their days, no destination to their lives. What incentive is there to earn a million dollars when you already have sixteen million?"

"But you grew up with lots of money. You're not like that."

"I'm an exception. My family flirted with the idea of disinheriting me when I chose to teach. They kept carrying on about how I didn't need to. They failed to grasp that I needed employment for reasons that had nothing to do with income. I needed a reason to get up in the morning."

That made Laura proud. She was now part of his reason for getting up in the morning. At the same time, it saddened her, because although neither of them had mentioned it, they both knew they were defining Jackson. He was a middle-aged man with no core or direction, and the same disquieting sadness that his friends showed.

There was something else that made Laura uncomfortable about these people. They seemed to universally hate the President—"that man!" as they often referred to Roosevelt.

"He's a traitor to his class!" was their most frequent and damning complaint. "Printing all that money and giving it away to the riffraff. I swear to you, a man came to the estate last week taking some sort of historical survey. I started asking him some questions and found out that he was actually *employed* by the government to write some sort of book. I ask you!"

"The next thing you know, the government will start handing out money to niggers and Jews just for being niggers and Jews!" someone once said at the dinner table.

There was a chorus of laughter and agreement. Laura

glanced at her grandmother and saw how thin and white Grace's lips had become. *She wants to tell them what we think of that kind of talk and can't because we need their money,* Laura realized, and for the first time she sensed what it really meant to Gram to have to turn her home into a hotel. It made her feel sick and cold inside.

It almost came to a head one night when a woman from Connecticut, a woman who wore a wig and false teeth and bottle-bottom glasses, said, "Well, I can say with a clear conscience that I never have and never will vote for that cripple in the White House. They keep saying it was polio, but everyone knows it was syphilis. And that terrible Eleanor! Why, she's about the homeliest busybody I've ever seen."

"I think I smell something burning!" Grace said, suddenly getting up and leaving the room.

Laura followed her and caught up with her in the kitchen garden, where Grace was walking back and forth muttering to herself. Laura fell into step with her.

"Oh, bunny, bunny!" Grace said, then bent and pulled up a weed and flung it away. "I sometimes think you might be better off learning to be a jug-marker."

XVIII

LAURA was reminded again of their former guests in late May. The newspaper headlines blared, "BONNIE AND CLYDE SHOT TO DEATH IN LOUISIANA!" Reading the article avidly at first, Laura was sickened to discover that Bonnie Parker was only twenty-four years old and had been nibbling on a sandwich when twenty-three bullets tore through her body. Laura remembered the day Gram had found her and Sonny "playing" Bonnie and Clyde in the barn. She wondered now how she could have ever considered such things joyful.

When Sonny came home for the summer, things were better between them, just as Grace had promised. This time, Laura had things to tell him, amusing stories to relate, people to point out. And he, too, had made some adjustments. "I was a real bastard at Christmas, Laura. I'm sorry," he said. "I just hated Mother and Dad and Gram so much for sending me to that place that it sort of sloshed over onto you."

"Do you like it better now?" she asked, suddenly uncomfortable. She didn't like having Sonny apologize to her.

"No, the place is rotten, but I've made some friends now and it's better."

"Who are they? Tell me about them," Laura said, a funny jealous feeling stirring slightly. As much as she'd hoped he'd make friends, she now feared they might somehow impinge upon their own closeness.

"Well, the best of them is a fella named Eric. He's a really good sort, Laura. You'd like him. He's poor like we are. You know, poor-but-not-poor. His dad's family is big stuff in Germany, with gobs of money, but Eric's folks came to this country in the war and don't have much to do with them. He hates sports like I do, but he's big and good at stuff and older, so nobody picks on him. And since he's my friend, nobody picks as much on me either. I'm gonna see if he can come visit us. You'll like him. Laura, why are you looking so sour?''

The summer passed quickly, far too quickly. Sonny and Laura had fun being children, truly children, for the last time. In a vague way, they knew this was a summer that would never happen again, and all the delight and silliness was tinged with a feeling both bittersweet and exciting. They would be sixteen on their next birthday—only their second birthday apart.

Sonny got along with Grace those months by avoiding her. Only once did they have a run-in and it turned out to have a very different effect than anyone could have anticipated. Once again the newspaper headlines screamed death. This time it was John Dillinger, ''Public Enemy Number One.''

''He looks different somehow,'' Sonny said casually of the photograph in the paper. Grace drew in a quick breath. They were on the front steps and several guests were talking over the headline.

''What do you mean?'' a man in golfing plaids asked.

Sonny, still unaware of the import of what he was saying, explained, ''Well, when he was here he seemed heavier.''

''Here! He stayed *here*?'' the man asked.

Before Grace could intervene, a woman who'd been listening called to a friend in the drive, ''Sylvia! Darling, come hear this. John Dillinger actually stayed here! Isn't that exciting? Imagine!'' She turned to Grace. ''Was he terribly wicked and interesting? Did he have a 'gun moll' with him? How utterly fascinating!''

To the family's astonishment, these people regarded the former presence of public enemies as ''too, too chic'' and begged endlessly for accounts of Ma Barker, Baby Face Nelson, and the rest of the thugs Grace had turned out the year before. Grace was stunned by this turn of events. ''They wouldn't be so impressed if they were still here,'' she said.

''But they're not still here, so make the best of it.'' India advised, rather more sensibly than anyone would have expected of her. ''Let them suppose it's part of the glamorous history of the house and don't mention the truth of how nasty and frightening they really were.''

About the time Laura and Sonny had regained all their

former closeness, resumed their former finishing-each-other's-sentences rapport, and discovered where they could escape the guests and be themselves, it was time for him to go back to school. This time it wasn't quite such a wrench. He didn't go eagerly by any means, but at least he wasn't fighting it every inch of the way. Nor was Laura as resentful of his departure. Most of her fears had been allayed. They could be apart, and their "twinship" could survive the parting.

This was proved the second Christmas he came home. This time they were instantly comfortable with each other. But the next summer, the summer of 1935, there was a change that took some getting used to. While Laura had, in feminine fashion, grown up gradually, Sonny grew up suddenly. He went to school in January a knobby, squeaky-voiced boy, with hands, feet, and head that looked too big. But he came back in May transformed into a young man. He'd grown an astonishing four inches that looked more like a foot. His shoulders had become broader, his voice deeper, his face fuller and lightly whiskered.

It was like getting back an individual that was, and yet wasn't, quite familiar. Instead of looking at him eye to eye, Laura had to look up to meet his gaze. He had gained a measure of self-confidence, too, that was strange to behold. It was evident in his long easy stride and wry wit. Even Grace, who had always been able to reduce him nearly to tears with a criticism, had lost the ability to intimidate him. "Now, Gram," he'd say, grinning, "you know you don't mean that. You're just trying to make me mad, and it won't do. It simply won't do." Several times he had her nearly sputtering with frustration when she tried to explain the error of his ways to him. "I've got to remember to thank Eric for telling me to try that," he confided to Laura.

One of the first things he did was get a visit set up for his friend. "His name is Eric and he's just graduated this year," he told his grandmother. "His folks have to go to Alaska in August for some sort of business and I'd like him to come stay here while they're gone. Is that all right?"

"I don't see why not," Grace replied. "We always have some extra rooms late in the summer. Have your mother correspond with his parents and arrange it. I'm glad to see you're making friends at school."

Grace was, however, less glad when Eric arrived.

Laura went to the train station with Sonny to pick him up.

"You're gonna like him, Laura. He's a great fella," he repeated for what seemed the thousandth time.

She waited in the car while Sonny went to fetch his friend off the train. She had a clear and rather jaundiced mental image of this Eric paragon. She knew he was a couple years older—he'd just graduated from high school and had missed a year early on due to illness. He was probably rather shy and inclined to nervousness, like Sonny.

But the young man who swung down from the train platform was a surprise. He was of average height with an athletic build that was oddly at variance with his thin, aesthetic face. He had streaked blond hair, a golden tan, and even from this distance his eyes were a startling pale blue—the sort of eyes that seem to see through secrets. He carried a big old-fashioned suitcase and a battered wooden paintbox. He set both down to shake hands with Sonny. As Laura watched, they talked a moment; then Sonny pointed toward the car. Eric nodded and gathered up his gear.

When he reached the car, he peered in the passenger-side window at Laura as though looking over an exhibit of some sort and then burst into speech. His voice was very deep. "Good God! Look at what a beauty you are! Sonny has talked about you until I thought I'd go mad. According to him, you're the most intelligent, sensible, loyal, and altogether wonderful sister in the world, but the ass never mentioned that you've got the best facial structure I've ever seen. Look at that serene half-smile, Sonny! If Da Vinci had known Laura Thorne . . ."

But it wasn't serenity Laura was feeling, it was utter confusion. First, there was the realization that Sonny talked to Eric about her just as he talked endlessly to her about Eric. That was a true salve to her hurt feelings. Second, and more important at the moment, this was the most compelling young man she'd ever met—not that she'd known many young men. His charm and effusive flattery washed over her like a tidal wave, knocking her flat. She felt the need to gasp for air.

"See, didn't I tell you you'd love him?" Sonny said, grinning as though he could read her mind. "Let's throw your things in the back, Eric, and buzz along to Thornehill."

Laura sat in the middle with Sonny driving and the overwhelming Eric on her right. He stared at her profile all the way back, commenting occasionally on her—according to him—astonishing features. "The essence of femininity," he said, "I'll bet you couldn't look cranky or small-minded if you tried. You will let me draw you, won't you, Miss Thorne?"

"Please, call me Laura," she said breathlessly.

"Oh, I am glad. Does that mean we're to be friends? I hope so. Sonny's made me feel that being your friend is a great honor, and now I can see he's right."

"Do you really think she's pretty?" Sonny asked, turning for a moment to peer at Laura. She felt like a biology experiment.

She went with them when Eric was taken to the library to be introduced to Grace. "Gram, this is my friend Eric from school," Sonny said.

Grace looked up from the ledger she'd been working on. Smiling warmly, she said, "I'm very pleased you could visit us, Eric. Sonny's been looking forward to having you here for a long time."

"Thank you, ma'am. I'm pleased to be here."

"I see you have a paintbox along. Are you an aspiring artist?"

"Much more 'aspiring' than 'artist,' ma'am. But I did get a scholarship to the Chicago Art Institute, so they must have had some hope that I could learn."

"How nice for you, Eric—I don't believe Sonny told me your last name."

"VonHoldt, ma'am."

All the warmth suddenly went out of Grace's eyes. "VonHoldt?"

"Do you know the name, ma'am? Perhaps you've met my parents, Rachel and George?"

"No, I don't believe so," Grace said. Her heart was beating in great alarmed thuds. How could the sound of a name do that to her? But that name—oh, what that name meant!

"Well, you might have heard about VonHoldt Armaments."

"I think I have. A German firm."

"Yes, run by Frederich VonHoldt. He's a second cousin or great-uncle or something. My folks don't talk about him much. They severed their ties with Germany and the family when they came over here just before the war."

Of course you're related to him, Grace thought bitterly. That thin face, those pale eyes, the hair, even the stance. Dear God, the times I've seen you in my nightmares, the times I've feared I've seen you in my son. Why don't they all know? Why isn't Sonny saying something tactless about how much his friend looks like his own father? Can't they see it? Pray to God they can't!

She realized he'd stopped talking and was waiting for her response. "It's nice to have you here, Eric," she said in a perfunctorily polite way. "Now, you boys better get ready for dinner. You can show your friend around after that, Sonny."

Laura hung back, and when the door had closed, said, "Gram, don't you like Eric?"

"I don't know him well enough to like or dislike him, Laura," she said curtly. "Now, run along."

"Gram, is something wrong?" Grace's face was pale and her manner strangely cold.

"Nothing is wrong, dear. Run along."

Eric VonHoldt's visit was not only the high point of the summer, but the high point of Laura's life so far. His charm, which in an older man might have been affected, was sincere. He was delighted to be at Thornehill. He found the family fascinating, the house magnificent, the grounds beautiful, and he said so, often.

Edmund declared him "an unusually bright boy." Adele found him "clean and polite." India, who had gone back to noticing "auras," proclaimed that his was positively glittering with promise. He knew enough about hunting to get along with Jackson, and his manners were so impeccable that Evelyn doted on him. Only Grace seemed utterly immune to his virtues. Not that she was ever rude to him; in fact, she treated him with a frigid courtesy that made Laura furious.

It was the only way Grace could keep from showing that she was terrified of him. This one seemingly harmless boy seemed to be standing at the very foundation of her life and was unknowingly planting the dynamite that could bring it down in rubble. Every time she looked at him, she was frightened by the similarities she could see and wondered why they weren't glaringly obvious to everyone else. She was counting the days until he'd leave. Knowing it was unreasonable, unfair, unkind, she despised Eric VonHoldt.

Laura was, of course, madly in love with him.

Fortunately, Sonny, who might have resented having his friend's attention and affection diverted to his twin sister. was delighted that Eric had so much interest in Laura. In fact, it was often he who threw them together. "If you're going to paint outdoors, why don't you take Laura along, Eric? She can show you some really nice views."

"Aren't you coming along?"

"Naw, I don't dare. I took apart Gram's favorite radio and I've got to get it back together before she notices. You two go on."

Laura accepted this sort of largess gratefully. She gave Eric a grand tour of the house, the grounds. the stables, the town of Eureka Springs, and, finally, the spring lake. "I don't think paint or ink could ever capture the tranquillity of this place," Eric said, leaning back on one elbow and munching on a ham sandwich from the picnic hamper they'd brought along. "I wonder how many other people have felt that way?"

"Sonny and I have always liked it here, but Gram wouldn't let us come by ourselves when we were young. She still doesn't much like us to come here. Dad says she had a sister who drowned and I guess it made her afraid of water," Laura replied, watching his handsome angular face.

"The Gorgon? Afraid? I can't believe it."

Laura stiffened. "Gorgon?"

"Oh, sorry. I forgot that you and she get along. I'm so accustomed to hearing about her from Sonny's view."

"She's different with Sonny," Laura said.

"I'll say. Why do you suppose that is?"

Laura looked out at the placid blue-green water. "I don't know. I've never understood it. Maybe it's that I'm a girl. It's always seemed strange and very sad that I could love Sonny and Gram and they both love me, but they don't much like each other. But then, Mother and Dad don't care for me as much as Sonny, so we figure it comes out even."

"No one who knew you could keep from loving you," Eric said, putting down the remains of his sandwich and taking her hand in his square strong one.

Laura's breath caught.

"You mustn't think Gram is mean to Sonny," she said, aware that she was babbling and unable to stop. "She loves him and wants the best for him, you know. They just can't seem to like each other very well. Just like Aunt Adele and India don't really like each other, but they love each other and are very loyal—"

"Loyalty means a lot to you, doesn't it, Laura?"

"Well . . . yes, I guess it does."

"Am I embarrassing you?"

"Yes . . . yes, you are."

"Well, I'm going to embarrass you a little more. Then I

promise to stop. I saw you with an artist's eye when I came here two weeks ago. To the artist, you were beautiful. A perfect arrangement of features, textures, colors. But since I've gotten to know you more, I'm looking at you as a man does. You're going to be an extraordinary woman someday, Laura Thorne. Extraordinary. You're honest without being tactless, loyal without being blind, sensitive without being 'precious—' "

Laura pulled her hand away. "Please, stop! You're making me sound perfect and I'm not any such thing."

"All right. I said I'd stop," he said, smiling fondly at her modest discomfiture. "Tell me all about this spring."

Laura's blush started to recede as she tried to remember all she'd ever heard about the history of the spring. "Well, they say the Indians used to come here . . ."

There was only one place Eric had not visited—the cottage. It was merely oversight, not design on Laura's part, though later she wondered if there was some mechanism of fate at work that she'd been unaware of.

Toward the end of August, when Eric had only a week of his stay left, he said, "I've got to walk that lunch off. Come with me, Sonny? Laura?"

"I can't," Sonny said with genuine regret. "I've got an appointment with Uncle Edmund to go over some math studies. He's afraid I've forgotten everything I learned last year and wants to send me back 'fully prepared to commence my work,' as he puts it. Why don't you two go down to the spring? There were some interesting ducks there yesterday. And, Laura, Eric says he's never seen the cottage."

"Yes, I thought I'd had the full tour but discover there's a place you left out," Eric said.

"I forgot about it. It's not very interesting. Just an old house. Last year my tutor lived there, but it's empty now."

"I need to do some architectural studies and I've already drawn the mansion from every angle imaginable," Eric said. "Lead me to this cottage."

"I'm afraid you'll be disappointed," Laura said later as they turned off the main drive onto the path.

"I'm with you. How could I be disappointed in anything?" Eric said, smiling. "Tell me about it."

"I don't know what there is to tell. Gram says it was here before my great-grandfather built the big house. Nobody knows who it belonged to first. It was vacant when I was little. Then, when the gangsters came to the hotel and Gram was afraid they were teaching Sonny and me terrible things, we moved down here for a year or two with India. That was a fun time for me. Sonny hated it because he wanted to be back in his room—''

"He told me. Your brother's an odd bird, Laura. Most of us want to get away from home at our age. Sonny wants nothing more than to stay home. I wonder why that—? Oh! Laura, is that it? What a place!''

Laura gazed at the cottage, trying to see why he was exclaiming over it. It was nice enough, and she had very fond memories of it, but what could a stranger see in it?

"Good Lord! It positively reeks of history, Laura. Can't you see that? Things have happened here. Someone built this with his own hands. Out of love, or duty, or vengeance— some strong emotion. It's obvious in the strength of the lines. Look at the craftsmanship of those logs!''

But Laura wasn't looking at the cabin, she was looking at him. His voice was low, almost reverent; his eyes were glowing. "I've never seen anyone look at a house this way—'' she began.

"Don't you feel it? Don't you see what I mean? No, of course not. It's too familiar to you. You've known the place all your life. It takes an outsider. Laura, this place says something to me. It has an aura—''

Laura giggled.

He looked at her for a moment, half-offended. "Oh, I get it. India's favorite word. Just the same, it *does* have a special air about it. May we go inside?''

"I guess so. It's not usually locked.''

"Wait! What's this in the grass?''

"A headstone, I think. It's been there forever.''

"Help me lift it up.''

"Lift it? It must weigh a ton!''

"No, it's thin. Look at the edge.''

Eric prevailed. Laura fetched a shovel to dig under the edges to get a purchase. After they hoisted it up and wedged it into place with rocks, she went for a bucket of water to wash down the face.

" 'Beloved Emily and Child,' '' Eric read. "I wonder who they were, this beloved Emily and her child. To think, they've lain here all this time, forgotten.''

Laura turned away, tears blurring her vision. She wasn't sure if she was sad about Emily or merely touched that Eric cared about the unknown pioneer woman. "Would you like to see the inside of the cottage now?'' she asked, her voice nearly cracking.

They went inside. "It's larger than you'd think from outside,'' Eric said. "It must extend back into the face of the cliff. Yes, feel this wall. It's cool. This is very nice, Laura. Which room was yours when you lived here?''

"This one with the white curtains at the window," she said, leading the way.

The room had been kept just as it was when they moved back to the mansion. The bed was even made up with fresh sheets, though no one had used it for a long time. Mabelann must come down here and clean from time to time, Laura realized. But her mind wasn't really on the room, it was still outside with the thin gray slab of headstone. Beloved Emily . . . Beloved Emily . . .

Eric was looking at the pictures on the walls, but Laura couldn't take in what he was saying. Was there anyone on this earth who remembered Emily? Anyone who could say: Oh yes, my great-great-aunt Emily . . .? Or was her whole being right out there? Suddenly Laura sat down on the edge of the bed, and to her surprise, tears started coursing down her face. "Poor Emily . . .'' she said softly.

Eric turned. "What did you . . .? Laura! What's wrong? Oh, Laura, I didn't mean to upset you with the headstone.'' He came quickly and sat beside her, putting his arm around her. "Laura, it's just a rock with an inscription. It doesn't mean anything.''

"But it does. It's all anyone knows of some poor woman who died here with her baby. Nobody cares. I didn't even care before. I've sat on that stone just like it was an ordinary rock—dozens of times! I never realized it meant there was a person under me. A person whose life ended and nobody cared—''

"But somebody cared, Laura. Cared a great deal. Do you know how hard it must have been to carve that stone? To get all those letters lined up so evenly? To chip out every one of them? That was a labor of love. Someone cared a great deal for Emily and the child.''

"Oh. Eric . . .'' Laura sobbed, burying her face in his shirt.

He wrapped his arms around her, patting her back, smoothing her disheveled hair. Then he kissed her temple. Once. Twice. Her arms, almost of their own volition, went around his waist and she drew back just enough to see his face. "I'm sorry," she said.

"For what?" he whispered. His breath was warm and sweet on her face.

"For being silly."

He ran one hand up her back to her neck. "You're not silly, Laura. Anything but silly . . ." The last word turned into a kiss.

His lips were soft, gentle as butterfly wings as they brushed so lightly, so tentatively against hers. "Beloved Laura," he whispered, pulling her closer.

Laura had seen movie kisses, imagined being in the embrace of a man, and wondered what it was like, but in none of her imaginings was it like this. This was real in a way that reality had never existed for her before. Her skin tingled where he touched her, and tingled more where he didn't. She suddenly wanted to be closer to him, though they were locked in an embrace. She could almost imagine they were part of one being, a cosmic "us-ness" she could feel but not define.

She wasn't aware that they'd fallen back across the bed until she realized that her shoes were off and her bare toes were rubbing against his shins. Her blouse had pulled loose and his hand was touching the skin at her waist. They were both wearing summer shorts and she could feel, with an awesome excitement, the hair of his legs softly against the smoothness of her own. And she could feel a hardness at the front of his shorts that made her want to push her pelvis against him.

What was this wonderful and terrifying feeling? It was love certainly, but not the sort of love she'd known all her life. This was a hunger, a sweet craving that half-frightened her; a power that made her nearly forget who and where and what she was. Was this what was meant by that heretofore meaningless word "passion"?

"Eric . . ." she murmured as his hand slipped upward, cupping her breast. "Ohhh . . ." Her head fell backward and he kissed her neck.

Suddenly a sound penetrated her steaming consciousness. "Miss Laura, what the hell you think you doing!"

Laura's body went cold, her mind froze.

Eric sat up quickly, dragging her along like a rag doll. Then, before Laura was fully aware of what was happening, Mabelann had grabbed her arm and pulled her to her feet. Her knees were shaking and she still had the phantom sense of Eric's hand, hot and firm, on her breast.

"You get youself back up to that house, missy, and straighten up them clothes and hair. You look like a whore who done had a bad night. I declare, if Miz Thorne had seed this, she'da whipped the stuffing outta you! I ain't sure Mr. Jackson ain't gonna take this boy out and shoot him!"

"Mabelann, it wasn't what you think—"

"What I *think*? Missy, I got eyes in my head. I seen that boy with his big ol' hand up your shirt and that man-bulge in his pants. I don't need no grass-green girl to tell me what I see."

Eric was on his feet now, his face flushed, but his manner relatively calm, under the circumstances. "If you're going to tell Laura's family about this, be sure you tell them it was entirely my fault. Laura had no idea—"

"No idea! And her writhin' round like—"

"Watch it!" Eric barked. "Watch what you say about Laura. She's an innocent and you well know it."

Mabelann was ever so slightly cowed by this. "Yes, I mind as she is. Knowed the child all my life, and she ain't never got near no man. But what Miz Thorne gonna think—"

"Mrs. Thorne isn't going to know about this. Nobody is," Eric said. "You and I are going to strike a bargain, Mabelann."

"Bargain?" Laura said weakly.

Eric paced the room, ferociously jamming his shirttail into his shorts. He didn't even look at her. "You know perfectly well that if you mention this to Laura's grandmother, Laura will be watched like a hawk for the next ten years. She's already almost a prisoner of that woman—"

"So?" Mabelann said, hands on hips. "Whatta you sayin'?"

"I'm saying I'm due to leave in a week anyway. I'll leave tonight instead."

"No!" Laura exclaimed.

He turned to her, heedless of the servant for a moment. "I have to go. I can't stay here and keep my hands off you, Laura. You're too young and innocent to know what that means now. You're a lovely hothouse flower in a rough world. Someday you'll understand."

"No, Eric, please don't go."

"Missy, he right. You ain't been around none to know what's goin' on here," Mabelann interrupted. "Aw right, boy, you get youself outta here tonight and I won't say nothing to Miz Thorne or Mr. Jackson 'bout this. Now, you scat on up to the house and get your things. Missy, you gonna stay here with me.''

Laura looked back at Eric. He smiled sadly and nodded. ''I'll go, Laura, but I'll come back someday. I promise.''

Laura threw herself back on the bed and sobbed, but Mabelann stood her ground. She'd waited out crying fits before and she could do it again. When Laura finally pulled herself together she said, ''That boy, he ain't gonna come back here—''

''Yes, he will. He promised! He'll be back!''

''If he do, you ain't gonna have nothin' to do with him, you hear?''

The rest of the family, less observant and far less devoted to and protective of Grace, had never seen the resemblance that haunted her during Eric's visit. But Mabelann, who had always sensed that Jackson wasn't Captain Jack's own blood child, had observed it. She'd been covertly watching Eric VonHoldt since the day he arrived, hoping to catch him out in something—anything—to use as a lever to remove him.

''Honey, has I ever told you a lie?'' she asked Laura, taking hold of her arm, just in case Laura considered flouncing away.

Laura sniffed. ''No.''

''Then I ain't tellin' you one now. That boy, he dangerous. Mighty dangerous. You can't go havin' nothin' to do with him. Never. Understand?''

''No! I don't understand. Dangerous? What are you talking about? What do you mean?''

''Ain't my place to say why. You just gotta take my word, 'cause it's true as true. Now, you run on back to the house and stay in your room till that boy done gone.''

Grace was weeding between two rows of carrots when Eric VonHoldt came up the path to the house. He was walking quickly, angrily, looking down at the ground. He didn't see her, but she sat back on her heels and watched him. She knew she had no right to hate him, especially when the rest of the family was so fond of him, but her long-festering humiliation had made it impossible to hear that name and see the shadow of those features without anger. Thank God Jack hadn't lived to see this boy in his house.

A few minutes later Laura passed. She, too, was angry. Her face was flushed and she appeared to be muttering to herself as she looked back over her shoulder at intervals. A hundred yards or so behind her, Mabelann strolled along, a thoroughly satisfied look on her face. She slowed to let Laura get inside as Grace gathered up her gardening gloves and padded knee board and intercepted her.

"What is this little parade, Mabelann?"

"Ain't nothin', Miz Grace. Jest been talkin' to that there boy. He goin' home tonight."

"Tonight? He wasn't due to leave for a week."

"He took into his mind to go sooner."

Grace stared at her a minute, then said, "Do you want to tell me why?"

"No, ma'am. I don't believe I do."

XIX

LAURA didn't see Eric VonHoldt again except as a blurred face in the front seat of the old Hispano-Suiza as it sped past the house on the way from the garages to the railway station. She never knew what explanation he gave for his hurried departure, nor did anyone except Sonny ever discuss it with her. He came to her room later that evening after he got back from taking Eric to Eureka Springs to catch a train. "So, what went on between you two? Eric wouldn't talk."

Laura sighed. No point in trying to keep secrets from Sonny. "We were at the cottage . . . uh, kissing. Mabelann caught us and was going to tell Gram. Eric made her promise to keep quiet if he left right away."

"I was afraid it might have been something like that. I'm sorry. I guess it's my fault for throwing you two together so much."

Laura flared up. She needed someone to be mad at, and Sonny offered a perfect target. "I suppose you think he liked me because you *forced* him to!"

"Still, he should have known better than to take advantage of a kid like you," Sonny went on, oblivious of her outburst. "He's older, a man of the world, compared to you."

"And I guess you think you're a man of the world too!" Laura said, flinging a stuffed animal at the door. "Lord, I'm sick of everybody telling me what a stupid baby I am! Why do you all think I can't learn anything about life without leaving here?"

"Well, you can't. You've lived in lamb's wool all your life."

"I have? What about you? Two years in a boarding school?

You think that's the world, Sonny? I meet more new people here in a year than you do there. The world comes to Thornehill, I don't have to go out and find it.''

Sonny picked up the stuffed animal and set it with the others on her pillow; then he patted her on the head in an affectionate way. "I guess you're right, Laura. But I'm sorry about Eric. That's all I came to say really."

Laura spent a full week pining over Eric. She imagined a hundred different ways it might have turned out. They could have married. He was certainly old enough and she was of age. Girls in the surrounding hills often married at sixteen or younger. She could have gone away with him to school in Chicago. They would have had a cute little apartment in Chicago while he went to school. He could paint in the day and they would love at night, like the afternoon in the cottage, but . . . more.

Sexuality, late in blooming, had burst forth in riotous blossom. She thought about those moments with him over and over again. The feel of his body against hers, his hands on her, inflamed her again and again. She even woke, startled and sweating, one night to find her own hand up her nightdress doing perfectly astonishing things.

Was this what Mabelann had meant by "dangerous"? she wondered, blushing. No, she didn't think so. The old black woman didn't mince words when she was referring to sex. The "dangerous" business seemed to mean something else entirely. But what could possibly be threatening about Eric? She'd never met anyone kinder, gentler, or more perceptive. For a moment she almost glimpsed the path to the answer. Gram's dislike of him had, she thought in passing, an edge of fear. But why? And then, as soon as she stumbled on the idea, she abandoned it. Gram wasn't afraid of anything or anybody. Besides the inate, unacceptable mystery of it, she was in no mood to examine or consider the deeper feelings of anyone else. It was her own frustrated passion that absorbed her, her own loss that formed the core of her days and nights.

But after a week of unrequited passion, Laura turned her frustration on Eric himself. Why had he left so readily, so . . . so eagerly? Almost as if he were glad of an excuse to get away quickly! He'd abandoned her without so much as a good-bye. Within a day she'd come to hate him nearly as much as she'd thought she loved him. He'd rejected her, tossed away her affection as though it were nothing more than

an afternoon diversion—which was probably all it was to
him. The beastly man!

At this point, she emerged from her room to take her
cranky, sullen place among the family, only to find that
they'd hardly noticed her absence. Everyone was busy and
half of them were every bit as discontented as she. Sonny
was getting ready to go back to school, studying with Edmund in the mornings, arguing with Grace about what to pack
in the afternoons. Packing was always a fight. Sonny wanted
to take as much of Thornehill as possible with him; Grace
believed in traveling sparsely. "But this isn't a little weekend
jaunt, Gram!" Sonny protested. "I'll be gone for months.
And I need a radio."

"That radio is half the size of Rhode Island and has never
worked since you took it apart anyway—don't give me that
look. I know you meddled with it. I found some of its innards
on the carpet where you'd dropped them."

Evelyn had some secret woe of her own as well. She'd had
a falling-out with one of her friends, apparently involving
Jackson, and she went about bristling like a hedgehog with
injured feelings, just asking to be injured further. She sniffled
and flounced and slammed doors. She picked a fight with
Adele about the sheets on her bed and fell out with India by
claiming she'd deliberately lost two edge pieces of a jigsaw
puzzle she was working on. "What do you think I do, nibble
them for snacks!" India screeched. "Just because Jackson is
playing footsie with your friends is no reason to jump on me,
Evelyn."

Evelyn slapped her and they didn't speak for two weeks.

Sonny was finally sent off to school, loaded down like a
ten-man Arctic expedition. Two weeks later they received a
telegram explaining that he'd gotten into a fight and fallen
down a flight of stairs. The other boy had been expelled. And
while Sonny wasn't seriously injured—only a broken right
wrist and two ribs—the authorities felt he'd better skip this
semester and recover at home. Evelyn, weeping over her poor
baby, was dispatched by train to bring him and his copious
luggage back.

Everyone was conditioned to act the gracious hosts in front
of the guests. The visitors that September and October never
knew about the overheated emotions that boiled just beneath
the surface, but the family's wing, the library, and the kitchen—
all off-limits to company—were a battleground.

Later, when she reflected on that disastrous autumn, Laura

realized that her father was at the heart of all of it. Jackson
had reached some private crisis in his aimless life. "A mid-
life crisis" people several generations later would call it. But
at the time there was no comforting label to apply to his
inexplicable behavior. He was merely "being an ass!" as
Sonny summed it up.

Jackson's interest in attractive women reached epic proportions. Instead of harmless flirting, he was bent on seduction,
and, as he'd run a bit to fat, it was a constant challenge. "We
cannot have you slobbering and pawing over every attractive
woman who comes here," Grace told him. "You'll drive
everyone off and we'll be back to eating rabbit stew for the
rest of our lives."

"Rabbit stew, indeed! Don't give me that bullshit, Mother!
You've made a fortune on these people. And you're still
packing away every penny of it. Evelyn and I live like
goddamn paupers while you go on squirreling away your
precious dollars."

"Jackson, you never have any sense of future, have you?"

"Dammit, this *is* my future! It's my past, my present.
You've stolen my life from me."

"Don't be melodramatic. You could have made anything
you wanted of yourself. You just never bothered."

By November, Jackson had subsided into sullen silence,
but it was obvious he was deeply troubled and unable to
understand, much less express, why. Edmund tried talking
with him, but came away shaking his head sadly.

On the eleventh of the month, they celebrated the twins'
birthday. "It was worth the broken wrist to be here for this
again," Sonny said, his mouth full of white cake with pep-
permint icing, his favorite.

"I notice it doesn't slow down your eating," India said,
watching as he expertly shoveled in food with his left hand.

Mabelann came into the dining room with another big bowl
of ice cream. "Somebody to see you, Miz Thorne," she said.
"I put 'em in the library."

"A guest? Some problem?" Grace asked.

"No, ma'am. Not guests, but a problem sure enough."

"Oh, Mabelann, ask them to come back tomorrow. We
don't want to be interrupted."

Mabelann set the bowl down and came around to whisper
something in Grace's ear. Grace listened, turned quickly to
Mabelann with a startled gaze, then said, "I'll be back as

soon as I can. Please go on without me rather than waiting."
She got to her feet and hurried out of the room.

Sonny and Laura had already opened their gifts, and after
everyone had finished eating, Laura slipped away. She tried
to tell herself she was merely going to thank Gram again for
her gift, but she knew she was really going to find out what
had happened to upset her grandmother enough to leave a
family birthday party—an almost sacred occasion that was
never slighted.

She approached the library through the small sitting room
with the private staircase. If she was going to eavesdrop,
which was her intention, she didn't want to be seen doing so
by guests passing in the main hall. The small sitting room
was dark and empty, but the door to the library was ajar and
Laura was able to see the people with her grandmother. There
was an older woman, a beaten-down ragged old soul. There
was a younger woman, fortyish, overblown, and clad in a
cheap taffetalike dress that was far too young and tight for her
buxom figure. The hem was out of the dress on one side and
her grayish brassiere strap was showing at the neck. She was
sitting in a chair across from Grace, who wasn't visible to
Laura.

Beside her stood a girl a year or so younger than Laura
herself. She was a remarkably pretty girl with curly blond
hair and a superb figure. She might have looked angelic
except that she had on makeup totally unsuitable to her
age—mascara, violently red lipstick, and clownlike pink circles of rouge.

"We wouldn'ta come to you if Smalley hadn't up and
died, Miz Thorne," the older woman was saying.

"I'm sorry to hear of his death. He was a good man,"
Grace said. Her voice sounded tight and cold. "But we have
no further business."

"No, Miz Thorne, we got lotsa business. Me and the girls
don't have no way of gettin' along in the world without
Smalley."

"I'm sorry to hear that," Grace said. She didn't sound the
least bit sorry. "But it's hardly my concern."

"Well, the way we see it, me and Iris, it's gonna *be* your
concern. You owe us somethin', Miz Thorne."

"I owe you nothing."

"You stole my baby," the blowsy women in the chair
said, leaning forward.

"I did no such thing. I adopted the child and gave her a

good life, which is more than you could have done. Look at the mess you've made of the one you raised yourself."

The teenage girl squinted myopically. "Is the old bitch talkin' about me, Ma?"

"Shut your face, Mae!" the older woman said, aiming a halfhearted slap in the girl's direction and missing. "We want what's owed us, Miz Thorne."

"You got all that was owed you, and more, seventeen years ago, Mildred."

Seventeen years ago? Laura thought. What was going on here? Who were they talking about? But as she wondered, she knew. She knew.

"What? A dirty old job with them cousins of yours? Smalley worked hisself to death on them damned gardens so them hoity-toity dames could walk around pickin' the roses. You think that's pay for what we give up for you?"

"Gave up? You gave up nothing but a child you cared nothing about, a child you would have ignored or mistreated."

Laura was trembling as she stepped through the door. "Gram, who are these people?" she asked.

Grace whirled in her chair. "Laura, go away. This is none of your business."

But Laura stood frozen as the older woman darted around the desk and grabbed her by the elbow. "This is her, ain't it? This is our own Annie."

"My name's not Annie," Laura said, taking a deep breath. Maybe, just maybe, she'd been mistaken. The horrible conclusion she'd come to was utterly wrong. They'd been talking about some servant or somebody she didn't even know.

"Maybe that ain't what *they* call you, but I'll bet my buttons you're our Annie. Lookie, Iris, this is your girl, ain't she? She's got your eyes."

"You are mistaken!" Grace all but shrieked, pulling Mildred's hand away and standing between her and Laura. "Laura, get out of here this minute."

"Baby!" Iris said, coming out of her chair with her arms open.

"Gram, you have to tell me—who are they?" Laura asked.

"You mean she don't know?" Mildred said. "Why, honey, you're my Iris's oldest girl. I'm your other gramma!"

Laura grabbed for Grace's hand like a trapeze flier caught in midair without support. "Gram!"

"Miz Thorne, you'd best tell the girl all about it," Mildred said, backing off with a cunning look, " 'cause if you don't pay up, ever'body in Eureka Springs gonna know by tomorrow.''

"Get out of here, you blackmailing fool!" Grace said. But there was defeat in her voice. "I'll see you at the kitchen door tomorrow at noon. If you dare get near the house or any of the family before then, I'll have you arrested."

"Like hell you will. Take an awful lot of explaining, wouldn't it, Miz Thorne? Take away this woman whose just tryin' to see her own grandchild what was stole from her."

"Get out."

"Is that my sister, Ma?" the teenager asked.

"Yeah, Mae. Now shuddup. Let's get outta here. We'll be back tomorrow."

"Yeah, we'll be back," Mildred added.

"Take them out the back way, Mabelann," Grace said. Laura hadn't even noticed that Mabelann had come in behind her.

As the door closed, Grace put her arms around Laura and hugged her so tightly she could hardly breathe. "Oh, bunny . . ."

"Is that awful woman really my mother?"

"Oh, Laura, I never wanted you to know. I could kill them all with my bare hands for doing this to you."

"But, Gram . . . I don't understand!"

"Let's sit down and I'll tell you. Come on, sweetheart, over here. That's right. You know, don't you, that your father tends to be . . . interested, let us say, in other women."

Laura nodded miserably.

"Well, unfortunately, Iris Smalley was one of them."

She went on, explaining as tactfully yet honestly as she could. And as she spoke, all sorts of things fell into place. "That's why Mother's never liked me, isn't it? She isn't really my mother at all. She's no relation to me!"

"She's your mother as surely as if she bore you, Laura. You mustn't forget that."

Suddenly the worst of it all swept over Laura in a single flesh-searing bolt. "*Sonny!* Oh, God! Sonny and I aren't twins at all."

"No, not exactly, but you are half-brother and -sister."

"Oh, no, Gram. Oh, no!" Laura collapsed against her, crying.

Grace didn't understand. "It doesn't matter, Laura. Nothing has changed."

"Everything's changed, Gram," she sobbed, leaping to her feet.

"Laura, sit down here until you've got a grip on yourself."

"No, Gram. I want to go to my room, by myself."

And without letting Grace have an opportunity to object, she fled the library, through the main hall, and out the front door. She ran until she thought her lungs would burst for want of air. Down the long drive, down the path, and into the cottage. She flung herself down on the bed where she'd slept for so long, the bed where she and Eric VonHoldt had almost consummated their love. She cried until she was so sick she had to go in the bathroom and throw up; then she cried awhile longer.

Eventually exhaustion overtook her and she fell into a fitful, agonized sleep. She had an insane dream of the revival, but this time everybody was pointing at her and saying, 'She's a bastard. She's not one of them. She's a bastard."

She awoke to Sonny shaking her shoulder. "Laura, everybody's looking for you. What are you doing here?"

"Oh, Sonny!" She flung herself at him. "Oh, Sonny, the most terrible thing ever! Terrible! We aren't twins. Mother isn't even my mother. My real mother is an awful, trashy woman with dirty underwear and a nasty mouth. I'm illegitimate. I'm a . . ." The word caught in her throat before she could say it. "I'm a *bastard*, Sonny!"

"Have you gone crazy, Laura? What the hell are you raving about? Here, wash your face, you look like a dead frog, all bloated . . ." He was trying to be very adult, but his face had gone white and his voice cracked.

Laura poured out the story, crying and hiccuping and losing her place and repeating herself. Sonny sat the whole time with his arm around her, the cast on his wrist cold against her neck. "How dare they all keep this from us!" he said when she finally stopped. "I guess Gram didn't intend to ever tell us."

"It wasn't just Gram, Sonny. They all knew. Dad. Mother. Everybody agreed to keep it secret. Aunt Adele and Uncle Edmund probably knew all about it too. Oh, Sonny, this is too terrible!"

Sonny got up and angrily trudged back and forth across the bedroom. "It just *doesn't* matter, if we don't let it."

"What do you mean?"

Sonny, unlike Grace, understood exactly what most upset Laura about these revelations. "We were twins for seventeen years, up until this evening, agreed? Did you ever doubt it before?"

"No, of course not."

"Well, then, what's changed? You were a . . . what you were, before that, and it didn't matter, so what difference does knowing make?"

Laura tried to sort this out. "But I'm not really your twin."

"Yes, you are! If you were my twin before we knew, you still are. The facts haven't changed, only the number of people who know them. See?"

"I guess so," Laura said, confused but comforted.

"It's just a question of blood. So, we'll fix that." He reached in his pocket with his good hand and took out his pocketknife. "Give me your finger."

"Sonny, that's stupid kid stuff."

"No, it's not. We have to do this, then our blood will be the same—shared. Put your hand out here!"

When they'd pierced their fingers and mingled the blood, Laura stood up. "We better go back. They'll have the sheriff out."

"That proves it, you know," Sonny said, wiping his finger on his pants cuff. "Nobody knew where to look for you but me. And I was sure where you were without even looking anyplace else. Only a twin could do that. Right?"

"Right, Sonny."

Laura spent most of the next day alone, roaming the grounds of Thornehill and thinking. At one point, she came across Mae Smalley by the spring. She was alone, sitting and throwing rocks at a flock of ducks. Conditioned to courtesy, even in the face of extraordinary circumstances, Laura said hello to her instead of slipping away.

"Oh, it's you," Mae said, her made-up face scowling.

"May I sit with you for a minute?" Laura said, still hoping she might find some common ground with this horrible girl who was her sister in the same degree that Sonny was her brother.

"I doan care. It's yer place."

"I like the spring," Laura said. "Do you?"

"I dunno. It's okay, I guess. Whaddaya call them shoes?"

"Saddle oxfords. They're new, and still making blisters on my heels."

"Wish I could have some new shoes. Ain't never had a new pair o' my own."

"I'm sorry." Laura felt she was somehow being coerced into giving away her shoes. That she would not do.

"Yeah, I'll bet you're sorry."

"Look, Mae. We're sisters in a way. Can't you be pleasant to me?"

"Pleasant, is it? I like that. You been raised like some damn princess here while I been eatin' crusts and wearin' hand-me-downs from rich bitches like your grandma."

"Nobody speaks about my grandmother that way, least of all the likes of you!" Laura said, getting up.

Mae jumped to her feet and ran after Laura. "We got the same ma, you and me, rich girl. The same ma. Don't you forget it. It ain't fair, you havin' so much and me havin' nuthin'. I'm gonna get even with you someday for it. You'll see. I'll get even!"

Laura started running, the girl's shrill invectives ringing in her ears all the way up the hill.

It might have all been, if not forgotten, at least pushed to the back of everyone's mind if Iris Smalley had taken the money Grace got together a few days later and left town. But instead, she sent Mildred and Mae ahead to a destination unknown to the Thornes and stayed in Eureka Springs to renew a few old friendships.

Unfortunately, she was coming out of the drugstore as Jackson emerged from a hardware store where he'd been buying some ammunition for his shotgun. "God above! I thought I'd gone crazy and was imagining things," he said later.

He'd missed dinner and come home while Grace, Evelyn, and the children were in the library listening to the radio for a half-hour before going to bed. He was very, very drunk and very, very angry. "She up and speaks to me, bold as brass, the slut! Says you gave her five thousand dollars, Mother! Five thousand fucking dollars!"

"Children, go to bed. Your father's not himself," Grace said.

"Jackson, what *are* you screaming about?" Evelyn asked.

"That slut Iris Smalley!"

"Children! Out!"

Sonny and Laura left with all the appearance of obedience, then ran around to the sitting room and pressed their ears to the door. "I don't think I want to listen," Laura whispered, straining to hear.

"You're right. You probably shouldn't," Sonny agreed. "Go upstairs and I'll come tell you what they say."

But they both knew she'd do no such thing.

Jackson was still shouting and they could hear him lurch into some piece of furniture that clattered. Evelyn was, characteristically, dealing with crisis by crying piteously. "Jackson, you know I never wanted to hear about that woman again. You promised—"

"Did you give her the money, Mother?" Jackson demanded.

"I did. What would you have had me do?"

"Throw her out. Call the dogs on her. She's nothing but a bitch in perpetual heat anyway!"

"Jackson, you can make your point with less vulgarity, even if you are drunk."

"Well, it's true and you should know it. Five thousand dollars! Goddammit, Mother, you keep us on such a short leash, then hand out that kind of money to that—"

"Jackson, I'm trying to be tolerant. Don't push me. Sit down and drink some of this coffee. I had to give her the money. She was threatening to tell everyone in town she gave birth to Laura."

Laura closed her eyes. How very like Gram to say "she gave birth to Laura" instead of "she's Laura's mother."

"So what?" Jackson shouted.

"So what? Jackson, imagine how awful it would be if everyone knew—"

"What would I care? I'm not the only man to have a few by-blows around in these hills."

"I wasn't thinking of your reputation. I was thinking of Laura's feelings."

"Of course you were. You always are. That brat comes before all of us. Well, I don't give a damn about Laura's feelings. Certainly not five thousand dollars' worth. It was your stupid idea to bring her into this house in the first place, not mine!"

Sonny lunged forward silently, clapping his hands over Laura's ears. Laura looked up at him, stricken, and clutched at his arms. Her heart seemed to have stopped, but she couldn't leave. Whatever more there was to this, she had to hear, no matter how terrible it was. What could be more terrible than Jackson's last words?

"To think, the whore was in my own house and I wasn't even told. My own house!"

Grace's chair scraped back suddenly. "Your house? May I remind you, Jackson, this is *not* your house. It's mine. Mine!"

"Of course it's yours, you old harridan. Everything in it is yours. The furniture, the servants, the family. We all belong to you, we dance to your tune, jerk when you pull our strings—"

"Oh, Jackson, please don't—" Evelyn cried.

"You too, Evelyn. You haven't got the spine to stand up to her, none of us have."

"Jackson, you're too drunk to know what you're saying," Grace said. "Go to bed. Sleep it off, and maybe we can talk about this sensibly in the morning."

"Oh, certainly, sensibly. Everything has to be sensible for you, doesn't it? The woman without a heart—only a steel-trap brain. Do you have any feelings for anyone, Mother dear? Anyone but that kid you dote on? Stupid question. Of course you don't. You don't give a damn about anyone but her. You've hated me for as long as I can remember—"

"That's nonsense."

"It's not, and you know it." There was a momentary silence, then a crash as Jackson fell over an end table. Then there was the jagged sound of male weeping. "Oh, God, Mother. What did I ever do to you but be born? I'm your only child. Couldn't you have loved me just a little? How can you love Laura so much and not me?"

"Jackson, you know very well how fond I am—"

"Not fond, Mother. Not goddamn fond, for Christ's sake. Love. I'm talking about love. Can't you even say the word?"

"Jackson, darling, come along upstairs." Evelyn was over her tears for the moment. "I'll fix you a nice sleeping draft . . ."

Sonny and Laura were frozen in place, clinging to each other like baby squirrels in a high wind. There was the sound of Jackson stumbling across the room, then the door opening and closing, then silence.

Laura laid her head on Sonny's shoulder, breathing in shudders. He rocked her, saying nothing. How was it, she was wondering despairingly, that utter strangers could find things in her to like well enough, and yet those who ought to love her the most didn't? Her father; her real mother, Iris; Evelyn—they all either hated her or, worse, had no feelings for her whatsoever. What had she ever done to them, she thought, echoing her father's words, except be born? Who among them would have laboriously chiseled on a headstone "Beloved Laura"?

Thank God for Sonny and Gram. They were her lifelines, her life.

In a moment, they heard a sound from the library like a kitten mewing. A soft, pitiful sound. Sonny pushed the door open slightly. It swung silently, revealing an almost dark room. But a single shaft of moonlight illuminated the desk where Grace sat, with her head and arms on the blotter, weeping.

Grace—weeping!

"Dear God," she cried quietly. "Why do we all love each other too much or too little? What's wrong with all of us?"

Sonny and Laura spent the night at the cottage. Sonny slept on the floor in front of the door, to bar access to anyone who might try to disturb his sister. No one missed them, and early the next morning they prepared to go back to the house. They hadn't talked about what they'd heard. Between them, there was no need.

"Whaddya think, kid?" he asked as they walked up the main drive. His tone was jaunty, determinedly we're-not-going-to-let-this-thing-bother-us.

"I think I'd like breakfast," she said, following his lead.

Apparently Grace and Evelyn had decided to take the same line and pretend that nothing out of the ordinary had occurred. Breakfast in the kitchen was a terse, unemotional affair. "Is Jackson coming down to eat?" Grace asked with the appearance of nothing but casual interest.

"No, he'd already gone when I got up," Evelyn replied.

"He ain't been into the kitchen," Mabelann said, putting a flat dish of bacon in the center of the table.

"I suppose he went for a walk or to the stables," Grace said, taking a crisp strip of the meat.

But a similar conversation went on again at lunch. This time a wiry thread of alarm ran through their words. "Sonny, go to the garages and see if your father took one of the cars," Evelyn said. "He must have had some errand in town."

But the cars were all there. So were the horses. Jackson didn't turn up at dinner and Grace started calling people he knew nearby. "He can't have gone far!" Evelyn exclaimed. "He didn't even take his billfold or anything. Grace, what do you suppose—?"

"I don't suppose anything. He must be on the grounds. Has anybody checked the cottage?"

"I was down there this afternoon, Gram," Sonny said. "Nobody's been there."

They called in help and started a search the next morning at dawn. Mabelann's brother-in-law Nathan found him in a hollow near the spring. Half his head was blown away, and brains were spattered for several yards. His shotgun, the only thing he'd taken along, was lying beside him.

The funeral service was held at the gravesite. Jackson was buried in a little family plot on the other side of the hill from the cottage and spring. He rested eternally between his grandfather Jeremiah and his four brothers and sister who hadn't lived past birth. Evelyn wasn't present. She'd collapsed and been heavily sedated. They didn't realize yet how much of her they were burying with him and that her tortured mind was already turning back more or less permanently to the 1920s—the time she'd been happiest.

But the rest were present, and Laura, in her turn, took up a handful of soil and let it dribble into the open grave onto the casket lid. "Good-bye, Father," she said softly.

Only Sonny was aware of the bitterness in the last word.

That night, after all the mourners had eaten their fill and left, Laura went to Grace's room to say good night. "It's a hard thing, Laura-bunny, to lose a parent," Grace said.

She gestured for Laura to sit down on the bed, but Laura stood her ground. "No, not for me it isn't. I wish I could feel sorry he's dead."

"Laura!"

"I'm sorry, Gram. But that's the truth. I heard—that night in the library. Sonny and I listened. Daddy shot himself—"

"Laura, it was an accident. You know that. He must have tripped and the gun went off—"

"He killed himself, Gram. I heard what he said that night. About how you didn't love him—but *he* didn't ever love *me*, and that's just the same. Gram, I'm glad he's dead. Now he can't ever hurt me again."

"Oh, bunny . . ." Grace said.

"You know, I've been thinking a lot today about overhearing what you and Father said to each other, but I've thought more about what I heard a long time ago. I was outside your door and he said he remembered when you loved him. Did you ever love him, Gram?"

"Yes, I did," Grace answered simply.

Suddenly she looked old and tired for the first time. Laura

asked no more questions and went away promising herself she'd never listen at another door. Things that were said behind closed doors weren't meant to be heard by others.

Grace considered going after her and explaining; she even went to the door and called to her—once, and very softly, too softly to be heard. She waited a moment, then went back to her room.

How could she have made Laura understand without telling her a truth she and Jack had tried to put away for all time so many years ago? No, it was too late. The truth was truly buried now, buried in the family plot, with her only surviving child, where it belonged. There was no need for anyone ever to know.

But Grace didn't sleep that night. She kept going back over that day when they made the snowman and she loved her son.

XX

June 1940

LAURA leaned back against a tree and closed the book on her lap. It was a new Steinbeck, *The Grapes of Wrath*, and portrayed a side of the Depression she'd never really seen or been aware of firsthand. Could it have been only ten or eleven years ago? That time seemed so far away, an episode of her childhood, utterly alien to the life of elegance and ease they lived at Thornehill now.

She looked around her. It was a picnic day at the hotel, and the whole family, together for the first time in many months, was joining in the holiday spirit with the guests on the balmy spring day. Grace and Adele were sitting in folding chairs chatting with some women who had been friends of Adele's in Boston. Edmund was fishing amiably with Evelyn, baiting her hook and advising her on how to cast her line. Sonny was taking a stroll around the perimeter of the spring with Freddie Hamble, an oppressively nice, doughy-featured boy who'd been proposing to Laura at regular intervals for two years and had accepted her turn-downs almost cheerfully.

It was nice to be back at Thornehill in a permanent way, but Laura was finding it unbearably irritating that the older members of the family kept referring to Laura's return as if she'd really been out in the world and had now returned—educated, "finished" properly, and world-weary. As if she'd spent the years in an artist's garret in Paris or something equally independent and brave.

Grace had finally relented on her policy of keeping Laura at Thornehill three years before. After Jackson's suicide and Sonny's return to school for the winter term, Laura had become moody and rebellious. Grace blamed the change on the death, never knowing it was what Jackson had said before his death that haunted his daughter. She arranged for Laura to take her senior year in high school at a girls' school in Kansas City and then two years at a very strict girls' junior college in Columbia, Missouri. Neither school was more than a seven-hour drive from Thornehill and every third weekend a chauffeured car brought her home.

Laura hadn't found that "going away" in that fashion differed significantly from staying home. The girls she met at school were girls of her class and kind, the supervision was too strict to allow any real adventure, and the education held slight challenge after years of Edmund's tutoring. So "seeing the world," as Aunt Adele kept calling it, was nothing more than seeing a larger dimension of the same existence she'd always known. It was a world of money and leisure, dancing and furs, three wines with dinner, country clubs and golfing. The boys were all attending or just finishing Harvard or Princeton or Yale, the girls were planning their debutante parties and searching madly for husbands who had both the financial charm to please their parents and the sexual appeal to please the girls themselves.

Now it was over and she was back at Thornehill. She'd added precious little to her mental equipment and hadn't even attempted to acquire a husband, in spite of Freddie's pathetic eagerness to fill that role.

Sonny flopped down next to her and said, "How ya doin', kiddo?"

Laura giggled. "How is it you're such a wonder with other languages and can hardly limp through a sentence in your native tongue?"

Sonny smiled and shrugged.

He'd been enrolled in French the semester he broke his wrist and had to return home. When he went back to school that year, he astonishingly caught up with all he'd missed and finished at the head of his class—in French, at any rate. That was the first hint any of them had that Sonny, the mediocre scholar, had a positively uncanny gift for languages. "It's like having an *idiot savant* around the house, isn't it?" he said to their questions.

He'd completed a four-year German course in the two remaining years of prep school and maintained a straight-A average in Spanish as well. India, who went through a spell of believing in reincarnation, built up an entertaining scenario of all the lives Sonny must have lived in the past to account for this remarkable gift. And he encouraged her by such techniques as putting his hand over his eyes and saying things like, "I see something—it's a big building, a castle. Yes, it's a French castle and there are people bowing to me as I pass."

Then there had been a battle royal over college. Grace insisted that he attend Harvard like his father, grandfather, and great-grandfather, but Sonny refused. "I don't like or do well in sports, math, science, or even literature. There's no point in enduring them for the sake of the languages when I can learn them better with private tutors."

Harvard had backed up his decision by flatly refusing the application Grace sent in under his name. "See, Gram?" Sonny had said placidly; then he rented a small apartment in New York and started setting up his own very personal college education. In three years he'd learned enough Italian, Polish, and Russian to read and write, if not speak, them fluently. A month earlier he'd returned to Thornehill with a crate of books he'd been commissioned to translate.

"Mostly German literature," he explained to Laura when she came home. "The government seems to think the clue to the Nazi mind is in this stuff somewhere. I think that's nuts, but I'm being paid nicely for it, so why not? I'm beginning to grasp why Hitler is a crazy man. If I'd had to read this stuff at a tender age, I'd be a lunatic too."

Sonny picked up Laura's book, looked at the spine, and grimaced. "Grim stuff, my girl. How about a game of baseball instead?"

"I don't dare. Freddie would want me to be on his team and if I agreed, he'd take it as encouragement."

"So he would. Poor Freddie. Oh, well, he says he's leaving tomorrow to go home to mama in Connecticut for the summer." Sonny set the book down and leaned back on his elbows, surveying the scene. "It never changes, does it? All of them . . ."

"I'm not sure. On the surface, not much, but . . ."

She looked at Grace as she spoke. To others she was the same as always, but those who knew her best were aware that she'd changed after "the accident," as she still referred to Jackson's death. It was as if something secret inside her that kept her young had shut off or lost its resilience. Her hair was nearly white now and she moved in a careful, old-lady way, as if constantly conscious of the fragility of her bones. And although she still ruled the house and family, there was less evidence of the old vinegar in her voice.

Evelyn had changed too. She'd always been rather solitary and self-absorbed, so it wasn't as obvious at first, but she'd slipped into a sort of gentle dottiness that was rather engaging to everyone but Sonny. "Good Lord, Mother, focus your eyes and really listen to me!" Laura had heard him say to her once when he was trying to explain something important to her. Laura understood his irritation, but had less trouble accepting Evelyn's vapid half-presence than he did. Laura had never called her "Mother" again after the revelations of the night before Jackson died, and Evelyn didn't seem to have ever noticed, much less minded, having her supposed daughter call her by her first name.

As for the others, Sonny was right. They hadn't changed much. Adele was still bustling about, happiest in a crisis. Edmund, his hair a little thinner, his stoop slightly more pronounced, was the same—always reading, studying, doggedly hoping to find someone who could converse with him on his own intellectual level. He'd lost his pupils when Sonny and Laura both went away to school, but had started a small class for some of the children of the hotel employees, which kept him occupied.

Dr. Howard Lee had aged with dignity. Grace's influence, or so Laura imagined the source, had given his usual good humor a wry and sometimes sharp edge, but it didn't make him seem the least unpleasant, merely more interesting. There were two younger doctors now in the area, one the young man from St. Louis he'd brought out and trained years ago. The other was a woman, an obstetrician. Their presence had made it possible for him to enter into a genteel semiretirement which allowed him to travel. Apparently this had long been a repressed passion which he could only now indulge. According to India, he always came back with interesting stories of the people he'd met. "Not always true, one suspects, but highly entertaining nevertheless," she'd told Laura.

India seemed constantly different and always the same. She was thirty-five now, as dramatic in her sudden enthusiasms as when she first arrived. She'd been a devotee of several different religions and philosophies over the years, and eventually lost faith or interest in most of them. Reincarnation had stuck with her and surfaced from time to time. "Grace was a queen in a previous life, of course," she declared, and no one disagreed with her. "But you, Laura, I can't figure out. An animal, I think. A fox, perhaps. Shy, slight, watching everything with an intelligent but wary eye. But not, perhaps, a terribly well-fed fox. You haven't the killer instinct to survive in the woods. That's a compliment, dear, don't look so put out."

Laura tried to take it as a compliment, but was depressed by what she saw as the truth in this assessment. She was, she feared, an observer of life more than a participant. Bound by an overdeveloped sense of duty and deep affection for the family, she'd come back—to do what? To fill in the years with fads as India herself was doing? To devote her life to the success of the hotel even though Grace's scrimping and inspired investments had long since restored the family fortune?

"Your thoughts must be very serious, my girl." Sonny said, prodding her arm with the corner of the book.

"Oh, Sonny, I just keep wondering what I'm doing here."

He nodded, understanding without explanation as always. "I could use some help."

"You know I can't translate anything. I haven't your gift with languages."

"No, but you've got fine fingers for typing, which I don't. I need a secretary desperately."

"Of course I'll help you, but that's not it."

"I know. You want to be doing something only you can do."

"Exactly. This war in Europe makes it worse, somehow. There are millions of people fighting for their lives, and here I've got mine lying on a silver platter and I haven't any idea what to do with it. I was reading in the papers last week about the evacuation of Dunkirk—all those people helping get the hundreds of thousands of soldiers off the beaches where the Germans had trapped them. I wanted to skipper one of those brave little fishing boats that dodged the bombs to save someone. Instead, I'm sitting here at a picnic, reading a book and dodging Freddie's advances."

"You could get married. That's what most girls have on their minds."

"To Freddie?"

"Of course not Freddie, but don't you want a husband?"

"I guess I do, in a vague sort of way. It's what I'm supposed to do. But I haven't found one I think I could stand."

Sonny nodded his understanding again. "We're both going to have trouble finding anyone. It's because of each other, you know. We're both expecting to find someone who can think as we do, in tandem. Finish sentences, understand allusions and family jokes.''

The picnic was breaking up. Several waiters were gathering up the picnic cloths, dishes, and chairs as the family and guests moved toward the house. Laura stood and stretched. Sonny's words hadn't changed anything, but his understanding had eased her depression. Seeing Freddie approach, Sonny took her elbow and leaned close to talk, indicating to Freddie that they were having a private discussion. "I saw Eric a few months ago," he said. "We've established quite a busy correspondence."

"Eric VonHoldt? Does he live in New York?" she asked. She had wondered about him lately, but hadn't thought to ask Sonny. She assumed they'd lost touch long ago.

"Was just moving there. He's been working in Chicago for an advertising firm. He's finally breaking out of the security of it and doing some real painting. We had an interesting talk. His family is changing their name."

"Because of the VonHoldt armaments?"

"Yes, they're getting tired of seeing their own name in the papers all the time in connection with Hitler. Especially since they've broken all ties. Eric seemed to think this was a good time to do it. He'd hardly want to throw himself into 'making a name,' only to change it later and start over."

"How was he?" Laura asked, remembering with a certain longing the handsome young man she'd known so long ago.

"Fine. Excited and scared about free-lancing. He's asked about you several times."

"What do you tell him?"

"That you are wonderful. He said he knew that."

Is he married? Laura wanted to ask, but said nothing.

Sonny smiled at her, reading her thoughts. "No, he's not."

Before Laura could reply, Freddie was at her elbow. "Will you be partner at bridge tonight, Laura?"

She tried to conjure up an expression that was neither encouraging nor openly rude. "I suppose so."

The VonHoldt name came up again barely a week later. Laura and Sonny came down from his room where she'd been typing and he'd been unwillingly straightening up bookshelves. It was a bit early for luncheon, but they were edgy and on the brink of arguing and had agreed a break was necessary. The library was empty but for India, who was staring into the dark cavern of a summer-naked fireplace as if seeking the answer to something in the traces of cold ash. "Is something wrong, India?" Laura asked.

"What? Oh, you startled me. I don't know, quite."

"What's happened?" Sonny asked, sitting down next to her and stretching his long limbs. A joint cracked and he grimaced.

"It's your grandmother."

"Is Gram sick?" Laura asked. She'd started to sit and got back as she spoke, ready to run to Grace's aid.

"No, nothing like that. But it's very odd. . . . Do you recall I wrote to you about the people who came here last fall with such a hush-hush attitude?"

"The government people who were meeting somebody mysterious?"

"Yes. An industrialist from Pennsylvania named Hargis and a pair of male secretaries and a man who was supposed to be a cousin and certainly wasn't. The so-called cousin was German and he had a couple of underlings with him as well."

"Government dealings, no doubt," Sonny said.

"Oh, yes. Hargis had been here before as a guest and I suppose he recommended to his department, whatever it is, that this is a safe, discreet place to have a meeting with foreign powers without the glare of publicity."

"Pretty Boy Floyd felt the same way," Sonny said with a grin.

"Well, we got a letter from Hargis this morning. He's apparently setting up another meeting for August. Asked that he be allowed to reserve all the rooms. They won't all be used, he said, but the guests he was booking needed privacy."

"That's happened before," Laura said, puzzled. "Besides, we're usually pretty vacant in August anyway. Nobody likes the hot weather."

"Yes, yes. I know. What's odd is Grace's reaction. I gave her the letter, just to get her approval before I confirmed the reservation, and she got quite pale and distraught. I think it was the foreign guest. Of course, he's not likely to be welcomed anywhere in this country, but still, if the government wants to meet with him, it would seem our patriotic duty—"

"Who is the foreign guest?" Sonny asked.

"VonHoldt. Frederich VonHoldt. The armaments man."

Sonny sat forward, rubbing his hands. "The devil himself! How exciting. Almost like giving bed and board to Hitler. What do you suppose this Hargis is doing? Trying to buy him out? Offer him more than Hitler has? God! What a fascinating thing. Thornehill might be in the history books as the place where momentous deals were struck! I can't wait to tell Eric that I've met his loathsome great-uncle, Frederich the Horrible!''

"Sonny, you mustn't tell anyone!" India exclaimed.

He subsided. "No, I guess not. Still, what a secret to keep!"

Laura had been silent. Now she asked, "What did Gram say?"

"She said, 'Jack wouldn't abide that man in his house.' Odd, mentioning your grandfather like that. I mean, he's been gone for so long. Do you suppose she communes with him still?"

Laura had a sudden vision of India trying to draw Gram into séances and all the rest. "No, I'm quite certain she doesn't. It must be because Grandfather died in a war that the VonHoldts made the weapons for." She didn't believe it, but hoped India would.

"Mmmm, maybe. At any rate, she said she'd think about it, and then an hour or so later she came down to the front desk and gave me back the letter and said I was to confirm the reservation. She said if there was a possible advantage to our country in the meeting, it was our duty to allow Herr VonHoldt to come. Herr VonHoldt. That's what she called him, and I can't tell you how cold and angry she sounded. Do you suppose she actually knows the man?"

Something clicked into place in Laura's mind with a faint snap, but it presented no picture, no understanding, merely a slippery sense that she should understand something and didn't—quite.

"I don't see how," Sonny was saying. "She's never been to Germany and I don't believe he's ever been here. I wouldn't worry about it if I were you."

"No, I guess not. Still, it was odd . . ." She got up and brushed down the wrinkles in her skirt as if brushing off the subject. "I think I hear the clink of silverware. Let's see if Mabelann will hurry lunch along."

Sonny was following in her wake, but Laura hesitated. She should, she felt, be able to grasp something that was just beyond the periphery of her understanding. It had something to do with the long-ago summer when Eric VonHoldt had visited and a feeling that Gram didn't so much dislike him as fear him. Now, there was again that thread of fear in Grace, even though Laura was glimpsing it secondhanded. She thought about it a moment, trying to rearrange the factors like letters in an anagram, but there was no way to make a word of it.

The forthcoming secret visit of the second-most-powerful "bomb king" of Germany remained a secret, even within the family. Laura once attempted to bring up the subject with her grandmother and was politely but very firmly snubbed. It was a matter of national importance and as such was not to be bandied about as casual, much less personal, discussion.

The summer passed more quickly than Laura had anticipated. The long decade of drought and dust was over. Finally the rains came and the land turned as richly green as her childhood memories. She revived some other childhood interests. Digging out a pair of binoculars India had given her years earlier, Laura got into the habit of taking an early-morning walk with her bird guide and a checklist. She also came across a small silver tatting shuttle with her initials engraved—a gift from Adele. With a refresher lesson from the older woman, Laura started making lacy edging for pillowcases. "Such a silly thing to see you doing," Sonny said. "So old-ladyish."

"I know," Laura said. "But you can't imagine how calming it is to have something mindless like this to occupy my hands. It has nothing to do with words."

Words had become her daily fare. For eight to ten hours every day she worked with Sonny on his translating. Sometimes he dictated as he read, more often he scribbled out his translation and she had the task of deciphering his sprawling handwriting. When they took a break from work, it was usually to eat and read the papers.

They watched with horror as Hitler rolled through Europe. On June 14 Paris fell and by the end of the month the papers were saying that the French had lost ninety-two thousand lives in the fight and had a million and a half of their citizens captured. Everyone knew that Britain was next on Hitler's agenda, and less than a month later the first large-scale attack began what would come to be known as the Battle of Britain.

Nobody at Thornehill mentioned who was helping the Krupps make the weapons that threatened to wipe out the civilization from which they had sprung. When the VonHoldt name was mentioned on the radio, the house's inhabitants sometimes made accidental eye contact but sheered away from it as quickly as possible. But August was coming and nothing could stop the inevitable introduction of the name into the isolation of Thornehill.

By the beginning of the month most of the guests had departed of their own will. Arkansas in August was not a desirable place for vacationing. The wealthy and pampered moved north to Wisconsin and Minnesota and upper New York State. They would return in the fall, when the heat had broken in the South and the cold had set in in the North.

And during the hot, humid interval, Thornehill would have a visitor whose very name struck terror around the world and a very special terror in one heart at Thornehill.

XXI

GRACE tried to get rid of Laura and Sonny. She suggested a trip to California, knowing it was something they'd sometimes discussed. Sonny, too preoccupied with plans of his own, didn't see anything suspicious in this offer, but merely brushed it off with thanks. "I've got too much to do, Gram. Maybe later. Good of you to think of it, though."

Laura, however, knew it wasn't just the thoughtful little gift Grace was pretending to present. She recognized it for what it was: an attempt to dislodge them during the visit of the German armaments manufacturer. She didn't want to give her grandmother unnecessary pain, but neither was she about to be shunted off. "You're so pale, bunny. I think the heat is particularly hard on you this summer. A nice rest—"

"No, it's not bothering me a bit," Laura insisted. "In fact, the thought of such a long train ride tires me to think about. I'd rather just stay here and be lazy. Perhaps in the fall sometime . . ."

Since Grace couldn't admit why she'd offered the trip, she had to accept this rejection. Laura felt guilty about thwarting her grandmother this way, but her curiosity was greater than her guilt. She would stay and see the monster VonHoldt no matter what. Someday she could tell her own children and grandchildren about it.

The afternoon before the anticipated arrival of the American representatives who would accompany VonHoldt, Sonny announced that he'd finished his current translation project. "I'm going to town. Can you finish up the typing today?"

"Sure. What are you going to town for?"

"To meet a friend at the station."

"The train station? You've invited someone here! Oh, Sonny. We're not supposed to have any guests. You know that."

"No paying guests allowed. This is a friend."

"Gram will have a fit!"

"You don't know the half of it." Sonny said, zipping out the door before she could question him further.

She understood at dinner.

They were seated and the salad course was being laid when Sonny came in. "Sorry to be late, but the May Never Arrive was living up to its reputation. Do you all remember my friend from school? Eric . . ."

Laura nearly dropped her fork.

"He's passing through and I asked him to visit us for a couple days."

Grace was nearly as white as the tablecloth. "I'm sorry, but Sonny seems to have failed to explain to you that the hotel is closed right now—"

"No, Gram," Sonny rolled on. "Eric's not a hotel guest, he's my houseguest and we won't be in your way at all. Just going to lock ourselves up in my room and jaw about old times. Uncle Edmund, Aunt Adele, you remember Eric . . ."

He proceeded with introductions like a courteous rhinoceros, impervious to the frigid looks Grace was giving him and his friend. Eric seemed less immune. He glanced uneasily at Grace, clearly not comfortable in the role of party crasher. Then he shook hands with the rest of the family, holding Laura's just a fraction of a second longer than required, and then took his place at the setting that Mabelann had thumpingly added to the table.

Dinner went on, but the conversation was strained to the point of incipient hysteria. Laura half-expected that before it was over someone would rise with a shriek and start tearing out his own or someone else's hair. Had Grace not been so seriously distressed, it would have been funny.

Laura wanted to study Eric, but every time she glanced at him, he met her eyes and smiled disarmingly. He'd certainly lived up to the promise of good looks he'd shown as a boy. The muscular, almost-but-not-quite-stocky build with the thin, sharply planed face was more fascinating than ever. His hair wasn't as fair as she remembered and he wore it longer, but his eyes—oh, those too-perceptive eyes. She hadn't forgotten that.

And suddenly she remembered the last time she'd looked

into those eyes: at the cottage . . . Mabelann standing between them . . . Eric's face flushed from aborted passion and anger and embarrassment . . . Laura herself in wrinkled clothes, still feeling the heat of his hands on her breasts—

"Laura, are you ill? You're so flushed."

"No, thank you, Dr. Lee. I'm fine," she said, mortified at being caught in a blush.

She couldn't meet Eric's eyes, and yet couldn't stop herself. His blue gaze caught hers and she knew he knew what she'd been thinking.

"I'd like to be excused, please," she said, standing up quickly. She ran upstairs, wondering all the while what the strange mix of emotions was that caused her heart to beat so strongly. She was glad to see Eric—how could anyone look at him without being grateful for the experience? But in an odd way, she was almost as angry as pleased.

All these years he'd been a memory she could take out and study. She'd remembered so often those few short weeks when he'd been here before, but she'd remembered them selectively and with a certain degree of creativity. Now, years later, she wasn't exactly sure how much of what she recalled had really happened and how much she'd invented. Now, here he was in a state of reality. He was no longer a memory, her creature to manipulate. He was a person who could make her heart pound by looking at her, make her hand tingle at his touch.

It wasn't fair to have taken her so unprepared, and she resented it. She'd been made to feel foolish, not just tonight, but all those months he didn't come back to her, didn't even write. Most of all she resented the fact that he'd seemed to know what she was thinking at dinner. No, that was only her imagination working overtime. He couldn't have known. He didn't know her at all. Or care about her.

Why, then, did she still find him so attractive? Why had she recalled with such hot vividness the last time they'd been in the same room? Why should he have the power to make her blush and run away from dinner?

She stayed in her room until well after dinner, and when she heard the sound of Sonny's door shutting down the hall, she assumed Eric was safely out of her path. She slipped down the back stairs, through the library, where Edmund and Dr. Lee were listening to the radio, Adele was sewing, and India was laying out a pattern of tarot cards. There was no sign of Grace, nor did anyone take much notice of Laura's passing. Stepping through the French doors, she went out on the stone-flagged walk to sit on the wooden swing Edmund had constructed earlier in the summer.

It was quite dark and she saw no one, but she knew from the way the swing didn't give when she sat down that someone was already sitting at the other end. Too late to leap up and fly back into the house. She wasn't a child who could get away with acting that way, nor had she any reason to be afraid of him. "I thought you were with Sonny," she said, turning to face him in the darkness and trying to sound merely polite.

"He went up for a pack of cigarettes," Eric answered. "Laura, I haven't the courage to apologize to your grandmother, but I've got a god-awful need to get an apology out of my system. May I deliver it to you instead?"

"What for?"

"For being here. If your grandmother had been able to lay her hands on a gun when I walked in, she'd have happily put it to my skull and scattered me all over Arkansas. I can't blame her, and yet I can't leave."

"Why are you here? Now, I mean?" Laura asked, feeling it would be stupid and pointless to deny his allegations about his reception. *I'll come back for you*, he'd said. No, that line of thought was even more stupid and pointless. It was adolescent melodrama spoken in the heat of passion, nothing more. Silly of her to have even remembered it.

He didn't answer right away. Was he considering his answer or allowing her time to complete her own thoughts? "I'm here because I have to see my great-uncle or whatever he is. I've grown up despising the man and I have to see him in the flesh. It's disgusting of me, like picking at a scab, and I can't help it."

"Sonny told you? He shouldn't have."

"No, he didn't tell me. He wrote at first and asked me to visit this week. I said I couldn't afford it, but he sent me money for the train and said it would be worth my while. There was someone I would be interested in meeting here. I don't suppose he thought I'd guess, but I didn't even have to puzzle it out. I knew who it was. I'm imposing myself on all of you—I know it and I'm sorry, but I can't help myself. Do you understand? Can you at least forgive me?"

She was suddenly angry. Not because he'd come to gawk at the uncle who'd made his name a dirty word—that she could understand perfectly well. Her fury wasn't that he *was* here to see Frederich VonHoldt, but because he *wasn't* here to see her. How idiotic she'd been even to consider herself part of the attraction of Thornehill. How childish and vulgar of her to suppose he remembered that day at the cottage.

"Of course I understand," she said stiffly.

"And forgive me?"

"Naturally." She sounded just like Grace in one of her coldly polite huffs. She didn't care.

"I've thought of you often," he said.

"Have you?" It was an accusation.

He made a tentative movement with his hand as if to touch her, but drew it back before he made contact. "Very often. And very fondly. You're even more beautiful than I thought you were going to be."

"That's an artist's compliment," she said, and choked back the rest of what she wanted to say: "not a lover's."

Now he was angry and she didn't know why. "I *am* an artist—that's why I think that way!"

Her eyes had adjusted to the dark now and she could see that he'd drawn himself up straight. She forced herself to relax and put a smile in her voice. "Let's start over," she said softly, and then regretted the words. She meant: Let's start this conversation over—but was afraid he'd read more into the remark than she intended.

Before he could answer, Sonny stumbled out the door into the darkness and there was a faint splat as a package of cigarettes hit the stones and skidded. "Well, here you both are," he said, squinting into the darkness. "Catching up on old times, eh? Say, help me find where those damned cigarettes got to, would you?"

Laura slipped away unnoticed.

She thought later about those few days and was struck with wonder at what a terrible influence time could have. If only she'd learned what she did of life during that time in slightly altered order, everything might have been far different. She also learned, too late, the very real value of ignorance.

The guests were to arrive at noon. She went down to breakfast early, ate hurriedly, and after selecting a book from the library, returned to her room for the morning. She didn't come out until she heard the cars coming up the long drive; then she went down the main staircase to stand by Gram.

Grace hardly seemed to notice her presence. She had on a

black dress, as if she were in mourning, and wore her hair pulled back into a severe knot at the back of her head. Without any jewelry or makeup and with her face set in an expression of haughty resignation, she looked like a statue. Edmund opened the door and suddenly the foyer was full of people milling about bumping suitcases and briefcases into each other's shins.

There was no mistaking Herr VonHoldt. He had a rigid, Germanic arrogance that made him seem the liner about which the tugs steamed. Laura half-expected a herald to precede him. He was older than she'd expected, in his seventies, she guessed. But there was nothing feeble or elderly about him. He seemed not quite human enough for something so common as aging. His face was hatchet thin, with hooded blue eyes, sleek white hair, and a slightly embalmed look of eternal preservation.

An American in his fifties—Hargis, Laura guessed—approached Grace, and VonHoldt followed a few steps behind. "Mrs. Thorne, allow me to present Herr Frederich VonHoldt."

VonHoldt put forward a languid hand as if to shake hers, but the movement seemed more like a gesture that invited kissing of rings. Grace's hands remained at her sides. She inclined her head slightly in acknowledgment. "How do you do, Herr VonHoldt." Her voice dripped ice and Laura imagined she could hear the words falling to the floor and shattering.

VonHoldt's eyelids lowered for a moment like the lenses of twin cameras recording her for future reference. "Have we met, madam?" he asked in unaccented English. No, not unaccented. There were British vowels in it.

"We have not."

Everyone was uncomfortable, sensing vaguely that something important was happening but utterly unable to identify it. Laura glanced quickly over her shoulder and noticed Sonny and Eric standing on the last step of the stairway—too removed for introductions, close enough for observation.

"Forgive me, madam, I thought perhaps—"

Grace addressed herself to Hargis. "I've prepared your rooms in the east wing. Your meals can be sent up on individual trays if you wish or you may have free use of the dining room. There are, as you requested, no other paying guests and the family and staff will dine elsewhere so you will not be disturbed. You have, of course, free access to the grounds, but I would suppose that your limousines probably attracted attention in the area and there may be local gawkers.

The decision to use the outdoor facilities is up to you, naturally."

Laura watched VonHoldt watching Grace as she spoke. He knows her, she thought, but can't place when they met. He turned his head slightly to Hargis and she stared at his profile with a vague sense of recognition. Had she seen pictures of him before? Was that why he seemed familiar? No, she thought not. He was mentioned in the news, but she couldn't recall having seen a photograph. Still, there was something in the sharp line of nose and the plane of cheek that she'd seen before.

Then everyone was in motion again. Edmund led Hargis and VonHoldt to their rooms. The secretaries bashed about with suitcases in their wake. Grace was still standing exactly where she'd been the whole time. Her face was drained of all color. "Gram, are you all right?" Laura asked, suddenly sorry she'd been a witness to whatever had just happened.

"I'll go to my room now," Grace said, not so much to Laura as to the empty air.

She made no move, however, until Laura took her arm. "I'll go up with you, Gram," she said.

Grace turned, walked, went up the steps—Sonny and Eric had silently disappeared from their observation post—like a machine. When they reached the door of her room, Grace glanced at Laura, and for a fraction of a second Laura could imagine in those swimming eyes the beautiful young woman she must once have been. "Gram, what is it?" she asked simply.

Grace twisted the doorknob, let the door swing open, and walked in. "I suppose . . . I suppose it's time you knew," she said softly. So softly Laura could hardly distinguish the words. "I didn't want you to know, but you saw it, didn't you? You're an observant person."

She went to the dressing table and sat down on the flounced bench. Only then did she look up and meet Laura's eyes again. "Tell me, Gram," Laura said, thinking she wanted to know the truth.

"I don't know . . . I hoped he'd gotten fat and ruddy and no one would be able to see it." She picked up a hairbrush and absently ran her hand over the bristles. She set the brush down, wound and unwound her fingers, and picked it back up to repeat the motion. It was unlike her to fidget.

"Tell me, Gram," Laura repeated, inviting the juggernaut of revelation. If only she'd stopped there, not urged Grace to go on. Nothing more would have been said and Laura's life might have been far different.

"I don't know if you should know. I've wondered for years. I've waited for something to give me a sign of what was right to do. I suppose the way you looked at him was the sign."

"He looks familiar."

"Yes." Grace sighed. "Yes, he looks familiar. And yes, you must know—from me, not from your own guesses." She put the brush down firmly, straightened her shoulders. "Laura-bunny, sit down."

She told it briefly, efficiently, coldly, like a surgeon coolly cutting out a tumor. "I met Herr VonHoldt, Frederich, in England many years ago when your grandfather and I traveled there. I was unhappy—it doesn't matter why—and I behaved very foolishly. Frederich flattered me at a time I needed flattering. He was attractive and attentive. I was stupid and gullible. We . . . we had an . . . affair."

Laura's knees gave out and she sat down heavily on the edge of the bed. "Gram . . .?"

"I know that's hard to imagine. And you probably despise me for it—"

"No, no! Of course not! Oh, Gram, don't say that. I'm just surprised. I always thought you and Grandfather Jack were so happy."

"We were. Later. But not then. I can't explain. It's too long ago for explanations."

Grace stared at Laura for a long moment. "You don't understand yet, do you?"

"I think I do, Gram. You're not the only woman who's ever made a mistake. But it doesn't matter. Not now. Not to me. How could you have thought I would hold such a thing against you? I love you, Gram."

Grace's eyes filled with tears and she opened her arms. Laura came to her, swamped with relief that the horrible confession was really something so innocuous. A fling, a short fling decades ago. She hugged her grandmother and then sat down on the floor beside her.

She thought it was done. But Grace began to speak again. "We came back to Thornehill and your father was born."

The words hung in the air, crackling with meaning.

Laura lifted her head. "What? You mean . . .?"

Grace nodded.

"My father . . .?"

Laura sat up straight and Grace reached out to touch her shoulder as if to grab and physically prevent her from drawing away. "He never knew. No one knew but Jack and me. And now you. You don't have to be afraid anyone else will ever know."

"That man—that horrible man—is my grandfather?"

"It doesn't matter!" Grace said. "It's biology. Nothing more."

But it was a great deal more. Laura felt her stomach churn with revulsion. Why had she asked for this? Why had she urged Gram to tell her the truth? And with that truth, other truths spilled out in front of her. Why Gram had never seemed to like her own son . . . why Herr VonHoldt seemed familiar. In that profile she'd seen her own nearly forgotten father's. And, in a slight way, Sonny's. She stood up slowly.

Grace had clutched a fold of her skirt. "Forgive me, bunny."

"There's nothing to forgive, Gram," she said, meaning it in a vague way. She didn't hold any of this against her grandmother—she didn't think. But there was so much she must consider, so many adjustments to make in her mind.

Grace let go of her skirt. "I've made an even worse mistake. Now I know. It was my sin, and I should have gone to my grave with it my secret. What have I done . . .?"

Laura heard the misery in the words, felt the weight Grace had borne for so many years. For a moment she stepped outside her own concerns and was able to say, "Gram, it's just a surprise. It doesn't matter. Really it doesn't. You're right. It's just biology. You were right to tell me. I'm glad you did. Really glad."

Liar, liar, her mind screamed in a dark recess. But she kept her face and voice and eyes sincere. She had to for Grace's sake. She'd carried the weight of this terrible secret for so long and had now transferred it. Laura had to bear up under the load—not only bear up, but smile and claim it was nothing. She owed that to Gram. It was the price for all those years of love and devotion.

"Let me help you into bed, Gram. You need a rest and I want to go for a little walk and think about this. Such a surprise, finding out I'm related to someone so famous!" She was sickened by her girlish gushing.

"Not famous, notorious."

"It's a sort of fame."

"You won't tell anyone—promise me you won't tell anyone."

"I won't tell Sonny. That's what you mean, isn't it?"

"Yes."

They both knew that Sonny wouldn't accept and bear the load in silence. He would bend, perhaps break under it. He would blame Grace loudly, continuously. No, Sonny couldn't know this. Laura had never kept a secret from him in her life, but this one she'd keep from him for the rest of her life. Not for Gram's sake entirely, but for Sonny's as well.

She got Grace tucked in for a rest and escaped. Mabelann was waiting in the hall, probably having heard every word. Probably having known all of this forever. Laura didn't speak to her except for a knowing glance. She left the house, heading first for the cottage and then veering away, afraid that Eric might decide to visit there. He was the last person in the world she wanted to see right now.

She went to a quiet glade she sometimes visited to watch birds. She'd never seen another soul there and sometimes pretended that she was the only human ever to visit this place. She sat down, put her head on her knees, and wept. Not from sympathy or self-pity or shock, not for herself or Gram or even her father. Not for any well-defined reason. She wept for sheer release. As if there were a poison in her that needed to be washed out.

Finally she mopped her face and looked up with reddened eyes. She felt alone, more alone than she'd ever imagined possible. She found herself wondering, almost objectively, just who she was. For years she'd thought she was the daughter of gentle, well-bred Evelyn Thorne. But she'd learned that was wrong, that her mother was that vulgar, dirty woman who'd come to blackmail Gram. She'd adjusted to that shock. It had been horrible, but the horror had passed and faded. She'd thought herself Sonny's twin and found that was wrong, but she and Sonny had managed to ignore the truth so thoroughly that she usually didn't even remember it.

She'd also thought herself the granddaughter of Captain Jack Thorne, the war hero, but now found, instead, she was the granddaughter of Frederich VonHoldt, the warmonger, the German monster. Could that pass and fade? Could she forget that?

She could certainly try. And she could make sure Gram never knew what a horror the knowledge was. She owed Grace that much, and more, for all those years when Grace made

her a secure, happy child, content that she was greatly loved—
even if not by her own parents.

Slapping a mosquito on her wrist, she noticed her watch
and was astonished at how much time had passed. It was
nearly the dinner hour and she didn't want to alarm Grace by
not showing up. She would stop at the cottage, freshen up
quickly, and be the gracious, cheerful granddaughter at dinner. She hurried back, slapped cold water on her face in the
cottage bathroom, brushed the leaves and grass off her skirt,
and got back to the house just in time to join the rest of them
going into the family dining room.

I could be an actress, she thought toward the end of the
meal. She'd carried it off well, helped in large part by the fact
that Sonny and Eric had eaten earlier and weren't present at
the table. Either of them, with their very different, but faintly
VonHoldt features, would have destroyed her performance.
She felt Grace's gaze on her the whole time and sensed the
older woman's relief as Laura forced herself to chat and laugh
with the family.

After dinner, she went down to the spring lake, taking
along a blanket and a candy bar she didn't want but felt added
to the apparent normalcy of the act. She spread the blanket
out, gave the candy bar to the ducks, and lay back. She
remembered a toy—a monkey, was it?—that Sonny had once
taken apart. It was all held together by a stout cord which,
when removed, let the thing fall to bits. Her own body felt
that way now, like some central adhesive had dissolved.

Someday, she thought as she let her eyes close, someday
this will just be a memory and maybe it won't even hurt. Too
bad she couldn't hurry someday along.

XXII

SHE must have fallen asleep, for when she opened her eyes again it was fully dark and she didn't remember at first where she was. She could hear footsteps—unfamiliar footsteps. For a second, still half-dreaming, she imagined it was Herr VonHoldt, coming to call her "granddaughter" and fold her in a cold, bony embrace. She sat up quickly, shaking off the dream. "Who's there?" she called.

"Laura? Where are you?" Eric's voice.

"Over here." For a minute it was as if the years hadn't intervened, as if they were taking up where they left off. But as he joined her, sitting down on the blanket, the moonlight— cold and blue—struck his features and made them old and sharp and dead. Sonny and I are more closely related to Frederich, yet Eric's is the greater resemblance, Laura thought, then forced the idea out of her mind. She was seeing Frederich VonHoldt in everyone. Next thing she'd be finding his chin on Adele, the arch of his white eyebrow in Edmund's features, the splay of his fingers in Dr. Lee's hands.

"Your grandmother was wondering what had become of you. I tried to ingratiate myself by offering to look for you, but it didn't work. She sent Sonny to the cabin and I sneaked out here to look."

Laura stretched, feeling that her joints had not only re-joined, but cemented themselves. "I'll go up now."

"Stay a minute. She wasn't seriously alarmed, only mildly inquisitive. Laura, I did something to make you mad last night. I don't know what it was, but I want you to know I'm sorry."

Last night? She couldn't remember that far back. Oh, yes.

On the terrace. "No, you didn't do anything," she said, wondering how she could have been so cranky and trivial-minded. He was just a friend of her brother's with whom she'd once done a little experimenting in growing up. It was nothing more—certainly not to him. And she shouldn't have built it up in her imagination to more than it was. "I just had something else on my mind. It was I who was rude. I'm sorry," she said.

"No, you weren't rude, but I was afraid I had been. This whole trip has put me off my stride. I feel like . . . Well, never mind."

"No, go on."

"Well, I feel like I'm a fool to have come here right now and for the reason I did. I have such fond—and important—memories of you and of Thornehill. I always thought I'd come back someday and it would be just like it was. But I waited until Sonny dangled great-uncle once-removed Frederich in front of me like some sort of obscene bait. Part of me knew I should never get near him if the unlikely possibility arose, and a part of me couldn't resist the temptation. I've done so much because of him, you see—"

"No, I don't. What do you mean?"

"Because of the name. That sort of infamy is hard to live with. It colors everything, no matter how much you try to forget it."

Don't tell me this, Laura thought, but could say nothing.

"We changed our name so it wasn't the same as his. That's an awful thing, to feel like someone has stolen your name and made a dirty word of it, and both my father and I have gone out of our way to be as unlike 'VonHoldts' as possible."

"Just what relation are you?" Laura asked. Why was she feeling so little sympathy and so much irritation?

"Frederich's first cousin was my grandfather. I guess you find it hard to understand, but it's a horrible thing to see that name in the news and know that his blood runs in my veins—and wonder: am I like him? I can't tell you how much it's upset me seeing him—"

Laura stood up and started to walk away.

"Laura! Wait, I just wanted you to know how I felt—"

"Dammit! I don't care how you feel! You can roll around in your petty problems by yourself!" she said. She was astonished at her own words, at her violent reaction, and yet she couldn't stop them. "Don't you see how self-indulgent this all is? Your blood, your name, your distress—you're hardly even related to him! I think you're enjoying this, looking at the monster VonHoldt and feeling sorry for yourself."

"But I'm related to him. Naturally I—"

"No, you're not! But I'm his—" She bit the words off, putting her hands to her mouth as if to muffle herself. She was horrified at what she'd almost said.

"You're what?"

"Never mind."

"I'm sorry I confided in you," he said stiffly.

"So am I! I wish to heaven nobody would ever confide anything in me. I don't want other people's problems and secrets and . . . Oh, Eric, leave me alone!" she finished on a sob.

She turned and ran for the house.

It had all happened so quickly, so senselessly, with such a terrible, unreasoning heat. By morning Laura knew she'd been horrible and despised her emotional outburst. She found the blanket she'd left by the spring folded neatly outside her door and almost burst into tears. What a bitch she'd been! He had no way of knowing what she was going through, nor of the awful irony of his words. Of course it was hard on him bearing the name. She had no right to be so rude. She couldn't rest easily with her own conscience until she'd smoothed things out with Eric. She wasn't sure how to do it without telling him the truth—which was out of the question— but she'd find a way.

She went to Sonny's room. "Is Eric up and about yet?" she asked.

He gave her a strange look. "Up and very much about. He's gone."

"Gone? Where?"

"Home to New York. Came in at midnight and asked me to drive him to the station. I told him the train didn't go through until eight in the morning, but he was determined to get out of the house. I assumed it had something to do with VonHoldt."

"It did, in a way. But mainly it was me."

"What happened?"

"I don't even know—exactly," Laura lied. "It's only a quarter after eight. If the train's late he might still be there. I'll call."

But for once the train was on time and Eric was gone.

Laura went straight to her room and wrote a convoluted letter of apology that made very little sense.

He never answered.

The meeting broke up that day as well. Apparently no agreement was reached because all the government guests went off walking a bit stiff-legged and speaking in very brittle tones. Grace didn't come into the public part of the house to say good-bye. Neither did Laura. Instead, she sat in a window seat at the front of the house and watched them get into their limousines. She was, she knew, being just as self-indulgent as she'd accused Eric of being, but she couldn't help herself. She had to see Her VonHoldt again. For a second she thought he'd sensed her presence. He seemed to look up toward the window where she cowered, but then looked away so quickly that she decided she'd imagined it.

Grace was clearly glad they were gone. When she emerged from her self-imposed confinement a few days later, she looked younger and happier than she had for some months. It was, as far as she was concerned, over. The past had been faced and defeated and her own long-standing guilt shed like a dead skin. She didn't seem to notice that now it was draped around Laura's shoulders.

By the end of the month, the heat broke and the usual guests started their annual migration back to Thornehill. Some of them had British children with them, children who had been evacuated from London to relatives and friends in the United States. They broke Laura's heart, those hollow-eyed boys and girls who pored over the papers with Edmund and stuck "bomb pins" in the big map of Europe he kept in the schoolroom.

By the middle of September they were calling it the "London Blitz," and even from a distance it was terrifying. In one night alone nearly a thousand bombers and fighters bombarded London in wave after wave. Hundreds of tons of bombs were dropped, killing thousands and thousands of ordinary citizens, many of them children who hadn't been fortunate enough to have relatives in safer parts of the world.

How many of those bombs had Frederich VonHoldt made and profited by? Laura wondered. How many people had he—her secret grandfather!—been responsible for killing?

"Don't you want to *do* something!" she railed at Sonny.

"Like what?"

"I don't know. I just have an overwhelming urge to help.

Not that there's any way I could. I've never even been in England, but I feel like it's my heritage that Hitler is trying to wipe out. Think of the buildings, the history, all the lives that can never be reclaimed!''

Sonny put aside the book he was poring over and slung his arm around Laura's shoulder. ''You're doing all you can. Teaching that little English girl in the blue suite to do that stupid tatting of yours is a service in a way.''

''That's nothing!'' Laura said angrily.

''For a few hours a day you're keeping her mind off the fact that her mother and father may be blown to bits any moment. Don't you think that's worthwhile? Now, quit crusading and get back to your typewriter. This book's got a military theme and might actually be slightly useful to somebody in Washington.''

Politics, particularly the politics of war, were a constant conversational topic at Thornehill. The privileged class of people to whom the hotel catered had not changed their minds about Franklin Roosevelt in the years he'd been in office. If anything, their hatred of him had become uglier and more vociferous. ''Never did a day's work in his life, lives on his mother's money,'' was one of the favorite complaints, expressed most often by people to whom the accusation applied equally.

The first lady's heritage and morals were another familiar topic. ''Nigger through and through,'' they'd say. ''Look at those lips of hers. That's where she got the clap, fooling around with the niggers.''

Laura would always get up trembling with outrage and leave the room when this subject was being hashed over. But Grace, who had once reacted the same way, had learned to let it flow past her virtually unnoticed, like bits of scum on a river—further evidence of the alterations age had brought to her. The one thing Grace still took an interest in was the subject of the war that raged across the Atlantic. ''We must not throw away another generation of our men!'' she would say.

Many of her friends agreed. Isolationism was a popular attitude that spanned class and age. Older men had seen the desolation and destruction of the last war; young men knew it was they who would have to fight this one if America got into it. Like many people, Laura had mixed feelings. She wanted to help the beleaguered Europeans, and when, in November,

Coventry was destroyed, she wept bitterly. She'd had an etching of the cathedral in her bedroom for years and it was as if something uniquely hers had been wantonly ruined. But she knew that American intervention would mean all the Freddies of her life would go, and so might Sonny. No, not might—Sonny, with his translating skills, would certainly go.

In December they had a visitor from Washington. "Laura, I want you to meet Senator Langley," Grace said. "You remember we listened to a speech of his last week on the radio."

Senator Archibald Langley was one of the premier isolationists in the country. With his thick white hair, patrician features, and liquid-gold voice, he was the ultimate elder statesman. He'd been mentioned as a presidential candidate a generation earlier, but for reasons of his own preferred to remain in the Senate. Cynics said it was because life in the White House would shed the harsh glare of public examination on his private life—a life of wealth and fanatically close family ties.

But the truth was that Arch Langley utterly lacked the common touch and was intelligent enough to know it. He was too elite, his inbred aristocratic features too obviously effete, to appeal to the voters. The American public was perceptive enough to sense that he could spend quite an enjoyable solitary evening reading Jane Austen and listening to Brahms, and they were, in his opinion, stupid enough to hate him for it. Yes, the average man could tell when a man was more comfortable in a yachting blazer than a Sears-catalog sport coat. So rather than face defeat in the polls, he'd remained the power behind the powers. A Republican to the core, he'd nevertheless stayed apart from partisan politics. Leaders of his own party hated and feared him for it. Democrats often forgot his rightist leanings in their respect for his culture, erudition, and eagle-talon tongue.

For many years he'd had—unofficially, to be sure, during the long Democratic administration—very nearly the final word on who was granted ambassadorial positions. His inquiries into the background and social acceptability of candidates were as incisive as a surgical knife and a number of men who thought their money and influence could buy a safe, comfortable post in an embassy found to their chagrin that their table manners and family lineage didn't measure up to Arch Langley's standards. Many a retired industrialist with dreams of a soft life in Bermuda slunk home to Indianapolis or Cincinnati cursing Langley.

He and Franklin Roosevelt had known each other for decades, and Langley refused to hear any of the gossipy criticism of him. Instead he spoke of the President, rather condescendingly, as a younger brother. "Frank's just a little off the mark there, I'll admit," he'd say. "But he'll come around soon enough. Brilliant man, really. He's finding ways of helping out our friends across the ocean without getting us in the middle of the conflict."

"Patronizing old buzzard," Sonny said.

"You don't like him, do you?" Laura said.

"Not much. Didn't you hear him spouting all that stuff about how the war's not really as bad as it sounds, that it's just that the press is riddled with Jews who are trying to drag us in? No, I don't like him."

Toward the end of his visit, Langley was joined by his nephew Stephen, and Laura forgot about politics. Stephen Highsmith Langley had, to an extraordinary degree, what a later age would have called "charisma." It wasn't just his looks—thick, dark hair, clear blue eyes, remarkably like Clark Gable, but with a patrician elegance overriding the earthiness—or his inherited wealth. It was an undefinable combination of generations of good breeding, a tailor's-dream physique, a rich, appealing voice, careful mannerisms, and an air of electric sexuality which he gave the impression of almost consciously keeping under control.

But all of that didn't explain his appeal completely. There was something else—an assurance, an unassailable calm, that brought it all together like a chemical reaction of powerful proportions. At thirty-four, he was in his prime and wore his self-confidence like a comfortable old jacket. A very well-made jacket.

Laura met him briefly as he arrived. "I'm here to meet my uncle, Miss Thorne. If you'll just point me in the right direction, I won't bother you anymore."

Bother me! Laura thought. "It's no trouble to show you up to his room. This way."

He was there only one day and Laura had no further opportunity to talk to him alone, which was just as well, because she found herself surprisingly tongue-tied in his presence. Instead, she was content to listen to him at dinner with the family, no other guests but the Langleys currently staying at the hotel. Under Grace's gentle questioning, he revealed his position. Trained in international law, he was currently serving in a nonelective post in the State Department. His uncle was his proud mentor.

"The men of our family have been in public service since we came from England in the late 1600's," Arch Langley explained. "Governors, senators, both state and national. Stephen's father, my brother, was under consideration as a Supreme Court appointment when he died during the Spanish-influenza epidemic. He would have been the youngest man on that esteemed bench."

"An impressive heritage," Grace said. "And what do you see as your destiny, Mr. Langley?" she asked Stephen.

"I'm going to be President," he said, spreading butter on a roll.

"President of what?" Sonny asked irreverently.

Stephen turned a startled blue-eyed gaze on Sonny. "Of America, of course."

"Now, Stephen . . ." Senator Langley said.

Stephen caught himself. Putting the roll down, he said, "If the people want me, naturally. I think I have a lot to give my country and the moral obligation to offer my skills."

"How old are you, sir?" Sonny asked, and only Laura heard the mockery in his tone.

"Thirty-four."

"It seems the Constitution specifies that Presidents must be somewhat older than that."

"And wisely so. I didn't mean to imply that I'm ready yet, nor that I have any grandiose ideas of supplanting Uncle Arch's friend Mr. Roosevelt. No, I've got several years of preparation ahead of me. I was merely stating my long-range goal. I hope I haven't offended you?"

"Not in the least," Sonny answered with a smile. But Laura knew him and knew that, for reasons that completely eluded her, Sonny *was* tremendously offended.

Laura was with Sonny, just coming back from a walk, when the Langleys left the next day. Stephen saw her and came over to speak as their bags were being loaded. "I'm sorry we didn't have any more chance to talk, Miss Thorne. I hope we'll meet again."

Laura merely nodded her agreement.

"I hope also that I didn't sound like a pompous ass at dinner. Talking about being President . . ." he said it in an almost boyish way, as if he were confessing to having talked too much about his marble collection. "I just felt so comfortable, so much at home here."

"I was very interested, Mr. Langley."

"Mr. Langley! Oh, no—that won't do! Please call me Stephen or I'll feel a hundred years old."

She smiled. "I was very interested, Stephen."

He grinned back at her, an expression that made her knees feel funny. "You're either the girl of my dreams or a wonderfully polite liar. We'll see each other again . . .?"

"I hope so," Laura said, hoping she didn't sound too fervent.

Silently she and Sonny watched as the hotel limousine wound away down the drive. "I've come to a realization," Sonny said.

"What's that?"

"It is my firm belief, held for a number of hours now and apt to last me the rest of my life, that men who want to be politicians shouldn't be."

"What do you mean?"

"I mean politics are something men should be forced into because of their particular talents. Against their will, if at all possible. Don't fall for him, Laura."

"Don't be an ass. I hardly know him."

"But I saw how you looked at him. I can't blame you. He's damned attractive. I imagine there are *men* who've changed their sexual orientation at the sight of him. But be careful. He's dangerous. Too ambitious altogether."

Though Laura had come to respect and nearly always share Sonny's assessments of people, she utterly ignored his criticisms and warnings this time. A great part of Stephen Langley's fascination was his ambition. He wanted something; he wanted to *be* something. He knew where he was headed. To Laura, bogged down in a swamp of pointlessness, this was enviable and exciting.

It was, she realized now, part of the reason none of the Freddies of her easy, circumscribed world had truly engaged her interest. They had no more idea than she where they were going or why or when. Even Sonny, her beloved Sonny, simply got from day to day translating his books, reading the papers, and chatting with family and guests with no purpose. Uncle Edmund had talked about it to her years ago—these privileged men with no reason to get up in the morning—and she was just beginning to realize that, except that she was a woman, she was one of them.

But not Stephen Langley. He was going to be President of the United States.

"What melodrama," she told Sonny. "You've had your head stuck in those gloomy German books for too long. Your mind is going! We'll never see him again anyway."

She wanted to tell him she envied and somehow admired Stephen for the simple fact that he knew exactly who and what he was, but she couldn't discuss that with Sonny. She couldn't say to him: I'm the daughter of Iris Smalley and the granddaughter of Herr VonHoldt, the Armaments King, whereas Stephen can look back at all his antecedents and be proud.

Why had Gram burdened her with this knowledge? She began to feel resentful, and with the resentment came an understanding: that much of her life and personality had been shaped and determined by the events of other people's lives. Her father hadn't loved her because she was born to an ignorant slut. His mother didn't love him because he was VonHoldt's son. Laura's own devotion to Sonny had developed, in part, because of the division of favoritism in their elders based on these events. She was still, for all her swimming lessons at school, afraid of water because Gram was afraid of water because her sister died by drowning over a half-century ago!

Did it always go on and on like this? Am I doing and thinking things that are going to determine the course of my own grandchildren's lives? Laura wondered. Will they inherit my guilts and fears along with the color of my eyes or the shape of my nose? Have I no control over my own destiny?

That brought her back to her own future—or lack of future, and that in turn brought her mind back to Stephen Langley and his particular attraction. He knew who he was, how he got that way, and where he was going. How wonderful for him.

And how magnetic.

Laura might have spent a good deal of her all-too-free time thinking about Stephen in the next weeks if something far more important hadn't intervened.

On Christmas morning the seemingly eternal, invincible Grace Emerson Thorne had a stroke.

Typically, she managed to have it privately and with as much dignity as possible.

Mabelann had been sent up to check on her when the rest of the family assembled for a holiday breakfast. The black woman came back to the room a few minutes later on a run. "She done taken terrible sick!" she gasped.

Edmund and Sonny went to find Dr. Lee while the women dashed upstairs. Laura was first into the room and found her grandmother barely conscious, her face twisted into a mask of helpless terror. Taking her hand, Laura was shocked that there was no answering pressure. "Oh, Gram! What's happened? Are you hurt? Please, say something to me."

Grace made a sound—not a word, but a response. Saliva trickled from the corner of her mouth. Laura grabbed a handkerchief from the bedside table and blotted it off her chin. Getting a grip on herself, she said, "Dr. Lee went out fishing early this morning. They're looking for him and he'll be along in a few minutes."

But it seemed like hours, like decades, before Howard was found, came in, and shooed all but Adele from the room.

"She's much better," he told the rest of the family later as they gathered in the library among the brightly wrapped Christmas presents no one had bothered to open. "Really. It was a very slight stroke and she's already enormously improved."

"Then she's going to be all right?" India asked.

He paused. "I can't promise that. She may live to a hundred and never suffer a recurrence—but it could happen again tomorrow. There's no way to guess. Of course, that's true of all of us, so I'd advise you to avoid treating her like an invalid."

After a very late dinner, Dr. Lee went up the darkened staircase to Grace's room with Laura. "She'll appreciate your company, Laura. I think she's more worried about you than herself."

"About me? Why me?"

"Because she has the idea that she must take care of you. Protect you from something."

"Protect me from what?"

"God only knows. The world . . . fate . . everything."

He stumbled a little on the top step and Laura grasped his elbow. He steadied himself a moment and said, "I'm sorry. Doctors aren't supposed to be frightened, but this has been a hard day for me and I'm getting old. I shouldn't have gone out in the cold this morning."

Laura caught the glance he cast at the door of Grace's room and, with blinding clarity, realized that he was in love with her grandmother. He probably always had been. "Why didn't you marry her?'' she asked before she had time to think what an impertinent question it was.

He put his arm around her and she could feel his hand trembling on her shoulder—or was it she who was trembling? ''There are people, my dear Laura, who love with such terrible intensity that they can love only one person at a time. Your grandmother loved her husband. Then she loved you. I didn't manage to slip myself in at the right time. Now, run along and visit with her for a few minutes. Then both of you get some sleep. It's been a long day for everyone.''

XXIII

*T*HEY'D been talking for hours, examining the events, speculating on the possible outcomes, and considering strategy for dealing with every eventuality. Normally, it made his blood move, his aging joints ease, but this afternoon it had merely wearied him. Was it age or the weather or just the prospect of this damned inevitable war?

Archibald Langley looked out the window at the rolling hills of Pennsylvania and opened the window a crack. For all the years he'd spent in rooms this way—plotting, planning, anticipating everyone's possible moves and motives—he'd never adjusted to the smoke that seemed inherent to politics. He'd tried a cigar once, thinking it might be pleasurable, but it only made him sick and dizzy like a kid smoking behind the barn.

"Hey, Arch, you're letting the goddamn outdoors in," one of the men at the table said.

He was an old friend. His banter usually warmed Archibald, but not this afternoon. "Sorry, but you boys are trying to choke me to death," Arch said, trying to disguise his snappishness and failing.

Someone laughed nervously, someone else got up and stretched, and the others were all suddenly restless. "I guess we ought to get back to the ladies. Supposed to socialize a bit," one of the men, a Republican congressman from the West, said.

One by one they finished their drinks, ground out their cigarettes, and left. All but Stephen. Arch studied him as he saw the other men out. Good boy, Stephen. No, not a boy anymore. And that thought reminded him of something he wanted to discuss before Bess got around to it. Smart woman, Bess Langley. Too damned smart sometimes. Arch had approved nearly forty years ago when his younger brother married her, thinking she had the extra spunk and drive he needed to get somewhere. But then when he died, she'd turned it all on Stephen. Too bad she hadn't considered remarrying, but then, she was a singularly sexless sort of woman. Always had been. Probably frigid as hell.

But if she'd had someone else—some poor sap of a husband—to lavish her energies on, Arch wouldn't have had some of the battles he had over Stephen. He'd never intended to be "co-mentor" to the boy. Of course they'd been in agreement on most of their aims; it was just a question of power and timing.

The last of the men had gone. Stephen had taken off his jacket and, clad in gray wool slacks and a red sweater over a freshly ironed white shirt, was now flipping idly through a newspaper. The clothes, the dark hair and penetrating blue eyes really did give him the look of a movie idol. It wouldn't hurt him in the polls. "You want to talk about something, Arch?" he asked without looking up.

There it was again, that hint of insolence Archibald had heard from time to time—or perhaps he was imagining it. "Yes, I do. You know this war is going to get us, no matter what crap Franklin gave the country all through the campaign about promising our boys would never fight on foreign soil again."

"Sure. What else could he say in an election year? You watch the polls. You know how opposed everyone is to getting into it. After that flap about the Conscription bill last September, he didn't dare say that he was going to ship all those boys off. He'd have every college campus on the country up in arms. I'll bet he's just praying for some aggression so overt it can't be ignored and the public begs him to declare war."

That was Arch's view as well, but it both saddened and irritated him to hear Stephen express it first. As if the boy was somehow getting ahead of him. He opened the window again and sucked in his stomach as he inhaled the cold fresh air. "It's just a question of time. But I want to talk about you. What you'll do."

"I'll join the army. If a man doesn't have the courage to defend his country, he doesn't deserve to have a place in its administration."

Arch glanced at him warily. All this courage crap was his mother's doing, and he'd wished a hundred times she'd laid off it. It was, naturally, just the right public line to take, but the boy seemed really to believe it. Or did he? Arch had never been sure.

"It'll take time out of the schedule, of course," Stephen went on.

The Schedule. The precious plan. The culmination of all the training and work and years of waiting. Arch felt the old stab of regret. Why couldn't this handsome, intelligent young man have been his own son, instead of a nephew? How the hell had his spineless brother ever fathered such an ideal politician?

"Going into the service needn't slow us down much, you know. We'll get you over there, get into some flashy action, then get you out again, then right into the Senate." Arch sat down across from him and was pointedly quiet until Stephen refolded the paper and put it down. "There's something else. You ought to be married. You're thirty-four now. In another year or two people are going to start thinking you're a faggot."

Stephen laughed. "I've been thinking about it," he said.

"I think it ought to be before you go. Give an appearance of stability. Girl back home, all that. Fighting for your country and the little woman."

"Have *you* got someone picked out?" Stephen said.

Was there mockery in the tone or did Arch imagine that, too?

"No, just that it's something we need to start thinking about."

"Have you talked to Mother about it?"

"Good God! Bess hadn't already got somebody lined up, has she?"

"Dozens. But she's rejected all of them. It doesn't matter, though. I've decided."

"Decided what?"

"Whom I'm going to marry."

Arch drew himself up indignantly. This was really too much. Every step of the boy's life had been carefully, intelligently orchestrated by Arch and Bess. Marriage, for a politician, was one of the most important decisions. Where the hell did he get the nerve to think he could just say, "I've decided"!

"Would it trouble you too much if I ask whom you've selected?" Arch said.

Stephen glanced up sharply. He was fully aware of his debt

to his uncle, and while sometimes it was oppressive, he neither wanted nor could afford to offend the older man. "Sorry, Arch. I didn't mean to ruffle you. I just meant—"

"Who?"

"Laura Thorne."

"Laura Thorne? Who the hell is . . .? Oh, yes. The girl in Arkansas. Why her?"

"Why not," Stephen said firmly. It wasn't a question.

Arch sat down, tented his fingers, and thought about it. Half a century ago he'd gotten into the habit of keeping a mental dossier on nearly everyone he ever met, even when he saw no need for it. Insignificant but nice-enough girl, as he remembered. Pretty, but colorless personality. Of course, that wasn't necessarily a bad thing. People were fed up with that ugly aggressive bitch Eleanor. Of course, the Thorne girl was awfully young. But they wouldn't be running Stephen until '48 or '52, even though he'd be old enough by '44. That would give her time enough to have two or three babies and learn the ropes politically.

"What do you know about the family?" he asked Stephen.

"Old money. The great-grandfather was Boston and Harvard. Money came from railroads originally, but he got out early and put it into stocks and property. They lost a lot in 1929, but the grandmother's brought the portfolio back above pre-crash level. The hotel seems to be something to keep her busy rather than a necessity now. The FBI has some idea there were some of Hoover's list staying there ten years ago or so, but it seems the Thornes cleared them out on their own before anything came of it. Nothing remotely questionable on the record since 1933."

Arch nodded. He'd underestimated Stephen. He'd done his homework. "What about that boy. Sonny? Stupid name . . ."

"He's Jackson Thorne III, actually. Doing translation work for Charlie over at the State Department. I only got to talk to Charlie for a minute, but it seems like it's mainly busywork. Nothing crucial, but they want to keep close tabs on him. He's apparently brilliant with languages and they want to know exactly where to find him if they need him."

"What about the rest of the family?"

"Laura's father died in some sort of hunting accident. Seems to have been a harmless sort. Her mother is, well . . . vague. Not crazy or anything. At least not enough to be an embarrassment. The grandmother, Grace, comes from an old

Virginia family. The Emersons. Wasn't your wife connected with them?''

"Third or fourth cousins. Have you talked to your mother about this girl?''

"I didn't think it was time yet.''

"Right. No reason to get her in a dither. Not yet. But I want to take another look at the girl. Why don't we go back next month.''

"I'll make reservations.''

Laura was helping Grace and Adele sort through a shipment of new bed linens. "Let me lift that stack, Gram,'' Laura said.

Grace hoisted it herself. "I'm not a cripple!'' The effect was ruined when she had to drop the bundle on the nearest table.

Laura picked it up without a word and tore away the brown paper wrapping and started counting out pillowcases. Gram had recovered from the small stroke in record time. Her walk had become a little springier and the slight slur in her speech was gone now except when she was unusually tired. But she'd aged noticeably. Her normally lithe movements were cramped and careful. Her handwriting had become crabbed and spiky. There were lines of worry and fatigue around her eyes that had never been noticeable before. She had developed a slight tremor that made it appear that she was always shaking her head no. It was all so slight, so subtle, that everyone else at Thornhill—except for Mableann, who missed nothing where Grace was concerned—believed she was entirely well.

But Laura had a special telepathy with Grace and sensed that the older woman wasn't at all well. And the specter of death shadowed their relationship, sometimes stepping between them so that they saw each other through a haze of regret and fear. Laura had talked to Dr. Lee about it, but he was true to Grace as a doctor and a friend. "If there were anything about your grandmother's health that she wanted you to know or that you needed to know, I would tell you,'' he said curtly.

"Then there *is* something wrong?''

"I didn't say that.''

India came in with a handful of mail and sat down to go through it while the other women finished their work. "The reservations are getting heavy for April and May,'' she said, slitting one envelope after another. "I think everyone's trying to get in one last vacation before the war starts. Here's one for March . . Oh, Senator Langley and his nephew again. And, Laura, there's a personal letter for you on the same stationery."

The three older women pretended not to pay any attention while Laura opened the letter and skimmed the few handwritten lines. "Well?" India finally said.

"Nothing—just a note saying he's looking forward to seeing me again," Laura said, feeling a schoolgirl blush creep up her neck.

"I'll bet he's coming courting," India said. "Imagine our little Laura married to a President. How divine! We could attend all the fancy parties at the White House and take turns sleeping in Lincoln's bedroom."

"India McPhee! Don't tease," Adele said grumpily.

"I've got to go help Sonny," Laura said, making her escape.

Stephen and the senator stayed only three days in March. Stephen returned by himself for a week in June, but had to leave when word came that the Germans were massing for attack along the Russian border. "This might be it," he said. "I need to be in Washington. I'd rather stay here. You know that, don't you?"

"I'm flattered," Laura said, trying to keep the tone light, for fear she was reading too much into his words.

"I didn't mean to flatter you. It's purely selfish. I've never felt quite so . . . so much 'myself' as when I'm here with you. Does that make sense?"

But Germany advanced, Russia retreated, and the United States stayed out of it and Laura started imagining when he'd return again.

She'd been astonished and somewhat embarrassed at the intensity of her disappointment when he had to go, just as she had been surprised at how difficult it was to sleep when he was there. She was forever thinking that time apart from him was time wasted, never to be recovered. Though he was never aggressively ardent—there had been only a few kisses, and those more respectfully friendly than passionate—there was no mistaking his interest in her. Nor could she mistake that she'd fallen in love with this energetic, determined man.

He managed to be both friendly and comfortable around her, but was always scrupulously polite. "You don't always have to open doors for me," she told him at one point.

"If I could think of bigger, better, more flamboyant things to do for you, I would. As it is, I enjoy leaping ahead and getting doors out of your way," he said with a laugh. "Is there something else I can do for you? Any dragons around I could slay?"

"None that I can think of."

"Pity. I brought my best set of armor along and haven't even had a chance to unpack it."

He filled the days as they'd never been filled before. An early riser, he was up and out looking for things to do before most of the rest of the household thought of getting up. "What a beautiful day. What shall we do?" he'd say as they ate breakfast in the nearly deserted dining room. And before most of the family and guests were groggily stirring, Laura and Stephen would be out—horseback riding, swimming in the frigid spring water, striding across the hills at his breakneck pace, or whirling through the lush countryside in one of the family cars.

It wasn't just physical activity that occupied him. Stephen Langley was a well-educated man who exercised his mind as strenuously as he exercised his handsome body. For the first time, Laura was challenged by conversation. He loaned her books of political philosophy as if he were bestowing life's treasures, and if she was less than vitally interested, she appreciated the generous intent and tried hard to work up an enthusiasm to match his.

"When did you decide you wanted to be President?" she asked one day.

He looked embarrassed. "I shouldn't have said anything about it. I know it sounds pompous."

"No, it sounds exciting. I envy you, knowing exactly what you want. Have you always known?"

"No. My mother and Uncle Arch have always had it in mind for me, but it didn't seem truly my own dream until a few years ago. The funny thing is, there wasn't any one moment when I said, 'Ahhh, that's what I want.' It was a gradual sort of thing, like loving your family. You always do, you just sometimes don't consciously realize it.

"Fortunately, because of Mother's dream, I was ready to accept the idea as a possibility. I'd been trained from the cradle, in a way."

"What do you mean?"

He smiled. "One of my earliest memories is my mother showing me how a family tree was constructed. She had one all mapped out and instead of nursery rhymes at bedtime, she'd tell me over and over again about my family, my heritage, and all the men who'd been important in some way to the government. You know what I did for my first 'Show and Tell' at school? I got up and recited the names of the Presidents in order. As soon as I got done, I realized I'd left out Jackson and I cried all morning. I can see now that it was a ridiculous thing for a child to be so upset about, but I was."

It was a strange childhood, Laura realized, but certainly no stranger than her own. Only different. As she thought about it, she realized that there was more of a bond between them than was immediately apparent. Stephen had become what his family had wanted him to become, just as she had grown to be the young woman Grace wanted her to be. Stephen had not only accepted, but wholeheartedly embraced the role and had made it his own dream. To accept might have been a weakness in some, but in him it was a strength. In a secret, unexamined part of her mind, his strength reinforced her own self-image. It was possible to be what others expected you to be and remain your own person. He validated her.

And when he'd gone, life became unutterably boring and pointless again. His letters were bright spots in her days even though they were seldom romantic by the farthest stretch of the imagination. In fact, they were somewhat frustrating. He was so open, so informal and easy to talk to in person, but his letters were careful, almost stilted.

In August he wrote that he was returning the next month. This time he was bringing his mother along to meet the family.

"You're being held up for approval," Sonny said sourly.

"That's ridiculous!" Laura snapped back. Stephen Langley had become a touchy subject between them. And Sonny kept coming back to it like a hangnail, picking until it bled.

"She'll want to check your teeth and your breeding papers," Sonny went on. "Yes, my girl, this is the final step. If Mama approves, you'll be getting that proposal you're so hot for."

"Don't be vulgar and obnoxious," she said, wanting to add the word "jealous." She'd be jealous too if Sonny had fallen in love first. It was only natural, as close and isolated as they had always been. It was her only regret about her relationship with Stephen—it cut Sonny out and created a barrier between them. But that was really Sonny's own fault. Stephen always tried to be friendly to him, and Sonny just kept drawing up like an outraged old maid when Stephen attempted to get to know him better.

"I can't imagine what you see in a stuffed shirt like him," Sonny said.

"Well, he's handsome and intelligent and treats me like a queen," Laura replied.

"Besides that?" Sonny said, finally smiling.

"He's charming and rich and Gram is crazy about him."

"Come on, Laura. You know you don't give a damn about rich and handsome. What is it really?"

"I can't define it, Sonny. I like being with him. He makes me feel happy. Isn't that enough?"

"That's romantic shit."

"You just want me to be an old maid."

"I guess I do. No, that's not really it. I don't mind you falling in love and getting married. I just wish you'd picked somebody I like better. Like Eric—you could have had Eric if you'd played your cards right, you know."

"He didn't want me," she said, meaning it to come out sounding light and frothy, but hearing self-pity in her voice. Still, it was true. Eric was convinced that being distantly related to Frederich VonHoldt had nearly ruined his life. Imagine if he'd known Laura's relationship to the man. It would have been like admitting to being the granddaughter of Attila the Hun!

"Didn't want you? Didn't you see the way his whole face turned to custard when he got an eyeful of you?"

"An eyeful! What kind of word is that?" Laura asked, determined to change the subject.

"Seriously, Laura, what went wrong between you two? I had high hopes of playing cupid."

"You'll have to play it someplace else."

"All right, I'll work on getting Aunt Adele set up with someone." He waited for a laugh, which didn't come. He went on, "I know you can't marry somebody for my sake, but are you sure Langley's the right one?"

"He hasn't even asked me—yet. Isn't it a little early for this sort of inquisition?"

"Doesn't it bother you that he never looks rumpled? I mean, it seems like he's got somebody running along behind with an iron. Every time he steps out of view for a second, he comes back looking tidier than ever."

Laura looked around Sonny's chaotic room. "I can see how that would irritate you."

"Well, all I can say is, you'd better be on your best behavior for this Mama-visit. I hear she's a tough old broad. She'll chew you up and spit you out if you don't watch it."

When Bess Langley arrived, Laura saw the truth in Sonny's predictions. She *was* on an inspection tour. "Such a very charming home," she said, looking over the front entryway as if surprised to find that it wasn't a mountain shack.

Bess had been born with more intelligence and drive and less natural beauty than was good for a woman in the latter decades of the nineteenth century. At the age of thirteen—pudgy, pimpled, and scowling—she had accompanied her family to a routine reception at the White House and she had realized she wanted to go back there as a resident, not a guest. From that day on, she structured her life to accomplish that goal. There was, of course, no thought in her mind of being a woman President. Such a thing would never happen. But she had to carefully select a man who could be elected.

At eighteen she made of list of attributes such a man had to have, and at twenty-two she met him. Jarvis Langley had the money, the looks, the manners, and the connections for it. All he lacked was the motivation, and that was what she could supply in full measure. He'd let her down by dying of the Spanish influenza, but after a short and intense grieving period, she'd realized she had twelve-year-old Stephen to take his place and her brother-in-law Archibald to fill in as father. So far, all the plans for him had come to fruition. Excellent grades in excellent schools, a thoroughly appealing appearance, and most important, the drive to make her dream come true.

But now he'd picked out a wife-to-be! Without even consulting with her in advance. She'd very nearly lost her head when he first talked to her about this Thorne girl. The words "I forbid it" were hovering on her thin lips when she caught a glint of determination in his eyes that frightened her into temporary caution. "We'll see," she said. "I want to meet the girl." And Stephen had acquiesced politely. It had been the right thing to do, for now if she found the girl intolerable, she sensed she could change his mind.

"How gracious of you to have us here at such a lovely time of year," she said to Grace, falling instinctively into the pretense that this was a private home.

That pleased Grace. "We're all so glad you could come. Here in Arkansas we're inordinately proud of our fall foliage and you'll probably be shown every tree on the property before you can get away. Ahh, here's my granddaughter. Laura, this is Stephen's mother, Mrs. Langley.''

"How do you do, Mrs. Langley? Stephen's spoken of you so often I feel we're already acquainted,'' Laura said, not very truthfully.

"How sweet of you, my dear,'' Bess said. The girl was stunning, absolutely stunning, with a valentine face, flawless skin, and toothpaste-advertisement teeth. Moreover, there was both elegance and strength in the fine jaw and large eyes. No wonder Stephen was so taken with her. Of course, looks were just an auxiliary benefit in a politician's wife. Nice, but not at all necessary. Eleanor Roosevelt proved that. "I'm looking forward to getting to know all about you, Laura. Stephen claims you are a a positive pargon among women,'' Bess said. The tone was jovial, but no one missed the implication: I'm here to determine whether you are a suitable wife for my son.

Laura hid her momentary terror of the woman and looked her in the eye. "How sweet of Stephen to give you that impression, but I assure you I'm not a paragon.''

Dinner was an inquisition.

A very polite inquisition, but an inquisition nevertheless. Bess didn't waste any time on banalities like where Laura had gone to school or what sort of grades she'd gotten. Bess already knew all that. A friend of a friend of a friend was close to the headmistress of Laura's preparatory school and a neighbor's cousin had once made a substantial endowment to the college she'd attended. Instead, Bess went after the sort of thing transcripts didn't tell—attitudes, morals, interests. "Do you ride?'' she asked.

"Not often.''

"I suppose if I were as delicate as you are I'd be terribly afraid of horses,'' Bess said with a self-deprecating smile that fooled no one.

"I'm neither delicate nor afraid, Mrs. Langley. Merely more interested in other things,'' Laura said with a smile as sweet as Bess's.

And when the conversation veered, as it inevitably did, to politics, Bess said, "All of this must be terribly boring to you, Laura.''

"Not in the least. Government has been a topic of discussion here since I was a child. A great many people have eaten at this table and aired their views.''

"And which of those views do you adhere to, my dear?''

"That government is best run by those who know more

about it than I do." She almost choked with a suppressed laugh at the sight of Sonny's face as she said this.

Bess wasn't sure what to make of this. It was, of course, precisely the answer she'd have suggested a future daughter-in-law make if she'd been able to script it herself, but was the girl sincere or merely making fun?

It was finally Sonny who put an end to the question when Bess Langley made some reference to Edith Galt and added, "Of course you know who she was, don't you?"

Laura replied, "President Wilson's wife."

At that Sonny pushed back his dessert plate and said, "Ah-hah! I saw that, Laura. You had the answer written on your cuff. No cheating on exams around here!"

Bess looked daggers at him and Laura laughed nervously before standing up and saying, "If you'll excuse me . . ." Before anyone could say anything, she was gone. Scooping up a sweater from the library, she slipped out onto the terrace. She was trembling with anger—but it was mixed with laughter. What a terror the woman was! Imagine asking her if she knew Edith Galt, as if it really were a school examination.

The door swung open behind her and closed softly. Expecting Sonny, she turned to find it was Stephen. "Can you forgive me?" he asked.

"Forgive *you*? What for?"

"For being her son," he said with a grin.

"You can't help it," she said, giving in to the laughter rather than the anger.

"She can't either, really," he said. Taking her hand, he led her to a stone bench that overlooked the long sweep of land down to the valley below where the spring flowed so endlessly silent. "I'm all she has, you see. That has got to be difficult for you to understand. You're surrounded by family, by people who love you and care for your every activity. Mother has only me. I envy you, you know. There's just me and Mother and Arch—the three of us against the world, she believes. But here . . . why, the Thornes are a whole world of their own. Uncles, aunts, cousins— "

"You're wrong. I do understand what it's like to have a strong-minded woman give you her full attention."

"Your grandmother?"

"Yes, Gram. She's the same way with me. She always has been."

"It's a sign of love. Great love. I tell myself that, and yet sometimes I'd love nothing better than to choke her. Still, it was intolerable for Mother to grill you that way. You know why she was doing it, don't you?''

"I think so." She was glad it was dark and he couldn't see her blush. It was silly of her to be feeling so girlish. She was a grown woman who'd gotten a number of proposals, most of them from poor Freddie.

"Laura, if this were a different time, I'd court you properly. You deserve it and I'd enjoy it. But there's this damned war coming our way. We can't avoid it very much longer and I can't face it without you. I want you to marry me, but—''

"You have to find out whether I passed your Mother's test?'' she asked, a splinter of annoyance preventing her from giving in entirely to the romance of the situation.

"Mother isn't asking you. I am. But don't answer me yet. I have to make sure you understand something. That night we first met, you remember . . . ?''

"You said you wanted to be President.''

"That's what I mean. I do want that. Besides you, it's the only thing I've ever wanted. I have to know you understand that.''

"Of course I do. Are you asking me if I object?''

"Yes. I'd give it up for you . . . I think,'' he added with devastating honesty. "But I don't know who or what I'd be without that dream. It's been a part of me for almost all my life.''

She turned and curled into his waiting embrace. "Oh, Stephen, I wouldn't dream of asking you give it up. It's part of why I love you, don't you realize that?''

"Then will you be my wife and help me?''

"Of course I will.''

It was a curiously pragmatic proposal and a shyly formal acceptance, but it was years before Laura could look back on that night and assess it accurately.

"How soon?'' he asked.

"As soon as you like.''

"Thanksgiving? It's only two months away,'' he said hesitantly. "I don't mean to introduce a grim note, but I'm selfish enough to want every possible moment I can have with you before the war comes.''

"You're sure we'll go to war?''

"Positive.''

"And you'll go?''

"Aside from not wanting to, there's no reason I should be excused. Nobody wants to go, but millions of us will have to.

The only thing that makes it bearable to contemplate is the thought that I'll have you—my wife—to come back to when it's over."

"Oh, Stephen . . ."

When they told the others, there was almost universal rejoicing. India was thrilled, Adele wept, and Grace's eyes shone more brightly than they had for months. For a few days Evelyn seemed to step gingerly into the present and be happy for Laura. She behaved as an exemplary mother and managed to weep a bit about "losing a daughter." Laura was touched and made no reference to the fact that she hadn't been Evelyn's daughter for years.

Even Bess seemed pleased, and Laura wondered briefly if Stephen had been somehow assured she would approve before he asked. But that traitorous thought was driven from her mind by Sonny's grim acceptance. At the first opportunity to speak to her alone, he said, "This is the biggest mistake you've ever made, my girl, but when you realize it, come to me and I promise I won't say I told you so."

"That's damned nasty of you!" she snapped. "Can't you be happy for me? You just don't like Stephen!"

"No, I don't like him. And neither would you if your hormones hadn't all gone to your head."

Before she realized what she was doing, she'd slapped him, and then, stunned, looked at her hand like it wasn't a part of her. "Sonny, I'm sorry . . ."

But he'd turned away, a pillar of offended dignity. Finally he spoke into the billowing silence. "I deserved that. I'm sorry too. Sorrier than I can say. I'll get along with your Stephen, Laura. I promise. I won't ever like the bastard, but I'll pretend for as long as you want me to. But, Laura . . ." He turned and gave her a bear hug. Speaking into her hair, he said, "If anything goes wrong, tell me. I care more about you than anything else in the world, and I won't ever let anyone hurt you if I can help it."

Laura walked her grandmother up the stairs that night. Holding the older woman's elbow lightly, she said, "Are you happy for me, Gram?"

"I'm delighted, bunny. He'll take good care of you."

Later, getting ready for bed, Laura thought about her grandmother's words. She might have said, "He'll make you happy," but instead had been concerned for her protection. Why did Gram always feel she had to be "taken care of"?

XXIV

SURPRISINGLY, it was Adele who first came out of the delirium of wedding plans to issue warnings of her own to Laura. "My dear, I wonder if you've thoroughly thought out what sort of life you're committing yourself to," she said hesitantly as she and Laura were driving to the dressmaker who'd been hired to run up a nice white wedding suit.

"What do you mean?" Laura asked, only half her attention on Adele and the rest on a tricky corner.

"Well, he is a politician. A politician's wife has a hard row to hoe, you know. There's always a lot of traveling—"

"I look forward to that."

"And you'll have to go live in his home state—"

"Oh, no. That's all been settled. There's already a well-entrenched Republican faction there. Stephen's going to live here and make Arkansas his home state."

That used to be the definition of "carpetbagger," Adele thought, but knew better than to mention it. What difference did it make if she liked or disliked the young man? He was perfectly respectable, an excellent catch in most people's eyes. And if Laura wanted to marry him, well, what right did she have to criticize his political morals?

"His mother and uncle agree," Laura was going on, "and I'm delighted. I won't have to leave at all. We'll move to the cottage, of course, until we can build a proper house of our own on the grounds someplace. That way I'll be here to help you and Gram anytime you need me. I've talked it all over with Gram. She's pleased at the thought of having Stephen here to help share the burden and someday advise Sonny on the proper way to run the estate. Didn't she tell you?"

"She mentioned it, but I didn't know the plans were all made. I don't suppose either of you has discussed this with Sonny, this business of having Stephen help him when the time comes?" Adele said wryly. Sonny was keeping to his vow not to criticize Stephen to Laura, but no one was blind enough to miss the fact that he loathed his twin's intended husband.

Laura looked away. "No, there'll be time for that later." At that inconceivable time when Gram is gone, she thought with a shiver.

"But that's not the point I'm trying to make, precisely," Adele said, no more anxious than Laura to discuss the questionable state of Grace's health.

"What are you saying?" Laura asked, sincerely perplexed.

"Just that you'll be in the public eye and under constant pressure of helping your husband attain his goals."

Laura pulled the car over to the side of the road at a spot where she frequently stopped to savor the beauty of the valley spread below. After turning off the engine and pulling on the hand brake, she swiveled around sideways and took Adele's hand in both of hers. "Aunt Adele, you're worrying about me needlessly. You all do that, all the time. You know, you and Gram are a lot alike, wanting to be busy and responsible. And I'm like both of you. But Gram has the family and the finances to watch over and you have the staff of the hotel to keep you busy. I have nothing but my typing for Sonny. Don't you see? I need a point in my life, too—a reason to get up in the morning, as Uncle Edmund once said. I know it's going to be difficult being Stephen's wife, and I'm eager for that difficulty."

But Adele wasn't satisfied yet. "All of us are a bit out of touch here. Thornehill has always seemed so isolated from the rest of the country, in spite of the many people who come here. We know so little of politics and you've never been much interested before."

"Nor am I now, to be honest, Aunt Adele. But I'm interested in Stephen and I can learn. Besides, not everyone has to be Mrs. Roosevelt. I can back him up in his career without having to be a part of it. In fact, I think he'd prefer it that way. His mother's involvement is something of a trial to him."

Adele kneaded the soft young hand and smiled. "You're quite right, darling. I shouldn't have worried about you. You do know what you're doing and I'm flattered that you should think we are alike. You're a fine girl, Laura. So good, so tolerant of having so many extra 'parents' to interfere in your life.''

"I've needed extra parents. My own were none too interested in me," Laura said. Then quickly added, "I didn't mean to sound pitiful, I don't *feel* pitiful. Evelyn did her best under the circumstances and if Daddy and that Smalley woman didn't care about me, well . . . that's their loss!''

"And now you're going to have a fine handsome husband to love. How fortunate for him. Oh, dear, I'm getting all weepy-eyed, just like a silly old lady. Start the car and let's get to our appointment before I make a fool of myself!''

Laura had assumed two months was more than enough time to plan a simple wedding, but the time flew by chaotically. Besides the activities she'd anticipated, she found that Bess had a few additions that she wouldn't have expected. For one thing, Bess was at Thornehill most of the time. Laura had assumed she'd go home and return in time for the ceremony itself, but Bess Langley spent only two weeks in Washington before entrenching herself at Thornehill.

She came armed with a stack of address books and boxes of stationery and invitations. "Mother, you can't possibly mean to invite all those people!'' Stephen said, looking over the guest list.

"They won't come, darling. It's just a courtesy.''

The other astonishing thing she brought along was a photographer. "There's a photographer in Eureka Springs we patronize," Edmund said to her, "and I've got my Brownie for informal pictures.''

"Ah, but we must think of posterity, Mr. Bills, mustn't we?'' Bess replied.

The photographer proved to be a thorough nuisance. Apparently on Bess's orders, he felt obliged to get as many candid shots of Laura and Stephen as possible and was forever darting out of the shrubbery or taking Laura unawares in the hallways of the house. Finally Laura had had enough. When a flash went off in her face as she came out of her room with a handful of lingerie to wash, she exploded. "If I see you again this week, I shall break your camera and burn all your film!'' she told the man.

She told Stephen about the incident, meaning to amuse him, but he was angry. "It was nothing," she reassured him.

"If it hadn't all been so hectic here lately, it would have just been funny."

The next morning, before she was awake, there was a light tap on the door. She stumbled over and opened it. Stephen was there. "Get dressed," he whispered. "We're going for a ride."

"A ride?" she asked, looking at her watch. "Stephen, it's five in the morning. The sun isn't even up yet. Why are you?"

"Just put on some clothes and meet me in the garages." He had the charmingly naughty look of a boy who'd found a cigarette to smoke behind the barn.

When she met him twenty minutes later, he had a car ready. There was an enormous picnic hamper in back. "We're running away," he announced.

"Oh, Stephen, I can't. There's too much to do."

"Somebody else will do it. You know that. I've left a note so they won't send the FBI out looking for us. Come on."

They spent the entire day just riding around the countryside. It was the only day Laura often looked back on in later years and remembered as the best. Not that anything important transpired. She could hardly even remember where they went or what they saw. But it was a day alone, a day without pressures, without anyone else interfering with them.

They talked about books, about people they admired and disliked, about their favorite colors and favorite foods, about pets and pet peeves—all the things that an extended courtship would have revealed in a leisurely fashion. But they, like many others of their generation, felt the hot breath of war down their necks and didn't have time to let these things blossom in their own time. The one thing they didn't talk about was the wedding and attendant preparations.

"So you don't like holidays," she said, laughing at his recounting of a disastrous Independence Day celebration during which the fireworks all went off at once.

"Some holidays are fine. Lincoln's Birthday, Groundhog Day, Arbor Day," he said with a grin. "You don't have to do anything about them. They just sort of roll around and you can ignore them if you want. But the big ones . . . I guess my mother did that to me. She's always made such a big production of Christmas and birthdays and all. She meant well, I know, but it made me feel like I was facing some sort of college exam. It was as if I had to have a frantically wonderful time or I'd fail the test."

"Yes, I can remember a birthday once when I had a cold and felt rotten. Nobody criticized me, of course, but they still made me feel I'd somehow let them down," Laura recalled.

"And the gifts! The awful gifts that you have to act like you're thrilled with. I had a sort of honorary uncle who kept giving me stuffed animals until I was fourteen. It was mortifying to have to act delighted with a fuzzy toy bunny at that age."

"Oh, Stephen! I was planning to give you that very thing for a wedding gift," she said, giggling.

"From you I would regard it as a treasure," he said with mock gravity, then laughed. "In any case, we've got years and years of stuffed animals stored up to give our children."

"You didn't keep them!"

"I didn't, but can you imagine Bess Langley ever throwing anything away? She is not inclined to discard. She's still got all my baby teeth, storing them up, no doubt, to string on a necklace someday."

"Oh, Lord!" Laura said, clutching protectively at her throat. "Who's suposed to wear them!"

"You, I'd guess. I can't wait to see how you look thrilled with that particular gift."

They pulled off the road, laughing easily over this nonsense while they got out the sandwiches and thermos of coffee. When they'd finished eating, Stephen said, "How have I managed to get through life this long without you? It's as if we're the two parts of one whole. It's a wonder I functioned alone."

Laura felt tears come to her eyes. "That's the loveliest thing anyone's ever said to me."

"It's the plain truth, Laura. Now, don't get weepy on me every time I tell you how much I love you or you'll spend the rest of your life crying!"

On November 30, the day before the wedding, three other photographers arrived. Bess had managed to convince several news services that in the midst of imminent war, the wedding of the scion of the house of Langley was a newsworthy event. Laura, surprised and mildly offended, managed to accept this as a natural part of the lot she had chosen.

That afternoon she went to the cottage to see that it had been properly cleaned and readied, not that there was any reason to doubt that Mabelann and Adele would have done a wonderful job of it. The plan was for Laura and Stephen to spend the first week of their marriage at the cottage, then travel to New Orleans for a proper wedding trip, returning just in time for Christmas with the family.

"Silly place to spend a honeymoon!" Sonny snorted to India. "He'll probably move his dear mama in with them."

"I don't think it's silly. Marriage must be something of an adjustment without having the nuisance of travel plans to cope with at the same time. Besides, it was Laura's idea. She likes that funny little old house."

Laura, however, wasn't thinking of it as a "funny" house, but as a place that had a very special significance to her. The new paint and wallpaper made it nicer, but no different to her. This was, she had now guessed, the place where she was born to the Smalley woman—her mother. How extraordinary! She would never be able to reconcile that she had any blood ties to such a person. It was possible she was conceived here as well. This was where India had taught her to play gin rummy when they were moved out of the proximity of the gangsters, and this was where she'd soothed her during that awful time when she suffered the nightmares.

This very room was where she nearly learned all about sex with Eric VonHoldt. The memory made her blush, not with shame but with excitement. Sex had been very much on her mind lately. Everyone made jokes, some more delicately than others, about the new role she would soon have. No longer the timid virgin, but the knowledgeable woman, was how India put it.

Timid she was not. Virgin she was—not entirely by deliberate choice. She'd had a number of boyfriends during her short three years away from home. There had been kisses, close embraces, some experimental fondling. Once she had allowed a young man to inch his hand up under her sweater, but his frantic fumbling had been so slobbery and pathetic that she had drawn away, disgusted and ashamed on his behalf.

With Stephen, the man she was to marry in a matter of hours, she'd had very little experience in such things. Their courtship had been brief and conducted largely through letters. Counting on her fingers, she started adding up how many total days she'd actually spent with him in the year since they met. Less than two months, and most of that time was recently with the constant threat of either her family or his or the abhorrent photographer popping up at any minute.

What would it be like? Her only real gauge was those stolen

moments with Eric so long ago, and she wasn't sure she could trust her memory. She'd been so young, so madly, foolishly enamored of him. She sat for a long time, remembering and wondering. It could have happened again when he came to see Herr VonHoldt. But it hadn't. There wasn't time, there was too much else going on both in her life and in his during those hectic, horrible two days.

Where was Eric now? Still in New York? Why had he never answered her letter and what might have happened if he had? What sort of life did he have? She wished now, more than ever, that she hadn't flown off the handle that night by the spring. She'd like to know what his life was like—it was a loose end that needed tying up, and she'd missed her one opportunity. Married ladies didn't look up old flames and ask them how life is—

Suddenly she stood up and started busily fluffing the bed ruffle. What was she doing, thinking so much about a man from her past—on today of all days?

It was a day rife with memories; they seemed to intrude on her at every turn. Two in particular kept coming back to haunt her. One was a mental picture of Frederich VonHoldt standing in the foyer facing Grace. That profile, the terrible revelations that had come as a result of his visit to Thornehill. But she had no need and certainly no urge to tell Stephen about him. She and Grace (and possibly Mabelann, who was more trustworthy with a secret than God) were the only ones who knew. None of them were ever going to tell anyone. Anyone!

Oddly enough, it was another, much older memory that troubled her more. It was the image of Iris Smalley putting out her plump arms and crying, "Baby!" She'd locked that loathsome picture up in a dark closet of her mind years ago and had almost succeeded in forgetting it. But now it kept coming back to her. She knew she should tell Stephen about her biological mother (she had never thought of Iris Smalley as her "real" mother). After all, even though it wasn't of the least real importance to her, it was a fact of her life he should know.

But with his tremendous pride in his own illustrious family, how would he like finding out that his wife-to-be was actually illegitimate? And the daughter of someone so unlike the Thornes? She was, she had to admit, afraid to tell him. Afraid he would see her differently if he knew. He wouldn't reject her, he wouldn't even consciously hold it against her, she believed, but it would disappoint him.

It wouldn't even matter, she told herself, even though a sensible voice in the back of her mind kept reminding her that she was to be a politician's wife—perhaps a President's wife—and her family would come under a great deal of public scrutiny sooner or later. Stephen should be warned that a distasteful truth lurked in her background. He would never know—no one would ever know—about the VonHoldt connection, but the Smalleys . . . ?

She went so far as to straighten her shoulders and try to find him to explain about the Smalleys. Unfortunately, he'd gone into town to pick up some flowers and send a few telegrams, and by the time he returned, her resolve had weakened.

She went back to her room and thought it all out again. If she didn't tell him, he'd never know. He'd never need to. She wasn't sure how much of the family knew, but she was certain none of them would ever bring it up. Nor was there any chance of the Smalleys turning up again. They'd either died or moved far away. They *must* have or they'd have been back to commit more blackmail. It had been a good five or six years since they'd come that first time. If they'd intended—or been able—to try it again, they wouldn't have waited all this length of time.

So she told herself, not really believing any of it, but afraid of losing even a tiny fraction of Stephen's love and respect. Years later, when she thought back to her marriage, it was this hour of mental gymnastics she most frequently remembered. How many lives might have been different if only Stephen hadn't gone to town for flowers! What might fate have served up to all of them if only she'd had the strength to lay out the truth that day?

She was often to ponder the question.

The wedding ceremony itself was a small tranquil island in a veritable storm of action. The hotel was full to overflowing, not with paying guests, but with actual company, mostly Arch and Bess's friends and political acquaintances. An amazing number of them had taken the wedding invitation seriously and made the trip without much regard for the gasoline shortage that was one sign of the war in the rest of the world.

Bess was in her natural element. Greeting guests, she almost gave the impression that this was her home, and Grace allowed it without a murmur. "I've asked Dr. Lee to give her a thorough checkup when this is over," Sonny told Laura when she expressed her concern about Grace's willingness to let Bess Langley roll over her.

"I know there's something wrong. Can you imagine, even a year ago, Gram letting someone take over that way? She'd have withered her with a word."

"She's given up on something—maybe everything," Sonny admitted. "I've often imagined such a thing, thinking it would be wonderful to have her subdued, not breathing down my neck like an irritable dragon. But oddly enough, I don't like it at all. But you don't need to worry about it. You just tend to getting yourself married and let the rest of us take care of Gram."

Sonny gave her away, kissing her tenderly on the cheek as he let go of her arm and turned her over to Stephen. India, clad in peach organdy and looking wonderfully young with her new, longer hairstyle, was her bridesmaid. Evelyn, who had been engrossed in her newest hobby, rug-hooking, to the exclusion of all else for several months, finally deigned to notice what was going on around her and did a very credible "mother-of-the-bride" act, sniffling becomingly as Laura said her vows. Grace, momentarily recovering some of her usual bite, was heard to say, "Evelyn, will you stop that disgusting noise so that I may hear Laura?"

Edmund and Adele sat next to them on the chairs that had been set up to simulate church pews in the large dining room. Bess and Arch sat on the opposite side of the aisle. It would have been difficult to say which side was prouder and more pleased. Bess had come around in the last two months and decided that Laura was the perfect choice of wife for her beloved son and even managed to give the impression that she herself had made the initial selection.

The rest of the day was a blur of festivities. The dining room was cleared for a magnificent dinner and then cleared again for an evening of dancing and merriment. When Stephen finally took Laura's arm and whispered, "Let's get away from here," she could hardly hear him.

The cottage was quiet, only a murmur of the noisy party drifting down the hill. Mabelann had taken time from her duties at the house to come down and start a cozy fire and turn down the big double bed. Edmund had made sure that there were plenty of good books in the living room and Sonny had seen to it that there were wine and fruit and tiny silver-wrapped wedges of cheese on the bedside table. Adele, ever practical, had put a new pink douche bag in the bathroom cabinet with handwritten instructions for its use.

Stephen tactfully stirred the fire while Laura went to change from her wedding suit into the filmy lavender peignoir India had given her. She slipped into the bed, feeling the coolness of the sheets, the slickness of the low-cut nightgown, the languorous warmth of the room. All her senses were alive as never before. She turned the light off and waited.

When Stephen joined her a few minutes later, he was naked, apparently having undressed in the living room. "It was a hectic wedding, wasn't it, love?"

"I suppose they all are to the bride and groom," Laura said, her voice breaking with nervousness.

He smoothed her hair back from her face gently. "Don't be afraid. I'll be careful."

"I know, Stephen."

He kissed her and slowly slipped the slender straps from her shoulders before cupping one breast in his hand. Laura kept waiting for the excitement to take hold, the breathless sense of freedom and longing she vaguely remembered from the other time in this same bed. But it didn't start—not then, not later. Stephen was gentle and considerate, but Laura acted her part mechanically. Waiting. Waiting.

She was still waiting when he penetrated her with a single sharp thrust that brought a surprised cry to her lips. "It's over now," he mumbled into her hair. "It'll never hurt again. I promise."

She closed her eyes, the pain already fading, as he sawed his way to contentment. She felt the moisture spring up on his skin and wondered why she wasn't feeling more than a mild discomfort. A muscle in her hip suddenly knotted into a charley horse and she whimpered and tried to ease it by moving her leg. Stephen took this as a sign of passion and plunged even farther into her, groaning. And for a second Laura was back in a parked car, with a silly freshman trying to find the hooks of her bra. The same sense of embarrassment swept over her and then was gone as Stephen raised himself on his elbows and looked down at her. "Oh, Laura, I'm so fortunate to have found you."

Suddenly she started crying, unaware of it herself until she felt the hot tears coursing down her temples into her ears. I'm a failure, she thought. Intercourse was supposed to be wonderful with a man you loved. Even Adele, in her prissy way, had made that clear in a euphemistic little lecture earlier in the week about not making a duty of what should be a joy. Why was this so boring? So uncomfortable? What was wrong with her?

In the next few days she told herself it was only because she was so tired and pressured from the wedding preparations, not to mention the fact that she had been a virtually inexperienced virgin. It would get better when she was used to it and they were both more rested.

But it didn't get better.

If they'd been forcibly kept to the cottage, there might have been leisure for learning, but there was still a houseful of guests, many of them important people. "We'll just go up for luncheon, darling," Stephen would say. "I know it's tedious as hell, having to be nice to a bunch of old fogies, but they came clear out here to see us and meet you and it would be rude to neglect them when we're right here so close. We probably should have gone to New Orleans straightaway—"

"Yes, it's my fault—"

"Not at all. I agreed, but now I've got to share you for a few days more. Sunday afternoon we'll go as planned and we won't talk to anyone but each other for weeks!"

"I guess this is one of the disadvantages of marrying a politician, that you and everyone else warned me about," Laura said, trying to sound lighthearted about it.

"It is, but I didn't want you to find out quite as soon."

Nor had he prepared her for the amount of time he'd be spending with his uncle and mother. "Sorry, darling, but there's word of another post opening up in the State Department and we've got to work out whether it would be to my advantage to seek to be appointed. Don't worry. Sunday night we'll be on our way and I promise not to mention another word about my work."

On Saturday night, a bride of six days, Laura started packing to go away from Thornehill and especially from the senior Langleys. On Sunday morning she rose refreshed and full of anticipation. Itching with impatience, she set the matched travel bags outside the door of the cottage for the estate wagon to pick up later. Stephen had risen early and gone up to the house, but he came back shortly after noon and jokingly complained that he couldn't even change his clothes for luncheon because she'd packed them all away.

"Your grandmother says they'll be ready to eat in an hour or so. How about a ride?"

"We'll smell all horsey and I'll have to unpack even more."

"A walk then?"

"Fine."

They got to the main house a little late and hurried in a side door closest to the diningroom, but it was deserted. The table was set but even the staff had disappeared. "Where is everyone?" Laura asked.

"I hear voices," Stephen answered, leading the way to the library.

Laura opened the door and said, "You've moved the party in here?" Then she saw their expressions. "What's wrong? What's happened?"

The room seemed full of people. Edmund was by the window. Adele was sitting in a wing chair with a stricken look. Bess Langley was on the sofa with her face buried in her hands, sobbing silently. Everyone was looking at the radio. Laura picked out Grace's slight figure and went to her. "Gram, what it is?"

Grace looked up, her face ravaged and old. "War," she said. "Another war."

Laura was speechless. Why should anyone be surprised? They'd talked about it for two years, but now that it had come she was stunned. Sonny stepped from behind his grandmother's chair and took Laura's hand. "The Japs have bombed a naval base of ours. A place in Hawaii called Pearl Harbor. There are hundreds of dead. It's war for us now. No question."

Laura turned, reached for Stephen, and stumbled. He wasn't looking at her, but was having a whispered staccato conversation with his uncle. Laura was too confused and distraught to understand the words until Arch Langley stepped over to talk to Grace. "Mrs. Thorne, you've been a gracious hostess, but we must ask another favor of you. We've got to get back to Washington immediately. May we use one of your cars to drive to Hot Springs to get the train? I'll send someone back with it in good order."

"Can't you take the MNA?" Grace asked, then caught herself. "Forgive an old woman. I forgot it hasn't run for several years. I'm getting my wars confused." The tone was singeingly bitter. "Of course. Will tomorrow morning be soon enough?"

"I'm afraid not. We need to leave within the hour."

"The hour? Stephen!" Laura cried, all but throwing herself at him.

"I'm sorry, Laura, but we've known this was going to happen. I have to leave."

"But our trip—our wedding trip? You can't leave me now!"

"Laura, there will be all the time in the world when this is over. We've got a whole lifetime ahead of us."

"*No!* What if you don't *come* back?" Then, as the words were coming out, she realized that she had said the unspeakable. Everyone looked at her with horror. One didn't say such things to men who were going to war. She flung her head up defiantly and took a deep breath. "Pardon me, please. That was a stupid remark. Of course we'll have our trip later. I guess I'd better redo the packing. Excuse me, everyone."

She fled before anyone could remark on her behavior, and was furiously redistributing their clothing when Arch and Stephen came to the cottage. Couldn't we have had at least this time alone? she thought, hating Archibald Langley with all her bruised heart.

He stood just outside the door, fidgeting nervously with the keys to the car while she and Stephen made their abbreviated farewells. She wanted to cling to him, hold him back from this terrible, uncontrollable thing. She wanted to cry out: Leave me something of yourself. Leave me a baby! Give me some memorable word of wisdom I can always cherish if I never see you again. If only there had been time. They hardly knew each other, they had everything to learn, and now she might never be truly one with the man she'd married only days before. Dear God! This couldn't be happening.

She felt herself flying to pieces and still sensed by the calm strength of his arms around her that he would hate hysterics. He counted on her to be a lady, to be in control. A future President's wife doesn't shriek and scream like a thwarted child because he's going off to serve the country he will someday lead. And yet . . .

By an enormous effort of sheer will, she was the first to pull away, her nerves strung so tightly she could hardly draw breath. But she managed to say, "I'll be waiting for you to come back, Stephen."

"I'll write as often as I can," he said, and for the first time she realized by the infinitesimal quaver in his voice that he was frightened too, and hated himself for the fear.

"I'll hold you to that," she said, and then in spite of herself asked, "Do you have to go? Isn't there any way you can stay here? At least for a while?"

"Laura, you know I can't. I've spent my life admiring the men of this world with courage, developing—I hope—the trait in myself. Fortitude is what separates man from animal. This war, horrible as it will be, is the test. I couldn't *not* go."

"Yes, yes, I understand. I just don't want . . . Never mind. Now, hurry before your uncle drives away without you," she said with a shimmeringly fraudulent smile.

Stephen drew himself up. "You're a good wife, Laura. Better than I deserve."

"Nonsense. We're both perfect and you know it. Now, go!"

The last word was shrill and she clamped her mouth shut. She didn't even cry until the car had disappeared from sight down the drive.

XXV

"*Y*ESTERDAY, December 7, 1941—a date which will live in infamy—the United States of America was suddenly and deliberately attacked by naval and air forces of the Empire of Japan. . . ."

President Roosevelt's voice came over the radio as he addressed a joint session of Congress. Laura sat rigidly in a straight-backed chair in the library and listened with the others in the family. Bess Langley had left with her brother-in-law and son. The few other guests, stragglers from the wedding a week before, had left that morning. Adele had given most of the staff the week off to be with their own people in this time of crisis. Now it was only the Thornes in the library, listening to the President's gloom-laden voice.

"Yesterday the Japanese government also launched an attack against Malaya.

"Last night Japanese forces attacked Hong Kong.

"Last night Japanese forces attacked Guam.

"Last night Japanese forces attacked the Philippine Islands.

"Last night the Japanese attacked Wake Island.

"This morning the Japanese attacked Midway Island."

Yesterday my husband left, Laura thought bitterly.

"I believe I interpret the will of the Congress and the people when I assert that we will not only defend ourselves to the utmost, but will make very certain that this form of treachery shall never endanger us again."

He sounded like a priest delivering a funeral oration. For a mass funeral, in advance of the inevitable thousands of deaths, Laura thought wildly.

"Hostilities exist. There is no blinking at the fact that our people, our territory, and our interests are in grave danger.

"With confidence in our armed forces—with the unbound determination of our people—we will gain the inevitable triumph, so help us God.

"I ask that the Congress declare that since the unprovoked and dastardly attack by Japan on Sunday, December 7, a state of war has existed between the United States and the Japanese Empire."

Grace, who had been sitting at her desk pretending to do paperwork instead of listening, suddenly rose and snapped the radio off. No one said anything for some minutes. The only sound was India's quiet sniffling into a handkerchief. Finally Sonny got up from his place in front of the fireplace, put on the winter jacket he'd had slung over his arm, and said, "Uncle Edmund, Dr. Lee? How would you both feel about a brisk walk. It'll clear your sinuses."

Adele took her cue from this. Wiping her eyes savagely, she said, "India, Laura, I've got an angel-food cake to make and I need someone to whip the egg whites. Come along."

Laura followed obediently, stopping for a moment by Grace's desk. "Gram, I'm sorry," she said, and then wondered what she was apologizing for. The state of the world, she supposed, as if she were personally responsible.

Instead of helping Adele, who didn't really want any help, Laura went back to the cottage. She'd slept alone there last night, in her empty bridal bed, and had no intention of doing so again. She'd taken along some empty cardboard boxes and unceremoniously dumped her things into them—the lavender gown, the douche bag, the garter with the pink satin roses she'd worn under her wedding suit, the books, and all the pretty little favorite knickknacks. She wasn't a bride anymore.

Sonny's draft number came up at the end of January. He said nothing about it, but merely disappeared one day, saying he was going to Eureka Springs on an errand. It was Laura, catching up on some typing in his room and wondering vaguely where he was, who found the note in his normally blank appointment book. After a moment of heart-stopping panic, she got a grip on herself and resolved to say nothing about his errand to anyone else. But she was in a lather of fearful anticipation all day long.

He returned during dinner, which Laura was picking at

disconsolately. Grim-faced, he sat down and said, "They've turned me down."

"Thank God!" Laura exclaimed.

"Who turned you down for what?" Evelyn asked. "Where have you been all day? I wanted you to help me move some furniture this afternoon and couldn't find you anywhere."

"I've been to see my draft board and they wouldn't take me. The damned asthma."

"I never thought I'd see the day I'd be glad of that affliction," Grace said.

"If they hadn't all known me from childhood, it wouldn't have mattered," Sonny said angrily. "I haven't had an episode for two years, but those damned old men all remembered me as a wheezing boy."

Grace put her fork down decisively. "Am I to understand you are disappointed in this turn of events?"

"Of course I am."

"But what would we do without you?" Grace asked.

Sonny stared at her with amazement. "Do my ears deceive me? What would you do without me? You, Gram, you think I'm a worthwhile addition to Thornehill?"

"Don't be fresh," Grace came back. "It's most inconsiderate of you, not to consult with any of us before going for your physical. The idea of you going into the service—why, it's just unthinkable."

"Oh, it's thinkable, all right! I'll find a way yet," he said, anger blotching his face in red patches.

"I forbid it," Grace said, picking her fork back up as if this were the end of the discussion.

"*You* forbid it! You haven't the right to forbid me anything. I'm going to find a way to serve my country."

"You'll have to do it without leaving here."

Sonny suddenly started laughing, a bitter, ugly laugh. "Do you appreciate the irony of this, Gram? I remember vividly, not very many years ago, when you made me leave. I pleaded with you to keep me here instead of sending me away to school. I begged you to let me stay here, and you shipped me off. Now I want to leave and you're carrying on like I'm needed here."

"You are needed here," Laura put in, but neither of them paid any attention to her. The rest of the family watched like spectators at a tennis match.

"That was different."

"Not very."

"Of course it was. You had to go to school to acquire a decent education. This time you merely want to go dashing off to get yourself killed somewhere for no reason. The draft board is right. You're not physically fit for military service. Nor mentally either. You haven't been raised to such things."

"Raised to such things? What does that mean?"

"Uniforms and marching—and killing people," Grace said, her voice shaking.

Sonny heard the quaver and took pity. "Gram, I don't mean to make you angry. Really I don't. But this is my decision and I have to go. It's my duty, as middle-class and tacky as that may sound to you. We've lived a terribly isolated elite life here, with virtually no association with our neighbors or any of the outside. But we *are* part of this country, like it or not. And this country is in trouble. Serious trouble. I'm going to do what I have to do and you'll have to accept it."

Grace, as if not having heard a word of his impassioned speech, merely took a bite of potato and repeated, "I forbid it."

Laura went to Sonny's room late that night. "I suppose you've come to attempt to harass me into staying here too?" he said.

"No, well . . . yes, I have."

"It's no use. My mind is made up."

"Everyone wants you to stay. Evelyn, Gram . . ."

"Mother will take up some new project when I've left and be ever so surprised to get a letter from me and discover I'm gone. You know that. She hardly knows where *she* is half the time, much less any of the rest of us. And Gram—she doesn't really care."

"She does, Sonny. She loves you and just can't say it."

"She just can't stand any of her possessions getting out of her grasp. Especially a name-carrier. Grandfather Jack died in the last war and Dad killed himself. Now I'm the only male Thorne left. That's her sole concern."

"That's not true!"

Sonny got up and walked to the window. "Maybe not entirely, but you know that's part of it. I'm not the least necessary here. My only role as far as Gram is concerned is to stay alive and father little Thornes someday. Maybe if I'd quickly marry some local girl and impregnate her, Gram would let me go more easily."

"Sonny . . . I need you here."

He came over and patted her shoulder absently. "You think you do. But that's only because Stephen has already gone. Laura, I'm counting on you to back me up on this. Don't you fight me too."

Her lip started trembling and a breath caught in her chest. She hadn't meant to cry. "Sonny, I don't see why you want to go."

"*Want* to go? Surely you don't believe that! Laura, you know if I had my way I'd never leave the house except for an occasional jaunt to town for a movie. I don't *want* to go away. Ever. But I have to."

"Then I'll go too."

"You? Why?"

"If it's your duty to serve your country, it's my duty as well. Someone who was here last week was talking about the possibility of women's branches of the army and navy."

"Don't be stupid."

"Why is it stupid? Aren't I as fit as you?"

"You know that's not it. You're worth two of me. But you *are* needed here."

"No more than you."

He started kneading her shoulders as he did when she'd get a stiff neck from hunching over the typewriter all day. "You're the most necessary person here. Gram's failing, Laura. We haven't ever talked about it openly, but that's the truth and we all know it. The responsibility for this place is going to fall to you more and more as time goes on."

"No. Uncle Edmund knows as much about the finances as Gram, and Adele knows more about running the house than anyone else."

"I don't mean in practical ways. I mean emotionally. You're the prop under all of them. Don't you see the way they all look to you? Even Adele at her busiest and bossiest is always looking to you for approval, though she tries to bluster around and disguise the fact."

It was true, much as Laura hated admitting it. For some time now she'd been aware of the fact that they were all, in subtle ways, looking to her more and more often, expecting her to make decisions. It was a weight she'd tried to shrug off and pretend not to notice, but it was there just the same, pressing down on her.

"Laura, back me up," Sonny repeated.

She took his hands, pulling his arms around her neck.

Leaning her cheek on his arm, she said, "All right. I think you're wrong, but then I thought you were wrong every time you ever took something apart—and I helped you over and over again. But, Sonny, don't do anything more dangerous than you absolutely have to."

"Good Lord, girl, I'm something of a fool, but not completely around the bend. I haven't got any impulse to go dashing off making a hero of myself. I'm going to fight like crazy for some nice safe desk job in Washington. If they give coward awards, you can be certain I'll come back weighted down with them."

"That's not true."

Sonny sighed. "No, I guess not. I hate to admit that anything Stephen says makes sense, or even that I listen to him, but all that talk of his about courage—well, I guess it's gotten to me. It is important to be able to think I'm a brave person who can and does stand up for what's right. Fighting off what the Germans are trying to make of the world is the right thing to do and I have to help. I really have to—for my country and for myself. Do you understand?"

"I suppose so. I hate, it, though."

"I know you do, but with the two of us united, Gram is sure to come around and accept the idea."

But he was wrong. Sonny's defiance of her wishes only raised Grace's ire, and she saw Laura's promotion of his idea as misguided and traitorous and blamed Sonny all the more for causing her defection.

Sonny's first move was a trip to the hardware store in town. He came back with a roll of wire. "To run a telephone extension to my room," he explained to Laura. He spent the next two days calling people. At the end of the time he emerged victorious. "I've pulled every string I could and I've done it. I'll be working with the code people in Washington for several months, then probably do the same in London, plus whatever odd translating jobs they need done."

Laura tried to act pleased for him. Grace made no such attempt. "Sonny, I warn you, I won't have it!" she said. "You get back on that phone and tell whoever it is that you've changed your mind."

"But I haven't changed my mind, and I won't."

Grace refused to hear him, and up until the day he left, she persisted in believing he would not go. Finally, however, Sonny was packed and the car was loaded and idling in the driveway with Laura at the wheel. Grace walked down the front steps, wearing a warm fur coat against the sleety pellets of snow that were falling. She leaned heavily on the cane which she had reluctantly agreed to use just in the last few weeks. Sonny dumped his last bag into the back seat and came over to give Grace a farewell kiss. She drew back.

"Sonny, this is your last opportunity to come to your senses and stop this nonsense."

"I'm leaving, Gram," he said gently.

"*You will regret this!*"

"No doubt. Good-bye, Gram."

Laura, in the car with the engine running, couldn't hear the words, but knew from their expressions the bitterness of the exchange. "What did she say?" Laura asked as she let out the clutch.

"Nothing much," Sonny replied, looking out the window.

When Laura returned from delivering Sonny to the train in Hot Springs, India met her at the front door. "We were worried about you driving in this weather. I'm glad you're back safe and sound."

"Whose car is that in front?" Laura said, coming in and stomping the snow off her feet.

"Willis Hawkins. Poor old man. Grace hauled him out here a couple of hours ago."

"What for?"

India shrugged. "She didn't volunteer that information. Just made the pronouncement that Adele was to summon him and he was to come no matter what. It says a lot for her strength of personality that he did it."

Laura felt an ominous shiver chase down her spine.

"You've got a letter here from Stephen."

"Thanks," Laura said, stuffing the letter into her pocket. "I'm going up to have a hot bath before dinner. I'm frozen clear through."

She opened the letter with a nail file after she'd sunk into the sudsy water. Stephen had been a regular correspondent since his abrupt departure. At first she had ripped into his letters eagerly, imagining them to be love letters. But after the first six or seven had arrived, she'd learned not to expect inked passion. They were informative enough—lots of chatty remarks about whom he'd seen in Washington and how they were; the problem was, Laura didn't really know very many of the people he talked about except as slight acquaintances, and their doings were of very little interest to her. He was also an avid reader of rather lofty nonfiction and always gave over part of his letters to a discussion of whatever he was reading at the time, often with a recommendation that she attempt to get a copy of one book or another from the local library so that she could discuss some philosophy with him via the mail.

But this letter, she quickly discovered, was different.

> *Dearest Laura,*
>
> *I've only got a moment before my train, so this will have to be regrettably brief. I'll write more tomorrow and fill you in on details of my plans. I got word today that I'm to leave for Europe in a few days.*
>
> *I had, of course, intended to come back there before I left, but I have such a short time that it would be taken up with traveling and we would have only a few hours together before I had to turn around and go straight back.*
>
> *Instead, I'm going up to Mother's place. I'm sure you'll understand and not resent my spending this last bit of time with her. She has no one else.*
>
> *The man's at the door for my things. Must go. More later, dear Laura.*
>
> *Love,*
> *Stephen*

Laura angrily crumpled the letter and flung it across the room. How dare he spend his last days in the United States—perhaps his last days altogether—with his mother instead of his wife! She tried, really tried, to control her anger and humiliation with sympathy and reason, but it couldn't be done. Yes, his mother had no other children, but Laura had no other husband. And Bess Langley had been seeing him all during the three months he'd been stationed in the East.

Even if he had to spend four days on a train to see his wife for a few hours, wouldn't it have been worth it? Laura would happily have done the same, given the opportunity. In fact, she thought with bitter self-pity, he must have known this was coming any day; why hadn't he invited her to come to Washington for his last weeks before shipping out? She could, come to that, have stayed with his mother the whole time.

Laura flipped the drain plug with her toe, and as the water started gurgling away, she realized another slight for the first time. That awful day when he'd left so hurriedly after the announcement of the bombing of Pearl Harbor, he'd had time to wait for his mother and uncle to pack and return with him. Why hadn't he asked Laura to come along? Why hadn't she had the sense to make that assumption herself? She was, after all, his wife. Her place was with him. But it had all been so fast, so hectic and terrifying, that she'd gone along with his plans without even questioning.

Now, however, she questioned. More than questioned. She was furious and hurt beyond physical pain. She should have been with him. He should have begged her to come along and share his final months before going to war. Why hadn't he? She would happily have made the long trip to Washington. There was nothing to chain her to Thornehill all the time. Granted, it had been understood since the beginning that she would live there, but she could have gone away for a few weeks without being missed. Why hadn't he suggested it? Did he care nothing for her?

She wept as she showered off the soapy water, but as she stepped out, the cold air in the room brought her back to her senses a bit. She was really being a sniveling fool. There was no reason to question his love. He needn't have married her, after all, if he didn't love her. A man doesn't wait until he's in his mid-thirties to propose and then do so without being quite certain.

But still . . .

She told the family only that Stephen was going overseas in a few days. She didn't mention that he'd have a leave in advance of departure which he could have spent with her and chosen not to. The rest of the family had their attention divided between this announcement and Grace's long afternoon with Willis Hawkins and didn't question Laura too carefully. She suspected, however, when she was given a piece of pie easily twice as large as anyone else's portion that Adele knew how deeply unhappy she was.

After dinner, she joined the others in the library as usual and took her current tatting project along to keep her hands occupied, lest she spend the evening wringing them. ("Better be careful, my girl," Sonny had warned just a few days earlier. "You take out all your aggressions in that silly activity. You'll have the whole place carpeted with it if you don't get control over yourself! You ought to take up welding. It's so much more practical.")

It was an endless evening. One radio show followed another and Laura heard none of them, so preoccupied was she with her secret grievances. Finally, when the news came on, she started putting away her shuttle and thread. The announcer was going through the usual dismal daily recitation of world disaster. After explaining that the battle for Java was lost and that the Dutch had been said to have destroyed all installations that could be of use to the enemy, he mentioned a report that the RAF had made extensive raids on Essen, a large city that housed the famous Krupp armaments works as well as one of the main branches of the VonHoldt armaments company.

"Must we have that horrible noise blaring away at us all night long?" Grace asked suddenly.

So, Laura thought, handing her secret over to me hasn't entirely erased it. Odd—the mention of that name used to bring Eric immediately to mind, and then for months after the German's visit, it brought old Frederich to mind, and now . . . now she was back to where she started, thinking of Eric for no good reason. As she undressed for bed that night, Laura wondered about him. Was he in the service too? Probably. Everyone seemed to be. What did the army use painters for? Dabbing camouflage on tanks? She had a mental picture of a man in a painter's smock and beret, standing back and surveying the effect of mud-brown blobs against a mud-green background.

For a moment she smiled.

But once in her cold bed, the light off, the smile faded and the tears, the hot, hateful, unwanted tears, started again.

It was a late spring, or so it seemed to Laura. The darkness of winter kept on in her heart far longer than it should have. It was only late March when they all began to realize the extent of another change in their lives. There was only a scattered handful of hotel reservations, most of them from people only as far away as Kansas City and St. Louis and many of them canceling before their arrival date.

By late April it was apparent that they couldn't continue to operate. "With the gas shortage, people can't afford to drive," Edmund said. "And if they ration gas as they're saying, we can't afford to drive anyone around."

"The newspapers and radio say the travel situation is awful everywhere," Adele added. "With all the soldiers taking precedence—as well they should—on buses and trains, it's nearly impossible to get anywhere unless it's an emergency."

"We'll keep on as long as we can," Grace said. No one wanted to dispute her. It was against tradition, and besides, it would soon become apparent, even to her, that it was utterly impractical.

The news in April was particularly upsetting. A month earlier the RAF had bombed Lübeck, destroying or damaging many ancient buildings and monuments that were dear to German people. Hitler was furious and ordered reprisal raids on England's most precious and beloved historic cities. Exeter was bombed; so were Norwich, York, and Bath.

"Bath? Bombed?" Grace said after the newscast.

"Have you been there, Gram?" Laura asked.

She was surprised at the look of pain on her grandmother's face when she answered. "Oh, yes. I've been to Bath. A very, very long time ago."

That was where she knew Frederich, Laura realized. Their eyes met for a moment of confirmation, but neither of them said anything.

In May, rationing started. First it was only sugar, which made Adele, who loved baking, very angry. Soon it was meat, butter, all fats, and canned goods. "Canned peas are rationed?" Laura exclaimed when she heard. "What makes the government think the men at the front would want to stuff themselves with peas?"

"It isn't the contents, it's the cans themselves," Edmund said.

"Oh, of course," Laura replied, chilled at the thought of the metal in common canned goods being turned into guns and tanks instead of innocently containing food.

In June they heard about a particular gun. "Big Gustav" belonged to the Germans and was being used against Sevastopol. This extraordinary gun had a barrel over a hundred feet long and fired a shell twenty-five feet long. It had a firing range of twenty-eight miles. "Twenty-eight miles!" India exclaimed when Edmund read about it aloud from the morning paper. "That's impossible, isn't it?"

"Not at all, I'm afraid. It takes fifteen hundred men just to aim, load, and fire it. Only the Germans could invent such a weapon. They have a national tendency to overdo everything," he added with masterful understatement.

Laura dunked a corner of toast into the yolk of her poached egg and wondered if Big Gustav had been built at VonHoldt Armaments. Sipping her unsweetened coffee, Grace was wondering the same thing.

*   *   *

In September the hotel closed.

The turning point for Grace was when two of the maids, sisters from Eureka Springs, came to her to give their notice. They were going to go to work in a factory in Hot Springs for better pay and fewer hours. "Factory work? Young women like you in a dirty, noisy factory!" Grace exclaimed.

"War work, ma'am. Lot of the girls are doing it. Helps the war effort more than making beds," the older sister explained.

Grace went on about it at dinner that night. Laura listened, suppressing a smile. Grace, a woman in many ways ahead of her time, couldn't possibly object to women in industry as much as she was saying. No, the whole act was staged out of fear that such an idea might enter Laura's head, and Grace obviously wanted to bludgeon it to death before it could take root.

"Two of the others are getting married, you know," Adele said. "That leaves me with very little staff. But then, we have no guests at the moment and only a few booked for the fall."

"Grace, it's simply not practical anymore," Edmund said. "The wages are actually outrunning the income this summer and things aren't going to change until this war is over. If ever. I don't think it's any secret that we no longer need the income from the hotel guests to be comfortably well off here. It's really quite foolish to continue when it's costing."

His words gave Laura a strangely warm feeling that she tried to analyze. Yes, it was the "we." It wasn't Grace's income or Grace's responsibility alone. It was all of them. All the Thornes whether they bore the name or not. Suddenly she remembered the day Edmund and Adele had come to live with them. So long ago, when life seemed so simple.

Grace was quiet for a long moment; then she looked up and said, "You're right, of course. I've wanted to keep as many people as possible in the house for as long as we could, but you're quite correct to say it's no longer practical. Are we all agreed?"

Still a family decision, Laura thought.

Grace smiled, an unexpectedly bright, naughty look in her eye. "India, would you cut up little bits of paper so we can vote?"

India stared at her for a minute, disconcerted, before she recognized the reference. "I was an ass, wasn't I? I can't imagine why you ever let me stay here!"

"Because you're one of us," Grace said firmly. "Well, if it's to be done, let's do it. Laura, you're the best letter writer in the family—except for Evelyn, of course," she amended, catching sight of that inveterate scribbler's hurt look. "But Evelyn is far too busy to be burdened with this particular job. Laura, write up a little piece about how we're closing the hotel so that our staff may take more important war jobs in industry, and send copies to everyone who has reservations."

Laura went to Grace's room before bed that night. "Just wanted to tell you good night, Gram," she said, poking her head in the door.

"Come in, Laura-bunny."

The room had the comforting smell of camphor oil, lavender water, and beeswax. A Grace smell. Grace was at the dressing table, brushing out her hair. It was entirely white now, but still thick and wavy. "Can I do that?" Laura asked, taking the brush. Grace smiled up at her. "You look very young and pretty tonight," Laura said truthfully.

"I don't feel young. I feel older than rocks."

"Are you sorry we're closing the hotel?" Laura asked, carefully brushing at a snarl.

"Not for myself. But Jack would be disappointed."

"Grandfather?"

"He liked the house full of people, and it has been for— how many?—twelve or thirteen years now."

"There. All done. Let me turn down your bed."

Grace took off her dressing gown and crawled into the high bed, her arthritic joints almost audibly creaking with the effort. "It ought to be like the boy and the calf."

"What?"

"Getting into this bed. You know, the story about the boy who picked up his calf every day, so that when it was a full-grown bull he could still lift it. I've climbed into this bed every night for more than half a century. It ought to be easier, not harder for me."

She shifted as Laura plumped her pillows, then settled back. "Almost half that time I've slept alone. Your grandfather died twenty-four years ago tomorrow. That's a long time to sleep alone. I'm tired of it."

Laura didn't know what to say.

"Hand me that glass of water and my pills, bunny. No, not the blue ones. They're for morning. The pink one and the two white ones with the creases in the middle. That's it. Now the light. Thank you."

Laura sat quietly for a minute, then kissed her grandmother's forehead, almost missing her in the dark. Then she went to the door. Opening it, she said, "Gram, I won't leave here—not to work in a factory, or anything else."

"Good," Grace said, the smile apparent in her voice. "I'm not needed here anymore, but you are. You always will be."

Those were the last words they ever exchanged.

XXVI

"*Y*OU go on back to the house, Aunt Adele. Sonny and I'll be along in a minute or two," Laura said, adjusting her black gloves.

"Of course, my dears. Don't be long, though. There's a chill in the air."

They waited silently until the rest of the funeral guests had gone, then after a last look at the place in the earth where Grace would spend eternity, went to the car and started back to Thornehill. Sonny had arrived only as the services were beginning, in response to her urgent telegram: "GRAM DIED THIS A.M. FUNERAL FRIDAY. PLEASE COME HOME."

"You look wonderful in your uniform," Laura said as Sonny opened the car door for her. "I hardly recognized you at first. Your letters never *sound* like you're wearing a uniform."

He smiled as he started the car. When they were out of the town traffic he asked, "Why did you have her buried here instead of on the estate?"

"You think I did wrong?"

"No, I just wondered."

"I called Willis Hawkins and he said she'd made no provision or request for a burial site in her will and it was up to me. Naturally, I thought first of that little private cemetery on the grounds. She was so determined not to leave Thornehill, but the last time I saw her alive she talked of Grandfather Jack and I decided to put her here with him."

"How did it happen? Can you talk about it?"

Laura took her gloves off and flattened them in her lap. How could she ever tell anyone, even Sonny, what a terrifying thing it was to realize that Gram—the invincible Grace Emerson Thorne—could actually die just like ordinary mortals. And how could she ever make him understand how the hour spent by her bed, listening to the labored breathing, doing nothing but waiting for the inevitable silence, seemed like years. Like her whole life relived.

She couldn't tell him, couldn't tell anyone how she'd wanted to cry out to her: Don't leave me! Don't you *dare* leave me with your secrets and your responsibilities and your past that weaves through my present. I'm not ready. I'm not sure I'll ever be ready. I can't be you—I can't take over for you. I know you meant me to, but you never told me how. Stay, Gram! Stay with me and help me be ready.

No, Sonny wouldn't understand. Or maybe he'd understand too well how lost and terrified she'd felt. All she wanted now was to put it out of her mind, pretend it hadn't happened. Or pretend she was enough of an adult to accept the loss and cope intelligently.

She drew a deep breath. "I can talk now. It was a shock, in spite of our knowing that it would happen someday, and probably soon. There's a big difference between knowing something in your mind and really understanding it with your heart. Once it was over, it wasn't so awful, or perhaps I've just been too busy with the necessary arrangements to really feel it. We spoke the night before and there was something very peaceful and . . . final about her. I guess in a funny sort of way I knew then, or I should have. She just gave up, Sonny. Dr. Lee said it was another stroke, but the real reason she died was that she was ready to. I think she willed herself to let go."

"It was sudden, then?"

"Not so sudden, but private, of course, and dignified. Mabelann took a breakfast tray in to her and found her almost gone. Unconscious, all tucked in, wearing her best bed jacket. Her hair wasn't even disarranged. I'd swear she posed herself. Your wouldn't have known she was alive except for her shallow breath and a faint pulse. I sat with her from then on. I kept talking to her, as if she could hear me—I think she could, even though Dr. Lee said not."

Talked to her? Laura questioned herself. Begged her to live, pleaded with her to come back and be a part of our lives forever. Laura was calmer now, had accepted the fact that her grandmother was gone, but she'd never forget the desolation she'd felt then, the sheer panic in the face of a world without

Grace Thorne bossing it. She'd never truly known until that hour how much of her life was shaped and fenced by Grace. But as tempting as it was to share her sorrow and the odd sense of anger, she wouldn't even try to express this to Sonny. This was something between herself and her dead grandmother. Another burdensome secret to carry through her life. Grace must have heard her pleading, but died anyway!

"Watch this stretch of road. The concrete is buckling and there doesn't seem to be anyone left on the road crew to fix it."

"How are the others taking it?" Sonny asked, slowing down.

Laura sighed. How to explain the chaos that seemed to engulf the house when they learned that Grace was dying? Mabelann's nearly hysterical crying, Adele's maddening busyness, India's reversion to all that old nonsense about auras, Dr. Lee's infuriating common sense in the face of his own desolation—and Laura's own realization that everything now fell to her. Instead of relying on Grace, she was the one being relied upon—an almost crushing responsibility, but one she'd had to shoulder before she even had time for her own grief.

"Very badly at first. I felt like the keeper in a mental institution that first day. They were like demented children whose mother had died. Even Edmund cried, and I had to have Dr. Lee give Adele and Mabelann sedatives to calm them down. It was as if they were all shocked to the core that Gram could die. But the second day I put them all to work and they pulled themselves together. Edmund straightened her desk and sorted out all the paperwork. Adele started cooking for the people who would be coming, and I put Mabelann to work sorting through Gram's clothing."

"And India?"

"Aside from all that silly rattling about reincarnation and auras, she's been wonderful. A real help. Especially with Evelyn."

"And how *is* Mother taking all this?"

"Fairly well. I don't think she's caught on yet what's happened. She dredged around in her closets and found an ancient black outfit straight out of the twenties, like a widowed flapper. All dyed ostrich plumes and black sequins. Ghastly, but it would seem to indicate she's periodically aware that there's been a death. But the whole time I was making arrangements, she was on me about how I shouldn't usurp

Gram's authority and should be consulting with her. She nearly drove me wild."

"I'm sorry you're stuck with her. It sounds like she's gotten a lot dottier since I've been gone."

"Yes, but in an entirely harmless way. Irritating, but harmless."

They rode in silence for several miles. Then Sonny asked, "How's it been, kid? Before this, I mean."

"Only moderately terrible. I miss you. Everyone does."

"Including Gram?"

"Yes. But of course she wouldn't admit it."

"What did she say about me?"

"Absolutely nothing. Literally. She never mentioned where you were or anything about the arguments you and she had about your leaving. When any of the rest of us talked about you, she'd listen with a sort of fixed smile and then move on to some other subject. I think she'd gotten over being so angry. Another month or two and she'd have accepted your 'defection.' I'm sure of it. She'd kept all your letters to her."

"She never answered them."

"Sonny, don't be mad at her now. She's dead, for God's sake!"

He put his hand over hers. "I'm sorry, Laura. I know this has been rough on you. I didn't mean to make it worse. Change of subject: what do you hear from Stephen?"

"Not very much. He's stationed in England. He can't say, of course, what he's doing, but I have the impression he's flying some sort of missions with the RAF. You know, he'd had a good number of hours of flying before this started. His letters are erratic, as if he's sometimes away from base for several days at a time, and there are a lot of references to the weather conditions."

Knowing how critical Sonny was of Stephen, she didn't confide how disappointing those letters really were. Granted, the censorship of mail imposed a strain. And a man as careful as Stephen wouldn't be very much inclined to pour out his heart knowing some army official would be reading it, but still, his letters (which he'd asked her to keep) read more like memoirs in the making than genuine communication. But then, he'd always been an awful correspondent. Even when they first knew each other, she found his letters disappointing. It was, she thought, his only failing.

"He sent me a picture," she said. "It was in *Time*."

"I saw it. Kissing his mother good-bye at the gangplank in

that article about all the rising young politicians who were risking it all to go overseas. Quite touching.''

"Oh, Sonny . . .'' Why couldn't he understand? She'd needed Stephen so much these last few days; the memories of him—especially the light, inconsequential moments—were all that had kept her going. When everyone else was in tears and hysterics and she began to believe the world had indeed ended, she could remember how he'd sat on the floor and taught her a lunatic variation on Parcheesi, or how he'd held her hand and nearly dragged her down a long slope and tossed her, shrieking and giggling, into a pile of leaves. Couldn't Sonny understand that those common, cheerful memories were the very things that kept her sane and that the hope of seeing him again was the only future she had to look forward to?

"Hey! Don't start crying on me now. I'm sorry I'm being such a bastard. I guess I'm another of the demented children you're burdened with. I promise I'll behave. Here's a handkerchief. Mop up, girl. Why isn't Bess Langley here? I thought she'd come to Grace's funeral. They hit it off pretty well.''

"I didn't tell her about it in time for her to get here.''

"Deliberately?'' he asked, cocking an eyebrow and slowing again to make the sharp turn into Thornehill's long drive.

"Yes,'' Laura said meekly. "I didn't want her here.''

"You're having trouble with her?''

"No, not trouble exactly. She writes all the time. Nearly every day. They're pleasant-enough letters, but . . .''

"But what?''

"Well, they're not letters to me, really. She never asks about how I'm doing. They're all just requests that I repeat the contents of Stephen's letters to her. She actually suggested a couple of times that I send them along to her to keep! Can you imagine?''

"Of Bess? Yes, I can. She's got all the tact and charm of a steamroller.''

"I try to like her.''

"That must be like trying to like smallpox.''

Laura smiled. "Smallpox is a friendly little disease compared to Stephen's mother.''

Sonny pulled up in front of the mansion and came around to help Laura out. Taking his arm, she looked up at the imposing facade of the house as if seeing it for the first time. "I can't believe she's not here anymore. This is Grace Thorne's house. How can it still stand without Grace Thorne? I half-expected to come back and find it had fallen in on itself now that the foundation is gone. Oh, by the way, Mr. Hawkins said we ought to have the reading of the will while you're here. Is this evening all right?"

"Sure. Pretty boring stuff, wills. She has to have left it to us. There's nobody else. Nobody in their right mind would put anything more than a nickel in Mother's hands. Come on, girl. If the house is going to fall down, we might as well be inside when it happens."

"Will you explain that again?" Sonny shouted.

Willis Hawkins fidgeted with his fountain pen, inadvertently splattering dots of ink on the document before him on the desk. Lord preserve him from another scene with the Thornes! Such difficult, emotional people! "Your grandmother has left the bulk of her estate to Laura. According to your grandmother's wishes, Laura may specify her heirs, but if she attempts to sell the property, she must sell it for a fair market value and the proceeds must go to charity."

"Damn her. Damn the old bitch to hell!"

"Sonny, please . . ." Laura said weakly. She had sunk, stunned, into a chair by the desk. "Mr. Hawkins, I'm sure there's a mistake of some sort. Gram wouldn't cut Sonny out of his rightful inheritance."

"That's exactly what she's done, Laura. Don't be so stupid and Pollyannaish about this," Sonny said. "She's tied you here so you can't ever get away with a penny to your name, and she's thrown me out."

"Don't *you* be stupid," Laura returned. "This is your home. You belong here."

"As a charity case? Not on your life."

"Charity—!"

"Now, now, children. Please lower your voices," Willis said. His head was pounding with the recollection of another day, another will, but this same room, these same hectic, bitter emotions. "Grace wrote this up herself, just after you went into the service, Sonny. I merely put it into legal terminology, but I wish to make clear to you what I told her. I don't think it would hold up if it's challenged. I confess, I didn't argue with her as strongly as I probably should have. I felt certain she would change her mind later, and I suppose I'd come to think of her, as many of us did, as immortal. For all my experiences with such things, I couldn't believe she'd ever really die. But she devised this while in a highly distraught state, which I would testify to, if necessary. While she lived, Grace was my client and my friend. My personal and professional loyalty was to her. But she's gone now—''

"Oh, she's gone, but her spite lives on," Sonny said, slapping his fist on the desk. Willis jumped back and Sonny turned away, running his fingers through his hair. "Sorry, Mr. Hawkins. I don't meant to take this out on you. It isn't the legality of it that upsets me, it's the intent. The hate and spite and vindictiveness. Dear God, she knew how I love this place. She knew that I fully intended to live out my life here, that I hated leaving it as much as she did—and she was a real fanatic about going away from home. What this will says is: I know what matters to you and I hate you enough to deprive you of it."

"She didn't hate you!" Laura cried.

"Laura, you're an ass if you can say that. Of course she did. I dared—I had the almighty goddamned nerve—to listen to my own conscience instead of her orders, and she hated me for it. You she loved. You did what she wanted. You stayed here, being the fawning, adorable granddaughter, you married the fool she chose for you, and stayed with her instead of going with him. You did it all the right way. Well, you deserve it. You've earned it, my girl. Thornehill. It's all yours, and good luck to you with it!"

He stormed out the door, slamming it so hard there was a sound of wood cracking. Laura sat staring at the door as if he might reappear. She was too shocked, both by the will and by Sonny's behavior, to move or even think.

"There are other provisions," Willis said.

Blinking, Laura dragged her attention back to him. "Yes?" she said numbly.

"Accordingly to the will under which Grace inherited from her husband, she had twenty percent of the bulk of the estate to dispose of at her own discretion. This is in stocks and she's divided it up between Adele and Edmund and your cousin India, with a portion in trust, the income from which is for Mabelann and for Evelyn for life. She has also specified that all five of them and Dr. Lee are entitled to live here as long as they wish."

"Of course they will. Where else would they go? I wouldn't dream of disputing that."

"Good. Miss Thorne . . . Laura, I don't think your grandmother acted entirely out of spite, as your brother believes."

"Why else would she do such a horrible thing?" Laura said bitterly, the tears finally beginning to flow.

"There, there, dear. Don't upset yourself. I merely mean that Grace never felt that Sonny knew how to handle money as well as you. She felt, with some reason, that you are the more practical and sensible child and that the estate would be safer in your hands. I've seen some evidence myself over the years that Sonny doesn't really have a good grasp of business principles."

Laura wadded up her handkerchief and dabbed at her eyes. Little as she wished to hear this, there was a kernel of truth in it. From childhood, Sonny had been reckless about handling money. No, not reckless and certainly not extravagant, merely uninterested. Any discussion of property, taxes, dividends, leases, or interest rates all but put him to sleep. "Still, it was horrible of her!"

"I agree with you. As I said before, I am *your* lawyer now, if you wish me to be—"

"Of course."

"—and I will regard it as my duty to do all in my power to execute your wishes in the matter."

Laura rose, her knees shaking, and shook his hand. "I appreciate your concern. It's probably better to do nothing at the moment. We're all much too upset to act reasonably. Mr. Hawkins, if you don't mind now, I'd be very grateful if you'd explain this to the others without me. I'd like to be alone."

"Leave it to me, my dear. Just ring me when you want to discuss this further and I'll be out here before you can hang up. I am so sorry that an already sad occasion should have been further marred by this."

Laura slipped through the hallway, avoiding the rest of the family, and went straight up to Grace's bedroom. Mabelann had gone through the closets, but the room looked the same. The portrait photograph of Jack in his World War One army uniform was on the dresser, Grace's slippers were under the pink flounced stool as if waiting for her feet. The bed was even turned down, ready. Laura sat down in the little upholstered armchair by the window and stared at the dresser, imagining Grace sitting there that last night of her life, brushing out her thick white hair.

"Why, Gram? Why did you do this to us? To me? We were so close and so happy only a few days ago, and you were, even then, harboring this awful, evil secret. It wasn't right and you must have known it. Causing Sonny a terrible pain like this—he'll never forgive you. And neither will I.''

She slipped off her shoes and drew her legs up, wrapping her arms around them and propping her chin on her knee. ''You were my mother and my father and my friend besides being my grandmother. I loved you so much. I depended on you and trusted you. We all did. How could you have done something so ugly and hateful? Was it to punish Sonny for going away? Or was it to create a conflict between us? I don't suppose you could ever accept the fact that I loved him as much as I loved you.''

Her voice echoed into the camphor- and lavender-scented darkness.

''Well, Gram, it's a good thing in one way. I can't seem to feel anger and sorrow at the same time. Maybe when the anger fades I can truly grieve you. God! I never dreamed it would be like this. I guess I thought you'd go out gently, but you never did anything gently in your life. You lived with a terrible intensity and I suppose this is a natural aftermath.''

She stretched her legs back out and rose. ''Good-bye, Gram. I do love you and I'll miss you forever, but if you're anywhere you can hear me, listen to this: you can't do this to Sonny. I will defeat you. *We* will defeat you.''

When Laura woke in the morning, she couldn't figure out at first where she was. Then memory returned. She'd been unable to face the rest of the family and had come down to the cottage to sleep, knowing Sonny would know where to find her. She went to the bathroom, threw on the clothes she'd worn the day before, and went into the small living room.

Sonny was slumped at the table, sleeping with his head on his arms. He stirred and looked up as she came in. His eyes were red-rimmed and his clothes and hair were in wild disarray. ''Got anything here to drink?'' he asked blearily.

''Whiskey?'' Laura said.

''Sounds okay,'' he said, disappearing into the bathroom. When he returned, looking only a little better, Laura had a weak whiskey and water on the table for him. She didn't drink enough to know whether she'd made it in the right proportions or not, but Sonny didn't drink enough to know the difference anyway.

He collapsed into the chair, took a sip, and grimaced.

"That tastes like shit, my girl." She smiled as he tried again.
"I was terrible last night. I'm sorry," he said.

"You don't need to apologize. I understand."

"No, you can't understand. I couldn't have until a few hours ago. I'm so consumed by hate and outrage that I'm actually nauseated with it. And I lashed out at you and said terrible things I didn't mean."

"It's all right. You could have slapped me silly and I wouldn't have held it against you for a minute."

"That's not right. It's my problem. I shouldn't have taken it out on you."

"Oh, Sonny, can't you see? I'm as outraged as you are. She betrayed me too. It was a horrible thing to do. And a lot of what you said *was* true in a way. I have always done what she wanted—not because she wanted it, at least I don't think so, but because it suited me as well. But the result was that she controlled my life, pushed me into each new door, and that will was her way of trying to control me and make my decisions after her death."

Sonny went to the sink, poured out the drink, and rinsed the glass. "I shouldn't have said anything anyway. I didn't mean it. I don't feel any resentment of her favoring you. I never have."

"I know that. But it's all behind us now. We need to talk to Mr. Hawkins again before you go to see what we need to do to break the will. He seemed to think it wouldn't be too difficult. We can go into town tomorrow—"

"No."

"Why not?"

"Because I'll be gone. I have to leave this afternoon."

"Oh, Sonny—"

"We'll talk about it later, Laura. Next time I'm back."

"I guess that'll be all right. Can you get away again for Christmas, do you think?"

Sonny came back and sat down across from her and took her hands. "Laura, I won't be back for Christmas. Maybe not for several Christmases."

"No!"

"Yes, I'm shipping out day after tomorrow. I only got this leave on the condition that I get back on time."

She clutched at his hands. "No, Sonny. I need you here."

"You'll get along fine without me. I'm not a bit of use. Never have been good for anything but cluttering the place up."

"Don't try to be funny! I mean it. I can't manage without you."

"And I mean it when I say you can. You *will* because you have to. If there's one thing Gram taught us both, it's duty. We are probably the most pigheadedly dutiful people on earth. My duty is to go where the army says to go, and your duty is to stay at Thornehill and hold things together until the world gets back to normal."

"Nothing's ever going to be normal again!"

"Possibly not, my girl. Possibly not, but we've got to pretend we believe it will. Now, stop that sniveling and let go of my hands before you cut off the circulation to my fingers."

Autumn passed into winter more easily than Laura had expected. By inventing work, she managed to fill the days to the point that there was little leisure for thinking—or feeling. She wrote to both Sonny and Stephen every day and was rewarded with replies. Stephen's letters were as impersonal as ever and came now more erratically. Whatever he did, he apparently did more of the time than before. Sometimes a week or more would pass between his letters.

Sonny's letters arrived looking like scraps of tattered lace. His natural, irrepressible indiscretion was the nightmare of the army censors. Some of his letters had, in fact, more words cut out than remained. He wasn't allowed to say where he was or what he was doing, but he did mention frequently that he was no longer stationed at (blank) and was now on his way to (blank). He said he was having to brush up on his (blank) and was finding it a bit tough. Laura knew the only European language he had trouble with was Serbo-Croatian and judged that this was what he meant. Did this message signify that he was going behind enemy lines? She lost several weeks' sleep over this possibility.

Uncle Edmund joined the local civil-defense volunteers and immersed himself in the ongoing search for scarce goods. It was like a nationwide scavenger hunt and Edmund wholeheartedly enjoyed it. He managed to collect a record amount of bacon grease for use in making ammunition. He doggedly peeled the tinfoil off everyone's cigarette packs, sometimes before they'd finished the cigarettes, which were getting to be in very short supply.

Just before Christmas he led a family raid on the attics in search of old silk and nylon stockings. "For parachutes or something?" Laura asked doubtfully.

"No, for powder bags for naval guns. Did you know by the way, that one old shovel head can be made into four grenades?"

"Fascinating," Laura said, thinking how much better off the world would be with more shovels and fewer grenades. But then, a shovel wouldn't do Sonny or Stephen much good right now and a grenade might, so she went to the stables and got a pile of old tools ready for Edmund to take to town.

Life was changing daily and in unexpected ways. Odd things became scarce; some made sense, some didn't. There was hardly a lawn mower left in the country, nor was it possible to purchase a new bicycle, Laura discovered when she attempted to buy one to save precious gasoline. Oddly enough, alarm clocks seemed to have disappeared as well as matches for lighting the increasingly rare cigar or cigarette. The Thornes learned to live by the motto the rest of the country had adopted: "Use it up; wear it out; make it do; or do without."

Adele devoted herself to teaching everyone within teachable distance how to cook with the meat, sugar, and flour allowed under the stringent rationing system. Fortunately, being in a rural setting and the owners of several farms helped them a great deal. They didn't suffer nearly as much from the restrictions as most city people did.

Evelyn heard that the soldiers at the front needed socks and went into a positive orgy of knitting. All the socks were huge and Laura found herself wondering if there were enough pituitary giants in the army to really make the best use of her handiwork. But it kept her busy and out of everyone's way. "She's working on needles that are far too large a gauge," Adele said.

"For heaven's sake, don't tell her that. Any change might make her lose interest. Do you want her helping you with your cooking classes?" Laura asked.

"Lordie, no!"

India, having grown up on the East Coast, took the blackout requirements very seriously. She hung hundreds of yards of black cloth. "India, there's hardly any reason to put shades in windows in unused rooms!" Adele sniped.

"You can't be too careful."

They hardly dared light a match in broad daylight without India jerking a shade shut, plunging them into darkness. "My dear India, I can hardly get these socks finished for Christmas without light," Evelyn would whine.

"Would you rather the Germans blew the hell out of the house?"

"The Germans? Why would they do that? I knew a delightful German couple when I was a girl . . ."

They all kept themselves busy and occupied and made a point of consulting with Laura on every detail. Sometimes these consultations became nearly unbearable. Laura wanted to scream: I don't care if you use turnips in the stew in place of carrots! I'm not interested in the fact that applesauce has gone from ten rations points to twelve! Knit some white socks instead of khaki if you want to! If the car has run out of gas and we have no more stamps, then we simply won't drive anywhere! Leave me alone! *Leave me alone!''*

But she held her tongue because she knew they were trying to involve her, keep her busy, prevent her from having free time to worry about her husband and brother or brood or her beloved grandmother's death.

Christmas was the worst, but even that was survivable. They made it as festive as they could and invited Willis Hawkins and his niece to dinner to swell the crowd and remember better times when there were more people at the table. Dr. Lee was in an especially good mood that day. "I'm going up to Kansas City next week to tour a hospital with a friend. You know, the army wouldn't take me, even as an adviser, because of my age, but this friend says he thinks there's a way I can be useful and wants me to come up and see him about it."

Willis Hawkins took Laura aside for a moment before he left. "I presume you've decided not to dispute your grandmother's will?"

"Not until Sonny gets back. He didn't want me to do anything about it now. Is there any hurry?"

"None whatsoever. I think that it's wise to wait."

The weather turned unexpectedly balmy the second week in January and Laura took advantage of the change to put on a jacket and go down to the cottage to pull a few weeds and set out new mousetraps in the closets. She got interested in a magazine she'd left there earlier and ended up lighting a fire and having a cozy afternoon by herself, reading. Toward dinnertime she vaguely noticed the sound of a car passing by on the way up the drive, but was too immersed in her story to get up and see who it was. A half-hour later there was a knock on the door.

She opened it and found Dr. Lee outside. "Come in. I

didn't know you were back from Kansas City yet. Did you have a nice visit with your friend? Can I fix you some tea?"

"No, thank you, dear. There was a call . . ."

"A call? What do you mean? What's wrong?"

"Sit down, Laura. Adele got a call this afternoon just before I drove in, and she asked me to come talk to you."

Laura's legs all but buckled under her and her ears started ringing. "What is it? Who? Sonny? Not Sonny!"

"No, Laura, it's Stephen . . ."

XXVII

STEPHEN had been flying a highly sensitive mission—dropping a half-dozen parachutists behind the lines deep in occupied France. The plane, according to another pilot who'd been flying just behind, apparently suffered engine problems and started losing altitude a few miles short of the drop target. As it neared the ground, enemy fire took out one of the engines and the observing pilot saw it go down in a small lake.

Missing and presumed dead.

The army description denied them even the comfort of a certainty. There were no bodies found, of course, because there was no way of searching. All this information came through Arch Langley. For reasons the Thornes resented but never fully understood, Arch and Bess had been informed of all this a full week before the dread telegram reached Arkansas. Bess herself never called Laura, nor did she write. With Stephen's death, any bond that might have existed between them was dissolved. Laura no longer had any purpose in Bess's life.

"I don't know about these things. Should we have a funeral or something?" Laura asked India ten days after the news came.

India shook her head. "Not a funeral."

"Then a memorial service. He must be honored."

"He has been," India said, fishing reluctantly for a letter in her purse. "I got this in the mail this morning. A friend in New York sent it."

It was a newspaper clipping describing the memorial service that had been held by Senator Arch Langley and his sister-in-law Bess for Mrs. Langley's only son, Stephen, who had died a hero's death in France. Stephen's background was explained: his tradition-laden family history, his exemplary college credits, his law degree, his career in the State Department. There was mention of his mother's family connections and his late father's life, but not a word about his wife. No indication that he had been married.

"As if I didn't exist," Laura said softly, handing the clipping back to India.

"It's shameful! You have every right to be furious with that bitch Bess. You know she fed them this information and kept you out of it so she could get all the sympathy and glory. Besides everything else, it's totally inappropriate. There's no proof that he might not still be living."

"Do you think that's really possible?" Laura asked.

India paused. She'd meant to give a little comfort, not false hopes. "No, I don't. From what we've heard of how it happened—the plane in flames, the crash into a lake—I think there's very little chance. Apparently Bess doesn't think so either. The very thought of that woman makes my blood boil!"

But though Laura was hurt, she couldn't work up to fury. Her heart was like a sponge that had been squeezed dry of all emotion. She was more numb than saddened. For the first two weeks she functioned fairly normally, getting up early as always, tending to her household duties, offering more comfort than she accepted. The family was pleased at how well she was taking it.

Only Dr. Lee was not. "It isn't normal," he told Adele. "The girl's been under a terrible strain the last year. She didn't even cry when I broke the news to her. Just sat there with her hands clenched, asking me sensible questions. It's not right. Do you think that she's not grieving because she's refusing to face the fact that he's dead?" he asked, leaving no doubt as to his own conviction.

"No, I don't think she's questioning that," Adele said. "The circumstances of what we've been told happened, the Langleys' memorial service—all of it seems pretty certain, and I think she sees it that way too. In fact, she's packed up all his things, the clothes he left and some books and such. That seems fairly final. What can we do for her?"

"I'm just a poor old country doctor. I can only sense that there's a problem. I can't prescribe a cure for a broken heart. Is there any word of Sonny today?"

"Not a letter for three weeks now."

"What does Laura say about it?"

"She won't talk about it. She meets the postman every day at the end of the driveway, then just brings the mail in without saying anything."

"Too bad he isn't here. They've always meant so much to each other."

Adele's eyes misted and she bustled around the kitchen where they were sitting. "Another cup of tea?"

"I ought to be helping Laura. Grace would have expected it of me. I don't seem to be doing any good, but I don't know what I can do for her, an old fogy like me."

In February, Laura started sleeping late. "Are you ill, dear? Perhaps a cold?" Adele asked her.

"No. Just tired. The weather's so dismal it seems pointless to get up early when the sun refuses to. Don't fuss. I'm fine."

But she wasn't fine. She started taking afternoon naps as well and her weight started dropping. "You must eat more, dear," Edmund warned. "You're already thin and need nourishment to help you through these bad times."

"Leave me alone!" she said with unusual curtness.

One night they were awakened by the sound of crying and found Laura huddled in the middle of the upstairs hallway. "It's so quiet and empty here. The house was always full of people," she sobbed as India and Mabelann led her back to bed. "Remember all the happy people, India? The gangsters and the rich people. There was laughter—there used to be things to laugh about. Nobody laughs anymore! Oh, India, why did they die? Gram and Stephen shouldn't have died. They shouldn't have done that to me. Everybody's leaving me."

"Hush, dear. Nobody else is leaving you. We're right here."

"Sonny's not here. Sonny's left me too. Nobody says anything, but I can tell. You all think he's dead too, and you just aren't admitting it. He didn't have to go! Everybody's going to die and leave me alone in this terrible empty house."

"Mabelann, let's take her to my room. I don't want her to be alone tonight."

They had a drink of brandy together, then another and another. At four in the morning they went downstairs, staggering and clutching each other for support, and raided the liquor cabinet in the library. By dawn they were both roaring, stinking drunk. India went outside and was sick in the snow, and Laura laughed so hard she fell down, tearing her night-gown and bruising her arm on the table she knocked over.

Mabelann reported this to Adele first thing in the morning. "You want me to fill 'em up some ol' black coffee, Miz Adele?"

Adele put on her housecoat and went down to look in on the chaos in the library. India was draped headfirst over Grace's desk, trying to count the roses in the carpet pattern. Laura was lying on her back on the floor singing "Praise the Lord and Pass the Ammunition" at the top of her lungs.

"It might be what Laura needed," Adele said, wrinkling her nose at the alcohol fumes that filled the room. "Let's just put them to bed and let them sleep it off."

But it wasn't what she needed. Even when she'd gotten over the hangover, Laura was grim and silent, refusing to refer to the episode in the library. Two days later she packed some clothes and books and her tatting and announced that she was moving into the cottage.

"No, dear. You shouldn't do that," Adele said.

"I'm going to."

"But if we need you for something. . . ?"

"That's one of the reasons I'm going there. I don't want to be needed for anything. I'm sick of being needed. I'm sick of everybody and everything, especially myself. Well, I can't get away from myself, but I *can* get away from everyone else."

"Maybe a nice little trip. A vacation. You could do some shopping or sightseeing. That would be a refreshing change. I could get away for a bit, or if you'd prefer India to go with you—"

"And hitchhike? How else would a person get anywhere these days? No, I don't need a trip. I need . . ."

Adele took her hand in a fierce grip. "What do you need, darling? If it's in our power, we'll get it for you."

At that, Laura's defenses cracked a little. "You're much nicer to me than I deserve," she said, hugging her aunt. "But I don't know what I need."

It wasn't a stay in the cottage, she soon discovered, but refused to admit it to herself. Alone there the depression that had clamped down on her tightened like a vise, nearly squeez-ing the breath out of her. It became almost a tangible pres-ence, a slimy creature who lived with her and whispered in her ear. It crept under doors, coiled in the blankets with her at night.

She slept as much as twelve or fourteen hours a day and it was miserable sleep that left her exhausted. The long nights were filled with bad dreams—not purging nightmares, merely anxious dreams. She was always almost missing a train, or forgetting an important appointment, or realizing she'd brought a suitcase on a trip and neglected to put anything in it. In her dreams she found herself in school assembly wearing only her underwear, or on a ship that was going to sink, or at Stephen's memorial service with her hair all cut off to her scalp.

She felt that her personality was compressing into a tight wad and she knew she needed help, but a terrible inertia had taken her and nothing seemed worth the trouble. She kept meaning to cheer herself up by fixing a nice meal, but she couldn't quite make herself get up and do it. She considered getting drunk again, but didn't like the taste of whiskey and couldn't work up the energy to walk up to the big house and get anything else. She got a snarl in her current tatting project and didn't bother to pick it loose. Long walks in the brisk early-spring air might have helped, but it was too much trouble to get out of her nightgown and into outdoor clothes, so she just sat at the window and watched the rain drip from the roof.

The family tried to visit her, but she ran them off. In fact her rudeness to them was the only definite, spirited thing she did. "I don't want to see you. Any of you. I don't want to see anyone. If you must bring me things to eat, just leave them outside the door."

India was the first to get fed up with this. "Look here, Laura, do you imagine you're the only person who's ever suffered a loss? What makes you think you have the right to be hateful to the people who love you and want to help you?"

"I don't want your damned help. What could you possibly know about being a widow! I just want to be left alone."

In late March a handful of letters came from Sonny. India ran all the way to the cottage to dump then in Laura's lap.

"He's alive?" Laura asked, running her fingertips over the familiar sprawling handwriting. India left her alone to read the letters and that evening Laura appeared in the dining room of the big house, her hair somewhat combed and a touch of lip rouge in a garish streak against her pale face. She talked with some animation about Sonny's letters and passed them around for the others to read. He'd been behind enemy lines for a month, helping to bring some important unnamed individual out. It must have been quite an adventure, for the letters were full of holes where the missing words had been cut out.

"I think the letters are a joke. You know, if he were really indiscreet, he wouldn't be trusted with anything this important. I think he's just deliberately giving some censor a bad time," India said.

Laura laughed briefly at this and they all exchanged happy, meaningful glances.

But even this apparent step to recovery was temporary. In another two days Laura had slumped back into the greedy arms of her terrible gray lethargy.

Howard Lee came to the cottage to see her the first week in April. It was midmorning when he knocked on the door. There was no response and he knocked again and waited. Finally he decided she must be gone and had started back up to the house when the door opened. "Dr. Lee?"

He stared at her in surprise. He'd thought India was exaggerating when she reported on Laura's condition, but all she'd said was true and more so. Laura was a mess—there was no other word for it. "May I talk to you for a minute, Laura?"

"I suppose so," she said grudgingly. He had that look, that zealous, reforming light in his eye she'd grown to loathe.

He came in and cleared a pile of clothing from a chair without waiting for an invitation to sit down and make himself comfortable—an offer he sensed wouldn't be made. "How about something to drink?"

"No, thank you."

He laughed. "I didn't mean you, I meant me. You're the hostess, I'm the guest."

"Oh, yes . . ." she said vaguely, and glanced around for a dirty cup to wash out. This was the part when his face was supposed to crease across the forehead and he would say: Laura, I'm worried about you.

She started some water boiling and sat down to wait for the inevitable. But instead he said, "I've been back up to Kansas City. The friend I told you about I was going to visit . . ."

"Yes, I remember."

"I wanted to tell you about it, if you have a little time."

"Oh, I have time."

Howard Lee went to the stove, took off the kettle, and poured himself a cup of hot water, then dunked a dented tea ball into it as he talked. "He's the administrator of a hospital there. He was telling me about some of their problems." He came back and sat down again, looking across at Laura's blank, apathetic face. "There's a huge number of boys coming back from the service with injuries, you know."

"I suppose there must be."

"The veterans' hospitals are under a terrific strain and the overflow is putting a like strain on the private institutions. You see, though a large proportion of the men coming in need intensive medical care, an equal if not greater number have had all the treatment that surgeons can deliver and need either a long period of recuperation or therapy. Laura, are you listening to me?"

"Yes, Dr. Lee," she said, abandoning her contemplation of the window and looking at him.

"Good. I want you to understand this."

"Why?"

He was momentarily disconcerted. "Because it involves you, or at least I hope it soon will."

"Me? How?" Her eyes had slid away soon.

"Just listen. The hospitals are running out of space. They have soldiers sleeping in the halls and X-ray rooms and along the edges of the dining rooms. And most of these boys don't need full-time medical care; they're simply not quite well enough to go home yet and resume a normal life. Many have lost legs, arms, hands. They have artificial limbs they don't know how to use and there isn't anyone who can take time from the medical emergencies to help them. And every day that atmosphere becomes more discouraging and oppressive. Their spirits are low and that further slows the recuperative process. Many of them who came in with a curable physical problem are developing mental problems as well. It's a terrible situation."

"Yes, it must be." She was staring at the window again.

"Laura! Listen to me!"

"I am!"

That was better. He'd made her mad. At least there was something still alive in her. "I imagine you're asking yourself: What can be done about this? Yes, I can see you are," he said with a wry twist to his mouth.

She scowled at him.

"Well, one solution is to move the men who are nearly ready for release into our institutions for the remainder of their therapy. Preferably not just another hospital, but something homier. That's where you come in.''

She was starting to look wary and was picking a ragged spot on the sleeve of her nightgown. "How so?''

"By letting the mansion be converted into such an institution. It's perfect. Plenty of room, all going to waste. Beautiful, serene surroundings, the spring lake where the men could swim in fair weather. Swimming is excellent therapy—''

She put her hands up in front of her face as if physically warding off a blow. "No, it's impossible.''

"Why?''

"It's just . . . just impossible. It would mean so many changes, such a great cost, and we're too busy!'' Her voice had risen shrilly.

"You know, Laura, this makes me downright glad Grace is dead.''

"How dare you say that!''

"It's true. Grace would turn in her grave if she could hear you talking this way—*looking* this way.''

"No!''

"Yes! Take apart what you just said and think about it. It would mean changes? Was she ever afraid of changes? Didn't she make enormous changes to convert her home into a hotel when it was necessary? As for the cost, you've got more money than you'll ever be able to spend because of her efforts. Do you honestly think she'd begrudge you using it in such a way? Of course not. If she were alive, she'd have come to me to offer rather than waiting for me to ask. She loved the house full of people. She felt almost a moral obligation to keep it full. As for you being too busy—''

"I am!''

"With what? You're dug in here like a slug in the winter. You certainly aren't spending any of your time on anything useful, not even bathing. This place is a wreck. It even smells bad. *You* smell bad, Laura Thorne!''

"How vulgar of you!'' she said, standing up suddenly.

"No, how vulgar of *you*. You haven't combed your hair in a week, I'd bet. The cottage is as filthy as you are. You don't remember, of course, when Grace lost her husband, but I do. Whatever private agony she suffered—and believe me, she suffered!—she didn't let herself go to pieces like you have. She would be sick at the sight of you. She raised you to be better than this. Now, you're coming up to Kansas City with me to meet with the hospital people.''

"No, I don't want to."

"Whether you want to or not makes no difference. You're coming. Now, get into the shower while I go back up to the big house. Mabelann is packing a bag for you and Edmund is coming along to discuss the necessary renovations and financing."

"You had this all planned!"

"Of course I did. I assumed I'd have your agreement."

"Well, you don't have it. I won't go!"

He stood, his look menacing and his voice more so. "I'm still bigger and stronger than you, my dear, even if I am seventy-two years old. Do I have to manhandle you into that shower? I will if I have to. I've known you since I treated your diaper rash. It wouldn't embarrass me a bit. Doctors grow accustomed to unpleasant scenes. Do you want to create one?"

Laura didn't reply, and he went on, "You know, I keep thinking about your husband—he was a great one for talking about courage. He died a hero's death, giving his life to defend and protect thousands of people he didn't even know. But here you are, unwilling even to help take care of your own people. I can't help but wonder what he'd think of you. Do you suppose he'd be proud of the way you're letting yourself go to the dogs?"

In the end she agreed to clean up and travel to Kansas City with him because it was quite simply easier than fighting his will. She sat in the back seat all the way, bolt upright and furious. Howard Lee and Edmund ignored her presence utterly. She got angrier with every mile. And with the anger, life flowed back into the mind and body.

They stayed an extra day, at Laura's request. She went to Harzfeld's and bought three new dresses in bright prints and a summer suit with padded shoulders and a beautifully draped orange striped blouse. She bought new shorts and halter tops. Then she had her hair cut and permed and her nails done with a brazen scarlet polish. She even managed to purchase two pairs of black-market nylons, which she didn't tell Edmund about. One for her, one for India, who, like many women, had taken to drawing a fake seam up the back of her legs with an eyebrow pencil.

Laura piled her packages into the trunk of Dr. Lee's car and they started back. "How soon can we have the house ready?" she asked Edmund as they left behind the suburbs.

Dr. Lee looked back at her for a second. "Then you're doing it?"

"Do I have a choice?" she asked with a smile.

"Of course you do. I just forced you to come up here so that you could make the decision intelligently. If you really don't want to, that's the end of it and no one will think the less of you."

She sat forward, leaning her elbows on the seat between the two old men. "You mean that, don't you? Do you honestly suppose after meeting that boy who'd lost his feet and had no one to teach him to walk again that I could say no?"

"Laura, you shouldn't make your decision on the basis of guilt. This war isn't your fault."

"No, I didn't start it and I can't do a thing to stop it, but I have the means of helping the people who are caught up in it and I want to. I want to."

"Are you sure you're up to it? You've had a rough time," Dr. Lee said.

"What is this reversal of position?" she said, laughing. "A few days ago you were telling me I was a stinky, sniveling, self-pitying brat."

"I didn't say that—exactly."

"But that's what you meant. And you were right. Don't you see, part of the reason I want this is purely selfish. I'm like Gram in that I like people in the house. I've grown up with it that way and I think the emptiness contributed as much to the state I was in as Gram's death and Stephen's. You've done me the best favor in my life, Dr. Lee. I'm grateful and I know Gram would be too, if she knew."

"You may feel differently after you get under way, Laura. This isn't going to be like having a bunch of rich, sophisticated people vacationing at Thornehill. Some of these boys are bitter, terribly bitter. And it could be very depressing to be surrounded day in and day out by cripples."

"Cripples who need help!"

"Still, I think you ought to consider it for a week or so more before you make any rash decisions."

"You're the doctor. Your treatment and advice have been excellent so far. I'll wait if you insist. But I'm sure of my decision, and if the rest of the family agree, we'll start making our plans in a week."

*   *   *

A group of hospital administrators came in and advised Edmund on the physical changes the mansion would have to undergo. They were to be more extensive than anyone had imagined. Elevators had to be installed for the men who wouldn't be able to manage stairs. The paths to the spring and the stables would need to be resurfaced for wheelchairs. Handrails had to be put in all the hallways, except the portion of the house that had always been reserved for the family's private use. Loose rugs had to be removed, urinals installed, electrical wiring updated, doors widened, and upper windows discreetly barred to discourage any thoughts of suicide.

Officials of the Veterans Administration came to look the house over, get Laura to sign a sheaf of papers, and leave a crate full of forms that would have to be filled out and sent in to them at weekly intervals documenting every patient's treatment and progress. An army nurse came to explain about linens, soaps, and pharmaceuticals, as well as the uses and care of therapy equipment. A professional nutritionist spent a full week with Adele, inspecting the food preparation and service areas and instructing her in a haughty manner that drove poor Adele nearly mad.

Once Laura felt she had a basic understanding of what she needed to know as the owner of the house/hospital, she and India went to St. Louis to take an intensive four-month crash course in nursing while Edmund was overseeing the renovations. It wasn't strictly necessary for Laura to have this education. Dr. Lee was busy hiring a staff, including a dozen nurses and nearly as many trained therapists. But Laura wanted to know as much as possible about the treatment the soldiers would be receiving and be ready to stand in briefly, should an emergency arise.

"Perhaps after we get into operation, I'll be able to go back and get a real degree," she told the old physician.

"I wouldn't count on that, my dear. The forms alone will be very nearly a full-time job."

"I used to wonder about those paper drives Uncle Edmund worked on. I couldn't understand what it was all needed for. Now I see," she said, glancing at the tottering stacks of forms that threatened to take over the library. "The army must use more paper than bandages."

India was taking special courses in crafts and skills for the handicapped. "Just think, there might be a potential artist in some trench someplace who doesn't even know he has the talent. If he ends up here, I want to be sure he has every opportunity to blossom.''

Thornehill Hospital opened officially on October 1, 1943—coincidentally a year to the day after Grace's death. Laura went with Dr. Lee and Uncle Edmund to meet the first group of patients. As she started out the front door, she paused and looked around. "What do you think, Gram?'' she asked aloud to the empty entry hall. "It's certainly different. Even all the fresh paint and handrails don't make it look like a real hospital, but it isn't quite the same old house either.''

As she spoke, Adele, wearing one of the white smocks she had decided to wear as an indication of her semiemployed status, came down the front steps. "Haven't you gone yet? Who are you talking to?''

"I was consulting with Gram,'' Laura said sheepishly.

"Do you still talk to her? So do I. She'd approve, you know. She loved this house, but never selfishly. I think she was happiest when it was being used and lived in. She told me once that she and Jack had intended to have at least a dozen children if they could manage it. I've always believed that was her greatest disappointment and made it so important to her to have people here. Now the men who are coming will be helped, not merely entertained, as before, when it was a hotel.''

Laura put her arm around Adele's plump waist and hugged her mightily. "I hope so.''

"You never know—'' Adele started, then clamped her mouth shut again.

"Know what?''

"Well, I probably shouldn't say anything, but I keep wondering if there won't be some nice doctor or even a patient who might someday take your fancy.''

Laura drew back in mock horror that was faintly underlaid with the real thing. "You old matchmaker, you! I'm not husband-hunting.''

"Of course you're not, dear. You're far too well-bred for that,'' Adele said, failing to see the joke. "But it can't hurt to keep an open mind, can it?''

"I'm going to be far too busy—thank God!—to think about men except as patients. Must dash, Uncle Edmund is honking the horn.''

As they rode to town, Laura's mind came back to this conversation. She hadn't really thought much about it, but she vaguely supposed she would remarry someday. Not soon, but she was still young. Adele might be right. There could be a man in her future. For the first time she began to wonder if she was legally a widow. It didn't matter to her now what the legal distinction was between "presumed dead" and "dead," but it might someday.

In her own mind there was no difference. Stephen was dead to her, and had been, she now recognized, since the week after their marriage, when he went away with his uncle. If he had survived even for a short time, she hoped he'd had medical care half as humane as the soldiers at Thornehill would soon be receiving. The thought gave her a cold chill because she knew it was a vain hope.

The Eureka Springs train station hadn't been used for passenger traffic for years; only freights passed through. But a string of special cars had been put on from St. Louis to bring the first group of soldiers and would be arriving once a week in the future. The townspeople had formed a committee to clean up the disused station and make it presentable.

From 1937 through 1940 the Crescent Hotel, where the Thorne family used to have luncheon on the Sundays that they went to church, had operated as a hospital under the direction of a man named Norman Baker, who claimed to have a secret cancer cure. But the townspeople seldom saw any of the patients there. They would arrive in private closed cars and never seemed to leave, except very late at night. Suspicion had taken hold and thrived on rumors of secret forays on moonless nights to ship off bodies of those who failed to be cured. In 1940 the Crescent had closed when Baker was accused of attempting to defraud people through the mails. Since then it had sat vacant at the top of the hill overlooking the town, a silent reminder of glib promises and unknown, unmourned deaths. It was even said to be haunted.

The people of the town were therefore glad to be even a small part of helping open up a medical facility that was both aboveboard and patriotic. The train station had been swept, painted, and had its windows washed. The station and town were hung with flags and banners and the high-school band was on hand to greet the train. Laura had contributed the money for their new red-and-white uniforms.

When the train finally huffed to a stop, half the county was waiting. Laura had to blink back tears when the first soldier, a boy of eighteen with an artificial leg and a hook for a hand stepped onto the platform. The band burst into a spirited

rendition of "God Bless America." The boy, leaning heavily
on an attendant, slowly raised the cold metal hook to his
forehead in a proud salute.

One by one the others disembarked, some under their own
power, others being carried in burly attendants' arms or strapped
to stretchers. After a few emotional speeches, the thirty-four
young men were loaded into the cars and trucks of those who
had volunteered to help with transportation and taken back to
Thornehill, where Adele had prepared a festive open-house
reception.

Laura went to the library to remove her coat and found to
her vast pleasure and utter astonishment that Sonny—half a
world away—had done the impossible. He'd managed, against
all the odds, to have a vast formal bouquet of roses sent with
a card saying "Happy the hospital with my dear Laura at the
helm. All my love, your twin, Sonny."

She sat down at the big desk that was now hers, had been
Grace's before and Jack's before that, and wept.

That night, before going to bed, Laura walked through the
house. Night-lights glowed in the halls and several rooms.
Smiling nurses raised their heads as she passed their stations,
and greeted her in the soft but carrying voices that only nurses
have. The old mansion was like a dozing giant, humming and
purring gently with life and hope and healing.

Laura slept that night in her old room, and for the first time
in over a year fell into a deep, dreamless sleep.

XXVII

LAURA put the last form on the top of the pile and pushed back her hair with ink-smudged fingers. At that moment one of the nurses came in the door with a folder full of papers. "No! Not more! Say it's not more!"

The young woman grinned. "Sorry, Miss Thorne, but it is."

Laura didn't correct her as she had once done when people addressed her as Miss Thorne. She had been Mrs. Langley for only a week, and that week was a long time ago. It didn't seem to have anything to do with her life anymore. She'd sent all Stephen's letters to Bess, since she wanted them and there was nothing particularly personal in them. Bess had answered with a short, courteous note, but since then there had been no communication between the Thornes and the Langleys except a single Christmas card with an engraved signature and no message. Laura had put her wedding ring into a little box and stored it in the attic with her wedding dress.

The nurse left as Adele was coming in. "Making progress, dear?" she asked, sitting down across from Laura.

"There is no such thing as progress at this desk. The work is Augean. As soon as I shovel a load of it out, another is dumped on me."

"You should be outdoors on a day like this. It's lovely, or so I hear."

Since the hospital had opened seven months earlier, Adele had been in a perpetual whirlwind. Happy and hectic, she had supervised all the meals and had even collaborated with India—a minor miracle in itself—to set up a row of beehives in order to supplement the sugar supply. India, sweeping about in

334

netting, tended to the hives and Adele managed the honey processing.

"I would like to be outside for a while. I'll see if Edmund has someone to drive the bus to the train station. It *is* Wednesday, isn't it?" The arrivals and departures of soldiers always took place on Wednesdays. "I want to do a little shopping, so I'll leave early. Anything you want from town?"

An hour later she was pulling into Eureka Springs in the unwieldy hospital bus. It had once been an oversized school bus, which the army had converted to their use. The front half still had seats and the back half was set up for a double tier of stretchers. It had also been painted a repulsive dark muddy green but had excellent, heavily treaded rubber tires and good springs, something few vehicles in the country could boast.

For once there were no soldiers being dismissed today, so Laura had only two companions on the way to town—Sergeant Walker and a nurse. Sergeant Walker was a big bearlike man with hammy hands that were as talented with handling clay in the therapy unit as they were in lifting and carrying the patients. He was a favorite of India's, and even Laura could see that his sculpturing had improved since he'd started attending her classes.

"I'm going up to the Basin Hotel for lunch. Do either of you want to join me? My treat."

"Thank you, no, ma'am," the nurse, a local girl, replied. "I'm having lunch with my aunt."

"I'll turn you down too," Sergeant Walker said. "I'm gonna look around for some more paintbrushes for Miss McPhee. Government doesn't realize they wear out and won't issue any more. I caught her yesterday givin' the fish eye to those cats that hang around the stables. Figure they're gonna turn up bald."

"I'll excuse you for a worthy reason like that," Laura said, laughing. "We'll meet at the station at two o'clock, then."

She ate a leisurely lunch, then walked up the hill to the old Crescent Hotel gardens. They were overgrown and neglected now, but still held a certain beauty in their wild growth. Laura sat looking out at the valley spread below for some minutes. The spring sun was warm on her back and the quiet solitude fed her soul the peace she needed. In a very little while she had managed to get the perpetual pile of government forms out of her mind and felt as refreshed as if she'd had a long nap.

The forms, boring and endless, weren't really so bad, she

realized now that she was safely away from them for a few hours. Aside from them and Sonny's absence, life was quite good now. The hospital had brought its sorrows, of course, as Dr. Lee had predicted. They'd had a suicide attempt, mercifully foiled, and several fistfights which didn't result in serious injury, but were upsetting and disrupting. And sometimes she lay awake at night unable to blot out the sound of one or another of the men sobbing raggedly.

But on the whole, the sense of doing something worthwhile outweighed the despair. Laura had learned the basics of braille and got tremendous satisfaction from helping teach this skill to those who'd been blinded in the service. She also spent many hours reading to those who'd not yet turned battle-rough fingers into substitute eyes. And if there was something missing, an empty area in her life . . . well, she had no right to complain. Turning the house into a hospital had given her work that pulled her back from the brink of a terrible abyss of near-madness.

She nibbled at a candy bar she'd been saving for two days, put the wrapper in her purse, and started back down to meet the train. Sergeant Walker and Nurse Edlin were already there having a game of gin with the worn deck of cards Walker was never without. "Want to take my place next hand, Miss Thorne?" the nurse asked.

"No, thanks. I think I hear the train, anyway. I'll pull the bus up closer."

The train was already in and Walker was helping the most ambulatory patients down the steps when Laura returned. She hurried to the other end of the special car. She reached up to take the first man's hand and felt her own gripped in a firm handshake. "It's really you, isn't it!" the soldier said.

She stared into that familiar face. "Eric!"

"You remember me. That's marvelous."

"Of course. I—"

"Come on, buddy. There's a load of sardines here wantin' out!" a voice behind him said as he stepped off the last step.

She lost him in the flurry of getting the patients loaded aboard the bus, but when she climbed back into the driver's seat she found that he was sitting just behind. She hardly had time to do more than smile at him when Sergeant Walker leaned over and said in a husky whisper, "We got a boy bleeding back here. Not too serious, but Nurse wants to get him back as soon as possible. So none of that stopping and pointing out the sights like you sometimes do."

"I'll hurry."

She drove all the way back hunched nervously over the big wheel and feeling that she was sitting on a time bomb—not the bleeding soldier: she trusted Walker's judgment that the medical situation was not critical. No, it was Eric VonHoldt's presence that made her feel giddy and girlish. Why hadn't she worn a nicer dress instead of just throwing on her everyday navy-and-white cotton? And stockings—she could have worn stockings. She had a pair she'd been hoarding for something special. And why did she think she could feel his gaze on the back of her neck?

She risked a quick glance in the rearview mirror. Yes, he was smiling slightly and looking at her left ear—or out the window. She couldn't be sure. Dear Lord, he was just as she remembered, but better. His face, so interestingly angular, had sharpened a little. His hair was still blond, but darker, and his broad-shouldered athletic build had certainly done justice to the uniform he wore. What rank was he? She wished she'd learned the interpretation of bars and stripes and stars better.

What, for that matter, was his name now? She remembered all too vividly the night by the spring lake when they'd had a falling-out over the VonHoldt name, but it took her a moment to recall that his family had changed it to Holt. Most important, what was he doing here? He didn't have an eyepatch, sling, or crutches, and in those few seconds when he disembarked, she hadn't been aware of any limp.

When they got back to Thornehill, Adele met the bus in a flurry of irritation about a domestic crisis involving length of sterilization of silverware. Once again Eric was swept away from her as Laura found herself mediating between Adele and a nurse. It was hours before she was free to go looking for him, and before she could do so, he found her.

"I was told this was your sanctum. May in invade it?" he asked from the door to the library.

"Yes, please do."

He was dressed in civilian clothes now, navy corduroy trousers, white shirt, and gray V-neck sweater. "The house has changed a lot," he said, glancing around the room as he came over and sat down across from her. "But it never loses its character. The last time I was in this room, your daunting grandmother was at that desk."

"Gram died almost two years ago."

"I know. I ran into your Uncle Edmund and he told me.

I'm sorry. It must have been a terrible loss for you. You've changed too. All for the better, though I wouldn't have believed there was room for improvement.''

"Thank you.''

"I thought I remembered everything about you, but I was wrong. I'd forgotten one thing. The accent.''

"I don't have an accent.''

"To my Northern ears you do, and it's delightful. You've become a beautiful woman, Laura.''

"Please—''

"Am I embarrassing you? I didn't mean to.'' He got back up and walked to the window. "I've remembered you and this place so often over the years. Especially the last year.''

"You promised to come back.'' The words were out of her mouth before she even realized she was thinking them. She could have kicked herself. Such a silly thing to say.

"And I have. I did once before, too, but I imagine we'd both rather forget that. Here I am again,'' he answered, not seeming to think the conversation at all odd.

"What *are* you doing here? Are you an administrator of some sort?''

"No, I'm a patient. A private one. That's allowed, isn't it?''

Laura nodded. Most of their patients were those who came directly from the VA, but a few were there by individual arrangement. "But you don't look . . .''

He resumed his seat and she realized for the first time that his gestures had all been with his left arm. His right hung motionless at his side. "Oh, no!''

"I was with Patton when he landed in North Africa last November. It wasn't even a war wound, exactly. A tank got loose, rammed into the side of the ship. I was in the way, or rather, my arm was.''

He spoke in an open, matter-of-fact way, as if describing something interesting but trivial, but Laura felt her heart aching for him. He was an artist, and right-handed. Now his right arm was useless.

"It might have been fixed better if it had been an industrial accident here in the States near a good hospital. But we were on a ship. Stormy seas and a patch-'em-up-to-send-home surgical unit. I'm damned lucky I didn't lose it.''

"But, Eric . . . your art. Your work.''

Something in his eyes warned her not to show too much sympathy. "That's why I'm here. I'll never use this arm again, not for painting at least. I can move it some and I'll get better, but if I'm ever going to paint again it'll have to be with my left hand. The army let me come here to learn to use the right arm for something—God knows what—and I'm determined to train the left one."

"India will be a great help to you," Laura said briskly, taking her cue from his tone. "She can't teach you anything about art, of course, but she's got excellent materials and equipment."

"That's all I need. That and a lot of time."

"And determination."

"That I brought with me." He said it rather curtly. Clearly this was the end of this line of conversation. "Where's Sonny? Is he in the service?"

"Army, yes. His last letter was from Edinburgh. He was on leave and wanted to see the Highlands."

"What does he do?"

"We don't know. Something to do with translating and refugees and escapees from war camps. On a few occasions he was out of touch for several weeks, and we think he was behind enemy lines, but of course he's not allowed to tell us anything about it."

"I haven't heard from him since a couple months before Pearl Harbor. He said you were getting married," he added, looking at her ringless left hand.

"I was married. For a week. He was shot down over Germany."

He, too, was aware of the brisk, nonemotional tone in her voice. "I'm sorry to hear that. You aren't Laura Thorne then?"

"No, Langley. But I answer to either one," she said.

"I'm awfully glad to see you again. Will I see you a lot while I'm here?"

"As much as you like."

Laura quickly learned what Eric's daily schedule was to be and planned her own work around it so that she could be with him whenever possible. She visited the art unit at least once a day and had lunch with him. Most evenings he had dinner with the family, and they would take a brief stroll around the grounds before the rigidly enforced curfew. Sometimes he'd help her catch up on paperwork so that she could be free, and he joined her braille lessons in order to increase the sensitivity of touch in his left hand.

They were always surrounded by other people, in the art room, the halls, her office, and even on the grounds in the evenings. Their talk was personal and friendly, but not intimate. Of the renewal of their once-affectionate relationship, nothing was said. Nothing overt. Nor did they ever refer to the short visit he'd made to Thornehill in 1940. It was something they needed to talk about sometime, Laura sensed. But there was never the right time, nor did she have the right words ready at hand. But it was still unfinished business, an opaque curtain of anger and misunderstanding that hung between them that—if they went on as she hoped—would have to be taken down sooner or later. Better later, she decided.

Eric told her about the years since they'd known each other—all but his war experience, which he never discussed beyond the brief description he'd already given of his accident. He told her things about his schooling and early career that they should have discussed the last time he was a guest, but hadn't. Laura filled him in on events at Thornehill, but said little about her marriage.

There were bad days, of course. The first time Laura saw Eric in a short-sleeved shirt, she'd been shocked at the network of scars on his arm and the depleted muscles. She'd been unusually bright and talkative to cover her reaction. "You don't need to gabble like a magpie, Laura," he'd said, understanding. "Take a good look at it now and get it over with. These jagged scars are from the injury and the first surgery. This neat, tidy one running through the others is from the surgery I had when I got back. There'll be another one along here someday. I've got to have a bone reset, but it can wait. It won't help the mobility, just alleviate some of the pain."

The worst pain, it soom became apparent, was mental. "I can still see in my head how I want it to be!" he shouted one day, throwing down his brush in uncharacteristic temper. "My right hand could do it, but this goddamn left one won't cooperate. I concentrate until my head aches and my muscles cramp, and I can't get what I want on the canvas."

"You will in time."

"Time! I don't want to get better when I'm eighty. I want it now."

"Eighty! You've only been here concentrating on your work for two months. And you *are* getting better. Even I can see it, and I don't know anything about art. India agrees. You would too, if you weren't feeling sorry for yourself." It pained her to say that to him, but she'd learned it was one sure way to get him back to work. He had a horror of self-pity amounting to phobia.

There were, however, slightly more good days for him than bad. His characteristic style came through even when his left hand wasn't cooperating as he wished. His work had a distinctly American flavor, somewhat like Thomas Hart Benton's work, but with more shading of color, more subtlety of line. His figures and themes were common and ordinary, but somehow epic and universal. A pencil sketch of a soldier fishing in the spring lake became a symbol of all the returning men; a watercolor wash of Adele in the kitchen was all women.

The one subject he didn't use was Laura herself. "I can't do you justice yet. It would be a sacrilege to try. Later on, maybe. Will you pose for me when I'm ready?"

"Of course."

One day in early August he said, "I can't work here anymore."

Laura's heart lurched. "What do you mean?"

"I'm being watched too closely. You look over my shoulder, India positively hovers, the other men comment and ask questions. It's too much attention. It's all done with the kindest possible motives, but I can't stand it. It's bad enough having the indignity of the struggle without an audience."

"I see." She said it very calmly, but inside her mind she was pleading: *Don't leave!*

"Don't sound miffed, Laura."

"I'm not miffed. I understand. I'm just sorry you're going to be leaving."

"Who said I was leaving? You couldn't force me out of here with a pitchfork at my back. I just wanted to explain all this before I ask a favor."

"What favor?"

"I want to rent that cottage down by the spring. I walked down yesterday, and it doesn't look like anyone's living there."

"No, they're not. That's a wonderful idea. But no renting. You can use it for as long as you want."

"Of course I'll rent it. You aren't running a starving artists' colony here. I wouldn't expect special treatment."

Have you no idea how special you are to me? Laura wondered. But she knew better than to tangle with his pride, so she said, "We'll work out a fair amount then."

"I'm going to check myself out of the hospital. I think the army's going to pitch me out pretty soon anyway. I can use my right arm for normal things like opening doors and such. That's all the therapy they owe me. How soon can I move in there?"

"I'll ask Mabelann to give it a quick cleaning today and I'll go down this evening and see if there's anything of mine still there."

"I wouldn't mind so much if some of your things were there," he said. "In fact, I hope you'll be there yourself as often as you can get free."

This time they were older, more sensitive to nuance and anticipation. There would be no ignorant headlong rush to passion this time. They both knew enough to prolong and appreciate each separate step before going on to the next. Up until Eric's move into the cottage they'd hardly touched, except by carefully staged accidents. Afterward, they held hands or walked with arms around each other's waists, and at the end of the day, before they turned away to go back to their separate beds, Eric would kiss her lightly, barely brushing her lips. Laura could feel the phantom tingle for hours.

Mostly they talked—about the weather, nature, the war, their families, their beliefs. And eventually, about Stephen. "You speak about him so coolly. Is that a cover for deeper feelings?" Eric asked one crisp October morning when they'd gone for an early walk by the spring lake. There were red leaves scattered artistically on the surface of the water and Laura wished she could paint so that she could capture the beauty of the scene.

"No, I hardly knew him. It took me a long time to realize that tragic fact, but he was almost a stranger to me when we got married, and then in a week he was gone forever."

"Why did you marry him then?"

"I loved him. Or I thought I did."

"What was he like?"

"I have no idea. I don't know what his favorite color was or if he liked brussels sprouts, and without looking at a picture, I couldn't tell you what side he parted his hair on. Isn't that sad?"

Eric picked up a flat rock and tried to skip it on the water. It hit and sank. "Do I like brussels sprouts?" he asked.

"You hate them. We had them last month and I noticed that you sent them back untouched. In fact, you covered them up with a leaf of lettuce so you wouldn't have to look at them.''

Eric laughed. ''What made you think you loved the stranger you married, then?''

''He was very courageous. It meant a lot to him to believe in something and then stand up for it. That's why he went into the service after Pearl Harbor and went overseas as soon as he could. I resented it then. In fact, I still resent it, but I understand it better and recognize how important it was to him and should be to all of us. You're very brave too—''

Eric wouldn't let the conversation shift to himself. ''But that was after you married him. What was the appeal before that?''

''I loved his ambition. I didn't recognize the truth then, but I do now. You see, he was fiercely ambitious. His life was focused on a definite goal, to be President.''

''Of what?''

''Of the United States. Don't look so skeptical. If you'd known him, you wouldn't be surprised. He'd have probably made it. He had everything it took, including a powerful family behind him.''

''And you wanted to be First Lady?'' Eric said it as if asking if she really liked brussels sprouts.

''No, I don't think I ever fully comprehended what my role would be. It was a very difficult time for me, before I met him. I was very immature for my age. Gram had kept me so protected. I was twenty-two, well-educated, well-groomed, and empty. I had no purpose, no goals of my own, no sense of my own worth. And Stephen made up for all that, you see. He was so sure of what he wanted, and I just adopted his goals instead of creating my own. Does that make sense to you?''

''I'm not sure. More than anything, it scares me.''

''Why?''

''Because in a way, I was like him before the war. Sure of what I wanted—I thought—living only for art and my almighty ego. Well, you know that, I suppose. Remember, I said something to you on the terrace, some compliment, and you said that was an artist's comment?''

''I remember.'' All too well, she thought.

''I flared up, all wounded vanity like the ass I was. Of course it was an artist's remark. Everything I said and thought was meant to promote that image. I was too busy working at being an artist to be a person. Everything was subjugated to my career. I can remember thinking one night: Should I leave my work to go to this party? How can anyone there help me? That's a terrible way to be. Of course, in my case, I was forcibly cured of it by a runaway tank. All those months in the hospital gave me time to realize I'd been well on the road to becoming a perfectly awful person. A very empty person. Life is meant for more than the accomplishment of one selfish goal.''

"You haven't lost your ambition."

"No, not the ambition, but I've lost the single-minded compulsion. Now that my one talent has been taken away from me, I realize that there are other very important things in life I was in danger of passing by without a glance. Things that make my life worthwhile. Like you,'' he added, twining his fingers with hers and walking along the path bordering the lake.

A soldier in a wheelchair was coming toward them and Laura had no opportunity to reply. They stepped aside, exchanged a few pleasantries with the young man, then went on. "How did he die, your future President?" Eric asked.

Laura told him.

"Then you don't know he's dead?"

"Oh, he's dead. I'm sure of it. According to his uncle, who had the story from another pilot flying just behind, there wasn't any way the crew could have survived both a fire and submersion in a lake.''

"It *is* possible."

"I know it is. But Bess, his mother, was sure he was dead. Sure enough to have a memorial service. And I'm sure, as close as they were, that she would have held out hope if there had been any remote reason to.''

"But what is your status legally? Are you officially a widow?''

"I don't know. It never really mattered before," she said, stopping and looking up at him.

"Does it now?" he asked softly.

"Yes, it's beginning to.''

They'd reached a deserted grassy spot along the edge of the lake. Eric sat down and patted the grass next to him in invitation. "Do you remember the last time we sat here?" he asked.

She nodded. It was time now. "Eric, I tried to explain in a letter—I don't know if you ever got it. I've never gotten over being sorry about the way I acted that night—''

"And I've never gotten over being sorry I couldn't answer you without offending you more."

"What do you mean?"

"Oh, Laura, I was such a fool then. Such a conceited, self-centered fool. You had the good sense to point that out."

"Not good sense. Rudeness. And I was even more self-centered. You see—"

He put his finger to her lips. "You don't have to tell me. I did see. That's just it. I was too busy pampering my terrible artistic ego to see with an artist's eye. It was a long time later that I realized . . ."

"Realized what?"

"The VonHoldt connection, of course."

Laura drew a long breath. Did he mean what she thought he meant?

"It was six or eight months later. I was doing some sketches from memory for an exercise. Sonny popped into my mind and I started penciling in his features. They turned into a cross between my own face and Frederich's. It was as if someone had hit me in the head. I would have seen the similarity right away if I hadn't been so busy being the 'sensitive ass.' Then I started really thinking—about your grandmother especially. I'd assumed, that first time I was here, that she hated me for my interest in you, but that was only part of it. My reception had been cool from the moment she heard my name."

"She was afraid of you," Laura said. "I thought it was dislike at first, then I realized it was fear."

"Was he your grandfather?"

She nodded and then looked at him beseechingly. "No one knows. Please promise you'll never tell anyone, especially Sonny."

"Of course I won't tell anyone."

Laura lay back in the grass and crossed her arms over her face. "Why didn't you write to me when you figured it out?"

"Because I'd made such a fool of myself, carrying on about having the monster's blood in my veins—God, it's embarrassing still to remember all the stupid things I said to you. You must have wanted to strangle me."

She smiled. "A little."

"Laura, I—" he began, but a nurse's voice overrode his.

"Miss Thorne? We have a problem in the office," she said, dogtrotting along the bank of the lake toward them.

Laura got up with a begrudging smile. "I'll see what I can do about it."

XIX

ERIC bought a car, beat-up mud-brown Plymouth coupe. Sergeant Walker dropped them off at the seller's farm on his way to the train to pick up soldiers and they drove it back to Thornehill together, Eric concentrating all his mental and physical effort on using the stick shift with his right hand.

Along the way he told Laura about his family. They'd been discussing the war and she asked why and when the break with their German cousins came about. "When my father told them he was going to marry my mother."

"The family didn't approve of your mother?" she asked, surprised. Eric often mentioned her in such fond terms, it was hard to imagine anyone disliking her.

"Of course not. She's Jewish. You see, VonHoldt Armaments and good old grandpa Frederich aren't supplying thirty percent of the war matériel Hitler's army uses merely for the profit in it, though that's substantial. Our joint second cousins are all multimillionaires, I should think. No, it's also their contribution to the dream they hold with hysterical fanaticism. The elimination of the Jews."

"I understand the name change better now."

"You thought it was merely patriotism combined with cowardice? Many of our friends did. But it was much more than that, a statement of belief. I'm only sorry my father didn't change it years ago. So is he, I think. How anyone could feel hatred like that for someone as kind and harmless as my mother just because—"

His voice had risen and grown quite loud. He stopped suddenly and smiled sheepishly. "Sorry. I do tend to climb up on my soapbox about it, given half a chance. Actually, it's nice having a name that takes a little less paint to sign my name to a canvas.''

Laura smiled back. ''I like your new name.''

Eric pulled the car over to the side of the road and turned off the ignition. ''I can't think about what my hands and feet and mouth are doing all at the same time. Do you mind stopping for a minute?''

''Not at all.''

''Laura, when we were talking before—about Frederich and that time I was here—we didn't finish. Or at least I didn't. There's something else I want you to understand. All that nonsense about being like them because of kinship was ridiculous. I know that now. And I know it was an appalling thing to say to you. Besides being dead wrong, it was hurtful.''

''Only because then it was all so new to me. I'd only just found out, you see. I hadn't fit it all into my mind yet, and I felt like you were telling me I was horrible because I was related to him.''

Eric rested his forehead on the steering wheel. ''I'm mortified. God! You should have pitched me right into the lake and been done with it. It would have been a mercy killing, shutting my mouth just then.''

Laura smiled at his overreaction. ''Does this mean you don't really care that I'm Frederich's granddaughter?''

''Care! Lord, no! I wouldn't care if you were Hitler's daughter!''

''Then there's something else you ought to know about me, while I'm sharing all my deepest secrets.'' She paused, wondering if he really wanted her secrets. Wasn't she doing just what Grace had done to her? Alleviating the weight of the past by passing it on to someone else.

He looked up. ''What else?''

She plunged in, heedless of the consequences. ''I'm illegitimate. A bastard.''

''Your father and Evelyn weren't married?''

''Oh, yes. They were married, but I'm not Evelyn's child. My mother was the estate gardener's daughter, a sluttish, dirty, stupid woman.''

He was smiling. Smiling! He was trying not to, but the corners of his mouth were turning up against his efforts to stop.

''You find this amusing?'' she said, sitting up very straight.

''I'm . . . I'm sorry.'' Laughter suddenly overcame him. ''I'm sorry, Laura, but I was thinking about Frederich and what the haughty bastard would think if he knew that his own granddaughter was also the granddaughter of an Arkansas gardener.''

Laura tried to stay offended, but the image of Herr VonHoldt's face came to mind. She could imagine the expression of horror . . . She started laughing too. She laughed until she was nearly sick with it. ''This really isn't funny!'' she kept gasping. ''At least it never has been before today.'' What a gift he'd unknowingly given her—the ability to laugh so heartily at her worries.

When she'd finally calmed down and was wiping the tears from her eyes, she said, ''You really don't care, do you?''

''I care about everything that concerns you, but I'm not bothered by it. In fact, it just makes you all the more interesting, and I didn't think until today that was possible. Laura, do you care about them?''

''I do, in a way. I don't mind so much who I am as who I'm not. Do you see what I mean? I loved believing I was Captain Jack Thorne's progeny. He was a man to be proud of.''

''But you're not anybody's progeny. Don't you see? You're Laura Thorne . . . or Langley. But you are yourself. How you got to be who you are doesn't matter. It's what you do and say and think today and all your tomorrows that matters.''

''You won't ever tell anyone?''

He looked offended at that, but only for a second. ''You don't need to ask. I'm enriched by sharing your secrets. I just wish I had some half as interesting to trade.''

They had a family party for Laura's twenty-sixth birthday, and on her insistence, set a place for Sonny. ''If he can't really be here, I'd at least like to pretend.''

''Would you mind if I invited Sergeant Walker to join us?'' India asked.

''He'd be a welcome addition,'' Laura said, thinking how pleased Evelyn would be. She'd taken to drifting through the hospital like a gently demented ghost of Florence Nightingale. She was under the impression that the soldiers were guests, like in the old days when she was a bride at Thornehill. The fact that they were all injured didn't make a ripple in the illusion. ''A riding accident,'' was her explanation for every handicap. She was actually rather helpful, spending many hours reading to the bedridden soldiers and pushing those confined to wheelchairs around the lawns. The soldiers were tolerant, even appreciative of her, accepting that she was one of those older ladies whose eccentricity had passed into sweet, well-meaning lunacy. She had recently taken a particular fancy to Sergeant Walker, believing apparently that he was a long-lost cousin who had just come back from World War One.

The dinner went well, everyone in high spirits. Evelyn prattled about the Kaiser, and Sergeant Walker nodded and smiled just as though she were making sense. Finally, over dessert India said, "Laura, Billy has something to ask you."

"Billy?"

"Sergeant Walker."

"I'm sorry, Sergeant Walker. I've never known your first name. What is it?"

"Well . . ." He stammered, most uncharacteristic behavior. Clearing his throat and glancing at India, he said, "Miss Thorne, I'd like to ask your permission to marry your cousin, Miss McPhee."

Laura gaped at him.

"Isn't it divine?" India said. "Billy and I felt it was only right to ask your permission, seeing as you are the 'head of the family,' so to speak." She was actually blushing clear to the roots of her fashionable hair.

"I'm flattered that you'd ask, and I'm thrilled for you! I just couldn't be happier. But you're not leaving, are you? I can't imagine Thornehill without you, India."

"That's why we felt we ought to ask you," Sergeant Walker said, his initial unease gone. "India wanted us to stay on here, but I didn't feel like we ought to make that kind of plan without talking to you about it first. It is your house."

"No, it's *our* house. India's home. There isn't anywhere you'd rather live, is there?"

"No, ma'am. I'm an orphan with no home to go back to. I'd be pleased to stay here, if you're sure it's all right."

"I'm positive! I think we need to break out some champagne and have a toast to your happiness."

Sergeant Walker left before India. She waited until he'd closed the door and said, "I wonder what my parents would have said if they'd lived? 'Who are his people, dear?' 'Well, Mama, he was left on a doorstep.' My marrying Billy would be a shock to them, I imagine."

"I don't see why. He's a fine man."

"Yes, but he's not what they would have expected for me. He's not what *I* expected—not when I was young. I always assumed that I'd marry someone 'of my own class.' You know, Andover and Harvard, sisters in school with me at Foxcroft. Not some orphan with no education, and a mere *sergeant* at that. How common!''

Laura looked at her, perplexed. ''You mind about that?''

''Lord, no, or I wouldn't be marrying him. That's just what I'm trying to say—I'm astonished to learn that somehow, over the years, I lost that inbred snobbism and didn't even realize it was happening. I have your grandmother to thank, in a way. If I hadn't come here and learned so much from her about what really counts in life, I'd be a dried-up old maid. I was afraid I was going to be anyway. But thanks to Grace, all of you, I've fallen in love with good old plain-as-can-be Billy Walker, and I'm so happy I could sing.''

Eric asked Laura to come to the cottage after dinner so that he could give her his present privately. ''You're thinking very deeply,'' he said as she tripped over a root on the way down the path.

''Oh, I'm sorry. I'm still trying to adjust to India and Ser . . . Billy Walker. I've never considered that she might marry. She must be nearly forty . . . no, perhaps only mid-thirties, and I very stupidly assumed she'd chosen to be a spinster. You don't think Billy will mind living here, do you?''

''How could anyone mind living at Thornehill? I think it's probably the only real home he's ever had. It's good of you to make him feel so welcome.''

''There's nothing 'good' in it. Pure selfishness. I'm very fond of him, and the family wouldn't be the same without India and her capricious enthusiasms. She keeps us all young.''

''Come in and sit down here while I put some wood on the fire. That's right. It'll be warmer in a minute. Want a lap robe? No? A cup of nice hot coffee?''

Laura laughed. ''You're gabbling like Evelyn. What's wrong?''

''Nervous about giving you your present. All right. Might as well get it over with. Close your eyes. Wait. Now, open them.''

''Oh, Eric, it's beautiful!'' Laura exclaimed, reaching out to take the canvas he was holding facing her. It was a portrait of her, done in soft pastels as if through a green spring mist. She knew the hours of pain it had given him to produce this work.

''It's not as good as I'd wished, but it's the best I've done since Africa. Do you really like it?''

"I love it. I only wish I were really so lovely as this woman."

"You are, Laura. You are."

"Only in your eyes," she said, rising and slowly putting her arms around his neck. "But that's all that matters. I wouldn't mind being a hag if you liked me."

"Liked you?" he said, arching an eyebrow. "I love you. You do know that, don't you?"

She nodded. "Yes, I suspected."

He sighed, pulling her closer with his good left arm. "We've waited a long time, Laura."

"Long enough . . ." she whispered. "I love you, Eric."

It was finally time.

They undressed there in front of the flickering glow of the fire, marveling in the discovery of each other. The passion that had been building for so long made both of them tremble, and buttons and hooks were not easily undone. Kissing, touching, rubbing thigh to thigh, breast to chest, they discarded their clothing and the reserve they'd so carefully maintained all the months since his return.

"Are you sure?" Eric asked.

"I've never been surer of anything in my life," she said, tilting her head up for a long kiss.

They made love quickly, frantically, like children ripping into a Christmas present; then, their appetites only partially assuaged, they started over very slowly, savoring each sensation. Laura wasn't even surprised at how different this was from her married experience. She'd known it would be ever since he took her hand and stepped down from the train. "I think I've loved you forever," she whispered against his chest as she twined her legs around him. "I can't remember ever not loving you."

"You can't imagine the times I've dreamed this—dreamed of hearing you say that. You love *me*! How astonishing!" He lifted her body onto his and ran his hands down her sides, making her shiver. "Ten years—it's been ten years since we started this evening."

"I remember. Oh, how I remember," she answered breathlessly as she arched her back and felt his hands cupping her breasts, brushing his thumbs across her erect nipples. "Ohhh, Eric . . ."

"Again?"

"Again!" she said, straddling him and gasping as he entered her. "I love you . . . I love you . . . I . . ."

"I don't know . . . which part is you and . . . which is me," he said, clutching her so hard she couldn't breathe and didn't care.

"Us . . . us . . ." she moaned into his shoulder.

Hours later they woke, tangled together in front of a dying fire. "Now I'm really helpless," he said as she shifted and freed his left arm. He flexed it, trying to get past the tingling.

She stretched luxuriously and suddenly realized it had gotten cold. Kneeling, she put another log on the fire and tried to concentrate on putting fresh kindling underneath. But she was hampered by the fact that he'd knelt behind her and had put his arms around her. His hands were roaming her body, one kneading a breast, the other straying down her stomach and between her thighs. He laughed as she writhed and gasped, trying to pretend to ignore him and failing. "I knew I was learning braille for a good reason. What does this say?" he asked, touching her with a tantalizingly delicate touch.

She spread her knees, then clutched them back together, trapping his hand as she leaned back against him. "I'm not cold anymore," she whispered, smiling so broadly it made the muscles of her face hurt. "Don't leave me again. Don't ever leave. Not for a minute. Let's stay here until we're old."

He laughed. "You'd get hungry eventually."

"I'm hungry now!" she said, twisting to face him. "We've wasted months and months. Why did we wait?"

"So it would be this good," he said.

"What do you suppose the law is?" Laura asked Edmund.

"Don't you remember? I discussed this with you earlier, a month or so after you heard. No, I don't suppose you were really listening then. In normal times you'd have to wait seven years and have him declared legally dead, but now—"

"But he *is* dead. I'm a widow."

"You don't know that. It's a logical assumption, but it isn't proven fact."

"The telegram said 'missing in action, presumed dead.' "

" 'Presumed' isn't good enough. The army says there have to be two witnesses to the death when the body is unrecoverable. In Stephen's case, there's only one witness and he can't be absolutely positive beyond any doubt. That's why there has never been any question of a will. In spite of Bess's memorial service, his death isn't legally established and won't be until the end of the war. If he isn't found then, he'll be declared dead and you won't have to wait the seven years. You could, of course, divorce him.''

"Divorce a dead man! A war hero? No. I can't consider that.''

"I knew you couldn't. I mentioned it only as an alternative, however unacceptable. I'm afraid that you're going to have to wait until the war is over. There'll be some sort of accounting then. There are thousands of young women in the same situation as you are.''

"I can wait. As long as I have Eric, I can wait as long as need be.''

He patted her head just as he had when she was a little girl. "It can't be for much longer. We're about to start a new year, and I predict that this war will be over before the year is.''

"I'm going to hold you to that!'' she said, kissing him on the cheek.

On Christmas morning they had a party in the ballroom. All the patients were brought down and given the fanciest breakfast Adele could devise under the restrictions of rationing. There was a huge tree that the nurses had decorated, and dozens of festive packages. Most of the gifts were trivial and homemade, but spirits were high enough to make up for that. They sang carols, draped wheelchairs with tinsel, and exchanged cards.

In the midst of singing "O Holy Night,'' Laura felt a light touch on her arm. "Yes, Mabelann?'' she whispered.

"Telephone, Miz Laura.''

"Oh, couldn't I call back?''

"Operator said it was long distance.''

"All right.''

She squeezed Eric's hand and smiled at him before slipping away. Picking up the phone in the library, she said, "Yes?''

"Long distance for Mrs. Stephen Langley,'' the operator said.

Laura glanced around, thinking a door was open, creating a draft, then realized it was only her imagination giving her a chill. "This is she.''

"Your party is on the line.''

"Hello? Hello?'' Laura said. But at first the only response was a stifled sort of gasp, as if someone was in the grip of a strong emotion. "Who is this?''

"Laura, dear. This is Bess. Bess Langley.''

"How nice to hear from you. Merry Christmas,'' Laura

said, trying to remember if she'd sent Bess a card. Yes, she thought she had.

Bess didn't answer for a moment. Then there was a muffled sob. "Laura, dear, it's Stephen. He's alive."

Laura felt like she'd been kicked.

"Oh, God!" she said softly. "Oh, my God!"

XXX

As it turned out, Bess's statement was based more on hope than evidence. An air-force pilot, forced down during a bombing mission three days after Stephen's disappearance, had been taken to a sort of temporary holding area and met an injured man who said he was Stephen Langley. Or Langston. Or Langworth. He wasn't sure. Within hours the bomber pilot was taken away to a prison camp, where he had spent a year before making a daring escape. He'd spent another year living under the guise of a simpleminded son with a sympathetic German family. Just recently he'd been able to get to France and thus to freedom. He'd made a report on the men he'd met in prison, and that was how Stephen's name had come up.

Through government and Red Cross connections, Arch Langley had traced the man down and questioned him closely, but there was little more to learn. The man had been through two years of hell since his brief meeting with Stephen—if it was he—and could remember very little except a general physical description that could fit Stephen. Or half a million other men. The prisoner he'd met, a man with a broken leg and a fever, had mentioned that he had a law degree and a mother who would be terribly upset. Bess found this sufficient ground to believe that her son was alive.

"This all makes me hate myself," Laura sobbed as she lay in Eric's arms that night. "When she said he was alive, my first thought was: No, please let him be dead! I've been praying for hours that he's dead. How can I wish anyone dead, especially my husband, who never did me any harm? What kind of terrible person am I?"

"The same kind I am," Eric replied. "I want him dead

too, and I've never even met the man. But, Laura, it isn't time to be so upset about this."

"Not time? Whatever do you mean?"

"Think about it. It's very likely it was someone else. The man doesn't even claim to be sure of the name. Even if it was Langley, it was a long time ago. More than two years. And he was injured, perhaps seriously. You have no reason to think he's alive, only that it's possible, and you've always known it was possible."

"No, I haven't. I believed he was dead. How could he have lived? A plane going down in a lake? In flames?"

"People have survived worse. If the lake was shallow, or the plane landed at the shallow edge—"

"Oh, Eric, what are we going to do?"

"We're going to wait. It's all we can do. You know that. When the war is over, you'll find out if you're a wife or a widow. Then we'll see."

This was an easy thing to say, a terrible thing to live with day after day. Laura began to torture herself with the newspaper accounts of the war. In January and February Buda and Pest fell to the Allies. In early March the United States took Cologne and Bonn. By the end of the month Frankfurt and Mannheim were in Allied hands, as was Müster a week later.

"Can't you keep that woman away from Laura?" Eric asked India and Adele.

"She's frantic. Nearly mad. After all, he's her only son and naturally she assumes Laura is vitally interested in her attempts to locate him. If only she didn't call every other day and report," Adele said.

"I've tried telling her Laura is out, but she just keeps calling back until she catches her," India added. "Every time the Allies take a few more miles, she thinks it might include whatever prison camp he's in. And she may be right one of these days."

"She may be, God forbid!" Eric said fervently, and the two women, understanding, nodded solemnly.

On April 13 President Roosevelt died and Laura burst into tears when she heard the news. It wasn't, as they all knew, that she had any more personal feeling for him than any of the rest of them, but her terrible nervousness needed an outlet. "I hardly remember there ever being another President," she said, trying to explain a reaction she didn't understand herself.

Nuremberg fell on Hitler's fifty-sixth birthday, the last he would celebrate. The only talk in the wards now was of when it would be over. Bets were placed; parties were planned. Within the last three days of April Mussolini was captured as he prepared to leave Italy and was executed, and Hitler took care of his own execution by committing suicide. "The devil is dead!" the hospitalized soldiers exulted.

On May 9 it was over in Europe. That the battles still raged in the Pacific meant almost nothing to Laura. Her heart and mind were focused eastward. I'll know soon! she thought with horrible anticipation.

"What now?" she asked Eric.

"Nothing. We wait and see."

Their lovemaking took on a frantic, guilty quality.

Bess was calling daily now. She had nothing of substance to say, but needed to talk endlessly about her efforts to locate Stephen. Laura's attempt to conceal the truth of her own situation from the older woman exhausted her. "Why don't I just tell her I'm in love with someone else?" she asked.

"Because there's no need," Eric told her. "Not now. Maybe not ever."

Every day that went by without word was a torture and a blessing. A letter arrived a month later from Sonny. The censor had let it through untouched. Sonny had been assigned as translator to the troops that liberated Auschwitz, and his description was heartbreaking:

> I cannot and will not ever be able to tell you what I saw. The inhumanity of man surpassed comprehension here. We thought we would perish ourselves at the sight of what these people have suffered. Time after time I've seen our soldiers collapse in sobs of despair. I've done so myself. It's bad enough for all of us, seeing those broken bodies and destroyed spirits, but I am the one who must hear their stories in their own words, their own language. I don't know how I'll ever sleep at night again— how these people will ever live a normal life. Laura, I'll be home as soon as I can. I'm mad with the longing for all of you and blessed Thornehill. Pray for me, Laura, and pray for these poor mutilated souls.

On June 1 the dreaded phone call came.

"They've found him! Laura, they've found him. He's alive and on his way home!" Bess Langley cried.

Laura went straight to Eric. It was late at night and he'd

gone to the cottage. "What are we going to do?" she asked for the hundredth time.

"We'll see," he said.

"No! You've been saying that for months now, but now we know. He *is* alive. I am married to him. He's coming back. You can't keep telling me to wait and see—Eric, don't you care?"

He grabbed her shoulders. "I care so much I can taste it! But what do you want me to say? That I hate the bastard for existing? Well, I do! I hate him, but that doesn't matter. What matters is what you think."

"What do you mean?"

"You'll have to decide what to do when he gets here."

"I . . . I don't understand."

"Laura, you married him. You loved him. You might still."

"No! It's you I love."

"You can't know how you'll feel until you see him."

"I can know. I do know." She was shouting.

"You *can't* know!" So was he.

"Is that why, all this time, you've refused to talk about us, about our future? Because you thought I'd be in love with him? I know lots of heroes, Eric. My house is full of them! Do you think I'm a silly schoolgirl who's going to fall down in a faint because—"

"You loved him before!" He'd dropped his arms and was striding back and forth across the small living room. His very posture spoke his fury.

"I didn't. I told you that. I explained it all a long time ago. I was enchanted by his ambition and purpose because I had none of my own. But that was over when the hospital opened. I grew up then, Eric. I learned what was in my own heart, and it wasn't love. It was never love. Not until you came. Eric, don't turn your back on me. I love you! Only you!"

"I know that, Laura. But I'm terrified. I don't think I was ever as scared in the war as I am at this moment."

She wrapped her arms around him, burying her face in his shirt. "Don't be. Don't ever doubt my love for you. Now, please, let's talk about this."

Eric pulled himself free and sat down heavily on the sofa. "All right. We'll talk. It's simple, really. You can stay married to him, or you can divorce him. It's that easy to define."

"Yes, it is." She sat down on the floor beside him and put

her head on his knee. "I wonder why I've needed you to say it."

He stroked her hair. "What's it to be, then?"

"I can't stay married to him."

"But you can't divorce him either?"

She looked up, her eyes filling with tears. "How can I? He's spent two and a half years in a prisoner-of-war camp. How can I meet him and say, 'Nice to have you back. By the way, I'm divorcing you'? I'd hate myself. I'd hate anyone who could do that to anybody."

"I've thought about that too. A hundred times, at least. You should make it fast and painless—but you won't. I do know you that well. That's why I say all you can is wait and see how it goes."

"Maybe he won't mind," she said softly, wrapping her arms around Eric's legs. "That's stupid. Of course he'll mind. Aside from everything else, it'll be a terrible insult. Even if he doesn't care about me anymore. And if he still clings to his ambitions, it will ruin him."

"Laura, don't agonize over it this way. You can't guess what's going to happen, how he's going to be, how you're going to feel." He stood up suddenly. "Now it's time for you to go home. Back to the big house."

"I'm staying here tonight. With you."

"No, you're not. Not until it's over."

"What do you mean?"

He took her arm, helping her up against her will. "You can't divorce a returning war hero; I can't cockold one."

"But—"

"But nothing. You're a married woman. Married to someone else."

"I didn't know you were so priggish!" she lashed out, stunned and insulted.

"I'm not. But you are. You've got a conscience, Laura. A terrible Jehovah-like conscience. Someday you'd feel guilty about it if you stayed, and you'd hate me for sharing your guilt—or refusing to. It would come between us someday. I can't risk it."

"You don't want me anymore?"

He glanced down. "How can you ask?" he said with a bitter smile. "I want you so badly you're lucky you're not being raped this minute. My hands ache from wanting to touch you. But I won't. Not until you're free to really be mine alone."

She stepped toward him. He backed up so suddenly he nearly lost his balance. "No. Go back home, Laura. Come back to me when we can marry."

"Don't do this to us. To me! I need you."

"And I need you, love. But I won't make love to a woman who's going to regret it. You settle things with your husband and then we'll have our whole lives together."

"That's blackmail!" she screamed.

"I guess it is, in a way. But I don't mean it like that. You have to be free of me to make your decision. It can't be my decision, my actions. It has to be you."

"You're not leaving?"

"Tomorrow."

She flung herself at him and he didn't dodge her this time. "No, Eric. I beg you, don't leave me. Please, please don't leave me. We won't sleep together if you insist, but please don't go."

"I can't stay here and watch you welcome your husband home."

"If I can suffer it, can't you? Can't you help me bear this terrible burden? I can't face the days without you. Oh, Eric, please, please—"

He pried her arms loose and shoved her toward the door. "I'll stay as long as I can stand it! But don't come back here. *Don't come back here!*"

She stood in the now-open doorway. "I love you, Eirc."

He put a hand over his eyes. "For Christ's sake, Laura, go away. I can't stand seeing you look like that. What did we do to deserve this hell? Go away. Go away!"

The next day a flock of reporters descended on Thornehill. At first Laura assumed their interest was in the hospital, and she was cranky about it. "We've been here all along!" she told Edmund when he explained that they wanted to see her. "Why weren't they interested in us before? I tried to get someone out here to get some publicity before, remember? We thought it might encourage other people to open up big homes the same way!"

"Laura, it has nothing to do with the hospital, not directly. They want to interview you about Stephen."

She never learned how Bess and Arch had done it, but they'd managed to convince several newspapers and magazines that the homecoming of the illustrious war hero and rising young politician Stephen Langley would be a touching story to cover. From then on, Laura was hardly ever free of reporters. She took to skulking around her own house and finally called Bess on it. "Get them out of here!" she shouted over the long-distance wires. "They are making my life miserable. It's upsetting to the family and the patients."

"Laura, dear, I've lived a great part of my life in the limelight. I know what an awful bore it can be. But it will be such wonderful coverage for Stephen. Such a help to his career. You don't wish to deprive him of the help you can give, do you, dear? I thought you understood all this when you married him. Of course, if you really feel that strongly . . ."

She let them stay. She even made an attempt to keep them away from Evelyn. "It won't help Stephen if they get wind of the fact that he has a dotty mother-in-law," she told India.

"Is she going to stay his mother-in-law?" India asked gently. "I don't mean to pry, Laura, but we're all wondering what you're going to do. We're behind you, all of us, but we wonder just where that is."

"I don't know. I just don't know! I haven't even seen Eric for three days. I've sneaked away from the journalists twice to go to the cottage, but he had the door locked and wouldn't answer my knock. I know he's there. That disreputable old brown Plymouth he bought was parked in front."

"I know you don't want my advice, but here is it: don't go to the cottage. It's hard on you, but it's just as hard on him. Don't risk driving him away."

"You've talked to him?"

"I didn't need to. It's obvious. Now, let's get some of this paperwork out of the way and not think about problems for a while."

Sonny came home first, and his homecoming was utterly unlike Laura had imagined. He called first from New York. "God, Laura, just let me listen to you. Talk! Talk!"

"I'll come meet you!"

"No, we'd just miss each other in passing. I'm starting home in an hour. I have a surprise for you."

"What kind of surprise?"

"You'll see. Ask Adele to fix some of that sour bread I always liked. About sixteen loaves. I've been craving it. And ask Mother to get out that tacky green flapper dress. I love seeing her in that."

"Sonny, are you all right? Really all right?"

"Completely, my girl. I'm back and that's all that matters."

"Sonny, when will you get h—" she said, but he was gone.

He arrived three days later. Laura was giving a lesson in her braille class when a nurse said, "Ma'am, there's a man downstairs who says he's your brother."

Laura flew down the stairs into his arms. "Oh, Sonny! It's really you, isn't it! I'm so glad, so . . ." She started sobbing in spite of all her resolve not to carry on this way.

He pulled out a handkerchief and mopped her face. "There, my girl, don't make a mess of yourself. Let me look at you! I was afraid I might never have the chance again!"

"Oh, Sonny, you're so thin and grown-up. I'm so happy you're back and—"

"Wait a minute. Don't you want to see the surprise?"

"You're surprise enough for me."

"Laura, this is Marysia . . . my wife."

She'd been standing there so quietly and meekly that Laura hadn't even seen her. Now, staring dumbfounded, she was speechless. The girl looked about twelve, skeletally thin. Her elbows and knees were big knobs and her face was disfigured by angry red scurvy scabs. With her huge, frightened eyes and half-inch-long hair, she was the ugliest individual Laura had ever seen. If Sonny hadn't identified her as a woman, Laura couldn't have ever guessed her sex. "Your wife?" she whispered hoarsely.

"My *wife*," he repeated firmly.

"I . . . I . . . How do you do . . . ?"

"Marysia. She doesn't speak English yet. But she'll learn. She speaks three other languages and is a whiz at learning. In a month you two will be jabbering away like girls together."

Laura stared at the girl and then at him. "Auschwitz?"

"She had no one left. They were going to take her to another relocation center. Another prison, if a kinder one. I couldn't save everyone, but I could save one."

"Do you love her?"

Sonny looked at Marysia with a wide smile, and still smiling, said, "It seems incredible, doesn't it? I haven't sorted out yet how much is love and how much is pity on my part and how much is simple gratitude on hers, but part of it is love and that seemed enough."

"You married her without even knowing her?"

"I'm not the only one who made a rash marriage," he said, still smiling. "And I do know about her—the external facts, at least. She came from a fine family, much like ours, in fact. Money, a private estate, a very sheltered, pampered, loving existence. When I learned that, and saw all that she'd suffered, I . . . well, I thought of you, Laura. I kept thinking: What if this were Laura? I'd have wanted someone to scoop you up and take care of you. But enough of Marysia and me. What about you?''

Laura paused. "You got my letters? About Eric and Stephen?''

"I did. Is he back yet?''

"Next week. So Bess says.''

Sonny put his arm around Marysia very gently and pulled her closer. She clung to him like a barnacle. "Are you going to meet him?''

"I thought I should, but Bess is determined that she's going to meet him and bring him here. No doubt with all sorts of hideous fanfare.''

"Won't he think that's odd? His mother meeting him, but not his wife?''

"Probably not. If Bess wants it that way, he won't question it.''

Sonny put his finger under Marysia's chin and tilted her head up. He spoke to her in a language Laura didn't understand and then said, "I told her you said you know she's going to become very beautiful and happy here.''

"And I hope she will.''

"She's earned it, Laura. Be as good to her as you can. I know she's rather horrible now, but with food and love . . .''

"We'll love her. We'll all love her somehow.'' She reached out to take Marysia's hand, but the girl drew back and hid her face and hands against Sonny's chest.

"She won't let anyone but me touch her. Yet,'' Sonny explained.

"It's going to be uphill, isn't it?''

"No. Laura, it's *been* uphill. This is the easy part. The loving.''

It was beautifully staged.

Stephen, his mother, and his uncle came to Eureka Springs aboard the Wednesday hospital train, and Bess had arranged it so that it appeared she had some vague role in the establishment and running of the hospital. She had also managed to get a large number of the townspeople to turn out. She and Laura had exchanged words about this. "Wonderful humble touch,'' Bess had gloated over the phone the last time they talked. "Getting off the train in his hometown, just like every ordinary soldier. The whole town can greet him. The reporters will love it. I've even got a man from *Life* coming in the day before. Be sure to wear something very middle-class but tasteful."

"I don't have anything middle-class!" Laura muttered.

"What was that, dear?"

"I said this isn't Stephen's hometown. Not yet. He lived here for six days. And the people of the town wouldn't know him from Adam!"

She expected Bess either to pretend hurt—she was good at that—or to act as if she hadn't understood. Instead she said, "The whole world is going to know my son . . . soon! You had better not forget it, young woman!"

This display of true colors shocked Laura, though it shouldn't have. She replied as frankly. "Bess, have you talked with Stephen about this ridiculous carnival you're putting on?"

"Of course not. It's impossible to get an overseas line, and he's in transit now, anyway."

"Then how do you have any idea he's interested in all this public display? I should think he'd find it extremely distasteful. I certainly do."

"I'm sorry to hear you say that. It's going to be the manner of your life from now on. And yes, I'm certain Stephen will approve of my plans. He's always counted on my guidance in political matters."

"But this isn't political, Bess. This is . . ." She stopped. She'd intended to say, "a man returning to his wife," but the hypocritical words stuck in her throat. Maybe she was right. He might think the presence of all these reporters at what should have been a private moment was a wonderful thing. She owed them that much. "Never mind. Arrange whatever you like but, Bess . . . don't ever tell me what to wear again. I won't tolerate being patronized. Keep that in mind." She hung up before Bess could reply.

Stephen called her from Washington before he started back to Arkansas. "Laura, are you there?"

He sounded exactly like before, and Laura, for all her warning time, hadn't formulated a thing to say. "I'm glad to hear from you, Stephen. Are you well?"

"Yes, entirely well. Except for the leg, of course. I've got a bit of a limp. It was broken."

"I know. Your mother told me."

"I can't wait to see you. We still have our honeymoon ahead of us, you know."

Laura shivered. "I . . . Yes, we do. It's been a long time, Stephen. We hardly know each other."

He didn't grasp her meaning. Or chose not to. "I've thought about you so much, Laura, I'm sure it'll be as if we were never apart."

If only you knew, she thought desperately.

He appeared on the train platform that Wednesday with Bess clutching his arm and Arch standing beside him. There were a few strands of grey in his dark hair and some lines around his light eyes, but he was still as handsome as ever. Laura had to push her way through the reporters to join him. "Laura!" he cried when he saw her. He strode forward, leaning on a cane and sweeping her into an embrace with his free arm. Flashbulbs popped and Laura had a brief cynical thought as they kissed. *He's posing for them.* Oddly enough, he wasn't in uniform like most returnees.

There was mercifully no time for personal conversation on the way home. Arch and Bess rode with them, as did three of the reporters. Stephen drove, his arm around Laura, answering questions as they covered the miles. "No, boys, I won't discuss my prison-camp experiences. Not now or later. It's too personal and painful. For now I want to try to forget and make a normal life for myself and my wife."

"Will you be going back into politics?"

"It's the only thing I know. I'm sure I will, but there's lots of time to make decisions. I want to find out first what the country is like, what the people think. I've been out of touch for a long time, you know. A politician's job is to represent the people, not himself."

"Are you going to run for governor of Arkansas? Or do you prefer to reenter on the national scale—Senate or Congress?"

He laughed. "No comment. I just want to be a private person, coming home for a rest for a while."

Laura had been afraid that Stephen would immediately sense her tepid response to him and know within minutes that something had changed drastically between them, but listening to his banter with the reporters, she realized he was oblivious of such personal nuances at the moment. He was in his element. Bess had been right: he was pleased at the public homecoming. But strangely, he didn't seem at all pleased to be asked about the war. But no, there was nothing strange in that. She had no desire to blab about the worst parts of her life; why should he? Bess, however, didn't seem to share this feeling or sympathize with it. It was she who kept bringing up his rank and reputation and didn't seem to notice how uncomfortable it made him.

Most upsetting was his obvious interest in politics. Somehow she had anticipated that his attitude would be altered, that two and a half years in a prison camp would have made him change his goals, but apparently the experience had only intensified his former interest. And this made her cringe with guilt.

When they got back to the house, the family and staff greeted him officially and warmly—especially considering that the family knew Laura's relationship with Eric and the terrible dilemma she was in. Stephen took a quick tour of the hospital itself. Laura started out at his side, where she belonged, but was soon aware that Bess was determined to crowd her out. She stood aside and let her. "Tell Stephen I'll wait for him in the library," she said to India. "If *you* can get close enough to him to say anything."

When Stephen and the family returned to the library, Laura ruthlessly refused to let the reporters in. Bess got stiff and white-lipped about it, but Stephen said, "Laura's right, Mother. This is the private part of the house. We've got to have a bolt hole of some sort. We can slip out the back door here to go to the cottage."

"The cottage?" Laura said, startled.

"Yes, isn't that where we're going to stay? Just like when I left?"

"Uh . . . no. I've rented it out."

"Laura, how could you?" Bess asked.

Laura gritted her teeth against the words that were fighting to get out. Words like: What business is it of yours?

"It doesn't matter. We'll share Laura's room here," Stephen said placatingly. "Where is it?"

"I'll have your things taken up," Laura said.

"No, no. I'll do it myself. You can come along and show me where."

Bess intervened. "Stephen, sit down and rest a bit. Laura can find someone to take your luggage."

He smiled. "Mother, I *want* to do it myself. And I want Laura with me. We haven't been alone together for a long time. You do understand, don't you?"

Now? Laura thought frantically. *Right now?* She went upstairs with him, feet dragging, mind spinning. She had to tell him, but how? How to say to a man who left two and a half years earlier a happy groom: "I'm in love with someone else. You went off to fight this bitter war and I forgot you." Laura was frantic with guilt—guilt so overwhelming it weighed on her like a wet blanket, blinding her, stifling her breath.

He took off his jacket, tie, and shoes while she fidgeted with opening his suitcase and putting out some of his things. "Stephen, we must talk."

He took a hairbrush out of her hand, set it down, and said, "Not now, Laura. No talk. No more words. I've been drowning in words. Just let me look at you, touch you. God! You're even more beautiful than I remembered. And so soft, so gentle and soft and feminine."

As he spoke he was quickly, almost frantically removing her dress. She felt like a shop-window mannequin, cold plaster limbs frozen and unfeeling. No, that wasn't it. She felt like a whore. Being touched and seen by a man she felt nothing but pity for. But that was wrong too. This man was her husband. He, not Eric, had the right to her body. And it wasn't just pity she felt. It was gratitude—it had to be gratitude. She owed him her gratitude. He'd risked his life for her and his country and their way of life. And she must feel admiration. His bravery and the bravery of thousands of other men like him had won the war, pushed back the monster and crushed his minions.

But as he dropped his clothes on the floor and pulled her onto the bed, she didn't feel gratitude or admiration or even pity. All she felt was clench-jawed guilt and self-loathing and a sense of embarrassment so severe she had to close her eyes to keep from seeing either her body or his locked in this terrible daylight embrace. As he entered her—painfully, for she was dry and tense—she could think only of Eric, so near, just down the hill at the cottage. She tried to stop thinking. They'd been so close, surely if she thought of him, his mind would somehow join hers and he'd know—he'd know!

She hated herself, she hated Stephen, she even hated Eric for a time. She wanted to scream. Stephen's body on hers was heavy and she began to feel a deep, horrifying claustrophobia, not to mention the pain that was tearing her apart.

Then finally Stephen rolled away, gasping, and she yanked the sheets up to cover herself. Her face was wet with tears of humiliation. She could have stopped him. She should have told him the truth. If only she'd had the courage soon enough.

Now it was too late. She'd made an unspoken commitment that she hadn't intended to make.

"If I live to be a hundred, nothing will mean more to me than this day," Stephen said quietly. "The years, the dreams of you, the awful, endless waiting to feel you in my arms—oh, Laura, I was so afraid all that time. Not of what was happening to me, but of what might be happening to you."

"What do you mean?" she asked, her voice shaking.

"I was terrified that I would survive and come back to find that you hadn't. That something terrible had happened to you. A car accident, or an illness. Death was so commonplace there, so much on our minds. Or, worse yet, that you'd fallen for someone else or simply gotten tired of waiting for me. I knew you must have thought I was dead. I went nearly mad trying to find a way to get word out to you that I was alive, so that you would wait."

"Stephen, I've got to tell you something—"

He put his finger to her lips. "No, you've told me everything I ever wanted or needed to know this afternoon. You waited, you believed in me. That's all I needed to know. None of the rest of it mattered—the reporters, the family, even Mother and Arch. All that mattered was you, here, still my wife, my future. Oh, Laura, things are going to be perfect now. The worst part of our lives is over. Nothing can ever be so terrible again. We weathered this and we can weather anything. You know, I worried about you before. I wasn't sure you had the courage and determination it took to be my wife, considering how much I knew I would demand of you. I hoped so, but I didn't really know. Now I do."

"But, Stephen—"

"You waited, you had faith I would be back, and so I am. And now we can get on with the future. Together. God, Laura, do you realize what this means to me? To us? So many lives wasted and ruined, and we survived it! Laura Langley, you're going to be the most wonderful First Lady there ever was, and if I can do it, you'll be the happiest!"

"Then you still mean to run?"

"Of course. You couldn't question that. It's always been my life's ambition, and I thought you shared it."

"Yes, yes. I do. I mean, for you—if it's what you want. But I thought you might have changed. All that time to think . . ." She was babbling stupidly.

"No, you needn't have feared that. I did have a lot of time to think, and it was a good thing, in a way. I'm sure of things now that I wasn't before. I want to talk to you about my plans. With Roosevelt dead and that ass Truman in the White House, things have changed.''

"Changed? How?"

"Well, Truman hasn't got what it takes to hold the party together. There's going to be room for Republicans to make names for themselves in Congress and at the state level without the shadow of Roosevelt blotting them out.''

"Do you mean you'll be running for national office right away?'' she asked.

"No, we'll have to do a bit of looking around, listening, testing the waters. I'm just saying that the years away had seemed lost time, but now I'm not so sure. All we'll do now is see how the press is going to react to me as a private citizen. A lot will depend on that. Don't worry, my dear. You look alarmed.''

"Just . . . just surprised. I really thought you might have changed your mind about all this.''

"I probably shouldn't have even mentioned it now. There's time for that later. All I want now is you, my wife.''

He put his arms around her and she used every muscle in her body to repress her shudder.

She was trapped. Caught as surely and as savagely as a wild creature in a steel-jawed trap. And all because she hadn't had the courage to speak in time.

XXXI

ERIC wouldn't let her in the cottage the next day. It was done very subtly but firmly with a few brisk, innocuous words about what a nice day it was as he stepped out and pulled the door closed behind himself. He led Laura to a wooden bench he'd built on the north side of the building. "Have you told him?" he asked bluntly.

"Not yet."

"I see." He snapped off a twig from the azalea bush next to him and started peeling the bark with great care.

"No, Eric. You don't see."

"Did you sleep with him?"

Laura cringed at the question. A matter of hours earlier it had seemed obligatory, an unquestioned if highly distasteful responsibility. Now that single reluctant act seemed the ultimate immorality. She couldn't stand the fact that she was imprisoned in the body she'd betrayed them both with. Once again, tears threatened, but instead of pouring out, they dammed up, blocking her throat as she fought for words.

"Eric, I love you."

"You did sleep with him." He didn't look at her, but merely nodded as if pleased with what he'd done with the twig.

"I . . . I had to. I didn't want to . . ."

"He forced you, I suppose."

"Please, don't be so cold. You're talking to me as if we're strangers."

"I feel like a stranger, Laura."

"Eric, he's my *husband*, for God's sake!"

"I know that, dammit! How could I forget? I spent all

night thinking about it. Imagining it . . .'' His voice was pure misery.

She reached out and he evaded her touch as if it were poison. ''Are you going to tell him?''

''Yes, yes. But I don't know how.''

''You just look him in the eye and say the words, Laura.''

''It will ruin him.''

''Not doing it will ruin me . . . and you.''

''No, it's not the same. I meant in a different way. He still wants to be President. It's all that matters to him, besides me. And I mean more to him than I thought.''

''I was right. You do love him now that he's back.'' Eric flung the twig away and started tearing up a new one. His hands were shaking.

''*No!* No, I don't. But he's not a bad person. I've been thinking he is because he stands between us, but he's not.''

''Sonny says he is. He thinks your husband is a bigoted—''

''You've been talking to Sonny?''

''Of course. He and I were friends before I knew you, or have you forgotten?''

''Sonny's always hated Stephen. I don't know why.''

''Sonny's opinion isn't the problem. Your opinion is what matters.''

''My opinion! Since when has what I wanted counted for anything?'' Laura said, suddenly furious. ''I made a terrible mistake years ago when I was young and lonely and stupid. I married a good man—the problem was, I didn't really love him. That was my mistake; now I'm paying. We're all paying, but my opinion . . . ? It means nothing. Nothing!'' Her voice had risen shrilly. ''All right, Eric. Here's my opinion: I can't destroy him. He doesn't deserve it. I'm the one at fault. Not him. He can't be made to pay the price for my error.''

Eric turned and looked at her with alarm.

''The one single thing that could utterly destroy Stephen's dream is a divorce. A divorced man could never be President. Never. A scandal like that would ruin him. And all he did . . . *all* he did was get caught by the Germans and leave his wife free to fall in love with someone else while he was suffering who knows what deprivations—''

''Laura, stop—''

''No, it has to be said. It might be well be now!'' She stood up and started pacing. She crossed her arms tightly, as if physically holding herself together. ''I can't divorce him. I can't do that to him.''

"No, don't say it. I pushed you. I'm sorry. I was just feeling pathetic. You *can* divorce him. We can be together—"

"We would be tarred and feathered and we'd deserve it! A woman who would throw over a war hero—he is, you know. All the papers say so. I'd be stoned as a witch! We'd never be able to hold our heads up."

He came to her then and it was Laura who stepped aside, afraid of his touch. "Don't get near me. I can't bear it. I've been expecting someone else to make the decision for me. That's always been my problem—I let my grandmother run my life for so long I hardly know how to run it myself. But no one else can decide, so I have. I won't divorce him, Eric. I can't!"

"You can't mean to throw your life away—throw our love away—on a man you don't care for!"

"I can and I do. I cannot abide cruelty, and it would be unforgivably cruel to discard Stephen simply for the sake of my own passion and pleasure. I took a vow—"

"You were young. You didn't know what you were doing."

"I should have known! I wasn't a child. I was incredibly naive and stupid, but I wasn't a child. I took the vow. I must adhere to it."

She was shaking so violently she had to sit back down. Eric put his hands on her shoulders. "Laura, this is my fault. I've been too busy being pathetic, wallowing in my own self-pity, to think of what you're going through. No, don't say anything else. Not now. I'm going to forget all this. Everything you've said."

"I meant it."

"No, you didn't. I pushed you too hard. We'll wait until all the homecoming furor has died down. I'll wait, Laura, because you're going to be my wife. Mine! That's worth waiting for."

"Oh, Eric—"

"No, no more tears. I can't bear it if you cry. It makes me want to scoop you up and carry you off—and you're right about one thing: I can't and won't decide for you. It's up to you, but not now. Not now, Laura. It's too soon. We've got all the time in the world."

"Do we, Eric? Do we really?" she asked, feeling that the world was rushing at her, fingers pointing, fists shaking.

Sonny had invited her along on a picnic, the first time since his return that he'd singled her out and demanded her attention. Marysia was, as always, clinging to his arm, and Laura felt a resentment she tried to repress and never could. "Are you ever alone?" she asked him, unsure just how much the girl could understand.

"Almost never," he answered cheerfully. "She's looking better, isn't she?"

Laura glanced at the girl and smiled. Marysia, perhaps sensing the falseness of it, shrank closer to Sonny. "She is." It was true. Marysia had put on a few pounds and her skin was looking better though still sallow. She might someday be pretty, as Sonny kept promising her. "Does she understand me?"

Sonny laughed. "No more than you understand yourself."

Laura stiffened. "What's that supposed to mean?"

"You know exactly what it means."

"Sonny, why can't things go back to how they were before?"

"Before what? Before the war? Before we grew up? Before Stephen came back? How long are you going to let him and his terrible mother stay here?"

"I don't want to talk about Stephen," Laura said firmly.

"Then tell me about Eric."

She looked at him, startled. "You've learned how to stick the knife in and twist, haven't you?"

"Laura, this is me. Sonny. Can't you confide in me?"

She glanced at the girl clutching his elbow. "Not like before."

He put his other arm around her waist. "Laura, you're jealous!"

"I guess I am. It's wrong of me. Unworthy. But it seems everything I think and feel these days is wrong and unworthy."

Sonny leaned sideways and put his head against hers. "Where did you ever get the impression that you're supposed to be perfect? Did Gram teach you that? Get it out of your head. You have just as much right to be selfish or jealous or spiteful as the rest of us. There's plenty of it to go around. Take your share and enjoy it."

Laura sighed and smiled. "How do you do it? Always make me feel better? Sonny, you're about the only person in the world who can make me like myself when I'm trying so damned hard not to."

"That's better. Now, let's find a place to eat and then we're going to show Marysia how to fly a kite."

* * *

Eric came to her a week later. "I want to talk to you, Mrs. Langely," he said from the door to the library.

"Certainly, Mr. Holt," Laura said. She had two of the nurses sitting across the desk from her. "We'll be finished here in just a minute."

When she had straightened out the error in a chart that had been plaguing her for two days and sent the two young women on their way, she said to Eric, "Where shall we go? The cottage?"

"No, I want to talk to you here."

Laura's heart felt heavy. She knew that this was it, the conversation she'd dreaded. He sat down in one of the chairs the nurses had vacated. "Sit back there where I can't touch you," he said.

Laura obeyed.

"You're leaving, aren't you?"

He nodded. "I thought I could wait for you. I can't. It's killing me. I've been offered a job. A mural in a hospital. I actually tried to turn it down, but they insisted and it's come to seem like some sort of heavenly order. I mean, a one-handed hack like me. I'm lucky to get a job that involves a paintbrush."

"Don't say that. You're good!"

"Good. Not great. I can never be great. I've come to accept that, just as I can almost accept that I've lost you."

"You haven't lost me. I love you."

"Don't say it again. It's useless, Laura. We've both known that ever since the day Bess called you to say he was alive. We've done our best to pretend it wasn't over, but it was over then and we're dragging a corpse around. That's a travesty."

"Eric, I'll leave him. Today. This minute!"

She started to get up, but he motioned her to stop with such a savage gesture that she sank back into the chair. "No, I won't have you that way. You're right: divorce would ruin him, and you'd never clear your conscience of it. I'm not even sure I could. It would be between us the rest of our lives. We can't stand up together in the bloody devastation of another life and love each other for it. You know, I loathe your damned sense of duty. Duty to your dotty mother and your cousin and aunt and uncle and brother and this house and all the rest. And at the same time, that's a big part of what I love about you."

"He might change his mind . . ." Laura said. Her voice sounded like dry leaves rustling in the wind.

Eric stood up as if she hadn't spoken. "Laura, I'll never love anyone else and I don't suppose you ever will either. We had something fine and precious, but it's gone. This way it can't get tarnished. I do and always will love you."

She clutched the edge of the desk, feeling an ageless desire to shriek or tear at her clothes. "Will I see you again?"

"No. Never."

And with that word and no look back, he opened the door and walked out.

Laura sat there, her heart and mind frozen, for nearly an hour; then she made up her mind. He was right about almost everything. Almost.

They were up late that night, listening to the radio accounts of the bombing of Hiroshima. While the others talked quietly about the horror of the unimaginable bomb and the inevitable end of the war with Japan, Laura sat rigidly, planning. When finally the house was quiet, she crept out of bed and dressed. She slipped down the kitchen stairway, glad she didn't run into anyone else, but not really caring.

It was a warm night with fast-moving clouds that kept dashing past a full moon. But Laura didn't need the moonlight to know her way. The path was as familiar to her as the palm of her own hand, and she moved quickly but with no nervousness or misgiving. There was the muffled beat of wings, and an owl swooped low, uttering a tremulous hoot. Laura didn't look up or veer from her path.

The cottage was dark; the door was unlocked. But she knew he was there, as with some very special sense of affinity. And she knew, as she stepped through the door of the bedroom, that Eric was awake. He didn't move or speak, but she had no doubt of his presence and knew as surely that he was watching her. Without hesitation she stepped out of her dress. Then he moved, but only to pull aside the light sheet and move over to make room for her as she lay down beside him. "It won't change anything," he said.

Or did he say it in words? Was it an exchange of thoughts?

"I know."

"Laura—"

"No talk. Everything's been said," she whispered. "All you said this afternoon is true. I couldn't ever walk out on my husband. You'd hate the woman I'd become if I did. We won't see each other again, Eric. Not after tonight. We don't have any future—it's impossible. But we have a here and now. Kiss me, my love, my beloved, my life . . ."

The clouds drifted, and flickering moonlight, like magician's lantern, shone through the window, illuminating them with cool blue light.

When Stephen had been reported dead, Laura had gone to pieces, but now she had no grief left. She had used up her lifetime quota. Eric was gone and she was the victim of a despair so deep that it was virtually impossible to feel. She was utterly numbed, placid, almost happy in a mindless way. There was a sort of horrible relief in having done what had to be done. She had listened to the voices of her childhood, Grace's voice, the voices of duty and loyalty and honor, and she had acted in the only way possible. She had let love go, graciously, for the sake of responsibility.

The essential Laura-ness of her had locked in place, barred the doors, shuttered windows to the world, and the external Laura went from day to day in her usual way. She worked in the library and in the braille class; she ate meals with the family, took walks with Sonny and Marysia, dosed Uncle Edmund through a bout of flu. The only time the barriers threatened to crumble was at India's wedding. She hardly got through it, and as India and Sergeant Walker looked into each other's eyes and repeated their vows, Laura got up suddenly and unobtrusively fled the room.

Only one thing was different. She didn't share Stephen's bed. At first she used excuses: She had a headache and couldn't sleep, she'd just stay in another room so she wouldn't disturb him. She was afraid of passing on Uncle Edmund's germs, so she'd sleep alone for a few days. She was so exhausted from last-minute preparations for the wedding that she wanted to be by herself. After two weeks, she ceased making excuses and simply took the remaining things of hers from her bedroom and let Stephen have it.

He came to her room the night she moved into it. She submitted dutifully to his lovemaking, but it was only an abortive attempt. He seemed angry for a few minutes, then apologized for bothering her and went back to his own room. He didn't come back again. Laura knew relatively little about sex and had no one to consult with, so she assumed that his needs were somehow less than other men's. Or perhaps men's desires weren't as great as they were generally thought to be. And of course, he had a lot to catch up on besides sleeping with his wife. She felt guilty, but didn't know what to do about the situation that wouldn't just create more, if different, guilt. The next morning he made a slighting reference to having disturbed her sleep—needlessly. "Stephen, it's just that so much has happened . . ." She was on the brink of telling him. But what was the point now? She'd made her decision and he'd never know.

But he misunderstood her anyway. "I know. It's been a long time. We have to get to know each other again. I enjoyed courting you the first time. I'll enjoy it all over again. I realize that in some ways this has been just as hard on you as it has on me."

"Don't say that, Stephen. You're the one who had to suffer for your ideals. I just hung on. You're the hero, not me."

"I'm no hero."

"Stephen, I know you don't like to talk about it, but can't you tell me what happened?"

He stiffened. "Nothing happened. The plane went down. Everybody but me died. I crawled away but was captured. That's it. There's nothing to talk about."

And after that brief exchange, he didn't press her about their sleeping arrangements. Laura's relief was enormous. So was her guilt. He was being so considerate, treating her like a reluctant virgin, when all along her reluctance was because she was an unrepentant adulteress.

He was too immersed in his own concerns to notice the eerie change in her that was so alarming to Sonny and the rest of the family. His mother had stayed on at Thornehill and his Uncle Arch had left for a short time and returned with several political cronies in tow. Laura often found herself unwitting party to their discussions and managed to pretend interest without absorbing anything more than a general idea of their plans.

Being in prison for so long had lost Stephen some valuable time but had made him a more noted figure in some ways than he might have been otherwise. The press, with whom his family had flirted so vigorously, was on his side. In spite of his firm refusal to discuss the war, he made good copy, the ideal American. Rich, but not ostentatiously so, handsome without any tinge of vulgarity, intelligent though not highbrow, young but not boyish, he had Eastern savvy and so-phistication with a rural Southern address. He also had a pretty wife and a home that had been turned into that most patriotic of things, a hospital for returning veterans. What more could they want. They buzzed about him like bees around a particularly aromatic flower.

He was becoming a name.

"People are going to get fed up with Truman quickly. No class at all. A dumpy little habedasher," Arch said. "There's a chance he'll win in forty-eight just because of this bomb thing. But we'll have to think about the vice-presidency then. It would get your name on the ballots. Even if you lose, people will remember in fifty-two. And of course, there's always the chance you'll win."

"That's crazy, Uncle Arch. I've got to put in my time in Congress or the statehouse first. But even when the time comes, I won't be put up for vice-president. They never make it on their own. I don't want to ever be idenfified as the man who ran *with* someone else. We'll stay with the original schedule—go first for Congress, the Senate, a governorship, dogcatcher! Any elected position except v.p.," Stephen said. "The worst thing we could do is try to hurry this thing. I won't even consider the presidency until I'm damned sure I'm in a position to win."

Arch frowned. The boy had gotten pretty stubborn of late. It worried him. Other things worried him as well—nothing definite enough to put his finger on, but he just felt uneasy sometimes. Stephen seemed to have secrets, opinions he almost ventured, then caught himself and shut down on. And Arch worried, too, that Stephen never, but never, spoke of his experiences in the war. The press boys loved him as it was. If he'd just open up and tell some good stories about it, he'd win them over even more thoroughly. Could it be the boy didn't realize that it wasn't going to be the people who elected him, but the press?

Arch suspected that whatever had happened was more upsetting that Stephen would let on. There were changes in him. Something haunted and wary that had never been there before. And of course, there was the very cool relationship with that wife of his who didn't seem quite human these days either. They weren't sleeping together. Arch was certain of it. But neither of them seemed to care. They were nice enough to each other—overly polite, in fact.

He knew, of course, about that crippled artist who'd lived down at the cottage. Laura had been sleeping with him. Everybody in the place knew it. Stephen must have been aware of it as well, though Arch had never discussed it with him openly. But now the man had gone away, and that should have cleared the way for Stephen to sort things out with her. Unless they'd fought about it. That seemed unlikely, though, in view of their strangely artificial attitude toward one another. It was as if they were actors playing at being the affectionate husband and wife, but not really engaged in the roles.

He said, "Whatever you think, Stephen. You might be right that there's a certain stigma attached to being v.p. Unless, of course, the party runs an old man who's going to die in office." It was meant as a joke, a tasteless joke that made Arch feel vaguely ashamed of himself.

Stephen just stared at him speculatively and Arch suddenly felt strangely old himself. And frightened. Something awful was going to happen. He sensed it like a sudden drop in the barometer.

Or perhaps it had already happened and no one knew it yet. The image of an actor came back to him again. That was what was bothering him. This man was Stephen physically, but mentally he was an actor playing Stephen Langley. What had happened? What had been done to him in Germany to make him seem so different? And, most important, just how different was he? Were the plans of a lifetime out of his hands? Was this stranger friend or foe?

"What's wrong, Uncle Arch? You look worried," Stephen said.

His tone was so concerned, so like the Stephen he'd known, man and boy, that Arch suddenly felt like a great fool imagining such foolish things. What kind of crazy old hen was he turning into? He stood up and slapped his nephew on the back in a hearty fashion. "Nothing wrong, my boy. Nothing at all!"

XXXII

*T*HE family had gathered in the library after dinner. Bess Langley, who was becoming, it appeared, a more or less permanent fixture at Thornehill, had retired to her room with a headache; Senator Arch Langley had gone back to Washington; and Stephen was upstairs making some phone calls, so tonight it was the family of old days—plus Marysia and Sergeant Walker. Laura was reading, or pretending to read. Actually she was watching her timid sister-in-law.

Laura had disliked her at first; not for herself, but for being Sonny's wife, his all-consuming interest and constant shadow when Laura had hoped to have him back to herself. It was jealousy plain and simple. Laura knew it and was ashamed of it, but needed Sonny's support. Gradually she'd realized that Marysia didn't interfere with their relationship—so long as Laura didn't let herself believe she did.

Now Marysia was one of the things that held Laura together. Every time she felt her control slipping and sadness at her loss of Eric threatening to overwhelm her, she forced herself to think of how much more Marysia had lost. Sonny had told Laura a little of Marysia's story. From a wealthy Catholic Krakow family, her uncle, a priest, had protested the Nazi invasion of Poland and brought the authorities down on the family. Marysia had been only eighteen, a bright but innocent girl with virtually no knowledge of the world outside the loving shelter of the family enclave.

Before it was over, Marysia had seen her mother raped, her father castrated, one of her little brothers shot, and the rest starved to death in the concentration camp. She herself had undergone some sort of ghoulish experimental surgery.

But Marysia had survived. Clearly damaged, she was attempting to build a normal life. Several times Laura had noticed that Marysia was actually making herself eat because she should, not because she liked the food. She'd managed, through sheer doggedness, to put on about twenty pounds. She was still very thin, unhealthily so, but she looked more human. Her hair had grown out a little, and Adele had trimmed it neatly. Laura had been in the kitchen that afternoon when Marysia looked at the results and pretended to be highly pleased. It was obvious that her experiences had submerged such trivialities as common vanity, and yet Marysia knew that she must recover even that small vice.

She had, as Sonny predicted, picked up English at an astonishing rate. Though she spoke infrequently and with a thick accent, she clearly understood the rest of them and was trying to be fearless and comfortable with them—not an easy task for one who had seen and suffered the very worst that human nature could serve up.

Marysia's example kept Laura from collapsing in self-pity, but it couldn't keep away that feeling that someone had grasped her heart in a terribly strong hand and squeezed every time she thought about Eric. Would that ever stop? It had been three months now since she last saw him, but if anything the agony was worse. She needed so badly to laugh, it was like a physical hunger. She kept thinking back to the times they'd shared laughter, as if those moments were a lifeline. He'd even been able to make her see humor in her questionable heritage.

Think about Marysia, Laura thought.

She watched her over the edge of her book. Sonny was trying to fix a clock and had its innards spread out on a card table. Marysia sat at his side, her hand always lightly touching him, her eyes never leaving him. He asked her to get a screwdriver from a drawer across the room, and had to explain to her what that strange new word meant.

She got up and went to get it, and it was touching the way her hand trailed behind, as if wanting to be ready to grab at him if he showed any signs of getting out of her sight. She came back and sat down and he very gently disengaged her from his elbow. He said something to her and she laughed softly and sat back with her arms folded. But in a few minutes one hand had crept free and was touching him again. There was nothing sexual in it, this constant clutching at him, but there was love, nevertheless. How lucky she was to have

Sonny, Laura thought, and how lucky Sonny was to have her. To be genuinely needed.

That, of course, was the difference between Laura and Marysia. The young refugee had suffered far worse deprivations than she had, but had found reimbursement—a man who filled her life. Whereas Laura had given up the love of her life for a man who kept her tucked neatly into a corner of his heart. A man whose primary interests and passions lay elsewhere, in the creation of a career. If only Stephen would sit by her and take apart a clock!

Sonny seemed to feel Laura's gaze and looked up from the destruction of the timepiece. "Something wrong?"

"No, just admiring Marysia's red sweater." That was another funny thing about the girl; she would wear only two dresses, both rather shabby, though she kept them clean. A holdover from her concentration-camp experience, Sonny had explained. A habit of having a few things only and refusing to give them up. She would get over it eventually, and in order to help her, Adele had knit her a bright crimson sweater which Marysia wore day in and day out, now that the weather had turned cooler. "You look pretty in vivid colors," Laura added.

Marysia smiled shyly and said, "Thank you, Laura."

"So what's the plan for the weekend?" Sonny asked, holding up a small cog and regarding it with a puzzled expression, as though he half-believed that someone had slipped it in on him when he wasn't looking.

"There's the parade in Hot Springs tomorrow, and Stephen's speech afterward, then Sunday all those political people are coming here for a big dinner."

"Why is Stephen the speaker? Doesn't Hot Springs have its own soldiers?" Sonny asked sarcastically.

Laura didn't reply. The "soldier" part of the remark stung. Stephen's attitude was slowly changing. At first she hadn't even been quite aware of it; then she'd started noticing that when people referred to him as a war hero, instead of vehemently denying it as he had before, he'd act as if he hadn't heard them. After a while he started saying a modest "Thank you, but I'm no more a hero than anyone else who went." And just three days earlier, she'd heard a reporter mention his heroism and Stephen had replied, as in the old days, "Courage, or heroism, if you will, is the one trait that distinguishes man from all the other creatures of the earth. If we're not willing to put our lives on the line for what we believe in, then we don't deserve to have been created humans."

She'd been puzzled by the change when she finally became fully aware of it, but on reflection, it made sense. Naturally he hadn't wanted to talk about his experiences when he first returned; the wounds were still too fresh, literally and figuratively. But with each day that passed, his leg healed, and so did his emotions. He was, after all, really a hero—Laura recognized that. He'd been flying a highly dangerous mission on a voluntary basis and had survived enemy capture.

The day after that interview, he got his uniform out and put it on, At Bess's request, to have a portrait picture taken. And had worn it later that day when they went to dinner in town. Laura was unhappy with this, however, and stayed up late that night tatting and thinking. She'd liked him better when he was working hard at putting the war behind him—behind all of them. There was, in spite of the limp, a bit of swagger in his walk when he wore the uniform. Or was she only imagining that? At least the press liked him better this way, and she supposed for the good of his career, that was important.

It had been a great mystery to her at first, too, this public interest in Stephen. But she was beginning to understand. Stephen, with the help of a very sympathetic press, had come to be a symbol. He wasn't just an individual, he represented "Returning Soldier," especially now that he was willing to accept the appellation. He was, as one paper had said, "a new Lindbergh." an essentially wholesome, quiet man with a deferential self-confidence that stopped just a shade short of arrogance. "Lucky Lindy," that great American hero of the thirties, had possessed the same qualities before the kidnapping of his child and his consequent hatred of the press that had once adored and later hounded him.

There was another reason for Stephen's sudden popularity, and Laura felt cynical for thinking it, however true it might be. Simply put, it was easier for people to accept and venerate a handsome, self-assured man with a slight and rather romantic limp than to cope with men like some of those in the hospital. The men with burned, disfigured faces, missing eyes, paralyzed arms, ugly, lurching limps—they weren't handsome. They were too strong a reminder of the true savagery of war. To many people they seemed to wordlessly say: Look what I gave up to defend you. You owe me something.

But Stephen Langley, Returning Soldier, demanded nothing of them and it was easy, oh so easy, to heap him with adoration. It sat so well on his broad shoulders. He was a man created and designed to be the recipient of respect. Even the soldiers themselves at the hospital seemed to be in affectionate awe of him. He was what they wished they were. He was damaged but whole.

And if he wasn't quite as whole as he appeared . . .

Laura tried to shake off the thought. It seemed downright traitorous to wonder if he was as well as he appeared. But there were things that worried her. He'd been having nightmares. One of the first nights he'd been back she'd awakened to the sound of strange guttural noises and found him thrashing as if striking out at something. Several times since she'd taken to sleeping in the room next to his, she'd heard him stumbling about and shouting in his sleep.

He had moments when he looked suddenly haggard. He'd given up reading, his consuming love before the war. He'd hardly touched a book since his return, and when she mentioned one of the books he'd recommended that she read years before, he'd dismissed it: "Oh, that nonsense. No point in wasting time on it." Surely he was entitled to have some residual effects of his experiences in Germany, whatever they may have been, Laura told herself. And naturally the war had changed him. It had changed them all, even those who stayed at home.

Laura stood up suddenly. That line of thought had led her back to Eric. She couldn't bear to think of him and yet couldn't stop herself. Was he thinking of her as well? Surely he was, and surely his heart was as sore and wrung out as hers. "Good night, all," she said, crossing the room.

"Wait, Laura," Marysia said.

Laura stopped, surprised. Marysia never spoke to anyone unless spoken to. The girl actually left Sonny's side and crossed the room. She put her hand on Laura's arm and said in a whisper, "I have been watching you, Laura. Don't be sad."

The girl suddenly hugged her with astonishing bony strength, then fled back to Sonny's side. He was grinning. Adele was sitting back with her knitting in her lap and her mouth open, Edmund was nodding his satisfaction, and India and Billy Walker were looking at each other with big smiles.

For a moment Laura remembered what it was like to feel happy.

* * *

The day of the parade started nicely enough. There was a big article in the morning paper about the unveiling of a mural in the VA hospital in St. Louis:

> In two weeks, the hospital will be having a special reception and unveiling of a mural that surrounds the central lobby. The public is invited. Many state and military dignitaries will be on hand and there is even the possibility that President Truman may be able to attend. Done by Eric Holt, the mural, titled *Medicine Defeats War*, is a masterpiece of patriotic art. The scope and sweep of the mural are massive, yet it is delicately detailed. The colors are clear and true, vivid with victory. The faces are the faces around us, the people one sees everyday. Not prettified, the work is nevertheless tremendously moving, a true tribute to the men and women, at home and abroad, who fought for freedom. The dignity of the human race is in every line, every scene in Holt's work. Holt himself is a veteran and lost the use of his right hand in the service. His own courage and determination shine through and will be an inspiration to the generations who will see this work. . . .

Laura set the paper down, her eyes clouding. How proud he must be! She wished she could have shared that moment of glory and praise with him. At least she might someday be able to see the mural. Tucking the article into her purse, she joined the others already assembling in the driveway for the trip to Hot Springs.

Stephen was in high spirits and Laura managed to pretend she was enjoying herself. The parade was endless, noisy, and something of a trial, but Laura endured it with good grace and even did a convincing job of appearing to enjoy the overcooked chicken at the big outdoor supper afterward. As the sun set, she and Stephen and Bess piled back into the car and drove a few miles to the place where the speeches and further festivities would be held. "Do we have to stay late?" she asked.

"We'll stay as long as we need to," Stephen said firmly.

"Of course, I just meant—"

"You can *get* tired, Laura, but you can't ever *look* tired during a campaign," Bess said condescendingly.

"I wasn't aware that this was a campaign," Laura retorted,

goaded by the older woman's attitude. "I thought it was a patriotic rally."

"Everything we do from this moment on is a campaign," Bess said, fixing her with a look that made her feel like a butterfly pinned to a board. "And you've got to do your part."

"Have you any reason to suppose I won't?" she asked angrily. "Haven't I ruined two pairs of gloves today shaking hands with people?"

"Aren't you feeling well?" Stephen asked.

She took a deep breath. "I'm sorry, Stephen. I'm just weary and unaccustomed to this sort of life."

"You had better get used to it," Bess put in.

Laura's anger hadn't dissipated by the time they reached their destination. Stephen should have come to her defense when Bess attacked her, she felt. But she got out of the car smiling anyway. This was his day, the first tentative step into the political arena, the true beginning of what he had always wanted. She could at least act the part of the happy wife for his sake.

The speeches were to be held in a tent, which made Laura uncomfortable, though she couldn't quite figure out why. The first two speakers were local "good ol' boys," who got a friendly reception, but Laura noticed that much of the crowd wasn't really listening to them; they were watching Stephen. And well they might, she realized, casting him a sideways glance. He was a very attractive man, and in uniform he was spectacularly good-looking.

Finally it was his turn, and he rose. There was a din of applause and he had to keep holding his hands up for silence. As the tent quieted, he started talking, his voice low but carrying, washing over them. Laura only half-listened, an intent half-smile fixed on her features. After a while she became dimly aware that he wasn't really saying anything. His speech was a sort of dictionary of patriotic catch phrases strung together by his fine voice. "No fear of oppressors," "brave boys giving their lives on the blood-soaked fields of Europe," "that the world never forget," "facing the future with the same courage with which we faced the enemy."

She looked around the room. Every eye was on him. He raised his voice and they all seemed to sit up a little straighter. He lowered his voice and several hundred people leaned forward or cocked their heads to hear his words. Eyes followed his every gesture, and as Laura, too, watched him, she began to have a vague feeling of recognition, a sense of *déjà vu*, as elusive as a scent.

As he started on what was apparently the last of his remarks, Laura noticed that people at the back of the room had stood up, the better to see and hear him. Others had moved into the aisles, and there was a subtle movement forward—closer.

"We must put this all behind now. It's done. We've served, we've suffered, we've survived," Stephen was saying in a rousing tone. "Now we have to link arms, join hearts, and stride into the future with our eyes clear and our spirits high! I thank you, ladies and gentlemen!"

He came back to sit by Laura, but the whole crowd was on its feet cheering, clapping, and shouting. With apparent reluctance, he rose again, held out one hand to Bess and one to Laura. They both obediently joined him at the front of the stage. Though it was late November and the air outside was crisp, Laura was sweating with nervousness and the oppressive human heat of the tent. In a lull Stephen raised his voice. "Ladies and gentlemen, my mother"—he bowed to her and she smiled radiantly—"and my beautiful wife."

They went wild. Everyone was crowding forward now. Hands were outstretched to shake his—or was it merely to touch him? Laura felt herself shrinking back, but Stephen had a firm grip on her arm.

Suddenly Laura remembered: the tent, the heat, the crowd, the surges of emotion—the revival! Stephen was the Reverend Johnny Heaven and she was instantly the little girl being crushed by the people. All those people! The crowd coalescing, melding, growing, pressing, pushing, the bloated many-armed creature of her nightmares come back to haunt her.

And now she understood what she hadn't then: that there was a strong element of sexuality run amok in this wild-eyed adulation, and Stephen knew, as the fundamentalist minister had, how to play on it, work it, and mold it like clay. And now the monster was coming at her. Stephen had stepped down into the crowd, pulling her along. People pressed closer, bodies jostled, hands touched, sour breath suffocated her. She became claustrophobic, frantic for room and fresh air. She gritted her teeth and breathed through her mouth to force down a rising nausea. Oh for India to pick her up and carry her out of here!

A voice from the back of the tent shouted half-seriously, "Langley for President! Langley for President!"

Stephen raised one hand, smiling tightly as if he appreciated the joke but didn't find it very amusing. With the part of her mind that was still able to overcome claustrophobia, she realized Stephen was angry—as if someone had given away a secret years too soon.

But the crowd was ready to fasten on a chant—any chant, and this one had a nice ring to it. Other voices picked it up, turned it into a chant that throbbed through Laura's very core.

Laura shivered violently and pulled her hand out of Stephen's grip. The crowd quickly swallowed her and dragged her away from him. She fixed her gaze on a side flap of the tent and started fighting toward it. Someone, some anonymous hand, cupped her breast momentarily and she shrieked in shock, but the hand was already gone, the faces around her all facing eagerly toward Stephen.

She lowered her head, crossed her arms over her chest, and plunged through them. Feet struck her shins, shoulders battered her as, salmonlike, she fought a life-and-death struggle against the tide of dehumanized humanity. Finally she got free, lunged for the tent flap, and flung herself outside. She ran a few steps, twisting her ankle painfully, then leaned against the cold metal of a car hood. She was sobbing, gasping for breath, trying to find some handhold on the hem of dignity.

Dear God in heaven, had she given up Eric for this? Was this to be her life?

The next morning brought further shocks. Breakfast was early and hurried. There were people coming later for a big party that Bess had planned. Laura had largely ignored the preparations up until now, but suddenly she found herself deeply involved. "We'll have dinner served buffet style outside the library if the weather holds. If not, we'll set up our tables in the library itself," Bess said, spooning up her scrambled eggs.

"No," Laura said.

Bess and Stephen both looked up sharply, as if they hadn't noticed her presence before.

"No, it can be served in the dining room, but not the library. That's where I work and I can't possibly get everything put away and fit for company." She didn't say what she really meant: that the library was private family space that must not be invaded by the Langleys' political friends. It was still, in a strange way, Grace's principality, and Laura had to defend its borders.

"It doesn't matter," Bess said, frowning. "I don't believe there's any chance of rain. You will, of course, have to keep the soldiers indoors—"

"I beg your pardon?" Laura said, stiffening.

"Well, it would be most unfestive to have all those pathetic creatures lurching around the lawns where the guests couldn't help but see them."

Laura dropped the roll she was buttering. "You're trying to make a joke, aren't you? You can't possibly be serious! This is a hospital. There are sick and injured people at a hospital. If you want a party atmosphere, have your party in a more appropriate place!"

"Now, Laura," Stephen said.

"Don't 'now, Laura' me. I won't have it! The patients have more right here than your political cronies. I won't have them locked away so your mother can impress strangers. Besides, she just wants them out of the way so you can get all the glory. Well, they deserve it too!"

Stephen stared at her for a long moment, then said coldly, "Laura, you have no right to talk to Mother that way."

"No right? No right! Stephen, have you lost your mind? Can't you hear the way she talks to me, as though I were some sort of unsatisfactory hired girl? I wonder how you could face the Nazis to defend your country when you can't even face your mother to defend your wife. Some hero! Your much-publicized courage is certainly an on-again, off-again thing! It doesn't seem to have come home with you."

Stephen looked stricken, with white circles around his eyes and mouth, and for a moment Laura felt ashamed of herself. But only for a moment. Everything she'd said was true and would have needed saying sooner or later.

"Mother," Stephen said stiffly, "we'll talk about the party arrangements later."

Laura got up. "You mean when I'm not here? It doesn't matter what your mother decides, I won't have the patients herded indoors like cattle in their barn. But I'll leave you two to yourselves."

She left the room shaking with outrage, and found herself face to face with Sonny. "Did you hear that!" she yelled at him.

"Are you surprised? Oh, my poor Laura-bunny," Sonny said, using Grace's old nickname for her. "You are so determinedly, pigheadedly blind. How do you do it? And why, for God's sake?''

She put her hands to her temples. ''Sonny, you're beyond all reason. Don't you know this is all hard enough for me without you perpetually yapping about how much you dislike Stephen?'' This, even she realized, wasn't quite fair. Sonny never pretended any degree of fondness for any of the Langleys, but he didn't openly deride Stephen. Only Laura, so closely attuned to Sonny's feelings, recognized that his hatred of her husband was intense and permanent.

''It isn't a matter of personal dislike, Laura. It's that the man simply isn't what you and most of the world think.''

''But you know something that the rest of us can't see?'' she asked sarcastically, allowing him to take her arm and guide her away from the dining-room door.

''In this case, yes. He is his mother's son as surely as if she ran him up on a sewing machine to her own design.''

''He's nothing like Bess!''

''He is everything like Bess—and more. You haven't been reading your history. A good seventy-five percent of all the truly important men in the world's history have been the adoring, obedient only sons of overpowering mothers. Look at General MacArthur. His mother moved with him to West Point and lived in a rented room next to the campus with a view of his window so she could actually see him studying. Roosevelt's mother was almost as bad and was equally adored. She treated Eleanor like dirt and FDR let her. No, don't say a word, my girl,'' he said, seeing the mounting fury in the set of her jaw. ''Forget I said all this, but remember: when you see the truth, come to me. I promise not to say I told you so. No, I'll say it once. Just once. Then I'll help you in any way I can.''

That afternoon Laura put on a heavy sweater and went up to the attic to hide. It was the only place in the house where she could count on not being found. She had a lot of thinking to do, but as the sun faded, she hadn't come to any conclusions. It was the first time she had really faced the idea of being Stephen's wife, Bess's daughter-in-law, *and* First Lady.

She had known in a superficial, purely intellectual way that this was a possibility—a distinct likelihood, actually. But in her musings it had always seemed a vague, distant thing. Something that might happen to her when she was older, more ready. Being President was something Stephen wanted, something *he* would do. Suddenly she realized it would involve her thoroughly—and possibly very soon. He was already campaigning, even though any overt move toward the presidency was several years in the future. There would be more campaigning, conventions, entertaining, public appearances, handshaking, hobnobbing with strangers, perpetually smiling—all anathema to her, but inevitable and unavoidable.

Most shocking (why hadn't she recognized it sooner?) was the realization that congressmen and senators and presidents live in Washington. Not Arkansas. Years yet. Don't think about it now, she told herself. But her mind kept coming back to it. He'd go to Washington. And where Stephen went, she would have to go. She had been so utterly absorbed in the hideous fact of giving up Eric that she'd spared precious little thought for what else she was going to have to give up—her privacy and her home.

Leave Thornehill? Unthinkable!

Her thoughts skipped back a step. Her home? Legally, yes, but morally, no. It was Sonny's home too. It was as dear to him as to her. Perhaps more so, especially now that he had Marysia to think of. This was Marysia's safe haven in a world that had served up a full measure of misery. Laura and Sonny hadn't talked about Grace's will since his return. There had been so many more immediate matters to attend to. She'd go see old Willis Hawkins tomorrow about it, she told herself as she went downstairs.

It was rather comforting to have something else to occupy her mind than her own fears and worries. She might not have very much control over her own life at the moment, but there was still one worthwhile thing she could attend to. She had no premonition of the things she would have to occupy her mind by the next day and for many stricken days to come.

The party was a nightmare to Laura. There were mobs of people, deafening music too much drinking, too much talking, too much everything. And through it all she smiled until her face ached. Stephen had been extremely irritated about her mysterious disappearance from the political rally the night before, so she was determined to do an exemplary job of socializing tonight.

Early in the evening she'd noticed him in conversation with a buxom blond, but didn't think anything of it until she noticed him talking to the woman again an hour later and then again near midnight. "Who is that woman?" she asked Bess when their paths next crossed.

"I'm sure I don't know," Bess said snappishly.

So Bess thought they were behaving suspiciously too. That was interesting, Laura thought.

Someone next to her at the buffet table said to a companion, "It's one thing to prosecute the Nazi leaders—don't get me wrong—I just mean those damned Krupps and VonHoldts ought to be strung up too. At least the Nazis thought they had a moral reason for what they were doing—an evil reason, but a reason. But the armaments manufacturers were in it for pure profit. If that awful Hun Frederich VonHoldt hadn't died, I could have killed him myself. . . ."

Frederich was dead? Laura hadn't known. She turned and smiled at the man who'd been talking. "Thank you," she said, and walked away leaving him wondering what on earth she was thanking him for.

Finally people began drifting away, some back to hotels in town, the privileged few to their rooms in the house itself. Laura slipped away to the library, ostensibly to catch up on some paperwork, actually to get away from the smell of tobacco and liquor and get her bearings. But as she slipped her shoes off and sat down in front of the fireplace, the image of the blond woman kept coming back to her.

She got up, pacing and trying to force the memory into focus. She went and sat at the big desk that had been Captain Jack's, then Grace's, and now hers. She always seemed to think better there.

The woman was familiar, but distantly so. She wasn't a local resident; Laura was pretty sure of that. Could she have gone to school with her? No, that was unlikely. There was something faintly trashy about the cut of her dress, the mannerisms, the open sexuality. The girls Laura had known in school were all terribly well-bred and brought-up. Besides, she could hardly have forgotten anyone with a figure like that! Where have I met her? Laura wondered. As she picked up her shoes to go upstairs, it suddenly came to her. Shoes. She and the woman had, as girls, talked about shoes. Shoes?

Dear God. That was Mae Smalley!

Laura's half-sister, the hateful, bitter little girl who had come along that time the Smalleys blackmailed Grace. She'd coveted Laura's saddle oxfords. And now, it seemed, she coveted Laura's husband. Stephen couldn't possibly know what a dangerous element she was. He had to be warned.

And in being warned, he had to be told the truth of Laura's birth. Not that it mattered, but it had never come up, and he might justifiably be hurt that she hadn't confided in him. There had never been time. Their courtship was so abbreviated, their marriage so short in actual time together. Certainly he would understand why she hadn't ever mentioned this almost forgotten factor of her past.

No, that was merely convenient self-delusion. There had been plenty of time; Laura had deliberately found justification for not telling him. First it had been for fear of losing his love, later for fear that he would be angry at her for having withheld the information in the first place. If only she'd known what real courage was when she met and married him. She knew now, though. If she could give up Eric, she could face anything.

Laura was still trying to figure out just how to explain about Mae Smalley when Stephen and Bess came into the library. She felt the all-too-familiar flash of irritation that they felt it was their room to make free with in whatever way they chose. Laura had some paperwork sitting on the sofa in sorted piles. Bess gathered it all up in a single scoop and dumped it on the floor before Laura could protest.

There was a knock on the door and the blonde from the party stuck her head in. "Hey, you nearly shut this thing in my face. Didn't you know I was behind you?"

"I beg your pardon?" Bess said haughtily. "I'm afraid the party is over, but if you need transportation back to town, we could probably arrange—"

"No, I'm not in any hurry to leave. I've got business to conduct."

Not yet, Laura wanted to scream. *Let me tell them*. But it was too late. What difference did it really make? The truth was the truth, no matter who told it.

"Oh, there *you* are," Mae said to Laura. "I was wondering where you got off to."

"You know this person, Laura?" Bess asked.

Laura nodded.

"Mother, please—" Stephen said.

"Oh, so this old gal is *your* mother," Mae said to Stephen. "That's funny. 'cause it's mothers I want to talk about. Mine and your little Laura-bunny's." The last words were said with such venom that Laura could taste it in the air. "That's what they call you, isn't it?"

"I cannot imagine what your mother and Laura's might

have to do with each other, but the fact remains that it's quite late, young woman, and—"

Bess's words were cut off by Mae's braying laugh. "You can't imagine, eh? Well, try this one: they are the same person. I'm your precious Laura-bunny's sister. Her mother isn't that dotty old witch in the flapper getup like you think. How do you like that?"

Bess gasped with disbelief and fury. "How dare you!"

Stephen took a step toward Laura, his face pale. "Laura, who is this woman?"

Laura had been feeling flushed and frantic, but now it was over, one of her two worst secrets was out. She felt an almost giddy sense of relief. It was as though this knowledge had taken root in a dark, concealed place in her mind years ago. Every now and then, in its irregular seasons, it had put out a painful, exploratory tendril. But now, with Mae's blunt words, the secret had been torn out by the roots. It was still a deadly plant, but not hers alone. "She's my half-sister. My real mother's legitimate daughter."

He seemed to lunge at her, so suddenly did he grab her shoulders. "Laura, you can't mean this!"

Mae sat down at the other end of the sofa from Bess, who was silent with horror and bounced up as Mae flopped down. "It's true, Mr. Hotshot Politician. And now that we've got it cleared up, we've got business to discuss."

"We have no business at all. Get out!" Stephen said.

"No, I don't think so. Not yet. As I see it, Mr. Langley, I've got your prick in a wringer. I'm wondering what's gonna happen when all those reporter friends of yours find out that your fancy, rich, oh-so-proper wife is really the gardener's bastard granddaughter."

Stephen exchanged a look with Bess, who had gotten a grip on herself and was sitting very straight and gazing into the middle distance, her lips white and her jaw clenched. She looked at him for a minute, nodded almost imperceptibly. He turned to Mae with a cold, collected look. "We will, naturally, want to talk about this privately. You can understand that."

"Sure. Sure," Mae said, scrabbling in her handbag. "I got a figure written down here that you'll want to think about. There's no bargaining, by the way. This is what I need to get my younger sister and me to California. She's a real beauty and she's got a chance for a screen test, but she has to have the right clothes and a good address, you know." She stuffed the paper in Stephen's palm and sauntered out the door. "I'll be waiting out here in the hallway. I'll wait for about fifteen minutes, and then I'll start making some phone calls." She smiled at Laura. "I'll leave a nickel by the phone for each one, sister. Don't want to take advantage of your hospitality." She laughed, a throaty, vulgar sound, and drifted out.

There was a long silence as Stephen crossed the room and closed the door. "Stephen, I'm sorry," Laura said. "I should have told you. I meant to. I really meant to, and then things got so hectic before the wedding and you'd gone to get flowers and then they bombed Pearl Harbor and . . . ."

His head hanging, Stephen sat down where Mae had been. This time Bess bounced clear to her feet. "Do you honestly mean to say that this . . . this *horror* is actually true?"

"Yes," Laura said weakly, but to Stephen, not Bess. He had his fingers laced together and was studying them. He didn't look up. The note Mae had handed him lay crumpled on the carpet.

"Can she prove it?" Bess asked.

"Prove it? I don't know. I suppose maybe she could."

"Where did all this happen? Your birth?" Bess demanded.

"Here. At the cottage."

"Oh, Lord," Bess moaned. "Probably half the county knows. Stephen, why didn't you find this out when you ran your check on these people?"

"Check? What check?" Laura asked. "Stephen . . . ? You investigated us? As if we were criminals?"

He looked up at her then, but didn't reply to her question. "How could you have kept this from me?"

"I meant to tell you, but I was afraid—"

"Afraid! You didn't have the common courage to tell your husband-to-be? I can't believe you're that spineless."

Laura felt as if she'd been slapped. "It *was* spineless," she said, her voice shaking. "And I'm sorry. Sorrier than I can say." In spite of the lingering anger over the unanswered mystery about the family being "checked," as Bess said, Laura really was so contrite that it was a physical pain. He looked like a man facing a firing squad for a crime he hadn't committed. "Stephen, I'll do anything I can. Tell me what—"

"Keep quiet. You've been very good at that so far," Bess snapped.

Laura looked to Stephen instinctively for defense, but of course there was none. For once, she couldn't blame him for not standing up for her against Bess. "What's the figure?" Bess asked, turning her back on Laura as if she no longer existed.

Stephen picked up the crumpled paper and smoothed it on his knee. "Five thousand dollars."

"She'd probably take two," Bess said, crossing her arms. "We can manage it, or better yet, little Laura can."

"No, Mother, it's too late," Stephen said. "Sooner or later she'd ask for more and more and more. It would never end."

Bess sat down beside him. "Stephen, darling, this has been a terrible shock to you. To both of us, and I hate to think what Arch is going to say, but you're not really thinking about it clearly."

"What do you mean?" There was hope in his face. Laura sat across the room still, locked into place, frozen with astonishment that this conversation was going on around her— not just around her, but because of her. Coward, fool! she kept telling herself.

"I mean this: the girl can and will take steps to keep you from getting elected to the presidency—"

"That's the whole point, Mother."

"Yes, but then what? Think, Stephen. Then nothing. There's no more threat. Once you're in, she can say anything she likes. Laura only has to be presentable until you get into the White House and then there's no getting her out for four years, no matter what anybody says. You can't be impeached for falling in love with the wrong woman."

Laura felt her face flushing. The Wrong Woman—it sounded the same as a Fallen Woman. And yet, she was that too, and they just didn't know it. Thank God!

"But in the years between, she could take us for a fortune!"

"Not us," Bess said coldly. "It's Laura's past, and logically her expense."

"I'd never get reelected."

"Of course you would. The story would be old news in four years. In fact, I think we might consider letting the story out ourselves—oh, say, six months or so into your first term. Just so everybody's gotten their teeth into it and gotten tired of it by the next election. She can either be kept well in the background, or she can be pushed forward to counter the implications. We'll have to see. But all we really have to do is keep this woman quiet until the election is over. Stephen, it's not so bad. I really don't believe it is. Now, we've got to settle with her and then roust Arch out of bed and . . . No, the other way around. You go up those back stairs, and I'll keep her off the telephone until you've explained it all to your uncle. Hurry.''

They rushed off in different directions, neither of them so much as giving Laura another look or thought. After a while Stephen came back in and found her still sitting, stunned, at the desk. ''You can write a check out for three thousand dollars,'' he said curtly.

''Stephen, do you really think this is the right thing to do?''

''You can ask me that? You, who kept this from me and my family all these years out of sheer cowardice? Just write the check, Laura.''

She wondered if the bank would honor it. The handwriting was so shaky it was barely readable. She watched as he left the room, waving the check to dry the ink. She hated herself and she hated him, but none of it mattered. She was cemented into this marriage now with a bond of duty and guilt and obligation. ''Oh, Gram, what have I done to myself?'' she whimpered, putting her head down on the old desk.

XXXIII

"*Y*OU'VE got to see one of hte doctors," Sonny said.

"I don't either. Stop nagging me. I'm fine," Laura answered.

"You don't look fine. You look like the dog's dinner. Ever since that party the other night you've been a mess. I've never seen you so pale. Come on, Laura. What is the matter with you?"

"What's the matter with me is that I'm a bastard!" she said, finally prodded into the words she hadn't meant to let out.

Sonny turned away, found her sweater, and dragged her out of the chair. "That's it, huh? Well, this is going to require some talk. Put this on and let's go down to the spring."

"Sonny, I don't want to talk."

"I don't care. I want to know what brought this all up again and I'd be willing to bet my last dollar it has something to do with Dragon Bess. Right?"

She'd poured it all out by the time they got to the spring. It wasn't, after all, such a long story once it was shorn to the essentials.

"He didn't know, then? I always wondered if you'd told him."

"No, and it was terrible of me not to."

"Nonsense, my girl. It was none of his damn business, or Bess's either."

"Yes, it was," Laura said, determined to be fair no matter how much it hurt. "It could cost him the one thing he wants in life."

"But what do you want?"

"Sonny, what I want isn't the point right now. I've thrown this horrible stumbling block in his path—just as if I'd been saving it up all these years. That's wrong of me."

Sonny kicked along a little rock he'd been nudging since they left the house. It plopped into the water at the edge of the spring lake. "You're not still trying to pretend you're in love with Stephen, are you?"

Laura sighed. "No. Love has nothing to do with it, Sonny."

"If you don't love him, why don't you get a divorce and be done with it?"

"Divorce? Certainly not. This business of my background is bad enough. Divorce would certainly destroy his chances politically."

"Who gives a damn about his chances, Laura? What about you and what you want of life?"

Laura sat down and wrapped her skirt around her legs. "Sonny, I made a bargain when I married Stephen—I agreed to be the lifelong wife of a man who wanted to be President. I took on that duty and responsibility with my eyes open. A lot of things have happened since then to make me regret that choice, but none of them were Stephen's fault. None!"

She was sick of hearing her own voice saying these things. She'd explained it all to Eric before, but she had to make Sonny understand. "Now, here I am, able to destroy him—by divorcing him—and God knows there's nothing I want more in the world than to be free! But I can't do that. I just can't. He can't help it that I've changed my mind about loving him and wanting to help him attain his goal. I had no goal on earth when we met and I willingly adopted his. Now I'm stuck with it."

"Duty! Shit! Laura, when are you ever going to start thinking about yourself? What you want and need and deserve, dammit! You've *served* all your life. You've done your duty to Gram and the whole rest of the family and this house and land and the hotel and the hospital. When do you get what you want?"

"Not now," she said, her jaw clenched. "And not at the expense of another person's dream. Sonny, he's got his faults, the main one of which is that is *isn't* Eric Holt, but he's a good, brave, honorable man. You've never liked him, but surely you can see that."

Sonny had sat down beside her. Now he stood up, shaking his head. "I've never met anyone so pigheadedly determined to throw her own happiness away."

She suddenly clutched at his leg. "Oh, Sonny, please understand. Please. I have to do what's right and I know this is the right thing—but I'm dying of it. I actually woke up this morning and was sorry I was still alive. Nothingness would be better than the life I see for myself, but I can't change things. I can't change me. Eric once said something about my having a Jehovah-like conscience, and I see now what he meant."

"Oh, bunny, I do see," he said, stooping and wrapping his arms around her. "You are who you are—and thank God for it!—but it makes me wild that I can't do anything to change your mind. You deserve to be happy, not miserable like this. Tell me something, anything, I can do for you that will help."

Laura wiped her streaming eyes on the sleeve of her sweater and sat up straight. "You can lend me your handkerchief and promise to listen to me the next time I feel like I'm going to pieces. Now, walk back to the house with me."

They went clear around the building, giving Laura time to get her emotions under control. As they got to the front entrance, however, Sonny shaded his eyes and looked down the road. "What is that? Do you see something on the road?"

Laura squinted. "It looks like a bundle of laundry fell off the truck. Let's go get it."

But it wasn't a bundle of laundry. It was a young man sprawled facedown. He was missing a leg, and a pair of battered cratches was lying beside him like butterfly wings. "Run up to the house and get help," Laura said, sitting down beside the man and feeling for a pulse.

"He's not one of our patients," she said when Sonny returned with a doctor and a pair of burly stretcher-bearers. "His pulse is good and he almost came to while I was waiting with him."

"How did he get here?" the doctor asked, pulling an eyelid back and studying the man's pupil.

"I have no idea."

They placed him on the stretcher and took him to the house. Laura went back to work for an hour on some forms she was filing, but she couldn't keep her mind on them. She went to the main desk of the second-floor wing and asked the nurse on duty, "That man they brought from the road—how is he?"

"Doing awfully well, Mrs. Langley. Just exhaustion, the

doctor said. He'd walked clear from Eureka Springs on one leg and crutches. His name's Schafer. Sergeant Schafer."

"I'll just look in on him quickly then."

She opened the door a crack, expecting to see the man sleeping, but he was awake and looking at the doorway. "I didn't mean to disturb you," she said softly.

"You're not, ma'am. The fact is, I was just wondering if I could have a drink of water."

Laura glanced at the chart hung at the foot of the bed. "I don't see any reason why not. I'll get it."

She came back with a metal pitcher full of ice water and a small tumbler. Schafer was sitting up in bed. "You look very spry, Sergeant," she said, handing him a tumblerful of cold water. "You had a long walk."

"I had to get here."

"There are better ways."

"You're telling me!"

"You lost your leg in the war?" she asked.

When the hospital had first opened she'd tried, with all kindness, to pretend that the injuries were nonexistent, or at least unnoticeable. Long experience had taught her that this was far more insulting to the patients than acknowledging their handicaps and asking about them. Some of the soldiers wanted to talk about what had happened, some didn't, but it was best to offer them the choice instead of closing down that line of conversation.

"In Germany. Prison camp."

"Oh?" she said in the carefully developed tone that meant: You can go on or you can change the subject—it's up to you.

"Yeah, I was captured. I was tail gunner in a bombing run, but we went down. I passed out, but my buddy Chuck pulled me out and got me up and walking away from the wreck. We got almost to these woods and a bunch of damned Nazi soldiers came jumping out. They already had our pilot. The German in charge—a big, dumb-looking blond—said, 'Look vat ve haf found,' just like that, in English. Then another of them came over and knocked Chuck down with the butt of his rifle. Socked it right in his stomach."

Laura swallowed and tried to look calm and interested. She'd heard these horror stories before and they never ceased to make her feel like she was being pulled inside out, but when a soldier needed to talk, someone needed to listen.

"They knocked me down too, but I got back up. Chuck was writhing around on the ground. I think they busted his ribs. This big guy started mincing around in this little clearing place, saying, 'Vell, vell, vell, ve haf three prisoners and only room in the vagon for vun more. Who shall ve take?' Then he goes over to the pilot and slaps him in the face and asks him. The pilot mumbles something I couldn't quite hear, then this Nazi bastard says, 'Vell, I guess I'll haf to decide for myself.' He goes over to Chuck—he was out by then, unconscious and breathing in this funny gurgle. 'He is nearly dead anyway,' he says to the pilot. And the Nazi goes over and empties his gun into Chuck's head. His brains splattered all over my leg.''

Schafer shifted his position slightly. He wasn't talking to Laura anymore, he was talking to the opposite wall. ''Then he walks back to the pilot and says, 'Now ve still haf two. Vould you like to come with us, or shall ve take him?' and the pilot says, 'Take him.' Just as easy as saying: Yeah, I'll have a cup of coffee. Take him. So the German strolls around me like he's thinking about it and goes back to stand next to the pilot. He held his gun in the pilot's gut and says, 'No, you look the more important. I think Führer would rather lose you.'

''Then the pilot—God, it still makes me sick to remember—he sorta doubles over and starts saying all this stuff nobody can hear. The German grabs him by the hair and jerks his head up. He's crying—I mean it, crying and blubbering like a goddamn baby, and saying he doesn't want to die and he's important and I'm not and if they let him live he can tell them all kinds of things about bombing-run schedules. I would of puked, except I already had.

''The moon must have been going behind some clouds, or maybe I was just blacking out, but it got darker all of a sudden and I was thinking how I might stand about a one-percent chance if I ran. Mostly I wanted to get my hands on the pilot. But I didn't do anything because the German shot me before I could make a move. Got me in the leg and I folded up. I heard him fire off another shot, but he must have missed. Then next thing I knew, I was waking up in this dark, stinking hole. A farmer had found me and dragged me in—at least I guess that's what happened. I don't speak German and he didn't speak English. I must have been there a week or so and I could smell my leg rotting, and my brain too. Somebody must have ratted on this farmer, because soldiers came and took us all away. I didn't even get a chance to thank this old man who was hiding me. The damned thing is, in a way, I was almost glad to see the soldiers. I thought at least they might take me to a hospital.''

Laura sat clutching the seat of her chair with both hands, half-fearing she might tumble off if she didn't cling to this one solid object. ''Did they?'' she asked. It came out like a croak.

''Yeah, if you could call it that. More like a big pigsty, but they must have known what they were doing—they took the leg off without quite killing me. I spent the rest of the war there.''

''Where do you live, Sergeant?''

''Nebraska. But I got relatives down here.''

Sonny, I need you here, Laura thought desperately. She took the tumbler, which Schafer still clutched in his hand, and refilled it. When he'd finished another drink, she took it back and set in on the stand across the room. It was time to ask:

''There are hospitals closer to Nebraska than this. What are you doing here?''

She wanted to put her hands over her ears so she wouldn't hear the answer.

''I'm here to get the pilot. The son of a bitch is going to pay me for my leg—one way or another,'' Schafer said in a matter-of-fact tone. *Yeah, I'd like a cup of coffee.* ''I hear he got a bad leg out of it, but at least he's got a leg. I don't.''

''You think he's a patient here?'' Laura asked, still holding out a hope.

''Patient? Hell, no, miss. He lives in this place. He's that Langley guy that's been in the papers.''

She'd known, even when he started his story, she'd known. Laura felt bile rise in her throat and forced it back down. ''Sergeant, I think you need to rest. You're looking pale. Let me help you get settled here. That's it. Do you want a light on? It will be getting dark soon.''

''Thanks, miss. Say, I'm sorry I spilled all this on you. It's not something I usually shoot off my mouth about. Will you come back and see me? You're a good listener and I have nicer things I can talk about. Give me a chance, huh?''

''I'll . . . yes, I'll come back soon. Now, you just rest and don't think about this until you're better,'' she said, and wondered if she could get out of the room before her legs collapsed under her.

''Say, miss, I didn't get your name,'' he said as she opened the door.

''Thorne. My name is Thorne.''

*   *   *

Laura was very busy the rest of the afternoon. She went into town first, made several phone calls and a visit, and shortly after her return sought out Sonny. "I want you to meet me in the library at ten tonight. Bess and Stephen will be there and I want you to listen. *Just* listen. Do you understand?"

Sonny looked at her blankly for a minute, then smiled slightly. He put his hand on her shoulder and turned her around slightly to look at her back. "Is this to say," he asked wryly, "that the ridge down your back is actually a spine?"

"It might be. It just might be. Be there? And be quiet!"

Bess didn't like being ordered around and she liked the mysterious element of Laura's summons even less. "What is all this hush-hush nonsense about?" she said, coming into the library and sitting down. "I've got a busy day tomorrow and I want to get to bed."

"You have a busier day than you know," Laura said.

Stephen came in just then. "Laura, Arch and I are in the middle of a card game. Can't this wait?"

"No, it can't. Sonny, would you hang that old 'Do Not Disturb' sign on the door? We don't want any interruptions."

"What *is* this about?" Bess demanded. "Have you heard from that awful sister of yours again?"

"No, this has nothing to do with Mae. It has to do with you and Stephen. No . . . it has to do with *me*." She glanced at Sonny and he smiled encouragingly. "I visited with a patient this morning, then I went to town and filed for divorce."

The word was hardly out of her mouth before Bess was on her feet. "You'll do no such thing, young lady. Not while there's a breath in my body."

"I already have. I've also called a number of your reporter friends and made arrangements for them to be here at ten in the morning. Stephen is going to announce that he is not now, or ever, planning to run for President or any other office."

Stephen stood up and put his arms out. "Laura, Laura, what on earth has come over you? Do you have any idea how foolish this all sounds? Are you ill? I can't imagine any other reason for you to say such outrageous things."

She dodged his threatened embrace and went around to stand behind the desk. "Imagine this, then, Stephen. Imagine a man whose whole life is based on courage, a man who is a hero, looked up to by thousands of people he's never met.

Imagine that man's plane is shot down and he's captured along with two of his crew, and imagine that the Germans who capture him ask him to choose between his own life and that of one of those men.''

Stephen's arms slowly fell as she spoke, and the color drained from his face.

"Imagine," she went on relentlessly, "that he allowed—no, *begged*—the Germans to shoot his men instead of himself, and offered the Germans secret information in return for his own life. And suppose that man came back to this country and let everyone believe he was a hero. Even his wife and mother.''

"Who told you this?" he gasped.

"Sergeant Schafer. He's a patient here. I had Willis Hawkins' partner come out this evening and take his statement. It's in a safe in the bank now.''

"What in the world are you talking about?" Bess shrilled.

"Shut up, Mother," Stephen said.

Bess plunked back down into the sofa like an overripe apple falling off a tree.

Laura leaned forward on the desk, her arms locked at the elbows. "To think that *I* felt guilty for being such a coward. And you let me! You dared to condemn me for my lack of courage! You, Stephen Langley, the most despicable coward of them all.''

"This is ridiculous. Schafer is dead. Has been for years.''

"You left him for dead, but he isn't. I can have him brought down here if you want. He's feeling well enough for a short wheelchair ride, I think. And he's very anxious to see you. I believe he intends to kill you, actually. At least he'd like to. And I can't blame him. You were his commanding officer and you told the Nazis to kill him instead of you.''

Sonny was sitting in the corner of the room, rubbing his hands and grinning, but true to his promise, wasn't saying anything. Bess had recovered from Stephen's astonishing remark to her and was on her feet again. "Stephen, she'll have to be put in a mental institution. We can say it's just for a rest or claim some sort of disease. Nobody will have to know that she's lost her mind, and then when she's better . . .''

Laura smiled at her. "Bess, you don't seem to grasp the situation yet. I'm not crazy. Stephen knows it. Ask him.''

Bess turned to her son, a furious look on her face. But it quickly faded to something else—something old and tired and sick—when she met his eyes. "Stephen . . . ?''

"Yes. It's true. In a way. But it wasn't like it sounds. I

thought they were just going to kill all of us anyway and I was just gaining a little time. Besides, it was just one moment of a whole lifetime—it can't count against everything else I've done over the years. Mother . . . Mother!''

She had buried her face in her hands, the first sign of human weakness she'd ever shown in front of Laura. Laura was curiously touched by it, but not swayed. "My whole life spent . . . gone . . . *wasted* on a traitor," Bess whimpered.

Stephen looked around the room wildly. He seemed suddenly stooped and sloppy and thoroughly defeated. "Mother, don't say that. Not you.''

Bess looked up. "It's true. You're still in the reserves. They can court-martial you. Our name will be dragged through the mud. Your uncle will be ruined, I'll never be able to hold my head up again.''

Laura sank into the big chair behind the desk. "I'm not sure of that, Bess. I have a statement typed up for Stephen to sign. In it, he admits the truth of Sergeant Schafer's statement and further agrees that he will never seek public office or any position of leadership. I think Sergeant Schafer might agree that this is adequate vindication. I can't promise anything, of course. If he agrees, I will keep Schafer's statement and a copy of Stephen's in the family safe-deposit box—along with the divorce decree when it becomes final. Now, Bess, you've got a lot of packing to do and, Stephen, you've got just twelve hours to prepare your statement for the press and leave here.''

"But, Laura—" Stephen began.

"There's nothing else to say, Stephen. Just sign the paper. Here's a pen.''

Out of habit, if nothing else, he looked at Bess. Her expression of loathing brought tears to his eyes. "I'd never do anything like that again," he said tentatively.

"You'll never have the chance," Laura said, and then, as a wave of pity swept over her, she added, "I think maybe some of us only have one opportunity per lifetime to know our own courage. You had your test and you failed. This night is mine. Sign, Stephen.''

Sonny sat in the corner where he'd been all along until they'd gone—Bess with her head still held high, Stephen with a defeated shuffle. Laura felt victorious, but deeply saddened at the sight of the man she'd once thought she loved. He could have had a brilliant career . . . No, he was never really fit for it. Born to it, designed for it, trained for it, but never,

never fit for it. "I do feel sorry for him . . ." and as Sonny started to object, she raised her hand. "It doesn't make any difference, but I am sorry—for him, for myself, for Sergeant Schafer. Even for Bess." Her voice trailed off into a silence that Sonny let stretch until she was ready to speak again.

"Now, Sonny, I have another document here. It's not official yet, but while I was at Mr. Hawkins' office, I asked him to make a statement too. This is a copy." She handed the flimsy carbon to him. "In it he appeals to the court to put aside Gram's will and divide the property equally between us on the basis of her unsound mind at the time she wrote it. He doesn't think there will be any difficulty. But he needs to see you in his office a week from Wednesday morning to sign some things."

"My Lord, you *have* been busy today!"

"Don't you want to know the terms?"

"I don't care, but you can tell me if you want."

"You get the house, half the land, and half the stocks if you promise to let all the relatives and Mabelann stay on for their lifetimes."

"You know I'd agree to that. And you, bunny, what do you get?"

"Clear title to my conscience. As well as half of the land, including the cottage, and the other half of the stocks."

"Do you really want to do this?"

"How can you ask? It's always been rightly yours. It was unforgivable of Gram to try to deprive you of it. Sonny, do you remember that time we saw her cry? She said there was something wrong with all of us—that we all loved each other too much or too little. I've been thinking about that and I think you and I are the only ones who've gotten it just right."

"That's because we're twins," he said, grinning. "Will you be coming in to see Hawkins with me?"

"No, I have somewhere else to be Wednesday."

"Oh?"

"They're unveiling Eric's mural. I would assume the artist will be present, and maybe I'll get the opportunity to fling myself at his feet and admit what a fool I was."

"Somehow I doubt you'll have to take such extreme measures."

It was raining that morning and the roads were slick and treacherous. Laura didn't get to the VA hospital until five minutes after the ceremony was to begin; then she couldn't find a parking place. She circled the block three times before finding a place. She squeezed in, ended up with two tires up on the curb, and abandoned the vehicle.

The lobby was crammed full. Some politician was droning on about the war. She slipped in and started working her way around the perimeter of the crowd, hoping to find a place she could see from. At one point she got turned around and found herself facing a section of the mural, which she had seen only glimpses of above the crowd. But now she saw herself, as if looking into a mirror. This part showed a grouping of nurses, their white uniforms pristine, their eyes gazing at a plane overhead. Eric had captured her exactly, even to the tiny mole next to her eye. More than a mere likeness, it was a loving treatment. Her eyes were soft in the picture, her chin vulnerable, her brow wide and intelligent.

She heard a familiar voice and turned. A space had cleared, and by standing on her toes, she could see Eric standing behind the elevated podium. "I'm gratified to see you all here today," he was saying.

Laura raised her hand tentatively as his eyes swept the room. He saw her and paused for a second, then smiled and went on, "There's one person I'm especially happy to see. . . ."

Epilogue

1950

*T*HERE was never much news to put into a Christmas-morning newspaper, which was the only reason the editor gave so much space to the story about Stephen Langley:

FORMER WAR HERO DIES

Stephen Langley, once mentioned widely as a presidential hopeful, died yesterday in a hospital in New York City from injuries sustained in a car accident. Langley's family had a long tradition of government service and Langley was considered by many to have been in preparation for a political career. Late in 1945, however, after his return from the war, where he had served with distinction as a bomber pilot, he withdrew from politics entirely and disappeared from public view. At the time of his death, he was employed as legal representative of a large tool manufacturer.

Laura put the paper down and shook her head. "Poor Stephen," she said.

Eric, who had already read the article, said, "At least they didn't mention the 'wicked woman' who divorced him like they did at first."

"The reporters *did* have a wonderful time making mince-meat of me, didn't they?" Laura said, as if they were discussing some slight acquaintance. It was very nearly true. She hardly remembered the tortured young woman she'd been during that awful year.

"Are you ready to go up to the big house?"

"As soon as I put my coat on. Have you got all the packages? Be careful of that one with the little glass orna-

410

ments tied into the ribbon. I'd hate for it to turn to shards before we even put it under the tree. Marysia puts such store by the fancy wrappings."

"Don't fuss, darling. I've never ruined a package yet," Eric said. "Are the twins ready?"

Laura put a finger to her lips and gestured for him to follow her across the living room of the cottage. She quietly opened the door to one of the bedrooms and they peeked in at the two little girls sitting on the floor dressing their new dolls. Named Adele and Elizabeth and called Addie and Liz, they were as cuddly and alike as a pair of orange kittens.

Eric put his arm around Laura and smiled. "If only they'd be willing to sit that still when I tried to paint a portrait of them."

At the sound of his voice, the girls leapt up. "Are we going now? Can we open more presents? Uncle Sonny said we could eat lots of cookies."

Eric offered to drive them up; Laura was in the last month of her second pregnancy, but she said she needed the exercise. When they got to the main house the girls ran ahead to find their cousins Rudie and George, Sonny and Marysia's boys. Unable to have children because of the surgery Marysia had undergone at the hands of the Nazis, they'd adopted the two little war orphans four years earlier. They were Polish brothers who'd lost their own parents in a camp like the one Marysia had been in. Marysia had become a model mother and Sonny adored the boys.

The big house still smelled ever so faintly of antiseptic, even though its role as a hospital had ended two years ago with the dismissal of the last soldier patient and Dr. Lee's well-deserved and long-overdue retirement to Florida.

Billy Walker met them at the door and relieved them of the packages. Since his marriage to India, he'd taken responsibility for the Christmas tree and gift distribution. In fact, he'd taken over a great many duties. While Sonny translated work after work of literature for several university presses, Billy managed the house and grounds and even kept their half-dozen family cars running.

"You shouldn't be walking around tiring yourself," he told Laura, who was puffing a bit from her exertions.

"Don't make me an invalid, Billy," she said. "I'm fine. It will seem strange without Evelyn this year, won't it?" Evelyn had died the January before of kidney failure and Mabelann had succumbed to pneumonia barely a month later.

"Yes, she always liked the gifts and food and singing as much as the children. Especially at the end. Come on, join us for a glass of wine before dinner."

They went into the library with him. India had pushed back the sofa in front of the fireplace and was trying to teach Addie and Liz a ballet step, her latest craze. Adele, plump and quite white-haired, was crippled with arthritis and unable to get around very well, but her hands were still agile and she was sitting by the window knitting furiously, as if to finish some present or other.

Sonny was sitting cross-legged in the middle of the floor, his boys across from him. The three of them were staring owlishly at the parts of a bicycle spread on the floor. "There must be some parts left out. Why didn't I buy it already assembled?" he was muttering.

Edmund rose from his favorite chair and came over to them. He was having digestive problems and the resulting weight loss made him look like an elderly crane. "I would wager you haven't bothered to read the instructions, have you?"

Sonny looked up so guiltily that Laura laughed. "You look just like you used to when you hadn't done your math homework!"

Sonny's boys, who were now Edmund's pupils, were fascinated with this information. "You mean Daddy didn't do his work when he was little?" Rudie asked.

Later that afternoon, replete with a Christmas feast, they gathered again in the library for the opening of gifts. Billy Walker distributed the presents one by one, drawing out the pleasure and anticipation as long as possible. The children loved the excitement and hated the delay. Laura, bulky and uncomfortable, sat in the middle of the sofa. Eric was on one side of her, Sonny on the other. Marysia, her features filled out now and quite beautiful, sat on the arm of the sofa, resting her hand on Sonny's shoulder. An outsider, seeing this lovely and tranquil young woman, would never guess what she'd been through.

"Do you remember the Christmas we had no money?" Laura asked. "I think it's one of my best memories."

Sonny patted her knee. "I remember. You gave promises. You said you'd do five of my homework assignments. I took you up on all five."

"Those five and another ten at least," she said, laughing.

"I still have the opera glasses Gram gave me that year. The twins play with them."

They sat for a moment in a little island of peace in the center of the Christmas mayhem the children were creating. "I've been thinking about names," Laura finally said.

"Baby names?" Eric asked.

"Yes. Since you refuse to let me name this baby Eric if it's a boy, I wonder how you'd feel about Jackson? Sonny, would you mind?"

"I don't mind in the least. But what if it's a girl?"

Laura hesitated. "I was thinking there ought to be a Grace here again someday. Would you hate that, Sonny?"

Sonny smiled at her. "You sound as if you're afraid to ask me. No, I wouldn't mind at all. Gram's been gone a long time. I can hardly remember being mad at her about the will. And she was, after all, our grandmother. I'd be flattered at a little Jackson and pleased at a little Grace."

Laura twisted awkwardly and kissed his cheek, then turned back to Eric. "You wouldn't mind, would you?"

"You know whatever you want will suit me. But you don't have to decide right now."

She smiled and took his hand, putting it against her tightened abdomen. "That was the next thing I wanted to talk to you about," she said with vast understatement. "We *do* have to decide pretty soon. Probably before morning."

This announcement created an upheaval. Eric tore off to get the car to take her to the community hospital. Sonny got busy on the phone trying to hunt down the doctor who had taken over the Thorne family's health concerns when Dr. Lee retired. India and Adele fussed over her until she escaped them to wait for Eric at the front door. As she stood there listening to the children's voices from the library, Marysia came out with a sprig of greenery. "For luck," she said, pinning it in Laura's hair. "Maybe we will have a Christmas baby. Shall I wait with you?"

"No, thank you. I'm fine."

As Marysia went back into the library, the sound of Billy Walker leading the children in singing "Silent Night" washed over her and Laura felt tears fill her eyes. Eric and the twins normally kept her too busy for the leisure of nostalgia, but standing in the warm, pine-scented darkness, she was suddenly swamped by memories.

She'd stood in this spot so many times. That door was the one she and Sonny had come in the day the stock market crashed and began the slow process of turning the house into a hotel. Later she'd opened the door to the man and boy on their way to Washington to tell President Hoover what he ought to be doing. Her grandmother and father had stood behind that desk pretending to make reservations for Melvin Purvis to clear out the gangsters. A few feet away was where she'd once stood and studied Frederich VonHoldt's profile, wondering why it was familiar. And this was where she'd been when Stephen Langley walked into her life. And she'd been about to come in this entrance when Sonny saw Sergeant Schafer lying the road. This, too, was where she'd paused one afternoon as she started out to the train station the day Eric came to Thornehill as a patient. She'd stopped and talked to Grace that day, she remembered.

She looked up the stairway again, imagining Grace there in the darkness still watching over her. "I'm happier than I ever thought possible, Gram," she said out loud. "And we're doing what you and Grandfather Jack always wanted—we're filling the house with children."

The door opened suddenly and Eric stood there, the perfect picture of a panic-stricken father-to-be. "Are you ready?" he asked.

Laura took his arm. "I'm ready for anything. What else could you expect of Grace Emerson Thorne's granddaughter!"

About the Author

Janice Young Brooks is a native Kansas Citian who lives there with her husband and two teenage children. Her last Signet novel, SEVENTREES, received the American Association of University Women's prestigious "Thorpe Menn Award" for literary excellence in 1981.